Just A
STALE MATE

JUST (e)STATE *Mysteries*

J. Ivanel Johnson

Black Rose Writing | Texas

ISBN: 978-1-68513-212-5
PUBLISHED BY BLACK ROSE WRITING
www.blackrosewriting.com

Printed in the United States of America
Suggested Retail Price (SRP) $21.95

Just A STALE MATE is printed in Sabon LT Std

*As a planet-friendly publisher, Black Rose Writing does its best to eliminate unnecessary waste to reduce paper usage and energy costs, while never compromising the reading experience. As a result, the final word count vs. page count may not meet common expectations.

Dedicated to the Rich-with-Joy Support Home Team, with many thanks for all you do, and have done.

And to my beautiful niece Sydney, whose eponymous grandfather was born in 'Sandytown' (Straffordville, Bayham Township). Perhaps this book will help her see the original 'setting' in which her ancestors created, dreamed and thrived.

CAST OF CHARACTERS

(Reader— surnames have intentionally been excluded; you'll see
why as you read on!)

Victoria, New Brunswick:

Polly Jane (P.J.), Philip Steele's godmother
Mary & Mort, married
Sheriff Chet
Betsy, P.J.'s neighbor, housed diagonally across her back-yard
Calpurrnia (Cal) the Cat

**West of Toronto, Ontario,
at The JUST *(e)*STATE
(home and farm of the Steele family for generations)**

Detective Inspector (D.I.) Philip Steele (Phil)
Hilary, (Lary), Philip's mother (Roger, her late husband)
Oliver, Philip's godfather, a beekeeper and landscaper
Paintpot, a therapeutic riding horse
<u>Visitors to the farm:</u>
Lila, from Michigan
Mandy, student
Sharon, Crispin's mother, married to Deputy Commissioner
(D.C.) 'Blue' Cobalt

Downtown Toronto

'Blue', see above, Crispin's father
Trevor (D.I. Ames)
Carl, Trevor's sometime-boyfriend

Bayham Brook House

Sela, nurse
Petra, her mother
Ruth, the cook
Karen (Kay)
Lucy
Monty
Dr. Jeremiah Flintwinch
Mitch and Jackie, artists, married
Della & Clara, maids, aides
Numerous animals incl. Tiny, the doctor's aging dog
Gerald
Crispin
Charlie
Latch
Annette/Anita
Walter (groom, former mason)
Bob & Martha, neighboring farmers
Daisy (former resident)
Officer Blake Biro, of the OPP
Owners, Chesters & Youngs (incl. D. Lawton, world-class tennis champ)

Edom's Creek

Rev. Peter Klassen, United Church minister
Daniel, masseuse, laborer

Port Dune

Cathy & Brian Nelson, siblings, own lodgings where Phil and Trevor stay (on tobacco farm)
Rev. Talbot, their Baptist minister

Just A
STALE MATE

PART ONE

"From morn to noon he fell, from noon to dewy eve,
(of) a summer's day, and with the setting sun
dropped from the zenith like a falling star."
-John Milton, *Paradise Lost*

CHAPTER ONE

1969, Victoria, New Brunswick

The scream came from downstairs, from inside the post office section of Polly Jane's cedar-shingled salt-box. She paused in her packing long enough to let it register, then calmly descended the stairs, stopping first to slide her petites into her "house shoes". (She hadn't worn her fuzzy pink slippers for months, since she'd tripped in them last winter and broken her ankle.)

As she neared the bottom of the steep steps, she heard the scream again.

"Cal? Calpurrnia?" she called, then noticed the door from the kitchen into the post office was ajar. She scurried into the front room, swaying her hips as only a former ballroom dancer could, to avoid the corner of the antique pigeon holes into which all of Victoria's mail was securely sorted for the morrow.

A flash of white caught her eye and she saw the cat heading for the kitchen again, then through the cat-flap she'd had installed over a decade ago when she thought the feral kitten had been both female and more inclined to become domesticated. Naming 'her', feeding 'her' and installing the flap had all been part of a plan gone sadly awry; Calpurrnia had turned out to be a tomcat who was hormonally overwhelmed, and who rarely wanted to come inside. Instead, he lived in her back garden, contently purring away on an ancient blanket in a corner of the potting shed and only occasionally – usually when he was chasing a rodent – venturing into her house. The black and white beast would not be tamed, didn't like to be touched never mind stroked, but would actually sit for hours in the shed or in the dilapidated gazebo while she went about her gardening work, listening to her discuss what bulbs she might dig up and transplant near the willow tree or which rose bushes she was thinking of cutting back to allow more light onto a side of the cedar-shingled, squat little home where she'd lived most of her adult life. Never one to descend into the habit of talking aloud to herself (as her godson Philip Steele was wont to do), Polly Jane was glad of the cat's constant company; most village residents passing by her fence knew their post mistress hadn't crossed the bridge into dementia-land, but was instead having an intelligent discussion with her mad mouser.

"I'll be gone for a few weeks, Cal," she shouted now to his fast-retreating backside. "Don't be coming in here while Mary's minding the shop, or she'll be calling the Fredericton pound, and the dog-catcher will come get you!"

Her postal assistant Mary Henry hated all animals, but especially the screaming and caterwauling of the feral feline when he was feeling amorous or enraged. P.J.'s widowed friend Betsy Lawford, who lived just through the hedge and two back-yards diagonally, would come up the flagstone path every few days to ensure Cal had food in the shed. As it was August, it was also possible the brook might dry up, so Polly Jane made a mental note to phone over to ask her to keep replenishing the old metal bowl of water near the outdoor tap as well. She'd better not forget, because calling New Brunswick from Ontario to remind her neighbor could be costly indeed.

Back to the packing. With her usual bustling energy, she trotted up the stairs again and considered what to put into the suitcase next. She'd already packed two pairs of shorts and three light-weight cotton skirts, knowing south-western Ontario was much more humid than her own Atlantic province. Though she'd be on the twenty-four-acre "JUST(e)STATE", a farm that backed onto a small forest, she knew the blackflies wouldn't be nearly as bad as they were here near the mountains. However, she did recollect that their mosquitoes could bite nastily. As her aging skin was more and more tender with each passing year, she grabbed her 'jungle' hat, a veiled affair she thought most romantic if only it was swathed in white instead of army green. That same hat had been part of her packing procedure since she'd worked in Sierra Leone when she was in her twenties. It went into her suitcase along with a spray bottle of insect repellent—although she knew there'd be plenty on hand at the Steele farm. The owner, her old friend Lary Steele, was currently running a riding school there, as well as the market garden and roadside stand which had been its mainstay for generations. So all that outside work meant there'd be lashings of ointments and sprays for every weather condition and eventuality.

Just as she was about to choose which of her closetful of blouses she wanted to take (–none of those polyester things! As she knew from past summer visits to the farm, polyester didn't breathe at all in that humidity and sometimes she wondered why so many marveled at its recent invention), there was a pounding knock on her front door. This was also the main door of the post office, locked today since it was Sunday.

"Tssk," she clucked as she wondered, with all these interruptions, if she'd ever get to the airport on time. She was paying Mort Henry to drive her down to Fredericton, but she knew he wouldn't want to hang about outside the salt-box in his hot Chevy while she continued to search the house for last minute items to pack. The man had no patience, despite having remained married to Mary for nearly 40 years. Or perhaps that was the *reason* he had no patience? Oh, she'd better remember to take the wrapped gift for her godson, Phil! Where *had* she put it?

Distracted, she pulled open the heavy door as mid-afternoon sunlight streamed in, causing her to blink several times to refocus. She couldn't see the figure on her stoop immediately, but the sound of Mort's gruff voice was an instant clue.

"P.J., I ain't gonna take youse in, if'n that's all right with you. Chet Anderson says he's got to head down for a police BBQ tonight anyways, somewheres south of the city. He'd be glad to take youse out to the airport."

Polly Jane thought for a split second and realized how lovely this news was; not only would it save her some money (she'd still offer to pay 'Sheriff' Chet for gas of course), but she wouldn't be forced to listen all the way to Mort complain about Mary, the rising price of groceries, and this summer heat wave. *And* in his discordant misuse of the English language.

"Oh, well, certainly Mort–that's just fine. Chet'll be over in an hour to get me then, same time?"

"Right you is, ma'm. His pickup's got bigger windows, too, so youse might get a better breeze goin' down the highway."

"I'll get the keys for you to give Mary now, then. Good thing you came by rather than called, or I might have forgotten!"

"Like as not the ole lady'd 'a- bin screamin' into the phone about 'em, never fear."

That was certainly true, thought Polly Jane ruefully, as she reached under the long oak post office counter for the main set of keys to the front door. Mary *was* organized – one of the few reasons she was good at her job. But she was also a nosy, gossipy and harshly critical woman and P.J. was going to make sure the door leading into the rest of her private abode was firmly locked, with that particular key taken along on her trip, just in case!

An hour and a half later, she and Chet Anderson were cruising merrily along the river road toward the small capital city, chattering about his most recent constabulary-related activities, just as she frequently did with her godson. Thinking of Phil reminded her that she'd left the present for him on the kitchen table. Ah, well, it had really been just a little gag-gift, nothing important.

Then, wondering what else she'd forgotten, she mentally kicked herself. She'd have to place that expensive phone call from

Ontario after all—she'd not reminded Betsy Lawford about filling Cal's water bowl.

•   •   •

Toronto, Ontario

Philip Steele's freckled, sun-burned face beamed when he caught sight of his beloved godmother coming through the gate at Toronto International Airport. He hadn't seen P.J. since Christmas, though they often spoke on the telephone, no matter where he was working across the broad expanse of the nation. She loved to feel a part of his cases and since his father's death several years ago, was indeed his primary sounding board outside of his investigative colleagues. While seemingly living an insular life in the small village in the wilds of New Brunswick, Polly Jane had traveled a great deal in her youth. Having seen much of the world, and being a first-rate judge of character, her ability to leap to the heart of a matter always assisted Phil in his solving of many a puzzle. But he missed hugging the blue-haired, graceful figure in person and as soon as she passed the barriers, he scooped her into his arms.

"P.J.! So glad you made it! Did you have a good flight?"

"Hello, dear–well, there was a fairly large man sitting beside me. Hush, now–there he is," Polly Jane nudged Phil and nodded in what she considered a subtle manner. She lowered her voice to say, "I think he was actually trying to flirt with me, would you believe? Since we were sitting so close anyway, thanks to his, er–heft, I'm sure he thought he'd make the trip all lovely and intimate. It just left me hot and exhausted!"

"Well, cool off in here while we wait for your luggage to come through. Then we'll brave the heat for about a quarter-mile as we walk to the brand new Plymouth Satellite the D.C.'s given me while I'm back in Ontario. Which, you'll be glad to note, is one of the maybe forty percent of new cars with air conditioning."

"Ooo, really Phil? Now that *will* be something, especially after being squashed on the plane! Aren't you getting to be treated like royalty these days!"

"Well, on a hot one like this, I'll admit I don't mind at all. Although I do miss the mountains and cool, dry air of the Yukon."

"Never mind. I know your mother's happy to see you back here. How did the Greenidge case end up, anyway?"

"Well, we got him on the murder of the young Mortimore boy. But myself and some of my colleagues still believe he's killed others. We just can't I.D. the bodies and thus it's going to go cold, I'm afraid."

"Remember when you phoned and asked me about poor Dickie Hovey?"

"Yes, the lad from Fredericton, whose folks haven't heard from him in a few years now?"

"Right. Is he one of the victims, d'you think?"

"I'm afraid he might be, P.J.," Phil said soberly. "He was new here to the big city, and naïve. There've been a couple of bodies of young men turning up. And some other missing teens – all gentle souls with – er – possibly those homosexual tendencies we were concerned about with the Mortimore/Greenidge case. It's worrying, but the D.C. has called a halt to investigations for now, since we at least have Greenidge banged up. Only on manslaughter, mind. But still…"

"And you've been able to have a break since then? Helping your mother on the farm?"

"Well, if you can call my yanking up the odd carrot and sitting with my book at the stand selling baskets of cukes all day, 'helping'." Philip grinned.

The two sat on seats facing the baggage carousels. "But the riding stable? Is that keeping your mother busy?"

"It is, P.J.–it's been really good for her since Dad died, you know. I mean, the ex-cons are still helping in the gardens and at the stand, but now she's got some of them volunteering with her new program with the horses, too. It's fashioned after the Riding for the Disabled programs they have in England. There's a lady in Michigan starting one like it, too, so of course Mother Dear is getting in on the ground floor of all that!" He took a folded mimeographed pamphlet from his shirt pocket and handed it to his godmother. Polly Jane peered at its blurred images and print, then reached into her purse for her glasses. Suddenly, she grabbed his arm in panic.

"Fiddlesticks, Phil–my specs! Oh, surely I haven't left them on the plane! That odious man yacking away at me…"

"P.J."

"… and then the rush to get my cosmetic bag and my purse and my book, which of course I never got a chance to read…"

"P.J."

"Yes, dear?"

"Your glasses are where you *always* find them. On top of your head."

She reached up in relief and they shared a chuckle, just as the carousel jerked into motion, laden with luggage. She put the pamphlet in her purse and said, "I'll have a look at this in your fine car with the air conditioning, on the way out to the farm. It sounds very intriguing!"

●   ●   ●

The sedan ride to the "JUST(e)STATE" was most luxurious for the slightly rumpled Polly Jane Whistler. After a brief sojourn in what her godson called 'Sunday evening traffic', it was clear sailing straight into the sunset as they headed west. With the outlying fields all being flat, and with more and more trees being hacked down all the time for what P.J. grimly coined 'regress', she had to admit it did make for a spectacular vista of the huge orange ball streaking the skies purple, pink and yellow. The air in the car was comfortable, the seat enormous and the leg room, even with her two handbags at her feet, unlike anything she'd experienced in a vehicle, save for her grandfather's old buggy.

She read with interest the pamphlet on her friend's latest equine venture while they waited for the line of cars to dissipate from the airport congestion. "Hilary Steele, Instructor, Now Offering Riding Therapy For Disabled Teens And Children At The "JUST(e)STATE" Farm On Jane Street, North Of Steeles."

Mrs. Liz Hartel was an accomplished rider in Denmark before she contracted polio in 1940. This left her with severe residual disabilities, confining her to a wheelchair most of the time. In spite of this she went back to riding, finally culminating her efforts with a Silver Medal for dressage in the 1952 Olympic Games in Helsinki. An organization called the Advisory Council on Riding for the Disabled was formed in Britain to coordinate groups at stables wishing to help. By 1966, 23 of these were present there. In North America, there are very few, the most developed being in Michigan, just across the border. Our program, "L.A.R.Y." may be the first of its kind to begin here in Canada.

Her friend's brochure then showed a grainy photo of a boy on a platform leaning over from his wheelchair, about to lift himself onto a horse's broad back, with adult helpers at either side of him, and one holding the horse.

Horseback riding for people with disabilities is "therapeutic" on several levels: As a physical activity, sitting on a moving horse causes the rider's upper body to respond to the movement of the horse's back. The rhythm of 80 — 100 steps each minute stimulates righting reflexes and balancing reactions. Overall physical condition is improved as muscles and tendons are exercised. Psychologically and emotionally, the thrill of being seated on a large, powerful animal that is trained to respond willingly to the rider's signals is reported by many as the most obvious benefit. Additionally, the rider must use their cognitive skills to relate to the space of the riding aren, including other riders and special equipment, and interact with his horse to navigate safely.

"How very interesting, Phil," said Polly Jane putting down the brochure. "I remember once when we were in Kenya, your mother saw a man whose legs had been cut clear off, being helped onto a camel so that he could feel the rhythm of the walk and enjoy being involved in some type of physical activity. I clearly remember her saying then, "I'd like to work with people doing that, back home." And I kidded her that she'd have to open some kind of zoo around Toronto if she wanted to bring in camels."

"Good grief, thank goodness she didn't take that seriously. Next thing we'd know, she'd have been calling it "H.U.M.P." for —I don't know—, for the Handicapped United for, um— Mobility Program!"

Laughing, they passed the Black Creek Pioneer Village, the quaintness and historical accuracy of which had captured Polly Jane's imagination nearly a decade ago when it had first opened. Because of that particular trip to visit her friends, she had returned to her Upper River Valley home and signed on to a newly formed board of directors, determined to build something similar in her own province. After several years of discussion, planning, grant-writing and purchasing, it was now well on the way to becoming King's Landing Pioneer Village and of that, she was very proud. She hoped within the next few years they, too, could open to the public. P.J. would plan an afternoon of her Ontario visit to see the latest acquisitions and programs at Black Creek. She wondered if they'd purchased one of Lary's old goats as they'd been proposing to do last fall...

As the Satellite slowed at that intersection, Philip clicked on the directional and they turned north onto Jane, really heading into the countryside proper now. Although nothing like the rural wilderness that made up most of New Brunswick, 'north of Steeles' (the major thoroughfare named after a great-great uncle of Philip's father, who had owned a pub in the area) was still a beautiful drive with its winding road, huge hardwoods on either side, and acres of pastures, hay meadows and corn fields.

Just five miles of further driving and Phil put his directional on again, turning into a wide gravel lot extended from the unpaved shoulder. Here stood a large board-and-batten shed with wide doors facing the road, attached to which an enormous white sign read: "Welcome to the 'JUST(e)STATE'. We are home to the *Just-Us on Jane*' Market Garden." This was followed by the Steele's farmhouse phone number. In smaller letters below this was painstakingly painted: "also– Hil's Horsie Haven" and in even smaller letters below that: "L.A.R.Y.: Lifted Ability for Riding Youth" beside which was an artistic picture of a girl on crutches petting a pony.

"Your mother's only offering this for children?" asked Polly Jane.

"For now, I guess—you know it's working with kids that keeps her feeling happy and needed. I think she gets more grants and sponsorship that way, too."

"Plus, if she runs the program for adults as well, she'd have to change the name! Not that that's ever stopped her before, has it?"

Phil grinned. How well P.J. knew his family! For years prior to his parents' marriage, his mother had been an alcoholic. Phil's father was one of the people who, as a concerned rookie in police college, had helped her put her addiction behind her. But in the ambitious and relentless way of many addicts, his mother drove herself to keep busy in a variety of charities, causes and home-based businesses. That sign out front had previously displayed an array of names for a dog kennel, a poultry-and-egg farm, a children's camp and a counseling center for American evaders of the draft. Plus, the estate still employed the seven or eight ex-convicts that had been vetted by Phil's own father as far back as the mid 1950s. He'd so believed in *Justice and Just Us*" and actively sought to rehabilitate those who, in his opinion as a distinguished Superintendent of first the Toronto Police Force and then the Ontario Provincial Police, deserved a second chance in society.

As they continued down the maple-lined laneway, Phil said "Mom wanted me to pull into the stables so you could say hello. She won't be back up to the house until about 9."

As they exited the car and stepped into the still-warm summer evening, Polly Jane gracefully side-stepped a pile of steaming manure. The stable lights pooled out of the two front windows, complete with ivy and geraniums in their window boxes.

"My, isn't it all looking lovely!"

"Mom and the men work hard, that's for sure. Remember my 'uncle' Olly?"

"Oliver Gandless, your godfather? How could I forget that old reprobate?" Polly Jane chuckled.

"Well, Olly told Mom he thought he was nearing retirement this year, so she made him the 'landscape gardener' instead. He lives in the cottage behind the farmhouse now, rather than in the bunkhouse."

"He's doing a terrific job with these window boxes!" Phil's godmother had plunged her forefinger into the soil of one. "I expect a bit of that manure, dried up nicely over the years, really helps the flowers as well as all the vegetables, doesn't it?"

"If they'd let you take a sack of it on the plane, P.J., I'd send some back with you," said a voice from behind her. "Not enough horses in New Brunswick for your wild English gardens?"

"Not nearly," laughed Polly Jane throwing her arms around her old friend's middle. "Lary! How are you, dear?"

"I'm well, thanks – glad you're here safely and not too sweaty like the rest of us in here." Hilary Steele waved a hand toward the steaming equine bodies that were being washed down in the aisle by children and their parents, all of whom seemed equally moist. "Phil, take P.J. on up to the house and get the kettle on. I put some of our lavender-jasmine tea leaves ready in the tea-pot."

"Oh, heavenly – you're growing jasmine now as well?"

Philip smiled proudly at his mother. "She's determined to pull it off, against what all the books say for our type of soil. She even pays the men extra to get out there at midnight to pick the jasmine petals. For the maximum scent, you know!"

"Oh, really, Lary – you don't, do you?" P.J. laughed.

"Whyever not?" her friend demanded. "They aren't all that old, still younger than I am. And I go out *with* them, in the damp!"

"My arthritis is acting up just thinking about it." Polly Jane rubbed her fingers. "But I'll look forward to tasting that tea."

"Let's go get you settled then, God-Mum."

As they exited the barn door, a low nicker followed them, echoing into the gentle rhythms of the cricket chorus just warming up in the fields beyond.

CHAPTER TWO

The next evening, after a hearty repast of Polly Jane's own cooking—always her way of helping out on her visits to the 'Estate', especially when Hilary seemed so busy with her businesses out of doors—the three friends sat in the library with Brahms playing softly in the background. This untidy but comfortable room had been the former domain of Roger Steele, the walls exhibiting floor to ceiling bookshelves which held tomes of every size and genre, as well as records from his classical music collection. On a nearby table, an antique dining one, with its legs cut off to lower it to about 2 feet 6 inches, stood a record player, radio and speakers. Next to it was a leather wingback chair, in which Hilary Steele sat curled up with two seed catalogues and a volume of Wordsworth poetry—neither of which she was reading as she was dozing with her mouth open, soft snores emitting from it. Across the room which had once been solely her late husband's, Phil and Polly Jane sat at a card table with a chess board before them. The card table was next to the window and Polly Jane looked dreamily out at an old orchard paddock and the ramshackle cottage which housed Oliver Gandless, while she waited patiently for Phil to decide upon his next strategic move.

"Your mother really works too hard for her age. *Our* age," she whispered.

"Hmm? Damned if I should have moved that bishop last time."

"Still swearing when you talk to yourself, Phil?" Polly Jane asked with a twinkle in her eye.

"Mom–ah, yes, she does work too hard. But she won't listen to reason. I'd love to see her take a trip – maybe a cruise to Alaska or to a beach in Hawaii."

"She used to love Europe when we were in our twenties, but she really hasn't traveled much since she married your father."

"He was the homebody, definitely. But over the years it must have been contagious, because now she doesn't go anywhere either. Not since we were teenagers."

"I can hear you, you know," said a voice from the armchair. "Perhaps before you both start commenting on the ten pounds I've gained since I last saw P.J. at Christmas, you'll just concentrate on your game."

The two chess players laughed. "It's only because we care about you, Mother. 'Care is heavy; therefore, sleep you. You are care, and care must keep you.'"

"But a little trip really would be so nice for you, Lary. Why not come out to me this winter?" said Polly Jane as she watched her godson move his knight up one and over two.

"I can't leave the men working here on their own. They respect the fact that I'm always here, pitching in with what's needed."

"What she means is, she likes to spend the winters pouring over new ways to use the farm to its potential. Next thing you know she'll be having a big old rock concert like that farmer in upstate New York did last week."

"Tssk. I read that they couldn't even make money from it, despite the numbers. Or I guess *because* of the numbers. The ticket-sellers had to just give up, with all the people pouring in."

"I thought at the time that we're about the same distance here from not only a major city, but the *Ontario* town of Woodstock..." said Hilary Steele thoughtfully, chewing a dirty fingernail.

"Uh-oh," her son tutted in pretend consternation.

"And my goodness, I also live an hour from Woodstock, New Brunswick, and an hour from *our* capital city! We could do a whole series of Woodstock folk and rock concerts in the east of North America..." Polly Jane Whistler, organizer of quaint pioneer villages, gave a sly wink to Phil, who grinned and rolled his eyes.

"I guess we'd need thousands of acres, though, not just 20-odd," Hilary mused.

"Not to mention that while the hippies loved the mud, I'm not sure they'd want to be rolling about in your horse manure, Mom."

In the adjoining kitchen, the wall phone jangled loudly. Phil sprang up, saying "Literally saved by the bell on this far-out topic!"

Both women chuckled, then Hilary called to her son's retreating back: "If that's a rider canceling for tomorrow's lessons, tell them I'm not doing any make-ups for them this week. I want to spend time with P.J. too, you know!"

She returned to her Wordsworth as Polly Jane's eyes tried to concentrate on the chess board in front of her. For a decade or more, Phil had grown too expert for her to be a real adversary, but she still liked to challenge herself. *Kept the aging brain tuned up,* she thought. She'd found no one in Victoria who was interested in anything other than cards or checkers. Phil's low voice in the next room lulled her however; she found it difficult to focus...

Suddenly, from the doorway of the library, Phil spoke with a catch in his voice and both dozing women snapped to attention.

"Mom. Mom, that was Blue. Crispin's dead."

Hilary sprang to her feet. "What on earth?"

Polly Jane also rose. "Crispin? Isn't that Blue's son?"

"By adoption, yes." Phil passed a hand over his eyes. At just over forty years of age, he supposed it wasn't dignified to tear up, especially as a hardened member of numerous homicide teams. But 'Blue', Deputy Commissioner Cobalt, had been best friends with his own father since they were rookies together and was the closest male friend Phil now had, considering how much he was forced to travel and live all over Canada. He was also Phil's indirect boss, the one who seconded Philip out as a consultant to so many outlying areas where the original homicide squads struggled to bring their cases to satisfactory resolution. Crispin had been adopted by the Cobalts when he was seven or eight years of age and, now in his early thirties, he battled addictions to drugs and alcohol as well as struggling with weight gain and a perpetually plummeting self-confidence. He hadn't worked a full-time job for most of his adult life and still lived in the Toronto home of his parents, Rory ('Blue') and Sharon Cobalt.

"What happened? Suicide?" Hilary asked. She did not go near Phil to embrace him; much as she worked vigorously for charities, and with children of all ages, she was not a touchy-feely type. But P.J., who was, moved forward and put her arms around her godson.

"I know. Suicide seems the most likely, doesn't it? Poor Crispin!" said Philip.

"What do you mean 'seems'?" asked Polly Jane, leading Phil to the leather sofa in the middle of the room. Her nose was twitching like the March Hare's, as it often did when she felt on the verge of hearing something puzzling and interesting. "You mean it mightn't be?"

"Sit down, both of you. I'll tell you what Blue just said."

Polly Jane sat beside Phil on the couch whilst his mother returned to her wing-back.

"Blue doesn't believe Crispin killed himself. He thinks he was finally in a better place emotionally, physically, mentally–after spending two months at a sort of spa-rehabilitation place in the country. They visited him every second weekend and both his parents had seen a marked improvement. He was even taking an interest in photography and origami again. But the OPP are ready to close the case after just four days."

"Crispin died four days ago and it's the first we're hearing?" Hilary asked.

"Five, apparently, according to the medical examiner. But Blue and Sharon were up north at their cottage. No phone. So it took the OPP some time to track them down and now Blue's hearing that this spa place didn't report the death right away. Well, not to the police, anyway."

"Tssk. Well, that already sounds suspicious!" said Polly Jane.

"I gather it was a matter of going through several channels, local doctor, and board of directors or some such. Anyway, the police down that way are saying it's suicide."

"And it wasn't in any newspapers?" Hilary wondered.

"It's south of Tillsonburg, Mom. The closest paper we might have seen would have perhaps been a Woodstock one, and you don't get that here, do you?"

"How did he–that is, what happened?" P.J. wasn't exactly taking notes, but she was definitely more attentive than she'd been at the chess board, Phil thought. He glanced at his mother, concerned.

"Maybe I'll tell you later, P.J...." His voice trailed off. His godmother was used to hearing details of his cases; he discussed them with her frequently. But his mother wasn't, nor had his father ever revealed details of *his* cases to his busy wife. On top of which, she'd known Crispin quite well, whereas P.J. had never met him.

"Don't be utterly inane, Philip." Hilary snorted. "I am not some delicate senior citizen whom you have to protect from blood and gore. I have to bandage up men's digits when they've lopped them off, before I rush them to Emergency. Not to mention picking a chunk of fencing out of a horse's neck. Not to mention their..."

"Yes, Mother. All right, fine. But it isn't pleasant hearing, especially when I know you had a soft spot for Crispin."

"Just go on."

He couldn't face her while he spoke, though, so he turned to his godmother, met her eyes. "Crispin's body was found near a creek, just off a main highway, right under a train trestle bridge. One of those really high ones. Blue says the equivalent of about twelve stories on an apartment building. His body was found by a farmer driving by at six a.m., who noticed a herd of his cows acting strangely down in their pasture and went to investigate. So that was early morning, and the coroner figures time of death was about ten hours before that."

"And they think, what—he jumped?" Hilary asked abruptly. "Poor little Crispin."

Crispin Cobalt hadn't been 'little' for about a quarter of a century, but Philip knew his mother was remembering the small boy who'd run about their farm squealing at the goats, chasing the chickens and climbing the orchard trees.

"He wasn't hit by a car and thrown?" Polly Jane added.

"The M.E. says not. Er–different type of injuries, and too far from the actual road." Again, Philip could not look at his mother.

"And this farmer—why didn't he telephone this accident to the police himself?"

"I gather from what Blue said that he and his wife are connected in some way to the spa place—the wife's a nurse and she was with him at the time—and they went to them directly and told them. The trestle bridge is partially on land that the center owns, Blue says."

"Is there to be a public funeral?" Hilary asked, no longer interested in the details of Crispin's actual death, as her old friend P.J. appeared to be.

"No. At least not yet. Blue is digging in his official heels and wants to send in a consultant to go over the case with the OPP first."

"Ahhh," said Hilary, now in full comprehension.

"Oh-oh!" said Polly Jane, also seeing where this was going.

"Yes, I'll be leaving at seven in the morning. Sorry not to spend as much time with you as I'd hoped, though, P.J."

"Never mind, dear. Perhaps I can persuade your mother to cancel a few lessons and take off a bit more time to relax with me."

"We'll see." Hilary stood and stretched. "I'm off to bed now, and I suggest we all do the same. I must call Sharon in the morning and see if she needs anything, or if she'd like to come over. I'm sure she's grieving in a very different way than Blue right now; he's probably just bullying his D.C. way into this and not even letting the shock wear off first."

Phil knew his mother was thinking back two decades to his sister's fatal overdose and the hell of disbelief and grief that overtook a family who had already suffered through addictions, broken promises, and personal remonstrances.

"We all must grieve as we best can," said P.J. sagely.

•   •   •

Trevor Ames was out of the downtown apartment—so stuffy in this August heat wave—at six a.m. Dawn had barely arrived; *the street lamps were still on, for Pete's sake!* But he was happy to be out of the filthy city and on the road in his little Beetle-bug. He took a last long drag on his Export A and tossed it out the window. Carl had been quite drunk after their bar sojourn last night and had stayed over—something they would have never normally risked. So Trevor had left him snoring away in bed, with the coffee pot on, and a note beside it saying he didn't know how long he'd be gone, to please lock up properly this time when he left.

While the D.C. had promised the team that had worked the Mortimore/Greenidge case some extended time off, Trevor was new to the homicide squad, freshly promoted to Detective Inspector, and a recent resident of Toronto in general. So he'd happily agreed when his supervisor told him that D.I. Steele had requested him on another job right away, one that was a personal favor to the Deputy Commissioner. Being inexperienced and at the bottom of the pecking order was rarely a good thing. It was one of many reasons the killing of Mortimore, and the disappearance of several other young men in the district he was coming to know, had terrified and sickened him so much. He was only marginally older than the eldest of the missing; Connor had been recorded as a 23-year-old. While none of his colleagues knew it, he had several other things in common with the young men, too: his love of song-writing and busking, his joy at sitting in an art gallery, and his romantic and sexual preferences. He was keeping all of these a well-guarded secret. He'd have to remind Carl again to be careful; Trevor's entire career could be at stake. But in the meantime, he was glad to leave his vacation and the city behind, to step in and take on another job.

As the sun rose behind him, its reflection was trapped in his tiny rear-view mirror, nearly blinding him. He reached up with his right hand and shifted it, then ran his fingers through his already-thinning hair. While he'd have liked to see if growing his hair into the latest, longer styles would keep his slight bald spot yet another secret from his fellow cops, "hippie" hair was frowned on within the force–unless of course one was working undercover. Thus he'd tried shaping it with Brylcreem, but he despised the smell. Maybe it was time to just give up and accept his fate; his father had told him, before they'd stopped speaking, that he himself had been mostly bald by thirty-five.

Anyway, wondered Trevor as he listened to Wilson Pickett's version of 'Hey Jude' on his VW's little tinny radio, why couldn't he just be more self-confident about his natural looks? Detective Inspector Steele, for instance, was a fine example of a man who oozed confidence–and he wasn't exactly a movie star. Trevor had worked the past seven months and through Greenidge's court case with the middle-aged Steele; he really admired the way the esteemed consultant not only pieced together seemingly unconnected clues and didn't suffer fools gladly, but stood up for any small injustices. He wasn't afraid to show his love of literature, history and the arts, either. The man was just average height, with thinning reddish-blond hair and freckles, too—but he could strut down the corridors of the headquarters on Jarvis Street as if he were Paul Newman. Maybe it helped that one of his best friends was Deputy Commissioner Cobalt. Or that he'd personally helped solve and put to bed so many notorious cases across Canada in his career?

While he'd miss Carl, he was looking forward to picking up 'Phil', as the D.I. insisted Trevor call him when they weren't questioning members of the general populous. They would take the air-conditioned Satellite the rest of the way as well, and as the day grew hotter, he knew that would be a blessing. Yes, he was rather looking forward to spending time away from what had become his "sordid little routine" as his father had called it, in this strange Ontario city.

·　　·　　·

Cathy put down the pruning shears and straightened her back slowly, vertebra by vertebra. The roses were looking quite withered, and the harsh winds off Lake Erie weren't exactly helping. But what more could she do to make the Port Dune Lodging House look charming and attractive? Or perhaps two tough city policemen wouldn't care, or notice? Certainly Brian wouldn't help her to pull that ugly old bench off the front porch. Perhaps if she draped an afghan over it and put the vase of daisies and coneflowers near it, the guests would overlook the peeling paint and crooked leg? Much like herself, she thought—only in her case it was more crinkling skin and crooked leg. Though the sunburn on her nose *was* starting to peel as well…

The share-growers were keeping Brian busy down in the kilns. Her brother was one of the first in the county to prime the flue-cured tobacco and the field workers were out first thing every morning, no matter the weather, no matter the day. This included their sacred church Sunday, which truly annoyed Cathy. Her Baptist minister, Reverend Talbot, was furious too, she knew; he tried to calm her when she spoke of it, however. That Jake Wiebe, their foreman, was responsible. His family was full of such hard workers, she had to admit—and the youngest daughter Sarah was certainly something of an academic genius—but it didn't excuse them deciding to work through the Lord's Day. Just because they'd come up from Mexico and missed a lot of Sunday meetin'-times on the long migration didn't mean they shouldn't start up again once they'd settled here.

Now, what to feed the detectives for breakfast in the morning? And would they go to Nellie's Bar and Grill between here and Sandytown for supper, or would they wish to buy groceries and keep some things in their big barn fridge? The Nelsons usually only offered their guests a morning meal, something she'd heard they did in Europe. They called them 'Bed-and-Breakfasts', apparently.

She wished she'd thought to ask that nice Detective Inspector Steele when he'd telephoned last night. And blast that Tina Van Doren, she just *knew* she'd picked up and been listening in on their party line. So it would be all over Port Dune and most of the county by now that the police weren't accepting suicide as the verdict in the death of that poor man who fell from the Black Bridge up on the highway.

"Cath?" she heard Brian's voice call from the other side of the barnyard.

"Eh?" she hollered in return—by way of letting him know her location between the rose bushes, not because she expected to carry on a conversation until he arrived at the garden fence.

"Cath! You there?"

She stepped out from the pricklies into the warm sun, stripping her hands of the gardening gloves as she walked to the fence.

"What is it, Bri? You know I got those police comin' any time now. And you know…"

"I've got plenty to do…"

"…Afore then." They finished together, not even conscious of the overlap.

"Stanley Fehr cut his hand and the first aid kit in the barn is out of BandAids. We got any up here?"

"Shore. Up in the bathroom."

"K'int youse get 'em? Don'wanna take my boots off."

"Oh, fine," Cathy huffed. "But you stay there and I'll toss 'em out the window. I ain't comin' back down and I sure ain't got no time to head to the barn."

Cathy limped up the stairs and tossed a tin of BandAids down to her brother below, keeping just a few behind for the bathroom shelf. Then she grabbed the most colorful afghan she owned from The Quay Room—Mama had knitted it in one of her last years in the nursing home, she remembered—and went back to the porch to drape it artistically over the bench before her guests arrived.

•   •   •

When the VW Beetle pulled noisily into the laneway of the JUST(e)STATE, Phil was standing ready, suitcase packed, at the front door of the farmhouse. Amused, he watched as the horse his mother was leading to a paddock spooked slightly. That must be a younger, greener one, he thought. She wouldn't be putting a handicapped child up on a pony that couldn't handle an over-loud little bubble-car. He was also tickled to see an arm shoot out the VW window, flick a cigarette into the gravel and wave cheerily to his parent as the vehicle passed. Phil couldn't see her face, but he knew his mother was glaring daggers back at poor innocent Trevor, the lad from Regina, now of Toronto. Likely never set foot on a farm in his life. Thank goodness he hadn't tooted the horn!

He turned as Polly Jane emerged from the kitchen, carrying a plastic cooler and small basket.

"I've packed you both a nice lunch, dear. There's enough in there to nibble on if you get hungry on the journey, too." They'd all been up since six, but Phil was still surprised she'd had time to do more than get dressed and sip her coffee.

"Thanks, P.J. We'll be there in two hours, though, before 9:30!"

"Well, you never know when you'll find a place to eat. And there's a thermos for you as well. Your mother said I could fill it with iced tea, but I know you prefer lemonade so I squeezed some specially for you. With some of your godfather's honey to sweeten it."

"Cheers, God-Mum. Now come out and meet Trevor. I doubt if Mother will."

Polly Jane smiled as the short and stocky 20-something wriggled his way out of his rounded Bug and reached behind for a gym-bag and briefcase.

" 'Morning, Trev," Philip said. "I'd like you to meet my godmother, fresh from New Brunswick. She's made us a lunch. P.J., this is Trevor—Detective Inspector Ames."

"Hi-ya!" Trevor bubbled, instantly regretting it. Oops, time to put on 'his act': the calm, slightly sullen macho performance he generally adopted for work colleagues. He lowered his voice a semi-tone. "Good to meet you." He shook hands with the elderly woman with the blue-tinted hair and gingham apron wrapped around a flowered cotton skirt. Had he just arrived in Mayberry?

"Mother!" Philip called out to the farm's sole owner as she headed back toward the stable. "I'm leaving now."

Hilary raised a hand briefly, distracted. "Be safe!"

Phil leaned down and kissed his godmother's cheek. "I'll call you every second evening, or so, with updates." He whispered, not caring for the young man waiting beside the Satellite to overhear. He nodded toward his mother's disappearing back, her clean-that-morning jodhpurs already stained with a green smudge on one beige buttock. "She'll probably want details, too—but she'll never admit it."

"I know, dear. I'll make sure she has some time to relax a bit more than usual, and perhaps Blue's wife will come and spend some time with us too."

"That would be nice for her. Although you'll probably end up doing the brunt of the grief counseling."

"That's fine. Wherever I'm needed."

Polly Jane stood in the laneway, waving her apron until the sedan disappeared behind the maple trees. Phil, who was letting Trevor drive the enormous new vehicle—part of the perks of having an assistant seconded to him; he might even be able to cat-nap!—stuck his arm out and waved back, wondering if he'd see her again before her Ontario holiday was over.

CHAPTER THREE

"I've put you in The Quay Room, and here's the *key*, Inspector Steele." Cathy Nelson chuckled. "Do you get the pun?"

"I comprehend the homophonic cleverness, Miss Nelson, indeed." Phil inwardly chided himself as he usually did when he sounded like a snob. But it was better than blurting out some satirical rejoinder, especially in the first minutes of meeting someone who had the potential to spit in his poached eggs every morning.

"The *what,* now? My brother and I are quite religious; we don't want that kind of behavior here. You *did* say you wanted *two* rooms?"

Phil pretended not to notice Trevor's reddening face when he met his eyes and threw him a sideways grin. He'd have winked, to ease the man's discomfort, if he hadn't thought it might evoke yet more suspicion from their hostess.

"Thank-you, ma'm. Yes, two rooms and a private place to use the telephone each evening, please."

"Oh, that ain't no bother. Though I told you we have us a party line here, didn't I? And a real nosy neighbor that likes ta pick up whenever she hears it jangle, like it does when you dial out sometimes."

"Well, we do appreciate the warning. We'll have to be extra diligent when we're discussing the case, and perhaps we'll be able to use a more secure line at Bayham Brook House itself?"

"Very likely. Though from what I hears, Jeremiah Flintwinch, the manager up there, ain't gonna be too welcoming of you-all.

Now, Inspector Ames, here's the key to The Dock Room. That's around the corner from the bathroom. My brother wanted to call it The Pier Room, but I said that was a pun too far. 'magine folk thinkin' we was peerin' at 'em, like some Peepin' Toms!"

"That's a pity. D.I. Ames rather likes puns. Or what he *thinks* are puns!" said Phil, remembering. "We look forward to partaking of your hospitality, Miss Nelson."

Cathy limped off down the stairs leaving the men to unpack their bags and settle in. She was glad Inspector Steele said they'd be eating out for most meals except breakfast. She'd checked the barn fridge and it hadn't been cleaned all summer and was chock full of bag lunches and sodas for the workers, anyway.

"Quite the maritime feel to these rooms, eh?" Trevor said as he tossed his gym-bag on his bed and looked around at the décor, complete with a ship's wheel and fishing net. He wondered if he should have brought his guitar, but figured he'd be lucky to have time to take even one stroll along the shore.

"Well, there are more harbors and ports along Lake Erie than up on Lake Ontario. Toronto doesn't have nearly the same reputation for freighter docking as they do down here, for instance. Or for fish and chips!"

"You've spent time down this way?"

"I've taught some courses at the Police College, yes. Nose to the grindstone all week, then on Friday nights everyone would usually come down to the lake for some dancing and perch."

"Wild times, man." said Trevor, grinning. "Wild times."

"Indeed. Let's get unpacked and head to the scene of this possible crime, shall we?"

•   •   •

Chugging smoothly along away from the lake again, this time toward Sandytown, a village surrounded by flat fields of tobacco planted in the loose sandy soil, Philip twisted the map in his hand. "We have to go through to just a few miles north of the village. It's half-way between Sandytown and another four-corner stop called… uh…" At this point Philip lowered his voice and started muttering nearly inaudibly, "Eden's Crock? Enter Crack? That can't be right…"

"You talkin' to yourself again?" Trevor asked, doing his 'cool' persona as he sucked in heavily on his Export A, then flicked ashes into the ashtray under the much-larger radio than his VW was equipped with.

"Oh, wait – I think that's Edom's Creek. Yeah. Anyway, we don't want to get that far north."

As the Satellite came to the top of a forested gully, the inspectors' jaws dropped as they saw for the first of many times, the 165-foot tall black-painted steel trestle bridge. The highway dipped down to go under it where a glistening golden creek wound gently along the valley floor; the trains were designed to find their way across the height.

"Pull over for a second, Trevor, please." They craned their necks, looking up through the windshield at the monstrosity. "Why the hell would anyone want to stand up there, never mind cross it? And the D.C. told me Crispin wasn't afraid of heights, but wasn't exactly an adventure-seeker, either."

"Must-a been trippin'," Trevor put in helpfully.

"I don't think so. He'd supposedly been clean for some months. But I guess it's our job to find out. O.K., let's go. Bayham Brook House is, according to this, just the other side of the valley there." While the men were officially now of equal rank, Trevor had no problem taking orders from the well-respected older man; he'd just play along through this case as if he were still a sergeant, he decided.

When they reached the top of the other side of the ravine, Trevor again let his foot off the brake. There was a large two-story house with a bright crabapple tree and low stone walls on the right, a meadow and forest sprawling out behind it. But on their left stood a towering four-story house, partly dug into a grassy hill, with windows, balconies, gables and terraces scattered all about it, presenting very little pattern or symmetry, it seemed to Phil. All along that side of the road for what looked like a half-mile, stretched a black wrought-iron fence. It was not more than three feet high and was supported every thirty feet by stone pillars of the same color as the walls on the opposite side of the highway. All along it ran strands of ivy, looking vaguely withered and wan now at the end of such a hot summer.

"There's a few driveways, but—look up there." Trevor pointed.

"Yup, that looks like the main entrance, and there's the sign: Bayham Brook House—Retreat, Spa and Natural-healing Center."

"You wouldn't figure it, out here in hicksville, would you? No pun intended."

What pun, for heaven's sakes? Phil wondered, as he often had when working previously with Trevor. Maybe puns meant something different in Saskatchewan, one of the few provinces in which he'd never plunked a boot. But he said only, "Oh, I don't know. It's not that far for the elite of Toronto to come stay, and I gather the area tobacco farmers—at least not the ones share-cropping—are making a pretty good dollar. Likely it's mostly their wives that want to come here and relax."

"So what was the son of a Deputy Commissioner doing here? If you don't mind my asking."

"Ask away, Trevor. It's our job. The D.C.— and I may call him 'Blue' sometimes in your company, if you'll pardon it—said they'd tried other centers and clinics, mostly up north of Toronto as well as right in the city. Those places would give Crispin methadone, to try to help with inevitable withdrawal, but they were often located too close to dealers, still. It was too easy to access liquor, despite all the AA meetings Crispin used to attend. The family thought this place was just far enough out to — what the *hell*? BRAKE!"

They had pulled into the main laneway, had been passing a tree line, with 2 clay tennis courts next to it, when he'd suddenly spotted a woman flying up from the woods and running diagonally across the courts. He was out of the car before Trevor had come to a full stop.

"Miss? Miss! Stop. I'm police! Are you all right?"

The woman, who appeared to be in her early 20s had long, stringy blond hair, matted with burrs. Mud, or possibly clay, covered her from head to foot, her loose-fitting floral dress streaked with gray muck and grass stains.

She was weeping, huge sobs wracking her body as she gasped for air. Phil put his arm around her and she simply sank to the ground on the court, leaning against his knees. Trevor, who was by now out of the car and no longer considering his macho act, skidded to his knees beside her.

"Hey, ma'm? What is it? Is something chasing you?"

"Let's help her up, D. I. Ames."

"Are you hurt anywhere?" Trevor asked. The girl shook her head vehemently and the two men raised her to her feet, steadying her as they each took an arm to support her. From inside the long, low clubhouse-type building along the tennis courts, they heard a door bang and then another woman's voice calling, "Karen? Karen, what's *happened*?" The outer screen door squeaked shut as this woman rushed toward them. Her ample curves were squeezed into tight blue jeans with the requisite belled bottoms and flat-sole sneakers. However, a starched white apron stretched across her well-endowed bosom and fell to just below her knees. A patch of reddish-brown showed plainly where the apron covered her thigh.

"Are *you* all right?" Phil queried, pointing to the stain.

"Me?" She glanced down, then waved her hand. "Oh, yes. That's just iodine. I was treating someone with a minor cut. Karen, what *is* it?"

The new woman, with curly wisps escaping from her dark brunette ponytail, slipped her arm between Phil and Karen; she and Trevor helped her to a park bench set along the edge of the court. Phil followed, clearing his throat.

"Ma'm, we're the detectives that were called in. You're expecting us? May we just question Karen for a few moments?"

"Of course, of course. I'm Sela Cowan, the resident nurse here."

Phil squatted to face Karen, who slouched forward on the bench, her face in her hands. With her arm, Sela wiped her own forehead which was beaded with sweat, tucked a stray curl behind her ear, then stroked the top of Karen's head as gently as though she were touching a newborn kitten for the first time.

"Easy, easy, Kay. Deep breaths, remember?"

Philip glanced at Trevor, who immediately took out his notebook. This was one of the reasons Phil had requested the young man; despite having just been promoted due to his sharp skills, he was also intuitive and—when he thought no one was looking—sensitively kind. Phil watched him lick the tip of his small pencil and knew he would be discreetly jotting phrases as the blond girl was quizzed.

"What happened, Karen? Can you tell us now?"

Still tearful, Karen nodded, not raising her face.

Sela said, "Mudfog marbles, three-five-seven!" and clapped both her hands sharply in Karen's ear. Startled, Phil and Trevor exchanged glances, but Sela Cowan looked up at them both and whispered, "Tell you later."

Phil, feeling as though he'd just slipped down the rabbit hole, asked again, "Karen, can you tell us, did you fall in some dirt? Some clay? When you saw something? Heard something?"

This time Karen looked up and studied him with calm, if slightly glazed eyes. "I saw Charlie. I found him. Charlie Squeers."

Trevor, intent on taking notes, asked "Charlie Squires?"

"Charlie Squeers," answered Karen. "I-I loved him, you know."

Phil frowned, still feeling like he was roaming about in Carroll-land. Squeers? Now where had he...? He said, "Where is Charlie now?"

Karen seemed in a trance as she answered simply, "In the ground. He's buried."

Weirder and weirder, thought Phil and glanced again at Trevor. But then the nurse spoke up to clarify. "Charlie Squeers was a client here, a residential client. He disappeared a few weeks ago and we thought he'd gone 'off program' and made his way back to the city. Unfortunately, it happens sometimes." The nurse shrugged and went back to stroking Karen's hair. "What do you mean Charlie is buried, Karen?"

"I'll show you, if you like." Karen got up, smoothed her rumpled skirt and steadily started walking in the direction from which she'd emerged in such a state of hysteria just ten minutes earlier.

Phil spoke up before moving. "Um. Should we—? Is she o.k.?"

"I'll explain more to you later, Detective _____?"

"I'm D.I. Steele. This is D.I. Ames."

"Well, come along gentlemen, we'd better follow and find out what's up."

It was at that moment that a scruffily bearded man in his thirties, a white bandage wrapped around his left forearm, sauntered out of the clubhouse-type building. Philip now noticed a sign reading: 'Tot'n'ham's Courtside' over its door.

"Hey, man," the stranger said, puffing a cigarette, but holding it between his thumb and forefinger as though taking a toke. This latter expression Phil had just heard in the past year, since his return to Toronto; in fact he believed it was Trevor who'd first introduced it to him. "What's the scene here? You cats the fuzz?"

Sela paused, pointing toward the main building. "Gerald, not now. If your arm's stopped bleeding, go on up to The Rookery and wait for lunch, please."

"Hey, yeah, that's cool. Don't wig out, Sealie, I'll split."

Phil stepped in with his typical formality, always used to balance his inwardly rolling eyes. "Thank you, sir. Please tell everyone at the house that we shall be in directly."

"No sweat, man."

Sela glanced at them as if about to roll her eyes herself, caught herself, then hurried ahead, calling over her shoulder, "Come on! Karen's disappeared down into the ravine!"

They waded into a forest floor more than ankle deep with the fallen leaves and twigs of hundred-year-old oaks, maples and elm, the latter of which were in imminent danger from the disease Phil had heard was making its way to Ontario woodlands. Almost immediately they dropped down a small but steep hill, about ten feet high, until they were brought level again onto a wide trail.

"Karen? Karen, where are you?" Sela called, apparently unsure which direction to lead them on the leaf-covered track. Hearing no response, the nurse turned toward the south and they walked in silence for a minute before she shouted again.

"Kay? Karen?"

"I'm here, Sela."

The three of them looked down into the gully that swept at least sixty feet below them now, seeing signs of a sunlit-sparkling brook at the bottom. There, about half-way down, sat Karen, on the ground beside an article of clothing. As they scrambled down the side of the hill, Trevor falling to one knee as a camouflaged branch caught him, Phil realized it was not an old tie-dyed shirt which Karen was clasping, however. A man's blackened limb was poking through the armhole of the fabric. A man who was half-buried in the hill's side, but whose right arm and leg were now sticking through the muck of a hole obviously dug in an effort to conceal his body.

It would appear that Charlie Squeers had not gone deliberately 'off program', after all.

·   ·   ·

Several hours later, after overseeing the Bayham Township Coroner's unit and two OPP officers as they collected samples, evidence, took photos and finally hefted the body up the steep incline on a stretcher, Phil trudged toward Bayham Brook House to join Trevor. He had sent the younger D.I. up there with Sela and Karen almost as soon as they'd seen the body, to first report it to the locals and the OPP. He'd then asked Trevor to contact Supervisor Flaherty, Trevor's direct boss in Toronto, and ask him to let D.C. Cobalt know of this change in circumstances. With a second dead man, Phil knew Blue would presume what they were all currently thinking: the deaths must surely be linked. Philip had then told Trevor to start questioning the residents and staff, primarily about Crispin's death, but also keeping 'an ear out and pencil at the ready' for anything that might pertain to two weeks ago, and the disappearance of Charlie Squeers.

While he'd waited for the locals to arrive, Phil had avoided his instinct to examine not just the body, but the area immediately surrounding it. This wasn't his case, not his job. Plus, Karen had probably disturbed the scene enough without him adding to it.

"Hell's teeth," he said through his own clenched ones and thought, *had she even done it on purpose?* To cover up something, add confusion? Or to remove something she knew might assist them? And what was with the suddenly calm act she'd brought on? Not to mention her words "I loved him, you know"?

Best let the coroner's team have at it; besides Squeers' body itself, there'd be layers of leaves to sift through and minutely scrutinize, potential clues to assess among the earth and composting tiers. He did, though, observe an opened channel of leaves where it appeared something had been dragged down the hill from the trail above. Was this how the body had arrived in its current resting spot? Or had someone pulled something else heavy along there? Or perhaps Squeers and another person had slid down themselves? Along this toboggan-wide track in the clay-soiled forest floor, he also caught sight of a packet of Belmont filters. He didn't go close, but recognized the familiar, though muddy, pack; his father had smoked them for years before quitting—too late, as it had turned out.

Once the teams had arrived and begun their work, Phil propped himself on a moss-covered rock and brought Dr. Manhope and an Officer Biro, the lead investigator sent from the local Ontario Provincial Police branch, up to date on his own and Trevor's presence at the retreat. While their groups worked below near the body, he relayed to the two men (both smoking cigarettes and dropping the butts into the dry leaves with a careless attitude that had Phil squirming), some of the strangeness they'd already observed since pulling into the laneway. Added to this recitation were some questions he'd considered while he'd waited for them to arrive. Then he'd watched from the road-like track as a coroner's assistant backed in an old station-wagon hearse from the highway, as far as they could, and hoisted Squeers' body on a canvas stretcher up the hill and into the back. He waited patiently until all the men had gathered their equipment and left the premises. *As if he'd been the host, when in fact he'd only arrived on the property himself.*

He sighed, grateful that Trevor had been with him, and able to keep everyone up at the main building so that there'd been no need to patrol spying guests, curious staff members, or lines of hippies, sitting cross-legged and doing yoga chants in memoriam.

"Stand guard at the portal of your *own* mind," he said aloud, scolding himself.

But now, glancing at his watch to find that it was nearly one o'clock, Phil felt too tired to be only about to start the actual job to which he'd been assigned. He walked a little way along the wide wooded track and noticed a rustic, wooden sign nailed to a tree. He'd missed that on their walk down, probably too anxiously searching for Karen at the time.

The sign was lettered in dark green paint which read: 'Cad's Hill' and Phil thought wryly, *I wonder if Charlie Squeers had been a cad? Was that an appropriate epitaph to the man whose body had just been lugged up Cad's Hill?* He turned and climbed the smaller hill, the ten-foot one that would bring him, he thought, to where the tennis courts should be. However, he'd over-shot his estimate; he emerged instead into a small stable-yard where three horses looked over the tops of their Dutch doors at him and an old German Shepherd, lying on the cool cement of his kennel, partially structured under a pine tree, did not so much as raise his head. A tabby barn cat stretched luxuriously in the sun, batting his paw lazily as a moth alighted on a straw bale. As Phil turned to get his bearings, spotting the tennis courts and his borrowed Satellite off to the left, a white rabbit hopped past the straw bale and disappeared into a hole in a door labeled 'Tack Room'. Well, that was certainly the first thing that made sense on this place, he smiled. If the rabbit had been wearing a tweed waistcoat and pulled out his pocket watch, Phil wouldn't have been surprised.

Reaching over the stable-yard's gate to unclip the latch, he admired the hedge on either side of it. Thick and still green in this heavy August heat, it served as an attractive entrance/exit to the barn. As he turned to close the gate, he read another natural-looking sign, painted to match the 'Cad's Hill' one, as well as the one he'd seen earlier above the clubhouse door. The stable sign said 'Furr-neville's Inn'. Well, it was certainly the home of several furries, he considered, and thought that his mother would be most amused. With both his parents' penchant for naming their farm and its businesses with fitting titles, he was sure she'd appreciate the English tradition of christening every knoll and outhouse presented here.

He stopped at the car and ate one of Polly Jane's sandwiches and a handful of grapes from the cooler in the back seat. They'd decided to keep rolls of film in a knotted plastic bag in the cooler as well, and to keep changing the ice block every few days. Phil then downed a cup of P.J.'s delicious lemonade, still cold after several hours in the thermos. If Trevor had not yet been fed, he'd send him out to relax in the shade somewhere to eat a lunch on his own. The young D.I.'s head was probably spinning by now, surrounded with buzzing voices and unanswered questions.

Reluctantly, but feeling at least more refreshed, Phil continued to the main building. Its four stories were not apparent from this angle; from where he stood now, it looked like only a huge two-story house. Had he not seen from below, as they drove up the highway's hill, that there were two other levels, the bottom and foundation almost completely of stone—and the other levels peppered with a mish-mash of terraces, balconies and dormers—he wouldn't have thought it looked so eccentric. From here it appeared to be a fairly normal, though somewhat modern and overly windowed, dwelling for a large family. He did detect a small turret on the rear side, though, reaching up even taller than these upper two stories to make what must be a fifth level to its entirety. One might have expected such a design to be entirely of stone or brick; however, these above-hill levels were simply white clapboard with a faded, black shingle roof. The only real color on the structure was noted as Phil neared a door; it was painted bright red. Beside it was a brick pigeon-holed structure and on the other side of this was another door, this one the same dark green as the letters on the rustic signs. Phil knew this because above this green door read yet another signboard: 'Bayham Brook House – Main Entrance'.

"Well, what the hell's the red door, then?" Philip muttered aloud. Why have two very different doors side-by-side? And painted two different colors? It certainly wasn't for aesthetics. But then, it would seem none of the building had been blueprinted for ease on eyes.

Phil also took in the odd door-knocker affixed to the thick green door. Sculpted in the form of a man's head, it sported a brass ring used to knock, which was threaded through the figure's teeth like one of his mother's loose-ring snaffles in her favorite mare's velvet mouth. The man stared at him with wide eyes, but through spectacles; his hair was messy and spiky. Feeling a strange familiarity creep under his skin, Philip Steele rapped sharply with this knocker, then simply turned the door handle and entered. It wasn't as though he was unexpected, after all.

CHAPTER FOUR

"If you're quite finished, Detective Inspector Ames?" Phil asked, a half hour later of Trevor, who had been sitting jovially at a banquet table in the oak-paneled dining room (signed 'The Melon & Cauli Tavern'). So much for thinking his younger colleague might need either a break in the shade for a quick sandwich, or time alone 'far from the madding crowd'. From what Phil had been able to tell in the last thirty minutes—he had helped himself to tea from a tea caddy in the corner and had just been standing listening as he sipped—Trevor had been busy most of the morning jotting notes as several people regaled him with a variety of uplifting tales. He'd managed to do this while scarfing down lobster salad, cold fried chicken and homemade rolls. Who needed P.J.'s white bread, chipped-beef sandwich with cream cheese?

"Certainly, D.I. Steele." Politely, and evidently forgetting the gruff exterior which Philip was always amused to see Trevor adopt when in the public eye, the younger detective stood, snapped shut his notebook and followed Phil out of the dining room. Outside the wide oak doors, Philip paused and lowered his head to Trevor's level.

"What's with the camaraderie? I didn't spend hours out in the heat watching a dead body be removed from among the maggots and shrieking cicadas so that you could be in here on your own having a jolly picnic with your new friends, did I?"

"Fear not. I've got lots of intel to share with you. Let's go to the office down the hall here." Trevor led him through a long corridor with several padded benches on either side of tall potted plants and with floor to ceiling windows on one side facing out to a pine tree-dotted ravine where Phil noticed several tiny and peculiar-looking buildings.

"Oh, Detective Ames, did you wish me for anything else today?" A pleasant male voice stopped them both and Trevor turned, facing a man in clerical collar who was just exiting from a room and locking the door behind him.

"No thank you, Reverend. You've been very helpful." Again, Phil was mystified at the change in persona; in the city, Trevor mostly turned up his abrupt and rough-spoken copper act. "Are you leaving for the day?"

"I am. I'm really only here for special occasions, anyway. And of course, when they called me about finding Char–a body, I came right over. Hello!" The minister extended a hand to Philip. "I'm Reverend Klassen, Peter Klassen."

"Good to meet you, Reverend. I'm D.I. Steele. D.I. Ames was just about to bring me up to speed, so I'm sure we'll be in contact soon."

"Any time. My church is the United, in Edom's Creek. If I can be of help and you can't reach me at the manse, I'll likely be in the church basement. We're renovating it." With a wave, the young minister disappeared down the hall.

"Nice fella," Trevor declared. "Told me I couldn't smoke in the dining room, mind you, but he did say I could in the offices and The Rookery. That's like their common room."

"But he doesn't actually work here?"

"I guess not. Sure seems pretty familiar with everything and everyone, though."

An orange-haired, middle-aged woman came out of another room as they continued their walk. She slammed the door behind her and glared at them, as if expecting them to arrest her for breaching the quiet. "*What?*" she snapped. "I suppose you think it's a good giggle to make fun of someone's weight, do you?" She poked a finger churlishly at Trevor's chest, but turned to address Philip. "He called me an elephant, did you know? I'll report him, I will! I'll report him. When the ice-cream van came last week, *he,*"— here she pointed again at Trevor—"said I wasn't to have the rum 'n' raisin!" With that she marched off down the corridor stomping her feet to emphasize her point.

The men looked at each other in bewilderment. Trevor shrugged and said in a low voice, "Haven't met that one yet. And I certainly didn't meet her last week!"

Just then Sela Cowan appeared. She was not wearing her starched nurse's apron now, but rather a short white lab coat over her tight bell bottoms, complete with name tag, upside-down watch fob, and walkie-talkie tucked into a pocket. Scurrying down a different hallway from a shorter wing of the sprawling house, she said, "I'm sorry, gentlemen. That sounded like Lucy Tox. And no, it's not short for 'toxic', although she certainly is. She is both delusional and a pathological liar. Pay her no mind."

Phil snorted. "Well, that's going to be tricky since we're here to question everyone on what are now officially two suspicious deaths on your property."

Sela smiled thinly. "Yes, I feel I should also explain about Karen and Gerald from earlier. You see, while many guests come here just for an overnight or weekend stay from time to time, to relax in one of our Earth-conscious villas, and take part in some of our sports or spa-offerings, we also have a number of residents who come for longer. And for more serious matters. Like poor Crispin, for whom you're really here, I understand."

"And Karen and Gerald?" asked Trevor, pulling out his notebook again, licking his stub of a pencil.

"Right. They are both here on a recovery plan of rehabilitation. Drug and alcohol dependency. We're one of the first centers in Ontario to try this live-in type of treatment and Dr.

Flintwinch is an extremely skillful counselor when it comes to rehab. His parents, Aaron and Lena Schneider were the founders of the Halfway-House movement in Michigan in the late 1940s. Amazing family."

Phil found he was about to retort, *And is it part of these amazing psychiatric idols' programs to have patients toppling off trestle bridges or being buried in shallow graves?* To prevent himself from such sarcasm, he slipped into his cool formality and asked, "When might we expect to meet Dr. Flintwinch, Miss Cowan? I understand, from the discussions I heard in the dining room, that he isn't available today?"

"He's in Toronto at a seminar, I'm afraid. I have telephoned to his hotel there, to leave an urgent message about Charlie, of course. He should return tomorrow."

"Thank you. D.I. Ames and I were just heading off to confer, if you'll excuse us?"

"Certainly. Charlie's body is—that is—I saw the hearse go by on the highway a while ago..."

"Yes, the coroner has taken him, but that area of the woods is strictly off limits for now, as it's a crime scene. Please make sure that everyone on the property knows this."

"Oh, I will. And were you," she said, directing this question to Trevor, "going to take D.I. Steele to The Growlery? It's really the quietest office, and Dr. Flintwinch is the only one that tends to use it, anyway. So help yourselves."

The Growlery? Phil thought with a jolt. *Now, really, some dots were connecting despite themselves...*

"Yeah, thanks." Trevor said, reverting to his abrupt manner and led Phil down the corridor again. Phil nodded at Sela then hurried after him, noticing cage-like elevator doors to his left. When they stopped outside the open door to a small office full of bookshelves laden with both binders and textbooks, Phil looked at the sign above the door. Sure enough. A shellacked wooden sign this time, but with the same green lettering which spelled out, 'The Growlery.'

"The Growlery," muttered Phil, cocking his head to one side, brow furrowed.

"Oh, man, that's perfect! 'Cause you're growling away to yourself again." Trevor grinned.

"Hmm. Come in and sit down for a second while I think on this."

"What is it?"

"Shut the door, will you Trevor?"

The younger man did so and they took seats at a polished table, the breadth of which spanned most of the room. A chessboard sat at one end, an ashtray in the middle. Trevor laid down his miniscule notebook, loosened his tie and collar, then poked around the office until he found some larger lined paper on which they could both write, if desired.

"The Growlery," Phil repeated. "Mean anything to you at all?"

"Don't think so. Should it?"

"It might if you like Dickens. There was a little place in— 'Bleak House', I think it was. Called 'The Growlery'."

"What was it? A dog kennel for the sad and mad?"

"No, a small library nook. So called because it was a good place for the owner to go be out of sorts on his own."

"Should I be writing this down?"

"Nooo. It's not a clue. I'm just realizing why some things have seemed familiar to me. For instance, you've noticed a lot of signs around? With green lettering?"

"Sure, who can miss 'em? It's like every place has a name."

"Right. The hill where Squeers' body was found was called 'Cad's Hill'. Dickens' estate in England was 'Gad's Hill'. Pretty famous. I'm pretty sure 'Squeers' was a Dickens' character name, too, though I'll have to check."

"O-kaay, but…?"

"Oh, it's no big revelation. I've just been struggling with some familiarity of things and now I see the connection to Dickens. In a few at least. Example: did you come into the building through the red door? Or the green?"

"Sela brought Karen and me in through the red door. It leads into the kitchen. I'm going to light up, o.k.?" Trevor took out his pack of Export A's, as Phil nodded.

"Well, right beside it—an odd place for another door, don't you think?— is a green door, and on that door is a knocker. I think it's meant to emulate Scrooge's doorknocker in A Christmas Carol. At least, the Alastair Sim movie version of it."

"Well, I *do* know that story. Bob Marley was in the door knocker, huh?"

Phil smiled. "Jacob Marley, but they were both Wailers. Of a sort."

"And you figure that's what all these signs are about?"

"We'll have to ask someone like Sela or Jeremiah Flintwinch. Wait. Flintwinch. I think *that's* a Dickens' character, too!"

"Hmm. Didn't she just say his parents' name was something different? Something German-sounding? Wait, I wrote it down."

"Ah, very good point, you're right!" Phil always tried to be generous when someone else, whether a colleague or his elderly godmother, 'got to it' before he did.

"Yeah, it's Schneider. Why would he change his birth name to a silly Dickens one?"

"A lot changed their names after the war. Didn't want to be connected to the Nazi movement. But it will be one of the first questions I ask him tomorrow, never fear."

"Well, I guess that partial degree you said you took, in English Lit., is gonna pay off in this case!"

"I doubt it," said Philip, sobering now. "I don't think any cute names of rooms or woodland glades is going to get us any closer to figuring out why a Deputy Commissioner's son went soaring off a sixteen story bridge."

Trevor inhaled one last long puff on his cigarette, then stubbed it out in the huge platter of an ashtray and leafed through his notebook to the front. "Well, first I'd better tell you that as soon as Karen went to her room to change her muddy clothes this morning, Sela told me why she coughed up some witch's mumbo-jumbo out there by the courts."

"Mudfog and marbles, and then some numbers?"

"Yeah, all that was missing was the boiling cauldron."

"What's it about?"

"Well, she said in layman's terms, for my benefit—though she wasn't quite so tactless—they sometimes hypnotize their patients, or clients, or guests, or whatever they call them. To try and get them to not want their heroin, or what have you."

"Dammit, *hypnotize*? I'm sure Blue wouldn't have gone along with that as part of Crispin's program here."

"Well, Sela said it was a new experimental kind of treatment. It's not exactly going under, into some kind of trance. I gather it's more like they are taught mantras and that's supposed to help them. Help them focus on something else besides a craving, or to help them get calm and get—" here, Trevor flipped a page back in his notes, " 'centered', she called it."

"And that's what she did to Karen this morning when she was hysterical?"

"That's what she says. She explained that they have key words, and that's what Karen's been taught to calm her down right away, apparently. Sela said she has always been pretty flighty and 'nervy', since she arrived here."

"So mudfog marbles, and then—" Philip interrupted himself. "Well, for *Pete*'s sakes!"

"You got something, Detective?"

"Just that I think Dickens even has something to do with a story, or anthology, or something about 'mudfog'. *Curiouser and curiouser, said the man who fell down a rabbit hole.*"

"You've lost me, D.I. Steele."

"I'm a little lost myself. Why don't I just sit back and you tell me everything you've learned from the beginning? And your impressions of the people, as you go. *If* you can have an unbiased opinion, mind you. I've seen you act differently with two groups–all warm and chatty with the lunch crowd and the reverend, but Sela seems to put your back up a bit."

"Wow, I heard you were observant before I ever worked with you on the Greenidge wrap-up. But that's pretty damned intuitive!"

"Some call it being in touch with my female side." Phil could tell that Trevor considered this might be an invitation to discuss his own proclivities, but that he was fighting against the urge. Better to keep it strictly professional, anyway.

"Yeah, I didn't really take to that nurse, can't explain why."

"Well, I've learned to trust my partner's instincts at all times, so point noted. It doesn't explain why you were so carried away with gleeful abandon over lunch. Just tickled to have fresh lobster?"

Trevor shook his head slowly. "No. Besides everyone simply being friendly toward me, except for the Elephant Woman in the hallway, I guess I just thought that since we don't even *know* D.C. Cobalt's son's death is a murder, I shouldn't come across as too accusatory or confrontational right away."

"No, but it would appear there was certain foul play in the death of Charlie Squeers!"

"Yeah, I realize that. But technically we're not here because of him, and aren't really supposed to have anything to do with that case. I'm assuming?"

"What did Blue—D.C. Cobalt—say to Flaherty, any idea?"

"No, Flaherty didn't call me back to say. And I wasn't going to ask him to."

"Sure. No."

"So I've mostly just been asking about Crispin, and trying to get a better understanding of what goes on here."

"It seems like a most, er–interesting place, that's for sure." Phil reached up to his throat and also loosened his tie. "All right, young fella. Begin."

●   ●   ●

After speaking to the two officers in the corridor, Sela Cowan hurried to the kitchen. She needed to talk to Ruth, the cook, about ensuring there was enough food for two extra servings at dinner. No doubt Steele and Ames would still be here by then, given all that had unfolded today. On top of which, she'd better arrange to have a tray sent up to Karen. She bit her lip. That girl, *honestly!* Announcing that she loved Charlie right in front of the cops—just blurting it out like she had some kind of ownership over the body!

"Ruth, what are we having tonight?"

Ruth McCorkle was a heavy-set almost mannish woman whose husband ran a tobacco farm just down the road toward Sandytown. She was one of the full-time staff at the retreat and felt lucky to have the job, as working in the tobacco harvest was just about the worst physical drain on a body anyone could imagine, she figured.

"We're havin' a hamburg and noodle cass'role, see? With cheese and tomato sauce, plus a big tossed salad. It's too hot to have the ovens on all afternoon for anything bigger and I ain't 'spectin' there'll be many's who're over-hungry tonight. Why?"

"I just wanted to make sure there'd be enough to feed the policemen if they stay. I don't expect them to make a habit of it, but I will 'invite' them for just this evening, if that's all right." Sela always felt she should tread carefully with Ruth. The woman could be downright intimidating at times and besides, it was always best to stay on the good side of kitchen help. If, that is, one didn't wish to find spittle, glass shards, or a June bug in one's Pasta Florentine.

"There'll be plenty, Sealie. Don't you worry none. Your poor mother comin' over?"

"It's too hot, I think. I'll just take her portion across when I go, thanks. The salad has lots of fresh veg?"

"Some picked from our gardens this morning, eh? And some bought Saturday from the Mennonites at the Aylmer Market. Della's cutting 'em up now." Ruth nodded her large hair-netted head toward her assistant who was standing across the kitchen at a huge, misshapen butcher block.

"O.K., great. Della, when you're finished those, would you take some coffees and maybe some ice water, into The Growlery for the gentlemen, please? And I don't expect Karen to be down for supper, so will you remember to take her a tray?"

"Sure, ma'm."

"Also, when you're in her room, keep your eyes open for any of her strange behavior again, all right? Now that Charlie's been found, goodness knows how she'll react. Make sure she isn't flicking that cigarette lighter on and off, or peeling her fingernails. And see if you can find that ring you thought you saw on her dressing table."

"I've never seen it since."

"No, I realize that. I know you'd have told me if you had. Have you asked Clara when she's taken in clean towels, if she might have?"

"Yes, ma'm. She says Karen's usually in there when she's been in, so she can't look around much."

"All right, that's fine. You're doing very well." Sela reached over and grabbed the tip of a carrot, popping it into her mouth. "Mmm, Mother will love these. Just a bit on the sweet side."

"Just like you's both is, dearie," finished Ruth, stooping to remove an enormous Green Giant can of corn from a bottom shelf.

•   •   •

Trevor cleared his throat. "Well, first of all, everyone I've spoken to so far seemed to like Crispin. Of course, they'd *say* that now, wouldn't they? Now that there's a murder investigation in earnest? But it does seem he'd made some good friends in the time he'd been here. By the way, no one knows him as Crispin Cobalt. The D.C. and Flintwinch told him he'd have to come with an alias, so he chose Clennam. Everyone here thought his name was Crispin Clennam."

Phil nodded. "Makes sense, I guess. Blue would want to protect the family's privacy, in addition to Crispin's own."

"And I've chatted with Gerald, tried to cut through all the hippie lingo. Asked how he cut his arm. He was out scything and a bolt came loose on the tool, so he was trying to fix it. Those that are here on a rehabilitation program have certain chores to complete each week. Helps them to have structure and responsibility, I guess. The two you saw me with in the dining room, though, a married couple, they're artists; they're here purely to relax and paint. Although I'm told Mitch likes to clean the horse stalls sometimes, and groom the beasts. They stay in one of the little huts—the artists, not the horses, I mean. Theirs is a straw bale structure, so they said. And, let's see," Trevor glanced at his note book. "They came the same day as Crispin, about two months ago."

"No starving artists-in-a-garret syndrome for them, I guess?"

Trevor smiled. "I did manage to glean that Mitch's family are well-off tobacco farmers, and they are happy to indulge the couple's artistic talents. Mitch said his wife Jackie has just had two landscapes accepted at a gallery showing in Toronto. So she, at least, must be pretty good."

Phil was taking notes on the foolscap Trevor had found. He'd likely need some charts and a series of recipe cards later, the way this was going, he decided.

"Then I met a sweet older man who just lost his wife, so his daughter sent him here for a vacation to try to put some 'sprit' back in his bones, he said. He's called Latch Lupin, and I can no more see him pushing a young man off a bridge than I can see him taking tokes in secret down by the brook. Where, I gather from the artists, those that aren't here for addiction treatment are often found."

"Well, that's got to go against the grain for Flintwinch, if he's intent on rehabilitating his addicts."

"Mitch claims they all keep it pretty secret from the others."

Philip Steele snorted. "In a place like this? I highly doubt it! And what kind of name is 'Latch', anyway?"

"I asked him, just chit-chatty-like. He said his father always told him he was 'latched on to his mother's apron strings'. So he called him 'Latch' and it just stuck, his whole life."

"Who else?"

"Well, I had a talk with a younger man, a bit like Gerald but not quite so tie-dyed, and hairy, if you know what I mean. He claimed to be best friends with Crispin, having arrived just a week after. So he's been here seven weeks and claims that Crispin's death may be what sets him back on booze again. He says he was doing well, not feeling like he needed a drink every hour of the day, and then Crispin fell. What's been his saving grace, according to him as well as Sela Cowan who walked in when I was speaking to him, is that we're miles away from the nearest LCBO."

"Yes, but if they're smoking dope in secret, I'm sure there're guests with stashed alcohol on the premises. They don't need an official Liquor Store."

"Well, maybe." Trevor lit another cigarette and took a short first drag. "But no one's admitted it so far, if so. And this fellow, Adam Tetterby, says he wouldn't know of any."

"O.K., good so far. You've made some inroads. Anyone else?"

"Yes, before I was first brought into the house, I met the fellow who found Crispin. He's a local farmer, has a general farm on the other side of the valley, above the trestle bridge. Name of—" Trevor consulted his scribbles with a neat flip of the pages, as if a practiced gesture by a T.V. cop actor. "Name of Bob Haggerty. He comes over here a few mornings a week to tend their garden that the cook uses. His wife's a nurse, Martha. She also works here part-time but I haven't met her."

"I suppose you didn't have time to question Haggerty about finding the body, or why they just came here to broadcast the news and didn't call the police themselves, that sort of thing?"

"No, I was whisked in by Sela, who was still worried about sorting out Karen, I guess."

"Well, Haggerty's one I want to interview myself, anyway, just to make sure I've covered the bases closely enough on that issue when I report to the D.C."

Trevor seemed about to wrap-up, closing his notebook and once again stubbing out his cigarette.

"Wait." Philip said. "Now you have to tell me what you think of each, your first impressions. These will help more than just introductions to each person and why they're here. Remember, you're not a sergeant anymore. So, let's hear it all."

"Oh, yeah. Well...You already know Sela rubbed me the wrong way right out of the starting gate. I mean, she's gorgeous, and seemingly very nice and helpful, isn't she? But maybe too much so. The artists are just relaxed and funny, I really liked them."

"Funny ha-ha? Or funny eccentric?"

"Aren't all artists eccentric? But I meant humorous—they had me smiling, and they have a way of quiet bantering with each other that's like a comedy duo. Also, I think they are so wrapped up in each other and their painting that they aren't liable to be too interested in the politics, or the counseling sessions, or the other goings-on of this insular, weird little place."

"Fair enough. And Gerald and Adam?"

"Well, both part of the hippie movement, obviously, and both certainly addicts. They have all the—"

There was a light rap on the door and Philip said "Yes?"

A girl about eighteen or nineteen opened the door, balancing a tray on top of which sat coffee mugs and glasses of ice water.

"Excuse me. I'm Della. Miss Cowan asked me to bring this to you."

"Oh, thank you, come in." Phil nodded. "I'm Detective Inspector Steele, and this is D.I. Ames, Della."

The girl nodded shyly and put the contents of the tray, incl. a tiny pitcher of milk and a sugar bowl, on the broad table.

"Good, I was getting parched. All this talking." Trevor picked up the water and downed it in two gulps.

"Oh, I'm sorry, perhaps I should have brought a pitcher of it?"

"No need, he can have my glass as well. The coffee will just hit the spot for me, thanks. Though I will need a bathroom soon, Della. I've had a lemonade and a tea all in the last hour, and once I slurp up this delicious-looking coffee…"

"There's one just two doors down that way, to your left, sir." Della pointed a graceful arm.

"Thank you. Do you work here full time, or part time?"

"I'm full-time this summer, sir. Just finished college in London."

"And you work in the kitchen?"

"The kitchen, and as a maid too. Or whatever needs doing. I do evening feeds at the stables before I go home, most nights."

"Well, you are a girl of many talents," Philip said, taking a sip of the coffee. "Ah, as I suspected—delicious. Did you make it?"

"Yes, sir."

"Well done. Thank you, Della. We'll see you again. We'll be interviewing all the staff over the next few days, in fact. So you can let them know."

"I think we all expect it, Mr. Steele."

"O.K. Thanks again." Phil looked at Trevor.

"Yeah, thanks." Trevor said, gruffly.

After the door had shut behind the girl, Phil said, "Now, Trevor. Don't take this as a lecture, it's just a bit of advice I've learned over the last few decades: If you want to do your tough copper routine with the prime suspects, and the upper echelons, that's fine. Probably will get you more information than having a laugh as you pick through the lobster with them." Philip held up his hand as Trevor was about to object.

"No, now hear me out, I'm honestly not lecturing. We all find our most efficient ways of interviewing. However, *always* be gracious with any staff, or workers, or volunteers. Without being condescending—just be genuinely polite and appreciative. Because I'll tell you, it's the staff of any facility or venue that hear things, that discuss things with each other, that have the inside knowledge we need about most cases. So, you want to keep them on our good side, no matter what."

Trevor nodded. "O.K., you're right. Good advice."

"Go on with what you were saying about our hippies."

"Just that Adam says he's not needing the alcohol, but it was almost all he could talk about when he was with me. And Gerald, well—you saw him. It's hard to tell how much the drugs have already fried his brain, or if he's just a nutter in his natural state."

Phil smiled. "I've lived in the Yukon for a few years, don't forget. Lots of the hippie crowd up there." Then, remembering his fiancee Rainey, he muttered, "It doesn't preclude their aptitude for murder, either."

"Sorry, Phil. I know you had someone close get killed—"

"Yes, yes. Thanks. Go on."

For a moment Trevor's genuine interior sensitivity battled with his exterior act, but he knew it was best to forge solidly on. "Gerald said a few things that did give me pause. I didn't write them down, because they didn't seem like anything we hadn't already noticed, but he said 'Karen's a groovy chick, man, but she's always flipping her wig, doesn't know how to hang loose, you dig?' Which we'd obviously already seen, although I'd say finding a body in the woods might cause most girls to react that way. If not a dude."

"We'll be having a very serious talk with that young woman as soon as she's deemed well enough."

"And then Gerald also said something to the effect of 'Kay's like a doobie-tube, man. Got a hole lettin' the good stuff out, you know?' Frankly, I think that's more a description of *him*."

Phil doodled on his foolscap, then starting drawing lines and arrows to some of his notes. "I'm going to start making charts of what you've told me so far when we're back at the Nelsons' tonight. You already told me what your instinct was about Latch Lupin. Anything more to add there?"

"Nope. I think he's exactly what you see – a sweet old widower who's lonely."

"Not one of us is exactly what others see, now are we?" Philip looked Trevor squarely in the eyes, but the younger man glanced down swiftly at another sheet he'd taken from his pocket while gulping down the second glass of water.

"Oh, yes, and I got the full roster of the staff and guests, part-timers even —the lot. Here goes, I'll read it slowly so you can write. There's a Ruth McCorkle, the cook. And a Clara Hopkins, a part-time maid, but she is here today, so we should fit her in, in the next few hours. Of course that's Della Taylor we just met. Then I mentioned the couple, Bob and Martha Haggerty who found Crispin's body. And you met the Rev., though he's only here if someone needs some spiritual support, or to do a prayer circle service outside once a month. Plus, there's a part-time guy that helps in the barn, Walter McDowell."

" Ri-i-ight. Got those down," Phil said as he wrote, and circled the Reverend Klassen's name.

"Oh, and I almost forgot, although she's clearly not a suspect. Sela's mother, Petra, lives across the road with her daughter. That place with the crabapple tree and stone walls? But she's in a wheelchair."

"I've convicted a wheelchair-user of murder before, Trevor."

"But not one who got on a hundred and sixty-five foot train trestle and pushed a full-grown man off."

They didn't laugh. It was too sobering. But both did their version of an harrumph.

"And guests or patients I haven't spoken with yet? Well, there's that freakish Lucy Tox. And someone named Monty Tigg. I thought that was a man, but Sela told me it's a woman in her fifties. The last one is Annette Micawber, another girl in her twenties, and let's hope not another hippie type. Sela said she *is* a recovering addict, though, so..."

"So those that were here for rehab and counseling were our deceased Crispin and Charlie, in addition to Karen, Lucy, Annette, Adam and Gerald?" Phil confirmed.

"Actually, I don't think Annette *is* here for addiction recovery this time. Sela mentioned she'd done that two years ago and was just back now to work on a magazine article she's writing for Chatelaine, talking about the spa-offerings, covering the plusses of the place. 'Scuse the pun."

There was no pun to be had, Phil wanted to snap, but instead remarked, "Well, I don't know when the last time was that I've had so many potential suspects all neatly lined up in one place. And I'm certainly glad the OPP will be looking more closely at Charlie Squeers' misfortune; we've got to make sure that for Blue's sake we're primarily concentrating on Crispin's death. Except of course, where they are linked... And surely they have to be?"

"I'd bet money on it." Trevor replied, not sure if he was being asked a question, or if D.I. Steele was talking to himself again.

CHAPTER FIVE

Since Trevor had been inside the main building most of the morning, the detectives decided it was only fair that Philip, with his fair skin, stay out of the grounds and the now-sweltering August heat. Trevor would wander from tiny villa to stables to clubhouse looking to discuss details with the maids Clara and Della, the journalist Annette in her cabin, and the groom/maintenance man Walter, while Phil would continue to conduct interviews indoors with Karen and Lucy Tox, as well as those he had yet to meet: Ruth the cook, and the woman named Monty. He would have to wait for the following day to speak with the Haggertys.

He was passing the common room dubbed The Rookery when he heard a woman's voice on the telephone from within. In what he immediately placed as a Yorkshire accent, he listened to the terse goodbyes as the woman ended a conversation.

"Right. On t'next, innit."

There was a pause and then she said, "Aye, I allus do."

And then after a three-second breath, "Nowt to do wi' me, lad. Tarra!"

Curious, Phil peeked into the room and saw a stout woman dressed in rust-colored riding jodhpurs with a thin yellow T-shirt pulled over a tight brassiere that must have cut into her ribcage most uncomfortably. She appeared to be in her mid-fifties, and as she hung up the receiver, she picked up a black velvet riding helmet and was about to stride to the door when she saw him and stopped short.

"Ey up! Thou makes a better door, than snicket!"

Phil smiled and moved gallantly aside. "Are you, by chance, Monty Tiggs?"

"It be 'Tigg', right 'nuff, but aye."

"I'm Detective Inspector Steele, Miss Tigg. I wonder if I might just have a word with you in here, as I've found you? I was going to be looking you up later but now will do nicely."

She checking her watch, flipping the back of her hand toward herself, pinky extended as if enjoying a cup of Earl Grey.

"Asked Walter ta have Odie saddled up for me at two. I daren't faff about much."

"Just a couple of minutes, if you would?" Phil gestured, suggesting they both sit in the plump chair and sofa with the rugged tweed fabrics. "You're from the north of England?"

"Got it in one!"

Philip nodded. "My cousin married a girl from Yorkshire, so I recognize your accent. Now, Miss—is it Miss, or Missus?"

"Thou just heard me bein' narky with me mister, on t'phone."

"I see. So, *Missus*?"

"Aye, right enough."

"Well then, Missus Tigg, I have your address from the list we received from the office here, but may I just have your phone number as a confirmation?"

"Tis 519-555-3357."

"And that's in the Brownsville area, is it?"

"We've an antique auction house thereabouts, aye."

"And you are here for—"

" 'nother three days, like as not."

"Oh, sorry, I meant your purpose for being at the retreat is…" Phil smiled as his pen stopped writing and he waited expectantly. The woman smiled right back.

"I 'reckon thou want ta 'ear summat like I'm an alkie, here for t'counseling. Nae addled in that way, tho'. Truth be, I jest bin right paggered. Needed a wee rest."

"I see, so you and your husband run a business and you've taken time out here for a bit of a holiday?"

"Used ta ride t'hounds in England. Like t'stables here, and massages, after ridin'. An' they've got one o' them new Jacuzzi Roman baths wi' jets."

"And how long have you already been here?"

"Five days, four nights."

"So you didn't meet Crispin, er—Clennam?"

"Poor lad. 'is body were found t'day afore I showed. Down t' beck. I rode down vale that afternoon, din't know."

"Oh, you heard about it later?"

"Aye, no one were talkin' 'bout lad's death, but I'll 'appen as 'twere later, at tea-time."

"Supper?"

"Aye, some folk were on about 'im then."

Philip made a few quick notes and underlined them before looking up again. "And what did you hear at that time?"

"Ee, I daren't say, 'xactly. Like as not they were on about summat like his goodly manners."

"They seemed to have liked him, then? *Every*one?"

"I gather 'twere a threp in t'steans 'e were gone, least-wise for t' retreat."

Phil's brow furrowed. "A threp in the...?"

"Thou knows: a kick in t'balls. It's hit 'em hard, I reckon."

Philip then asked her several more questions about whether she'd seen or heard anything unusual, especially in the night. She did stay in the main house, she confirmed—didn't really care for the little villas with no running water—but had been sleeping well after her days in the sun riding and walking in the woods, and having her relaxing spa treatments. So she'd seen nothing she would consider suspicious. Philip intentionally did not mention the discovery of Charlie Squeer's body that morning, nor did the woman bring it up. Although Phil thought that a bit odd, he also knew from his cousin's wife that Yorkshire folk kept their dignified noses to themselves, answered questions only when directly asked. He decided he'd probably been lucky to get as much information as he'd already garnered. Thanking Monty Tigg and wishing her a good ride, he escorted her to a glassed exit in the sunny corridor.

Next, he wandered toward the kitchen and strolled in through a swinging door. A broad-shouldered woman was sitting at a small geranium-laden table by the window, sorting through what appeared to be a recipe box. Phil was reminded that he'd need to stay up late that night, doing much the same thing. Although ingredient lists and measurements wouldn't be on *his* cards.

"Mrs. McCorkle?"

The woman stood, dusting flour off her apron in a white puff cloud and extending her palm.

"Yes, sir."

As Phil shook her hand he said, "I'm D.I. Steele. If I could have a word?"

"Been expectin' youse. Take a load off." She pulled up a stool and sat back down at the table.

After double checking her address at their farm near Sandytown, transcribing her phone number to his notebook and asking how many years she'd worked at the retreat (four, since it had first opened, she'd said), Philip proceeded with some of the questions he knew a woman of her position in the facility would know best.

"Was Dr. Flintwinch the manager here right from the beginning?"

"Sure was. The owners took him on before the place ever opened to the public. Him and Sela, 'course. They both hired me."

"Ah, Miss Cowan has been here that long, has she?"

"Oh my, yes. An' before, like. Sealie were practically raised here."

"What do you mean by that?"

"Wal, the folks that built this place, back after the war, they was called 'Hogarth'. And them an' Sela's mother, Petra Cowan, they was best friends. They built that place 'cross the highway, there too, for Petra. She'd lost her husband in the war, see, and she were pregnant with Sela about the time the Hogarths were building here, so they just added that cottage on for a place for the two of 'em. An' ole Neville Hogarth, he deeded it to Petra so she and Sela could keep livin' there. Then, when the new owners bought this here property, Sela got the job as nurse for the center, as she'd just finished up her qualifications."

Philip took a deep breath, hoping it might encourage the cook to do the same. He realized this interview was going to be in direct contrast to the condensed answers the Yorkshirewoman had given him.

"And these new owners? Are they here much?"

"Nah, hardly a-tall. They're two couples, some rich folks from Toronto, who bought it as a tax write-off, so's my old man sez. The Hogarths wanted to sell up, you see, after Neville passed. So these new owners—"

"Could you tell me their names?" Phil asked, fairly sure Blue already had their details, but not wanting to overlook anything when he reported to to his father's friend.

"Wall-ll—there's Mr. an' Mrs. Young. Gary Young, I think he is. Owns some investment company downtown, I b'lieve. An' his wife was Donna Lawton, you know. The tennis player? She's a bit of a star, played that there Billie Jean King a few times and wanted the clay courts to practice on when they came out of the city. The first year or so, when they were building the business up here, anyways. An' the other couple, I ain't quite...oh, wait a sec, now—" Ruth McCorkle got up and crossed the kitchen to a small desk in a dark corner. She fished in a drawer and pulled out a lime green, plastic address book. Returning to her spot behind a red geranium, she said, "I wrote down all that info. back when I was hired on, just in case somethin' happened to Sela or the Doc., an' I was in charge. Yeah." She leafed through the book with long, chapped fingers. "Here they is: Mr. an' Mrs. Chester. They's some kind of lawyers, I think, s'what I heard."

Phil jotted down the names of both couples. Then he said, "But since the retreat has been up and running you haven't seen much of them, is that right?"

"Not hardly never. Maybe once, twice a year, like."

"So Dr. Flintwinch, he runs things here most of the time?"

"Yes, sir. An' when he ain't 'round, our Sealie steps up and takes over. But mostly it's the Doc around, seein' to things. 'Cept the more domestic stuff, you know? Like Sealie'll check on the meals, make sure the rooms are being cleaned right, n' all."

"Let me ask you now about the night before Crispin Clennam's body was found, I understand, by Mr. Haggerty?"

"Right enough. Bob Haggerty and his wife Martha, they both help out here a few days a week. Own a sweet little farm over the highway and up the other side of the valley. Yeah, they was drivin' through, under the bridge on their way here, and was checkin' some cows down by the creek, the little Otter Creek, eh? An' Bob, he got out an' found him. Martha had a headache and—"

"Sorry, if we could just talk about the night before? What do you remember?"

"Oh, wal, my shift usually ends at 5:30, see. I just get the dinner finished and ready to be wheeled out on the carts. Then it's up to the girls that live here, Della and Clara, to put it up on the buffet tables, and all the guests an' then the live-in staff, they help themselves. Then Della and Clara clear up afterwards, like. That's why they get time off in the mornings and afternoons. They have a lot of dishes to wash in the evenings!"

None of this was, of course, important to Phil. But he knew enough not to get on the big woman's bad side. He let her ramble.

"Any-hoo, that there night weren't nothin' unusual in my mind. I ain't sayin' there weren't some discussions, or shoutin'— there usually is, if there'd been an afternoon 'session', as Dr. Flintwinch calls 'em. Counseling an' all, for the rehab. folks. Them as are addicted to what-not. Yeah, those sessions can get a bit loud and rowdy, even. An' I do remember some yellin', mostly by that Tox woman, and maybe Adam that day. Or Gerald. But again, that ain't abnormal."

"I see." Phil took a second to write a few sentences before looking up. Ruth McCorkle was staring out the window, her face scrunched in obvious concentration.

"Now I *think*, wouldn't swear, mind, that that were the same day as how Crispin—such a nice young feller, really—he got a call in The Rookery from his folks. An' he were in there talkin' on the phone, like, when I got Della to ring the dinner gong. 'Cause I were just on my way past in the corridor, about to take in the coffee urn. Least-wise, I think it were his folks. I did hear him say somethin' like "That's not right, Dad. I don't think so."

Phil frowned at this. He knew Crispin had always called Blue 'Pop'. He made another note, putting a question mark and asterisk beside it. Ruth kept on, without pause.

"Then the girls got the carts ready and pushed 'em out, and I 'member as how Crispin walked in then—I'm sure it were that night—and sat with Adam, like usual. And then…"

At this moment a young girl's voice was heard outside the red door from the front area, speaking as she opened it and entered.

"Ruthie, I've just been talking to that young copper out at The Vines. I told him 'bout Charlie an' Kay, was that—"

She stopped short as she caught sight of Phil, who rose to his feet. Ruth stayed seated, waved her hand dismissively at the newcomer, and said, "Clara, this is D.I. Steele. He's chattin' with me now, so you go on up to your room 'til it's time to serve. An' don't be gossipin' up there with Karen or any other guest, you hear?"

"Ah, come on Ruthie, you know I don't."

"Fine, then. I'll see you at dinner. These two nice policemen are invited to eat with us tonight. I don't know if you knew?" Here she glanced at Phil.

Philip smiled. "Thanks, Mrs. McCorkle. I wasn't aware, but just for tonight that might be appreciated. We have so much to do."

As Clara disappeared into the corridor, Ruth continued with her story, "And then I got ready to go home. I didn't drive that day, I 'member, so Fred, my ole man, he picked me up. An' that was it. The last time I saw that Crispin, poor feller. Until I watched them come an' load up his body. That's two hearses I seen in a week leavin' here, sir. What on earth's goin' on, like?"

Phil knew he would have many more questions for the cook in the forthcoming days, but as he was already standing he said, "We certainly mean to find out. Very soon I hope. Thank you so much for now, Mrs. McCorkle. I look forward to tasting your delicious cooking in a few hours. Now, I wonder if you might point me the way to Karen's room? We've given her time to get over her shock now, and I'd like to..."

"Ooo, I better not send you up there lessen Sela's given the o.k., Mr. Steele. How about I just check with her, eh?" She went to a walkie-talkie, picked it up and said into it, "Kitchen to S.C., D.I. Steele wants to go to Room Two. Please advise."

When there was no immediate answer, she repeated the exact phrase and at that moment Sela Cowan appeared through the swinging door.

"Hi," she said rather breathlessly. "I was just on my way down here when you called. Yes, come along, Detective. I've given Karen a mild sedative and she is fine to see you now."

•　　•　　•

Polly Jane Whistler heard Hilary Steele put down the phone receiver with a final clink. All afternoon, the JUST(e)STATE had been bustling with workers in the field and at the roadside stand, and with several volunteers grooming and leading the horses about in the ring, practicing for the next lessons with handicapped children. But Hilary had been sitting most of those hours on the back patio with the long phone cord pulled through sliding glass doors, and P.J. marveled that only once in all that time were they disturbed by a question from anyone—a teenage girl wanting to ask where a beach ball was, to toss at the horses to de-spook them, she'd said. P.J. was impressed with the efficiency with which this place was running. She knew her friend had always been a powerhouse behind many businesses and charities but after decades of seeing a variety of activities based here, she thought the woman had finally found her niche, and the right people to support her in it.

She opened the patio doors. "Lary, dear–my oatmeal raisin cookies are just about to come out of the oven. Would you like a few out here?"

"Oh, I'm coming in now, thanks, P.J. How you can bake on a hot day like this is beyond me." Philip's mother gathered up papers and the phone and, pushing her bare feet into sneakers, entered the dining room and dumped everything in her arms on the already-cluttered table. "Mmm, smells great, though!"

"I'll admit it's hotter and more humid than New Brunswick's ever been, but with the windows all open, there's been a nice cross-breeze. Did you get all your administration work finished?"

"Indeed, and I've a little surprise for you. A woman from Michigan who has been running a center for riding for the disabled down there, is driving up tomorrow for a few days. I was hoping she'd come last week instead, but I think you'll enjoy seeing her in action. She can help me with one or two students I'm especially concerned about, and give me some advice about the wheelchair ramps in the stable. But coinciding with that, I've just spoken with Sharon Cobalt and convinced her to come out here for the whole day tomorrow. If you don't mind helping be a support system for her, I think it will do her good to see some of my students riding. Give her a bit of hope, you know?"

"Certainly, I'll do whatever I can," Polly Jane said as she took a tray of cookies from the oven and started placing them on cooling racks. "How did she seem, poor thing?"

"Oh, a tad teary-sounding when she first heard my voice, but the thought of the drive out here on her own has given her something to look forward to, I think. Blue's been so busy trying to organize the investigation that he hasn't had time to just absorb Crispin's death *or* to just sit with her. That was my take on it, anyway. She had a piece of news I know will be of interest to you, though." Hilary's eyes twinkled at her old friend, whom she knew loved to help her godson piece together his cases, as much as she thrilled when solving a Perry Mason on the television.

P.J. put down the spatula and turned. "Yes? Have they already heard from Phil?"

"In a roundabout way, it seems. That D.I. Ames called his boss, who called Blue. Or something like that. There's been another body found at the retreat place. Right when Phil arrived, apparently!"

"Imagine!" said Polly Jane, and absentmindedly gave her friend a cookie without a plate and poured her a glass of orange juice instead of the iced tea she'd obviously meant to pour.

"Yes, I expect Phil will phone this evening, but if he doesn't, certainly Sharon will know more when she arrives tomorrow. Now, will you be able to sleep tonight, I wonder?" Hilary asked, teasing.

"Another body, just imagine!" was all P.J. was able to say.

•　　•　　•

Cathy limped to the front of the parlor, where she knew Brian would be sitting with his newspaper. He usually ate a late lunch, read a bit of the paper, then had a quick nap before returning to oversee the men in the kilns until evening.

"Just had a call from that older policeman, Bri. He said they'd not be comin' in tonight 'til around eight. Guess they got an invite to stay at Bayham Brook House for their suppers."

"Yeah? Just been..."

"Readin' the news. I can see."

"Wal, says here that-there case of the Crispy Crackles feller ain't gonna be closed 'til our guests say so."

"Quit yer callin' him that. I told ya he weren't named after no cereal, and it..."

"Ain't right ta make fun of the dead. I know, ya done tol' me a-hunnert times, Cath."

"Well, we already knew they was comin' here for somethin' important."

"Guess they figger our own cops don't know what's what."

"More like that Crispin guy weren't just some dope addict. More like he were a big-wig. Maybe some television star?"

"Well, the Tillsonburg News don't say nothin' 'bout that."

Cathy snorted. "Would ya 'spect they'd tattle that secret to all-an'-sundry?"

"Nah, guess not. You gonna tell 'em, about Ruth 'n' all, though?"

"Depends."

"On what?"

"On iffen they ask me," Cathy said, as though it was obvious.

"Hmph. Well, you know best. I'm just gonna..."

"Have a nap now and then..."

"...Get back to the yard."

.   .   .

Philip was led by Sela Cowan to Karen's room upstairs—Room Two (he was mildly surprised each door didn't also have a name painted in green letters outside its frame). Sela tapped lightly and then just opened the door and entered. Phil followed and saw the curled up figure of Karen, now freshly changed into a turquoise sundress with huge orange sunflowers on it. A ceiling fan rattled above his head and, outside the open window, a hint of a breeze touched the branch of a tall cedar. Perhaps Trevor would have some relief from the heat if a thunderstorm was brewing out there, he thought.

"Karen. Kay? D.I. Steele would like to speak with you now," Sela said.

The young woman raised herself on her elbow and looked at them with damp eyes. Then she further pushed herself up and sat, cross-legged on her bed, facing the hard-backed chair where Phil seated himself. He nodded at Sela, who was perched against the dressing table, as if she might stay.

"Thank you, Miss Cowan. I'll find my way downstairs when we're finished here. Would you please telephone the Haggertys and mention that I'd like to see them when they arrive in the morning–probably about ten o'clock?"

"Certainly. Although they'll be here by eight."

"Ah," said Phil. "But we won't. Thanks so much."

Sela exited with a nod at Karen, even though the latter wasn't looking her way.

"Now then, Karen. Are you feeling any better? A little more rested?"

"Yes, sir."

"I know it was a terrible shock. Maybe it would help you to tell me about Charlie?"

"Oh, he was just the most wonderful!"

"You knew him well?"

"We–we knew each other in Toronto a bit, yeah."

"Oh, I see. So you didn't just meet him here for the first time?"

"No, no. We'd gone to the same counseling group in the city, a few years ago. And Charlie, he was excited to come here. He was the one who told me about Bayham Brook, said he was sure this was going to be the place that made him clean. He said he thought it would really help me."

Didn't help HIM much, said Phil to himself.

"And do you find it has? Helped you, that is?"

"Oh, I'm ever so much better physically, you know. I'm really not having any cravings, not for anything."

"That's good, Karen. Were you feeling better mentally and emotionally, too? Until this morning's terrible shock?"

Her eyes welled once again. "I was! I really was! Charlie and I–we, we went and…" She stopped, unable to continue.

Phil sat quietly for a few moments, then urged gently, "What was it you and Charlie did?"

"We–um, we swore to each other we were going to get through this together. And now he's gone!"

Philip didn't believe for one minute that that was all Karen had been going to say, but he let it slide for the moment.

"Why were you in the woods, in that spot this morning, Karen?"

"Oh! Oh, I was just—you know—walking. It's so cool and lovely out there."

"But you found Charlie quite a bit off the trail. Or road, or whatever it is down there."

"It used to be what they called a corduroy road. Laid out with logs. It was the main buggy road before they put the big highway through, Sealie says."

"I see. And now they just use it for walking and riding?"

"That's right, and to get down to the brook and to the Little Otter, too – down where they found…" her voice trailed off as she stumbled again.

"Down by the creek under the black bridge? The trestle bridge?"

"Yes, that old road goes right down there." She sniffed.

Phil realized he and Trevor would have to get some sort of map the next day, and do some hiking and exploring of their own— both to the top of the railroad bridge, and below by the brook and the wider creek where the body had been discovered.

"So why were you off the old road trail?"

"Well, I thought I saw—something."

"Clothing you mean? Charlie's clothing?"

"No. I thought there was something farther up from him. Like a black mound. I thought it was maybe a trapped baby bear or something."

The girl may know about historic road building, but she hadn't a clue about the flora and fauna here, Phil thought. *Bears, in south-western Ontario!*

"What was it?"

"Well, it was a bit of earth, a dug-out bit in the hillside. And some old bits of glass. Just trash, I guess. But then I slipped..."

"You slipped down the hill? That's when you found Charlie?"

She dabbed ineffectually at her eyes, sniffed again. "Yes, I practically rolled right on top of him. I–I was freaked out, like, at first. Then I couldn't believe it, but I recognized his shirt. Through the leaves and the earth, you know. And I just ran like mad to get Sealie or someone to come help. I guess–I think maybe I thought she might save him somehow?" Karen shook her head in short, sharp rhythms, as though trying to jolt herself again from the nightmare. "I know that's silly, man. I know. But I wasn't thinking straight..."

"Perfectly understandable."

"Then I got up through the short cut to the tennis courts and there you all were."

"Now, Karen—the last time you saw Charlie alive. Could you tell me about that?"

"Oh, Charlie! Oh, he was the best! He brought me some flowers he'd picked down by the brook. That was about, maybe, two weeks ago? I could check in my diary." Here Karen reached over the bedspread and under her mattress, pulling out a small white book with a little lock and clasp on it. "I have to keep it hidden because I think that maid Clara's been snooping." She opened it and read a few passages, then flipped several pages. "Here, mister. Here it is. Charlie brought me the flowers on July the 28th. He kissed me that evening, too, after our counseling group in Selwood Terrace. That's our group meeting room. Then we said our goodnights at about nine, because they like lights out by ten. So Charlie needed to get back to his room, down in the men's wing. And the next morning he was just gone. Gone!"

The tears started again, and Phil decided perhaps she'd had enough trauma for one day. He stood to go.

And it was at that moment that a long, pale snake seemed to fall heavily into the cedar tree just outside the open window and Karen let out a terrified scream.

CHAPTER SIX

Detective Inspectors Steele and Ames sat exhausted in The Quay Room, Phil's slightly larger bedroom at the Nelson's farmhouse/inn in Port Dune. The rest of the afternoon had been fraught with activity which, they realized now, appeared to be irrelevant to the case and more of a distraction to the interviews on which they should have been concentrating. They were both annoyed at the amount of time wasted and spoke of little else on the drive back to Port Dune in the growing dusk.

After establishing that Lucy Tox, the 'Elephant Woman', (as Trevor now seemed determined to call her in private) was the person responsible for sending down a cascade of knotted-up sheets from the servants' floor storage cupboards at the top of Bayham Brook House, in a delusional attempt to escape into the cedar tree, the two men had sat quietly on their own during supper in the Melon and Cauli Tavern dining hall. Other guests had gathered at their usual tables and while the atmosphere in the big room was subdued, there had been enough patter of voices to allow the detectives to discuss some general points from the day, without going into details.

Over ample helpings of hamburger casserole and fresh green salad, Trevor had laughed and said, "I was half expecting to be served cantaloupe and cauliflower."

"Oh? Oh, the name of the dining hall, you mean?" Phil had asked. "Do you know, I think after discussing A Christmas Carol with you earlier, I've remembered that Scrooge goes off to have a miserly meal at a pub called The Melancholy Tavern. Clever, really—I'm guessing it's meant as another connection to Dickens."

"Well, what the *dickens* is going on with all these names?"

"I meant to ask Sela before she left to go across the road to her mother, but we can find out tomorrow. We got a bit side-tracked, there, with that Tox woman—"

"Tox-*ic,* you mean? This time, when I was picking cedar branches from her hair, she said— in front of Gerald and Adam, mind— that I'd raped her last Thursday. And asked, had I enjoyed the ride?"

"Yes, er–mm, I'm starting to think it doesn't much matter that I didn't officially interview her as planned today. Between both her delusions and the lying that Miss Cowan mentioned, I'm not likely to get much sense from our Lucy."

"Woman should be in the nut-house, not bunking in at a retreat like this."

"Quiet, now, Trevor— we can discuss it all later." Phil had nodded toward the table where Lucy Tox, seeming perfectly relaxed, had her orange head bent over a mounded plate of casserole. One would never guess that just three hours prior, she had been trying to shimmy down a rope of bed linens from four stories up. While Phil had run to find Sela Cowan for help, Karen had stopped screaming and gone to her window to holler for Gerald and Adam, smoking just below on one of the terraces. They had come running and had joined Trevor who, already finished his interviews out in the grounds, was entering the building through the main green door. Sela and Phil had hurried back to Karen's room in case Lucy made it that far, but she had climbed no more than three feet down the 'rope'. The two 'dippy-hippies', as Trevor referred to them, had helped Trevor pull her back up and into Clara and Della's shared bedroom.

Now, back at the little inn, Phil took off his tie and shoes and lay on his bed, arms behind his head, head stretched back on two pillows as he gazed thoughtfully around the room.

"There, Trevor, take off your tie as well, and kick back on that bean-bag chair. There's a footstool sort of thing here by the closet door. Get your feet up. I think some hiking's in order for us tomorrow, so rest those puppies while you can."

"You have your notes with you there?"

"Oh, damn. No, pass me those folded foolscaps on the dresser, please. I tossed them there with the room key."

After his partner was settled and both men had their notes in front of them, Phil volunteered the little he'd managed to learn that afternoon, 'before the orange orangutan started jungle-gymming', as Trevor put it. He gave details about his common-room talk with the horsewoman from Yorkshire, Monty, and about how Ruth had told a bit about the building of the two houses after the war, by the wealthy Neville Hogarth and his family, how the cottage across the road had then become a permanent home for Petra and her daughter, Sela.

"Yeah, I got a bit of that from the groundskeeper, or groom, or whatever he is. Walter. After I got used to his stutter, I realized he sure knows a lot about the history of the building of this place. Seems he did the masonry work on the foundation of the house, as well as the stone walls across where the Cowans live."

"Stutter, eh? He wasn't just nervous?" asked Phil.

"Nah, it's a hell of an impediment. Took a lot more time to get through a few simple questions than it should have, but I was patient and charming, like you said to be with the staff."

"Exactly right, that. Now he's...," Phil took a moment to flip back through his papers. "Walter McDowell, right? And you say he's been here since the end of the war?"

"Lived 'round here all his life, he says, and has been working on this place doing various duties from '46 on."

"I see. Well, good to have a few that know the full chronicles. Now, to continue, Ruth said a funny thing about Crispin; I starred it here. She thinks he was talking to his father around suppertime the night he must have gone up on the bridge. But Blue never mentioned he'd been talking to him the night before and I'm sure he would have. The cook said she heard him say 'Dad'."

"So, couldn't it have been?"

"Don't think so. Crispin always called Blue 'Pop'."

"Uh-*uh*! said Watson to Holmes."

"And then Ruth said there'd been some kind of squabble between one of the men and Lucy, after one of their counseling sessions. But she assured me, rather too pointedly perhaps, that that was normal."

"I had Della tell me that there was an argument that night between all three men that were here for rehab – Crispin, Gerald and Adam," said Trevor. "She said it went on during dinner. I mean 'supper', as they call it here."

"I see. Did she say what it was all about?"

"She only heard bits and pieces. Because she and Clara were in and out with serving caddies."

"But what was her impression?"

"She thought it was about something that had happened in the counseling session, and also to do with Charlie, because his name had come up, she said. By then he'd been missing for about—" Trevor checked the scribbles at the front of his notebook, then licked the stub of his pencil. He ticked off marks, counting, as he said, "about ten days."

"Hmm. Well, let me tell you about Karen, and then you can go ahead with everything you've found out. This Karen strikes me as a lot more intelligent than she sometimes portrays. Either that, or she's half-hypnotized, or on something. But she seemed quite lucid this afternoon. Sad, but lucid. However, she's definitely keeping something from us. She and Squeers were in some kind of group together in Toronto. Like AA, I gather. Claims he was the one that got her in here. And she saw him the night he disappeared, at nine o'clock, upstairs. She pulled out her diary to find the entry. I'd really like to get my hands on that diary, but without a warrant…"

"You think she's hiding something important and that it's in that diary?"

"I'm sure of it. You go ahead now. Where did you find the two girls?"

"Three, really. 'Cause that Annette Micawber, the journalist, is really only a young girl herself. Pen name: Anita MacElburns, by the way. But if you mean the two maids—Della was doing up the Saffron Hill Hut, the straw-bale affair that the artist couple stay in. Clara was in The Vines Villa, that's a little mud-hut shack where Latch Lupin is sleeping. Della says the villas and cabins are for the guests that *aren't* here for rehab. Guess it makes sense to give the spa guests more privacy and keep the addicts in the main building where they can keep an eye on them."

"They haven't done a terribly good job of that, have they? Two deaths and a woman who's so bonkers she tries to climb out a forty-foot window into a shrub."

"I know. Doesn't it seem like they're a bit short-staffed? Especially with Flintwinch gone?"

"It does indeed," Phil said. "I was about to ask that question of Ruth, but then Clara came in to say she'd been talking to you. She saw me and choked right up. That's another thing I wondered about. What did she say to you, about Karen and Charlie's relationship, exactly?"

"Well, I sort of had to drag it out of her, but she said Karen was always following Charlie with her eyes, always putting on more make-up and eye-shadow when he was going to be around. She admitted she'd seen a few things in Karen's room that didn't seem 'right', either—not for someone who hadn't left the property in weeks. There was a new issue of Chatelaine, but Annette Micawber told me later that she'd given it to Karen herself, since she sometimes writes for them. And some stashed chocolate bars. There were a couple of empty glass vials, but I asked Della about them, and she said they did an arts and crafts night twice a week down in the games rooms, and that they used the vials for little memory-capsule ornaments, or something. But the thing neither Clara nor Della could explain was that Della had seen a diamond ring one day on Karen's dressing table; neither of them had seen it before or since."

"They seem like rather nosy maids, don't they? Good for us, I suppose; not great for the guests here, though."

"Della let it slip that Sela Cowan and this Flintwinch character asked the staff to keep a sharp eye out for anything unusual with the rehab. guests. It's part of their so-called program, apparently. They know they aren't supposed to keep secrets from the staff, or to have what might be considered contraband goods, or to be up to any bad old habits that might lead to feeling the need for drugs or alcohol."

"Like what?"

"Della said Karen used to chew on, and peel, her fingernails, and Gerald used to poke holes in his ears."

"For God's sakes!"

"Those were just a few examples she gave. But it's all part of being an addict. I know, because I have a–a friend who used to shoot coke. And he'd sit and shake his leg for hours, drove me nuts."

Phil thought of his sister, who'd over-dosed on the same substance but was also a teen alcoholic, thanks in part to their parents' strict upbringing and their mother's past propensity for addiction. But he only smiled at Trevor and said, "A friend, eh?"

Trevor blushed. "Yeah, we were roommates for a while. In Regina."

"I see."

Quickly changing the subject, young D.I. Ames said, "Anyhow, the point is that this diamond ring was never worn by

Karen and was only seen the once on the little table. So, what do you make of that?"

"Couldn't it have been an heirloom? And she hides it where she keeps her diary, under the mattress?"

"Why not wear it, then? It's not a prison—they don't take everyone's jewelry off them when they arrive, or anything."

"What ideas did Della and Clara offer?"

"Well, again—neither was overly forthcoming, but Clara, who seems the most romantic and naïve of the two, said she thought Charlie had given it to Karen and wondered if they were engaged."

"Oh, yes?"

"But then Della said that was unlikely, since she thought Charlie preferred 'more mature women' and had spent a lot of time going for walks with Cowan and Tox."

"Well, how old is this Annette, then?"

"Oh, I'd say about twenty-two, twenty-three. But she's a tiny slip of a girl, really looks more like a teenager."

"Right. What else did she have to offer regarding Crispin?"

"She's only been here for ten days and is leaving tomorrow. If we let her, that is. And she had indeed been here a few years ago as one of the first guests in Flintwinch's rehabilitation program. She got so much out of it that she swore, when she got some writing jobs, she'd come back and do an intensive article on the place, with photographs and all. She was only here a few days before Crispin died. However, and this might be key—she'd planned to interview him officially the next day. He'd volunteered to be one of the first."

"Hmm, I wonder if he'd have let it slip who his father is. I hope not, but I know Crispin, and he wouldn't have liked to keep anything secret, not when he was on a wellness path. Different, of course, when he was spiraling downward."

"You think he'd have blabbed his real name, and his connection to the police? That mightn't have gone over too well with the other addicts."

"It might have been a worry, certainly, if it was to come out in a national magazine. Did Miss Micawber have anything else?"

Trevor flipped through his notes and was about to answer when there was a rap at the door and Cathy, their landlady, poked her head in. Philip got off the bed and went to open the door wide, remembering her homophobic reactions from that morning. Behind her stood her brother Brian, whom they had met when they'd come in that evening.

"We're on our way to bed now, detectives. Me and Bri get up early…"

" A'fore the sun," finished Brian.

"Bein' farmers," they said together and then Cathy continued with, " an' all. But just wanted to check if you's needed anything?"

Phil turned and looked at Trevor, sprawled on the bean bag chair with his sock feet on the footstool. Trevor shook his head slightly in a return glance so Phil said, "No, thanks, Miss Nelson. I think we're both set very comfortably. I wonder if we could ask that our breakfast be just a bit later than we'd discussed, though? We've got a busy night of discussion still ahead of us."

"Oh, yeah, what's later?…"

"… later?" put in her brother for good measure, in case they hadn't heard.

"Perhaps nine?" said Philip.

"Rightie-o, then. Have a …"

"Good night" they both said and went off to their respective rooms.

"Good," said Trevor. "I hadn't wanted to climb out of bed for her 7:30 breakfast. Not if we're staying awake half the night."

"I really should go telephone through to Blue before we keep on, I guess. Don't want to wake up the Nelsons on the phone later."

"And don't forget – she told us that there's some neighbor on the party line that likes to listen in."

"That's definitely going to be a problem. I think I'll have to ask Flintwinch tomorrow for a place to report to Blue at the end of each day, from Bayham Brook House. Of course, I'll still need to call home from here some evenings."

"But at least you won't be saying anything about the case then."

Phil threw a crooked smile toward Trevor before he left the bedroom to descend the stairs. "Oh, you don't know my godmother P.J.!"

.   .   .

While Philip was gone, Trevor took the opportunity to lay back his head on the puffy red bean bag and consider. Did he want to make a habit of calling Carl? He hoped he'd remembered to lock up properly, when he'd left Trevor's apartment that morning. Hell, was it *really* just that morning? He was so tired, and it seemed days ago already.

And why did Philip Steele always make him squirm whenever he mentioned a single thing about his private life? Did he suspect? Trevor supposed he hadn't gotten to be a top investigative consultant without having a nose for people's characteristics and what made them tick. He'd certainly dropped some subtle hints and glances in the time they'd worked together in all the last long months...

No, Trevor decided. He wouldn't phone Carl while he worked this job. He'd felt lately that Carl was getting a bit too needy and clingy, anyway. It would be better for them both to have some space, some time apart.

Trevor Ames closed his eyes and took a short cat nap while he waited for Philip Steele to return.

.   .   .

Sela Cowan had brought the dishes from their supper back into the kitchen. Her mother had only eaten about half of what Ruth had sent over for her, and Sela hadn't felt much like eating either. Still too muggy out, they'd decided, and with Sela relaying some details about the finding of Charlie's body, it would have felt wrong to be scarfing down noodles in tomato sauce, regardless. She started to run the water into the sink to do the few dishes, but Petra called out to her from the patio in the back of their cottage.

"Coming, Mom!" She stirred up the suds, then tossed the mugs and plates in to soak. "What is it?"

"Oh, darling. Could you just reach that hook on the stone wall for me? I wanted to hang a potted plant Charlotte brought for me today, from town. It's over there in the shade."

"It's lovely, Mom. Some ivy and little geraniums? And what're these?"

"Calendula. And I believe some trailing verbena."

Sela handed the planter to her mother, knowing the woman would want to do whatever she could for herself. Petra reached up from her wheelchair as Sela pulled down the hinged hook. Together they successfully hung the planter and backed up to admire it.

"Will it get enough shade there, do you think?" Sela asked.

"I'm sure, and I can wheel out here most mornings and water it just after you leave for work. That'll be my reminder. As soon as you leave, I have something important to get to!" Petra smiled at her dark-haired daughter. "Would you bring our teas out here, darling? It's too hot to go inside yet."

"Sure, Mom. Just let me quickly wash up the dishes and I'll put some ice cubes in the tea with a few mint leaves I brought from across the road."

Sela returned to the kitchen, quickly wiped the dishes and put them in the rack to dry, then took out a pitcher of cool tea from the low shelf of the refrigerator where everything was kept within easy reach for her disabled mother. Except for the ice, of course.

It was up in the freezer where Petra could no longer access it as she once had done when they'd first purchased the appliance many years ago. Sela grabbed the ice tray and was about to dump all the cubes in the pitcher when she saw the plastic bag at the back of the freezer. She'd nearly forgotten, in the day's craziness. She took it out, put the butt to her nose and inhaled. *Ah, it still smelled the same!* It had been over a week since she'd last checked it. She was grateful that her mother could never reach the freezer, because this would stay so fresh here. The other items in the bag were also best stored in the cold, rather than in her room or elsewhere on their property.

As she slammed the freezer door shut, the menorah on top of the fridge jiggled and she grabbed it, along with the pitcher and two plastic glasses.

"Here we are, Mom. And I had a bit of a brainwave—let's light the menorah and I can keep reading from The Edible Woman out here. Plus that much smoke from the candles might keep the mosquitoes away."

"Oh, honey, I know we don't practice anymore, but it still doesn't seem quite right to light it any old time."

"Mom. It's fine, really. We haven't read Atwood for a while now, so unless you've been cheating and reading it on your own…"

"No, but I did wonder about having a bath tonight. Might help me cool down a bit."

Sela sighed. "I'm really too exhausted from this insane day, if you don't mind. Let's do your bath tomorrow night, can we?"

"Of course, my darling. Here's the book, in my bag. I think we were just starting Part Three…"

•   •   •

Phil returned to The Quay Room to find a gently snoring Trevor. "Sheesh, I wasn't even gone ten minutes!"

"Eh? What's that? Oops, just havin' a little shut-eye. What did the D.C. say?"

"Just let me shut the door so we don't keep the Nelsons awake." Phil did so, then climbed back onto his bedspread. "We didn't touch on a lot of details. I warned him about the party line right at the top of the call. Blue wasn't any too impressed that we're going to have more 'inept OPP' all over the grounds again, because, of course, solving Crispin's death has become his only real priority. I think he's forgotten he's a top-cop. This week, he's just a grieving father."

"Well, speaking of 'father', did you ask him if he'd talked to his son that night?"

"I did. And he hadn't. So whomever Crispin was speaking to the same evening he bizarrely went and climbed up on that trestle bridge, it wasn't the D.C. Unless Ruth is lying, and I don't see why she would, not about that."

"You mentioned 'bizarre' and I've been thinking..."

"Have you? I thought you were snoring," Phil laughed.

"I'm equipped with the skills to do both simultaneously. I was thinking, you don't think Crispin might have gone up on that bridge, and maybe even thrown himself off, because of some kind of hypnosis, do you? I mean, the Cowan woman admitted that they use some hypnosis as part of their therapy?"

"Hmm. It's a thought. But I understood it was more like repeated mantras, a sort of conditioning to certain sounds. Also, I think when the Toronto coroner has done a more thorough autopsy than the local doc, we might find out if there were any drugs in his system that could have caused him to do something so freakish."

"Oh, that's happening now, is it?"

"Yes, I told you that Blue was going to try for the Blexdale doctor to step in, and as of today Crispin's body is going straight to his lab. The provincial police can have Charlie's body done locally, but if there're similar findings..."

"So you think it's either hypnosis, or hallucinogens that made Crispin go up there?"

"Not necessarily. Maybe the poor guy was just taking a walk, felt like some adventure, despite what his parents say. I mean, they all knew the train times around here—there aren't many, I understand—so there was no real danger for him to cross the bridge then. Maybe it was a good place to watch the sun set?"

"And you're saying you want to hike up there tomorrow afternoon?"

"After our other interviews, yes. Or I'll go up, and you can go down to the brook, follow it to where it opens into the creek. Check out where you heard they go to smoke weed. Then you can be right under me when I'm on top."

"As long as you don't want *me* to go up on my own. I wouldn't mind crossing it with you, but definitely not on my own, thanks very much."

"You prairie boys don't like heights, eh? No problem. Now, when the Nelsons interrupted us you were about to say what else the Micawber woman divulged."

"Oh, right. Well, I would hardly call it 'divulge'. But since she was here a few years ago in rehab, and since she's been really trying to experience every nuance of the place now for her article, Annette did bring up a few interesting points. I wrote them down in the order she told me, so no particular sequence here. One: all the guests' last names, even those who are just staying for a relaxing retreat-like holiday, are fake. That is, no one uses their real surnames, for the sake of anonymity."

"Oh, for heaven's sakes! Yes, I should have guessed, especially when we heard Crispin wasn't using his. And when I thought some other names seemed literary."

"Shouldn't the Cowan woman have been up front about that right away?"

"Not if one of her main concerns is to protect the privacy of all her patients and guests."

"But why wouldn't the OPP have told you this morning out in the woods? That seems like something they should have known, no matter how inept D.C. Cobalt seems to think they've been."

"You know, I don't really think that's fair to them. They've done their best with the information they've been led to, which was that it was a suicide. Plus, if people here are all going to harbor secrets, including their real last names…"

"Yeah, I suppose…The county coroner wasn't even called in on this until the D.C. got involved, so I shouldn't jump to conclusions."

"What a nuisance, though. I guess anyone that seems in the picture for a suspect, we'll have to do a background check based on a whole different set of last names. What a confusing mess!" Phil pulled some foolscap toward him, crossed out a lot of surnames and made a note under his list for Flintwinch on the morrow. "And number two?"

"Two: Annette said their counseling sessions can be scary. She admitted to giving full credit to Flintwinch and Cowan, and their program for helping get her clean. But she says it certainly doesn't work for everyone."

"Nothing's guaranteed when trying to help people with addictions." Philip thought once again about his sister Vicki, how his parents had tried so hard to get her the right help. *Over twenty years ago, and it still hurt like hell to even picture her face.* "What did Miss Micawber mean by 'scary', exactly?"

"I gather it's hard core. They sit on the floor and there's some serious soul-searching and even brow-beating. Beating other things, too—like the floor, in rhythm, she said. Like a drum circle, whatever that is."

"Has she been in on them lately?"

"No, of course they won't let someone not currently in the rehab. program join them, especially someone about to do a write-up. No matter how much she appears to wish to promote the place."

"I just wondered. Did she mention if there'd been this mantra mumbo-jumbo partial hypnosis stuff going on a few years ago?"

"We didn't discuss that. I guess I should have asked."

"Not a problem, we can double check tomorrow," said Phil. "And three?"

"Three: Annette says that on top of overhearing the loud discussion in the dining hall on Crispin's last night, she woke up in the middle of the night and thought she saw someone go past her villa. She's in a vertical log deal, called Sorrel Close Cabin."

"What time was this exactly?"

Trevor checked his notebook again. "She thought about three a.m. But she also thought it might have been a deer, or that maybe one of the horses had got loose. She was sleepy, she said, and she wears glasses, so couldn't see properly. Plus, in her cabin, there's a lower bunk and one on top. She'd have been looking at it from the top bunk where she chose to sleep, and the window is lower down and quite small."

"Well, it's certainly something to keep in mind."

"I spoke to Walter after I chatted with Annette. He stuttered his way through an explanation of how even if a horse breaks out of its stall or paddock at night, they can't get down to the area with all the little earth-friendly huts. That's all fenced in with the garden to keep wildlife out."

"So, it wouldn't have been a deer, *or* a horse, then?"

"Highly unlikely, according to him."

"Is there a number four point from the loquacious Miss Micawber?"

"Nope. Just those three."

"Well, I'll leave it to you to tell her that we don't want her to leave tomorrow. I've already mentioned to Sela that no one should be planning to go home for at least a few days yet."

"Right you are."

"Anything else from your interviews, either this morning or later?"

"I think I've covered every point that might be relevant, or which was niggling me."

"Me too," Phil said, stretching his arms above his head. "At least for now. I'll maybe spend another hour or two going over notes, and making up my recipe cards into categories. You go on to bed, Trevor. And thanks."

"Oh, I'll be off to the Dock Room. But I'll likely stay up, organize my notes a bit too."

"See you in the morning, then. Hope breakfast isn't a duet of those two siblings finishing each other's sentences or saying the same thing at the same time. It's hard to concentrate on who to listen to, when they get that double act going."

"Still better than the Elephant Woman and her nasty lies."

"Sleep well, Trevor."

"You too."

The detectives parted ways, but each of their bedside lamps stayed on until close to midnight as they hunched over their cast of characters and potential clues.

CHAPTER SEVEN

At breakfast the following morning (waffles with locally tapped maple syrup and two sunny-side eggs each), Cathy Nelson limped back and forth from kitchen to their table on the porch.

"May I help you at all, Miss Nelson?" Phil asked, feeling a little guilty.

"Oh, bless youse, not at all, Detective. If you're worried 'bout my bein' a cripple, don't. I had polio when I was four, so I've been like this most o'my life. Plenty used to waiting on a couple folk at a time. But I appreciates the offer, I most shorely do."

While Trevor and Philip had agreed not to discuss the case in front of their landlords, that all changed when they saw Cathy's brother Brian come out of the barnyard and head to the house.

"Cath!" he bawled from about thirty feet away.

"Eh?" she squawked back from the porch steps.

"Need more bandages – some of them bigger wrap-'round 'uns, like!"

"Oh, for goodness sakes, Bri. Again?"

"It's Sid Vanderbrugge this time. Wrist. Might be a sprain, but he's cut, too."

Brian came up the porch steps and nodded to the men sitting in the early sun. "Gen'lemen"

Trevor jumped up. "How about I grab those for you, Miss Nelson?"

"Oh, I'm fine thanks. They ain't upstairs, them ones. I'll go grab 'em from the laundry room." Cathy disappeared and her brother leaned against the porch railing.

"You gents sleep all right, did yas?"

"Fine thanks, Mr. Nelson. How's the tobacco harvest?"

"Slow-to-middlin'. Workers keep hurtin' 'emselves, so gotta keep stoppin'. Gotta wonder iff'n they's fakin' it, like."

Phil suddenly put down his fork, an idea striking him. He pulled out some smaller recipe cards, shuffled through them like a deck of cards and made a note on one, putting it by his plate.

"Did Cath talk ta you's 'bout Ruthie, yet?"

Trevor, seeing Philip was still occupied in his mind, said, "About what, sir?"

"Oh, nuthin'. Just that Ruth, the cook at Bayham Brook, she's…"

"…our cousin." Cathy finished, returning to the porch with a roll of fabric which she handed to her brother. "Ruth often comes down on her day off and chats about up there at…"

"…at the house," said Brian. "And last month she had us…"

"…do a little job for her."

Phil was looking from one to the other, trying to understand. He looked at Cathy, hoping she would sit down and explain rather than bustling back and forth.

She looked over at her brother and said, "Best get on back to the barn, Bri. Wrap Sid's arm up and let me know if he needs a ride inta town later. These policemen been 'right nice to me, an' I guess as how I better tell 'em …"

"… what we know. For the best, Cath."

Brian nodded at the men again and took his leave. Phil stood and held out a stool for Cath to perch upon. She accepted willingly, now that their breakfasts were nearly finished.

"See, I wasn't gonna tell youse we was connected to Ruthie, 'cause we took an oath of silence on this favor she had us do. But last night, me and Bri heard 'bout them findin' Charlie Squeers's body up there, an' I called Ruth—she's our second cousin, her daddy bein' our Great-Uncle Mel, an' all. Well, by marriage, like."

Phil was tempted to roll his eyes at Trevor but instead calmed himself with his cool decorum, always prevalent in situations which invited, at least in his estimation, scathing sarcasm. "I see. How marvelous to be encompassed by such a close-knit familial relationship." He tried not to look impatient and could tell Trevor was doing the same; the younger man was tapping his fork lightly on his empty plate, head down.

"Yeah, mostly we has us a good, friendly kinship, but about five weeks ago she asked for somethin' a little more than maybe she should-a done. She drove that Charlie Squeers down here to Port Dune, and he applied for a marriage license, like. That were on one of Ruth's afternoon's off. An' then a few days later, she drives down here with Charlie and his bride-to-be, Karen-somethin'. So then our minister, Reverend Talbot, he married 'em. Ruth had asked me to set that all up with him, and he weren't none too keen, as he didn't know 'em, nor nothin' 'bout them, 'cept they was likely both addicts. But Ruth vouched for 'em, and Bri and I witnessed. We took our foreman Jake Wiebe and his girl Sarah along, too—she'd made the bride some flower chains for her head and neck. Then we gave them all some sandwiches here on the porch afterwards, as a little send-off. Though where they was 'sending-to' beats me. They just went right back to Bayham Brook House, o'course."

Cathy stood again and started collecting their plates. "We was thinkin' of tellin' youse last night when we said good night, but I thought you looked too busy with other stuff, and I chickened out a bit. But Bri was pushin' as how I oughten't ta let any more time go, and when I called Ruth last night, I got her to agree we should say. 'Bout the weddin', an' all. It's just too sad that little girl's already a widow now, an' I kinda liked Charlie. He seemed a jolly enough feller, gave me plenty of compliments on my special angel food cake I'd made 'em. But it's just too sad, with them two boys' deaths up there, an' Petra Cowan needin' that surgery, an' ole Walter's heart attack an' all. Just too much sadness up there right now, like."

She started to carry their dishes through the screened door, held open by Phil, but he took some from her pile and followed her. "What surgery is Petra Cowan needing?"

"Oh, her disability left her in lots of pain. She got hit, you know. On that busy highway up there, 'crossin' over from the big house to go back home. That were, what—near ten years ago now, it were. Some car driven by a coupl'a local hoodlums. An' so ever since, Sela—that's her daughter, you like-as-know—she bin tryin' to save up extra money for to take her mother to New York City for a special surgery to alleviate the pain in her spine. She's got some bones pinchin' together, I gather, so Ruthie says. An the only doc here that can do it proper, is in Toronto and he's got a two-year waitin' list, or more. So Sela wants to get her over the border."

"I see," said Philip. "And Walter—he's the stableman and groundskeeper, is that right?"

"Yes, sir. He's from down here in Port Dune, though I bl'ieve he went ta school— just ta grade 8, like as not—in Sandytown."

"You said he'd had a recent heart attack?"

Trevor had followed them now and answered from the doorway to the kitchen. "Forgot to say that besides his stutter, the poor guy has quite a weight problem."

Cathy Nelson nodded. "Poor old Walter hasn't had much of a life. Always teased and bullied. Good enough with his hands, though —he's a good mason and a good gardener, too. Yeah, about six months ago he collapsed in the manure pile, muckin' out them stalls up there. An' Jeremiah Flintwinch, he done that there rescue breathing on him, and we heard was thumping on his chest in that new way, too, until the ambulance got to him, Ruthie says."

Seems like this Jeremiah Flintwinch is on a pedestal with everyone—like a bloody god, thought Phil.

"Certainly seems like they're having their share of hardships at Bayham Brook House, Miss Nelson," said Trevor. "Thanks for filling us in."

"Just a moment. Miss Nelson, did you or your brother happen to see Charlie's or Karen's last names when you witnessed at this wedding? On the papers you signed?"

Cathy thought for a minute. "Think it just said Squeers, like. But no, now's you mention it, I think we didn't see their names at all. We was both just tryin' to sign our own names neat and proper and I think the Bible was laying at the top anyhow."

A short time later, in the car heading north, Trevor looked over at Philip and said, "So, that's one big secret out. Imagine that Ruth, keeping it to herself! Or Karen, for that matter."

"Well, I blame myself," Phil said. "I must be losing my touch. I knew they were both hiding something, but I didn't dream it was the same thing, and I thought my interview skills were better than that. How I didn't find out about that marriage yesterday is shameful."

"Ah, not really, Philip. I mean, we don't know if anyone else on the place even knew about it, and obviously anyone who did was sworn to secrecy, like Ruth and the Nelsons."

"Wonder why, though? Why the big secret?"

"Well, for starters, I don't think the rehab. guests are supposed to leave the property for longer than an hour to get some health snacks at the stores in Sandytown or Edom's Creek. They aren't allowed candy, but Della told me they go for granola, and nuts and all sorts when there's a car goin' for errands or to the post office."

"So, I'm guessing Karen *does* keep her wedding ring somewhere on her person? Just not where nosy maids will see it and gossip?"

"Likely on a chain, or something. Hey, there's that Nellie's Bar and Grill Cathy told us about. Shall we plan to come back here for our lunch, after this hike you've got planned?"

"Sure. We can maybe order some kind of takeout and eat in the car. That'll give us more privacy to discuss things."

For the rest of the journey, Trevor drove in silence as Phil bent his head over his recipe card notes.

•   •   •

"Mr. and Mrs. Haggerty, good of you to come together like this for us so promptly. I'm D.I. Steele and this is D.I. Ames, whom I believe you met briefly yesterday, sir. Please sit again, both of you."

They were back in The Growlery at ten o'clock sharp, and the middle-aged couple who owned the farm which connected to the top of the black trestle bridge on one side of the valley, were already waiting for them in the little study with the enormous table. Sela had told the detectives from her broom-closet of an office near the front door to expect to find them there. Four mugs of steaming coffee and a plate of shortbread sat in the middle of the table, the ashtray having been pushed down to one end. Apparently the Haggertys did not smoke.

To assist Trevor in gaining experience with his interview skills, Philip generously offered to let him take charge of the questioning whilst Phil himself would remain mostly quiet, taking notes and interjecting just occasionally.

"Now, I have your address here from the staff directory. If you'd please just confirm your phone number as well, to add to our notes? Mrs. Haggerty?" Trevor asked of the buxomly woman in a nurse's uniform, with a name tag above her left breast labeled 'Martha'.

"We have two different numbers, Detective. One for the house, one for the barn. It's in the milk shed. The first is 866-

9732, and the barn where you'll usually get Bob, or our son, Bob Junior, or the hired hand, Andy. That's 866-9733."

"Thank you, Mrs. Haggerty. That's very helpful as we only have the house number from the list. Now, tell me please—how long have you each worked here part time?"

The couple exchanged glances. "About three years, and a few months. About when the retreat started to get busy 'cause they'd been advertising so much in the cities. Both in London and Toronto," Bob Haggerty said. "Once they realized it was going to take off, so to speak, and they could make a go of it, they needed help with the vegetable gardens and chickens, and I'm the closest general farmer in these parts. So many others have turned to tobacco now. I could easily walk over here, but most days I drive to save time. After I'd been here just a few weeks, I mentioned that my wife worked part time as a nurse at the Tillsonburg Hospital. So they offered her more work here, and for far better pay than she gets at the hospital, isn't that right, dear?"

"Well, the owners can certainly afford it."

"Have you ever met the two couples who own the place?"

"No, sir. They mostly stay clear. Let Doctor Flintwinch and Sealie do it all. An' they're both good at their jobs, so why would they interfere?"

Mrs. Haggerty added, "Yes, the doctor is well known for his work with rehabilitating addicts and of course Sela Cowan, well— we've known her forever. She's a pretty special gal, very caring."

Phil needed to know an answer to something that had been bothering him since Brian came to the porch and asked his sister for a bandage earlier. He said, "Mrs. Haggerty, if you were going to wrap an arm that had just been cut—would you use iodine? Here at the retreat?"

"Oh, not likely, sir. That's very messy and old-fashioned. We like Ozonol as an ointment. A good Canadian standard, and it's both soothing and disinfecting."

"Hmm, yes. And would you wrap the entire arm with a cotton bandage, or just put on a few sticky-plaster types?"

"Well, of course if the cut was very deep we'd do stitches and apply a white bandage as extra protection. But usually the little cuts and scrapes we see around here, they just get some stick-on Band-Aids."

Phil made a mark on one of his recipe cards, nodding at Trevor to continue.

"You say Dr. Flintwinch is well known in his profession. Is it as 'Flintwinch', or perhaps 'Schneider'?"

"Oh, I see you know about the name-thing," said Bob Haggerty. "The doctor's certificates on his wall are all for Jeremy Schneider, but he's always been known in Ontario as Jeremiah Flintwinch, I think."

"*You can have your droll name again... setting you apart,*" muttered Philip Steele, quoting from memory.

Trevor looked at him quizzically. Phil mumbled to him, "Later. Go on."

"And Mrs. Haggerty, you find he's professional in his medical practice as well as his psychiatric work?"

"Oh, indeed, sir. I know some of his ideas are controversial, but that's just because they are so new. He's very compassionate, even if at times he might seem strict or overbearing with his behavioral therapies."

"Are you ever involved in the group counseling sessions?"

"Rarely. Only if Sela can't be in them for some reason, and if I'm available."

Trevor turned to Bob Haggerty, "I wonder, sir. On the morning you found Crispin's body—and we'll be getting to that in a moment—did you happen to notice any deer or horse hoof prints around the garden?"

"I don't think... no, I'm sure I'd remember seeing that, and there's been no trampled produce or anything. May I ask why?"

"Oh, we just heard there might have been a loose animal that night out by the little villas. Not important. Now, Mr. Haggerty, please tell us in your own words what happened the morning you and your wife drove down from your farm and came under the bridge and saw your cows—on the wrong side of the creek, was it?"

"Wal, no. Most of them were on my farm's side, but about five had broken through the bit of fencing under 'the tunnel', the little bridge for the highway, so they were on my farm's side of the creek, but on the wrong side of the highway, if you get my meaning. Those five were all staring across the creek and two or three had waded down into the water when I looked down from the road. So I pulled over to go check."

"And you saw Crispin Co—Clennam, on the ground?"

"Yeah, I had walked down from his side, not the cows'. He was right there, all broken up..." Bob glanced at his wife and Martha put a comforting hand on his leg.

"I was in the car, not looking, Inspectors. If I'd seen Bob gesturing for me, I might have gone down, even in my white uniform shoes. But I just assumed it was the usual hole in the page wire issue that the cows had pushed through, and that he'd soon fix it and be back up."

Bob said, "Nothing you could have done for the boy anyhow, Martha. He was deader than dead by then." The farmer shook his head, then took off his smudged and faded baseball cap, wiped back his greasy bangs with a broad, calloused hand, and replaced the hat.

"Would you be willing to take me down there and show me exactly where you found him, a bit later, sir?" asked Trevor. "I'm sure the OPP markers are still visible down there, but I'd like to get your impressions and descriptions while we're on the scene."

"I can do that, sure," said Bob Haggerty agreeably. "Anything to help, especially now that Charlie's body's been found as well."

Trevor thought the man was subtly fishing for more information, so quickly added in an effort to sidetrack him: "D.I. Steele plans to go across the brook, up the other side and follow the tracks along over the Black Bridge. I'd like to plan it so we were underneath at the same time. Shall we say about eleven-fifteen? Where should we meet you?"

"You can find me in the garden, down by the cabins, there." Obviously no self-respecting south-western Ontario farmer was going to use the term 'villas'.

"Right. I think that's it for now, Mr. and Mrs. Haggerty."

"Just one more thing, if you don't mind," Phil added. "And please understand I'm not laying any blame at all—I'm just curious how things work here." He intentionally left the 'here' unqualified; he could have meant Bayham Brook House itself, the county, or in fact the entire rural provincial area for which the OPP were responsible. "Why did you and Mrs. Haggerty not immediately go to a telephone and call the provincial police, to report the death?"

Bob was pensive for a moment, then said, "I guess, since I recognized his body and since here was the closest phone, anyway, other than back to our place, I just thought I'd tell Doc Flintwinch, expecting he'd look after the rest right away."

Martha added, "Bob was very shook-up, anyhow. Not sure he could have made much sense over the phone at that point."

"And was it to Doctor Flintwinch that you *did* report it?" Phil was trying hard to get the exact details of those hours, especially before meeting with the manager, the 'great man' himself, later that day.

"Wal, now. No. Sealie was right at the door in her little cubby-hole office. So Martha and I just blabbed it all to her, and she told Martha to take me in to Ruth and we could sit and have a sugary tea. For the shock, you know. She said the doc was in a private counseling session right then, and she'd just go pull him out quietly and tell him. She headed off down the hall, but then I heard later that the doc called the owners about it. That took some time, I gather, and it was then the owners who decided how to approach the police. Did I do wrong?"

Phil was reassuring. "Not at all. I'm sure you did exactly what felt natural. It's just that it took both Crispin's family, *and* the OPP, a little longer than it should have, to find out. So, we're trying to understand if we can rectify this sort of thing in future. Please don't worry, sir. You've both been very helpful."

The Haggertys stood to go back to work for an hour and the detectives faced each other.

"Well done, Trev. Now, before we go off hiking, I'm thinking one of us needs to confront Sela about why she and the good physician didn't call the OPP themselves, while the other needs to confront Ruth in the kitchen about why she wasn't forthcoming about the secret marriage. Obviously, we need to talk to Karen about it again, or I'll let Officer Biro know he needs to question her, since that's more about his case at this point. But we need to find out what else Ruth might be hiding from us. Loyalty is one thing, but it can go too far..."

"You can say that again. I really need a smoke, so how about I go ask the cook to join me outside the kitchen door for a chat, and you can take on Nurse Ratched?"

Phil smiled at the reference. "Oh, you've read that novel, have you?"

"Your interest in literary pastimes isn't exclusive."

"Meet you down in the garden in an hour."

•　　•　　•

Philip went on the hunt for Sela Cowan, keeping an eye on his watch. He met Della in the hallway with a stack of towels in her arms, coming from the "Bubble & Squeak Room, Clutterbucks Welcome". From inside, Phil heard the roar of a whirlpool bath and smelled chlorine from a pool.

"Ah, Della. I'm looking for Miss Cowan, have you seen her?"

"Mornin', Inspector. I think she's upstairs in the men's wing. Want me to show you?"

"No, that's fine thanks, I'm assuming it's in the opposite direction of Karen's room?"

"That's it. Right above where we're standing now, rightly."

On his way up the polished wooden stairs, he looked out at the vista of the valley below, appreciating for the first time the views from higher up in this magnificent but unconventional building. Rather than mar the scenery, the towering black bridge in the near distance actually enhanced it. As tall pines and oaks appeared to hunch in diminutive subservience to the trestle's majesty, the Little Otter Creek wound its quaint way through the valley floor, catching golden glints from the morning sunlight.

Up on the third floor where he'd been interviewing what he now knew to be a less-than-merry widow yesterday, he turned left and padded silently down a faded-scarlet Oriental runner of a carpet, protecting the hardwood floors that poked out from either side. He was about to pass by a partially open door, Room Five, when he heard sounds of drawers opening and closing from within.

Peeking in, he watched for a moment as Sela took clothing from a chest of drawers and placed them in boxes. While she moved with the efficient confidence of so many in her profession, he noted that her shoulders were slouched, her chin tucked in to her chest. He rapped on the door and pushed it open fully to enter; he then saw her stand firmly tall and erect. Body language was so important to observe in his line of work and P.J. was forever complimenting him on his capable reading of it. But in this instance, he wasn't sure what he was reading.

"Ah, Detective Inspector Steele, how are you today? I decided I'd better clean out Charlie Squeers's bedroom now that his body's been found. We had already cleared poor Crispin's a few days ago.

We're expecting two more guests coming in the next few days, that is if you all will allow the change-overs to happen."

"We'll have to see about that, I'm afraid. Certainly, as I mentioned to you, no one can *leave* in the next forty-eight hours."

"I understand. But I expect when Doctor Flintwinch arrives later on, he'll come with instructions from the owners to try to carry on as normally as we can. These two deaths will be a rotten blow to the retreat once word gets out. It could seriously affect our future bookings."

"I just had a few questions that have arisen. I wonder if you could help me with them?"

"Certainly, have a seat." Sela tucked a curly lock behind one ear and gestured to a desk chair while she perched on the side of the bed, rubbing her hand over the bedspread to smooth it.

"First of all, D.I. Ames and I were just wondering if you weren't too short-staffed? It seems to us that with Doctor Flintwinch gone, and Martha only working part time, the medical responsibilities of Bayham Brook House is mostly falling to you?"

He'd tried to formulate this question as tactfully as possible; however, Sela instantly stiffened defensively. "I've tried to keep everything running smoothly. Nothing like this has ever happened before when the doctor's had to be away."

"Of course not, no. I wasn't laying blame at all. We just realized that with Lucy Tox trying to climb out the window yesterday, and of course with these two deaths—well, shouldn't you have more help?"

She took a deep breath and let it out slowly. "I have, in fact, asked for an orderly for some time and we're supposed to be advertising in Toronto papers for a live-in. We did have a man that worked full time as one, but now he only comes in as a freelancer, and just as a masseuse."

"We don't have a record of this individual," said Phil. "He wasn't on the list you gave Trevor yesterday."

"Oh? Oh, well I am sorry for that oversight. It's just that he's not officially on staff anymore. His name is Daniel Blevan. I can give you his phone number when I'm downstairs next."

"All right, thanks. My second question may also seem that I'm somehow laying blame. I certainly don't wish you to take it that way."

Sela sat up even straighter and thrust her shoulders back even more, were that feasible. The whole movement couldn't be called a squirm, more a 'bracing', Phil decided. He said, "Bob Haggerty tells me you went immediately to Doctor Flintwinch with the news of finding Crispin's body at the creek. However, I happen to know Crispin's father personally and it was a number of days before they were told about the tragedy. They laid the blame with the OPP, but an Officer Biro told me yesterday that they didn't get the call until the following day and that the crime scene had by then been compromised by animals, and such."

Sela stared at him. "I can't understand why that would have happened. Doctor Flintwinch put the call in to the owners right away, I'm sure. As soon as I told him! And I thought I'd heard that Crispin's family had been up north somewhere, and out of reach?"

Phil let that slide and continued, "You thought it best to follow some sort of line of command, did you? Rather than calling from your office right when Bob and Martha told you?"

"Certainly. That's how we've always done everything around here. If it's regular issues, I report to the doctor and he either deals with it himself or tells me how he'd like it dealt with. If it's something out of the ordinary, like Crispin's death—and Charlie's now, too, of course—he phones the owners and they advise on how they'd like it handled."

"And as far as you're aware Doctor Flintwinch called the owners right away?"

"Oh, I'm certain of it."

"Fine. I assume I'm set to speak with him later today?"

There was just an infinitesimal pause, Phil thought, before the nurse said, "He'll probably feel very overwhelmed upon his return, but yes, he knows speaking with both you and the OPP officers is priority."

"Lastly, Sela, I'd just like to ask," Phil leaned forward to close the distance fractionally between them so that he could examine her eyes, "were you aware that Charlie Squeers and Karen had secretly married?"

The shock that registered on the nurse's pretty face could not be feigned. Her jaw dropped open, her cheeks drained of color and her eyes grew into open orbs that stared intently back into his own.

"I take that as a 'no'?" Phil said.

"I–I—when? How? How on *earth*?"

"Our landlady is a cousin of Ruth's, and apparently your good cook was party to the entire affair, helped Charlie set it up in Port Dune, right on the lakeshore there. About five weeks ago? So you suspected nothing, even?"

"Oh, I knew they were friends, of course! That Charlie had recommended us to Karen. I knew Karen had what I'd call a bit of a crush on him, but I–I never…"

"D.I. Ames is down having a word with Ruth right now. We feel she should have been forthcoming with this information yesterday."

"Never mind yesterday! I'll have to tell the doctor she'll need to be let go. Staff can't keep secrets like that around here!"

"Why don't we just wait on that right now. At least until some other things are settled. She and her cousins did say they'd all been sworn to secrecy."

"But she had no business agreeing to help them in the first place!"

"Perhaps she is a romantic at heart, felt a little like Friar Laurence in Romeo and Juliet?"

Sela spluttered, "Ruth McCorkle!? *Romantic?* You must be joking!"

"Well, regardless, I suggest you take some time to digest this first. Of course I can't stop you interrogating Karen or recommending that Ruth be fired, but may I just ask that you do neither today? We need time to question them again, without any impetuous emotions or fear of reprisals interfering."

She thought for a moment, standing to continue packing boxes from the bureau. "Fine," she said. "I'll agree to wait on that, but I'll be discussing this with Doctor Flintwinch in detail as soon as you've had time to interview him this afternoon."

"Thank you. I'm now meeting up with D.I. Ames and Bob is taking him to the creek while I explore up above on the trestle bridge. Did you mention that you all knew the train schedule here?"

"Yes, there's usually only two a day now—both freights. The first is about 10:00 a.m. and the second is about 4:30 p.m. So you should be safe."

"Well, we'll see you after lunch then."

On his way to meet Trevor and Bob in the vegetable garden, Phil bumped into the Englishwoman, Monty Tigg. She was again in riding breeches, but without her boots, and was returning from the area of the stables. Long cotton socks were pulled up almost to her knees and she had slipped her feet into a pair of red sneakers which, Phil thought, clashed violently with her rust-colored jodhpurs.

" Ah, Mrs. Tigg. Have you had a good ride?"

"Oh, aye. Lovely morn for 't, innit?"

"I was going to ask you yesterday—you mentioned that you like your massages here. Tell me about the masseuse, would you?"

They paused at a picnic table in the shady lane and Monty put her foot up on the bench as she set down her riding crop and scratched at her behind. "I'd a nanglin' wasp bite me on t'arse," she explained, unembarrassed.

Hiding his smile, Phil said, "I'm sorry to hear it."

"Naw then, Daniel, he be t'masseuse yer on about, I reckon. An' there be nowt wrong wi' 'im, neither, as some'll say!"

"What do you mean, exactly?"

"Well, I booked ta come for nine full days, so's I'd get three massages from 'im. But when I reserved me spot six month ago, 'e were still 'ere workin' full-time, like. An' I guess summat 'appened, as I was only comin' fer a week, original. Then I gets a phone call sayin' do I wish to do a nine-day special, so to have the three sessions with Daniel Blevan?"

"I see, so this fellow used to work here as an orderly, from what I've gathered from Miss Cowan, but now you say he comes only every three days?"

"He were sacked for summat, I dunno. But I tell you this, he be one fine gripper o' t' body chunks when it come to a massage."

Phil was beginning to enjoy his conversations with the Yorkshire woman. He thanked her and moved off again, down the path toward the variety of naturally-built guest huts, in the direction of the garden. He glanced at his watch. He'd just have time to stop at the car to tighten the laces on his hiking boots and grab a thermos of water that could be clipped to his belt. He had a long, hot hike ahead of him, he knew. Perhaps as much figuratively as literally.

•   •   •

Sharon Cobalt leaned against the top rail of the riding ring at the JUST(*e*)STATE with Polly Jane Whistler. They had had a pleasant morning with Lary, sitting under the shade of the monstrous maple behind the farmhouse, sipping iced tea and nibbling P.J.'s oatmeal cookies. While Sharon's eyes had welled with tears several times, the other women had allowed her to talk about her son Crispin without her feeling pressed to do so, or wriggling uncomfortably when she did. They were now watching Lary and the founder of the Michigan riding for the disabled program, Lila Sponwin, teaching a ten-year-old thalidomide girl to ride. Mandy had no arms, just hands attached to her shoulders, and no legs, just feet attached to stumps that grew from her groin. But with the help of three of Lary's dedicated volunteers and one of her quietest geldings, Paintpot, Mandy was learning to steer through a series of poles and was laughing with glee.

Lila Sponwin had been planning this trip to help Lary Steele with a few of her students for some weeks, and now Lary and P.J. were happy to see Sharon become really distracted and even smiling at Mandy's sheer joy.

P.J. said softly, "This is quite a life-affirming experience, isn't it?"

Sharon nodded, her eyes now shining. The volunteers leading Paintpot and helping to support Mandy, perched on the top of the saddle, all burst into applause as a particularly difficult maneuver was navigated. Sharon clapped in delight also, and P.J. called out, "Well done, Mandy!"

"You know," said Sharon, "I always thought Crispin might want to spend more time out here on the farm. We brought him often when he was a child and he really seemed to love the animals, and being around the Steeles. But our necessary location, so close to downtown, really made it hard for an adopted kid, who already struggled with feelings of inadequacy, to stay away from the peer pressures."

Polly Jane put her hand on the woman's arm. "I completely understand. You and Blue can't feel guilty. Drugs have become such an epidemic these days, it seems. I watched Hilary and Roger struggle with the same guilt when Vicki became addicted..." She wanted to say more, but stopped herself. Comparisons never helped when someone else was grieving.

"You know, the last time I talked to him, he thanked me for helping him so often, for finding him the spot at Bayham Brook House." Sharon's eyes overflowed with salty wetness, ironically sparkling in the sun's rays. "He said he really felt they'd helped him there."

"I'm sure they did, Sharon. But why the two murders, I wonder? Do you think Crispin saw or overheard something he shouldn't have? Or was someone jealous of him recovering, being ready to return home?"

Phil's godmother knew full well she shouldn't be prying into this now, but she simply couldn't help herself. It was just in her nature to dig when the soil was soft.

Sharon seemed neither offended nor dismayed. "You know, Blue and I did have a short discussion about the motive. I–I can't believe it's possible that anyone would want to hurt Crispin himself, but Blue certainly has lots of enemies. People he's seen jailed over the years, witnessed against, helped put away for life…"

"You think someone pushed Crispin to get back at Blue for something? Well *done*, Mandy!" Both women on the rail applauded again as Mandy said 'whoa!' to Paintpot, now standing with his brown and white front feet in the middle of a hula hoop on the ground. Mandy had managed to lean back with her shoulders, thus manipulating her hands to pull back on the specially-added loops in the reins. Her instructors, mother, and volunteers again rallied with enthusiasm.

"Well, we did just wonder. But we're not sure how anyone would have found out his real identity. All the guests at Bayham Brook, whether they are there for treatment or just a spa holiday, show up with pseudonyms already in place."

"Do they?" P.J. hadn't heard this particular bit of information and found it most interesting. Up to learning of the second body found the day before, she too had wondered if the motive for killing Crispin might not have lain with his father's illustrious career path.

"Yes, so Blue has asked them to delve deeper. We think it's got to be something else. Crispin also said, that last afternoon we spoke, that I was to tell his Pop when he got home that Crispin would have some kind of 'information' for him. I thought he just meant about another treatment program, or a new type of machinery, like those new Jacuzzis, that he might want us to purchase. I never imagined it might be something to do with a case!"

"What did Blue make of that when you told him?"

"Oh, he was fairly dismissive. He tends to be that way, especially if a woman makes a suggestion about his work. And with this being so personal..."

Thank goodness dear Phil didn't have that misogynistic attitude, Polly Jane thought gratefully, or she'd never have been allowed to help him so much as he shared details of his commissions with her through the years.

"When was this last time you spoke with Crispin exactly, Sharon?" asked P.J. as Mandy was led indoors and Lenny, a boy with cerebral palsy, was brought out atop a stout pony she recognized as Folly.

"Two nights before he must have been—killed."

"And neither you nor Blue had contact with him after that night?"

She shook her head. "It's one of the things that really bothers Blue; the last time they spoke, Blue had had his mind on a case, been a bit abrupt with him."

"What had made him abrupt?" P.J. asked.

"He says Crispin said something about some hypnosis techniques that were being offered with certain drugs as 'supplements', and he felt it should be looked into. He told his father he'd said 'no' to the experiment, that he was perfectly satisfied with the counseling giving him the support he needed, but felt there shouldn't be *any* other drugs on the premises. Blue just thought he was making that up, though. After all, he told me the other night—who would feed addicts *more* drugs when they were trying to get them off?"

Who indeed? P.J. thought, hoping that while her godson had not telephoned last night, he would certainly do so tonight.

CHAPTER EIGHT

Philip huffed along, slip-sliding through the deep layers of leaves into the wooded gully not far from where Charlie Squeers's body had been located. Bob and Trevor's hike would be worse; they were going to be mostly in hot sun all the way to the meadow down at the creek. At least Phil had the protection of the cool forest as he approached a quaint hogs-back bridge over what was surely Bayham Brook itself. The bridge had the now-familiar rustic wood with green-lettered sign, dubbing it 'Blackfriar's Bridge'. He crossed it, then had to nearly crawl up the other side of the steep gully whereupon reaching the top he saw that another sign read: 'Bloomsbury Ridge' and in smaller letters, 'BBH property line'. He'd been given directions by Bob, but hadn't realized that the railroad tracks would be almost immediately at the top. He could clearly see why the property line had to end there; the Canadian National Railroad must own this next stretch.

He turned left and hiked along the tracks for another ten minutes, stopping only once to take a long pull from his thermos. He had double-checked with Bob about the train times—it never paid to trust just one person, especially when there were so many suspects in a place. So, as the top of the trestle bridge came into sight he felt no nervousness.

He stepped out carefully onto the solid railroad ties with nothing but a one-hundred-and-sixty foot expanse of air underneath. Glancing down only once, (because he knew that could cause dizziness or, at minimum, a change of mind), Phil made sure to move deliberately, placing his shoes flatly on top of each tie so that a toe in the spaces between couldn't trip him up. After about fifty ties he came to the first pedestrian's emergency cage, a little balcony built out over the side with a single bar railing around it. These were built in case a train came along, but they were hardly a sturdily appealing place to want to pause. He couldn't begin to imagine it with a metal monster whizzing by only feet away.

Oh, what the hell, 'the fears are just paper tigers!' said Phil aloud. He stepped out onto it, grasping the railing firmly with both hands and not yet looking down. Instead, he directed his gaze straight across and saw only the very top story of Bayham Brook House, the old servants' floor from which Lucy Tox had decided to make her descent. There were only small windows up there— highly unlikely anyone would have been looking through them at the time Crispin and someone else were on the bridge, because he'd already made his mind up that that had been between 7:00 and 9:00 that evening. He saw the end of what would have been the corduroy road, the old trail which was obviously the original buggy road that would have headed toward Edom's Creek and Tillsonburg, originally winding behind the Bayham Brook House property rather than the paved highway now leading through the front. Across the road, he could just see the crabapple tree and the tail end of a pretty stone wall at what was the Cowan's bungalow.

He gripped the railing more tightly. Had the wind suddenly picked up? Surely the bridge was swaying?

He'd been told that the OPP had not ventured here. Therefore, no fingerprints had been taken and he swore at himself for not thinking of it, although the chances were slim that it was from this balcony which Crispin had toppled. Why would a killer have added the extra problem of a railing/barrier, no matter how flimsy it might seem to the man currently clutching it for dear life? He was also annoyed with himself for not bringing the camera; he'd offered it instead to Trevor to take shots from below, and to try to get a straight line on him when he signaled from above.

Phil closed his eyes and reminded himself that his surname was meant to represent what his nerves were made of. Steel. He breathed in, then out, slowly counting to fifteen. He opened his eyes again and this time looked down, with 'soft eyes', a phrase he'd heard his riding instructor mother call out to students while cantering up to a jump. Staring hard at something meant you were tense and unfocused. Softer eyes would help him relax.

He blinked a few times and scanned the lay of the land below, continually reminding himself not to gawk intently at anything for over one second. That's when dizziness would settle in, he knew. Not directly below him, but just off to the right, farther along toward what would be nearly the middle of the bridge, and almost where the pavement of the highway began, were two tiny figures standing at the edge of the Little Otter. So, if Trevor and Bob were examining the exact spot where Crispin had been found, and if his trajectory had been straight down, Phil's guess that he'd been pushed (or thrown?) *not* from here on this cage must be correct. Fingerprints wouldn't have mattered. He blinked several times again, took another deep breath in and out.

"Ahoy!" he shouted. But a car was passing by underneath and he could tell the men hadn't heard him. He'd been conscious of that car coming for at least a full minute, so he now understood why someone could have risked a push from above and be sure not to have witnesses. They'd have simply been able to do it when there was silence in the air, or rather only the soothing sound of crickets and cicadas. No vehicles. And, as he knew no one would be stupid enough to cross this bridge in the dark, he was sure that the fatal push, or struggle, must have occurred between supper—when Crispin had last been seen—and dusk.

Phil waited until the car traveled south, up the hill toward Sandytown, then tried again. "Halloo!" he called, immediately thinking of Monty Tigg and her Yorkshire fox-hunting. This time both Trevor and Bob looked up. Trevor (he could only just distinguish who was who by the glare of his colleague's white dress shirt) raised both hands over his head and waved them from side to side, then pointed down at their feet and walked a small circle. Evidently, he was indicating the placement of Crispin's body. Phil, keeping his right hand firmly on the metal rod, made a large gesture of a salute to show he understood, and that Trevor should snap a photo or two focusing straight up. He then looked down the tracks and decided that since he was here, he'd better continue on. It was most improbable that any sort of clue would have remained up here after nearly a week with two trains a day whipping past, and the night winds gusting in from the ocean-like turbulence of Lake Erie. But being thorough was how Philip had risen quickly from mere constable to staff sergeant in his early days in the RCMP. He'd never allowed that habit to slip.

He moved off the balcony and started along toward the center of the Black Bridge, once again purposefully planting each foot down flat as he trudged along, like a choreographed dance of a mime in a quagmire. When he got to the approximate middle, he stayed inside the two steel tracks for safety, but did risk looking over to check the line he was in, in conjunction with the highway's painted white stripe. Slightly to the right. If Bob's cows had gone under the road tunnel by escaping through their page wire fencing to graze the other side, then it made sense that they'd have been spooked by a body on the opposite bank. Perhaps they'd even been witness to the fall, heard something from above them. If only they could bear witness, how easy his job would prove, Phil considered wryly. A movement caught his eye; he saw Trevor and Bob Haggerty heading back to the main house, but following a different route. This time they weren't going back by the old road laneway. They were climbing a hill just atop the highway.

Phil kept slow-motion marching along the evenly spaced ties. The second pedestrian safety balcony *was* actually more like a cage. This one was barricaded better, with a chain-link fence underneath the railing and a black, much-tattered plastic tarp covering the interwoven wires. He wondered why there would be a difference between the two safety overhangs. Perhaps the first one had had these extra precautions at one time but they'd deteriorated and the CN crews hadn't bothered to replace them? Phil looked back the way he'd come and suddenly, in the midday sun, saw a sparkle that was not from the steel tracks nor their partly rusted, massive spikes.

He breathed slowly, keeping his eyes 'soft' again. He stepped carefully back the twelve or so feet to where he'd thought he saw the tiny glint. Although he hadn't wanted to look straight down through the wide cracks between the railroad ties, knowing that wouldn't help any feeling of vertigo, he now kept his head bent searching. He couldn't see it, so got down on his knees, tilted his head near one of the rails and looked for the sparkle from that angle. And there it was!

Drawing out the tweezers he always kept in the little leather pouch in his pocket, he inched forward, still on his knees and realizing the creosote would probably never come out of his trousers. He picked up the tiny object with the tweezers and examined it closely. It looked like a sewing needle, perhaps a little thicker, but without the eye. Instead, the non-sharp end had a tiny whirl of a twist to it, like a miniature corkscrew. He couldn't imagine what this object was, and doubted it could be a clue although it was certainly very close to the area from which he'd decided Crispin had fallen. But he wrapped it in a tissue and put it and the tweezers back in his pocket. While still on his knees he looked in that same section for other potential clues but saw nothing.

Feeling he'd been brave enough for one day, he decided not to walk back across the entire bridge in order to go through the gully as he'd come. Instead, Philip simply walked the remaining forty feet to where the tracks met with firm land again. This side, he knew, was now on the Haggerty farm. Although he was well aware that the walk home in the hot noon sun, first down a dusty gravel road to the highway, then up the same highway's hill, with visible heat waves rising off the pavement, would be much more uncomfortable physically (as well as longer), it was with a huge sigh of relief that the detective planted his feet on the dried-out grasses of the bridge's opposite bank and happily stretched his legs in a long-striding pace.

· · ·

An hour later, Trevor and Philip, the latter now exceedingly grateful that Blue had thought to rent him a new car with air-conditioning, sat in said car, parked underneath a willow tree in the lot at Nellie's Bar and Grill. Trevor was munching a huge cheeseburger with French fries, while Phil had ordered a Hero sandwich, with a side order of slaw. They hadn't unrolled the windows yet, hoping to keep some of the cool air from the air-conditioning inside as long as they could. It also allowed them more privacy to converse, should anyone be passing by on their way in or out of the truck-stop-type restaurant.

Phil put down his heavily laden sandwich for a moment and pulled the handkerchief from his pocket. Unwrapping it with care, he held it in front of Trevor's face.

"Found this up there. Any ideas?"

Trevor finished chewing his mouthful, then took the pin in his fingers, still holding it between the layers. "Not a clue. I mean, it might well be one, but I don't know what the hell it *is!*"

"I found it just about where I think Crispin must have gone over, to land where you were standing. Although I'm wondering if it's possible someone just beat the crap out of him and hoped we'd all *think* he fell? We'll know in a day or two, of course, with the new coroner's report. I'm sure they'll be able to tell, damage to lungs, angle of his legs, that sort of thing."

"Yeah, poor old Bob said his body was pretty badly twisted. How the hell could someone do that by just beating him? Bob said it looked more like he'd been tied to a car and dragged."

"Well, I just don't understand having now been up there, why Crisipin or anyone else would willingly go across that crazy thing." Phil put the pin back in his pocket and took another bite of salami, provolone and soft bun.

"I had a good look around the OPP markers down there, Phil. They'd trampled quite a bit carrying him up and out, so I wasn't expecting to find anything in the way of clues, but Bob did show me where the so-called secret spot is for the joint smokers."

"Thought that was done by the brook?"

"Right, just near the end of the old road trail and where the brook joins with the creek. Could you see it from up there?"

"I saw where the road ended, but nothing else."

"Yeah, it's still back in the woods several feet. They've got a few logs pulled around for seats, and butts lying everywhere. You were right, it's hardly a secret, but maybe they keep closer tabs on the people in for treatment?"

Phil was glad to see Trevor had stopped referring to them as 'addicts'. "One would hope. Although with two of them dead and one having tried to climb out a window, I think we're back to the very short-staffed issue."

"And what did our Miss Cowan have to say about that, this morning?" Trevor asked.

"She admitted that they were, that there was usually a full-time orderly on duty as well. Apparently the guy that comes in to do massages, one Daniel Blevan, had been laid off his duties. Other than coming in every three days to give a massage to whomever had signed up for one."

"And what did she say about no one reporting Crispin's death to the provincials?" While Trevor had seemingly let go of the term 'addicts' and was technically correct in calling the Ontario Provincial Police 'provincials', Philip was quite sure the irony in the double meaning of the word had not escaped his colleague, that he was using it on purpose to cover both.

"Just that she'd definitely immediately gone to Doctor Flintwinch and reported what the Haggertys had found. I'll be double-checking with him later, of course."

"What about the secret marriage?"

"She seemed genuinely shocked. Hard to blanch your face if you're faking it. What did our good cook Ruth have to say on the matter?"

"Hm. Ruth. I don't know how to take her, she seems so 'in charge', even when I'm meant to be. I had thought getting her out of her kitchen might help but she only stayed long enough for me to have a quick smoke and she was right back inside chopping celery. I managed to get a slightly embarrassed look, just for a matter of seconds, that she hadn't told you yesterday. But then she got fiery and defensive, so I eased off. The gist of it all was that she'd made a solemn oath to keep that a secret from *any*one, including staff here. And that she always kept her promises."

"I don't know… when I was interviewing her yesterday, Clara barged in saying something about had it been o.k. to tell *you* about Charlie and Karen. Since you said she'd mentioned that damn ring, I wonder if more of the staff hadn't made some assumptions at least? Wouldn't Ruth be the first to know the ring had been spotted? Della and Clara both seem to be her little minions."

"I'm finished," said Trevor, wrapping up his greasy hamburger papers and tossing them into the hamper into which, just yesterday, P.J. had packed their lunch.

"Let me just eat a few more spoonfuls of this cole slaw, it's delicious."

"Don't mean to rush you. I just want to get back and have that chat you promised I could have with our Weeping Widow. Also, if I *have* to do the Elephant Woman for you, I will. Even if they have to put her in a strait-jacket first. I know you'll likely be with the great doctor most of the afternoon."

"And that really will be illuminating, I suspect."

"Providing he's forthcoming and doesn't pull patient confidentiality on you."

"Providing."

•   •   •

When the men entered Bayham Brook House after returning from lunch, Sela met them outside her little office and gestured down the hall. At the very end stood a figure in a two-piece suit.

"D.I. Steele, Doctor Flintwinch has returned and is happy to see you now."

"Thank you, Miss Cowan. I wonder if you'd show D.I. Ames to the women's wing upstairs? He has more questions for Karen today in light of what we now know, and if Lucy is feeling less delusional, perhaps he can attempt a conversation with her as well?

"Certainly. This way, D.I. Ames."

The pair disappeared toward the stairway and Phil headed down the hall in the opposite direction, wishing he'd thought to put on his suit jacket which was still in the Satellite's back seat. The air-conditioned and shady-treed respite had been pleasant after his sultry hike, but he was aware that he must still have soiled armpits and a wrinkled shirt, not to mention the creosote-stained knees of his pants. At least he'd straightened his tie and combed his auburn hair.

As he neared the man at the end of the hall, who had raised a hand in greeting, Philip looked him over with an interested eye. The man was everything Phil was not: the clichéd 'tall, dark and handsome' with just the right amount of cleft and dimple to make him teeter on the balance of human rather than god. He was the type Phil would have expected to see with a woman clinging to each arm, eyes raised in adoration. Yet here he stood alone, on the estate he managed alone. The wrong sort of 'dark', perhaps? Philip wondered. Remembering his lunch, he added mentally what he'd like to have muttered aloud: "*A Hero, with a side of 'flaw'.*"

Thus his first words to Jeremiah Flintwinch, although formal, were delivered with a smile that surprised them both. "Great to finally make your acquaintance."

Inside the doctor's private office (door sign read: 'Chesney Fold') Phil and Flintwinch shook hands cordially and the doctor quipped, "Welcome into the fold". Not for the first time, Philip was quite certain.

"But isn't it actually Chesney '*Wold*'?"

The doctor stared and then a wide grin spread across his face. "Have we a Dickens fan in our midst?"

"Well, a literary fan, at least."

"It's my own little joke about the two types of people we welcome here to Bayham Brook House. In Bleak House, Dickens says of Chesney Wold, 'I have mentioned the strata of society. Let us now shoot through the layers from the very bottom of society to its very pinnacles.' I'd have it on a plaque in here if it wasn't guaranteed that some of my patients would take offense! And I just thought it was more welcoming to call my space 'the Fold'. Do have a seat."

Phil looked the office over as he arranged himself, apologizing for his appearance and explaining that he'd spent the morning hiking and on his knees on the tracks. Behind the doctor's head, where the dark-haired man sat behind a desk much smaller than the table in The Growlery, were a number of diplomas and certificates. On some, Phil could read 'Jeremiah Flintwinch'; on older-looking ones he could just make out 'Jeremy Schneider'.

"Tell me about your own name-change, first, please, Doctor."

"Ah, you've noticed? I guess I can see why you're at the top of your field. Yes, my parents moved to the States from Germany in '46 and they had family friends, originally from England, the Hogarths. Neville Hogarth and his wife Jane and children Char– and Cheryl, had moved to Canada before the war and built

Bayham Brook House as a private estate in the early 1940s. My parents, and sometimes me, used to visit here regularly. Neville was a first cousin of the great-grandchildren of Dickens' wife, Kate."

"Well, *there's* a connection!" Phil said.

"Yes, and the man was a stalwart member of the Toronto chapter of the Dickens Fellowship, right from the time he moved to this country. You probably know that Bayham Brook was so named because not only are we in Bayham Township here, but Bayham was both a street on which Dickens lived, *and* his character's first name in Bleak House–Bayham Badger."

"And how did you come to manage the property which had been owned by your parents' friends?"

"Mostly a happy coincidence, although I believe Jane did recommend me to the new owners. Anyway, because Neville had already named several spots on his property after Dickens' place names or characters, I kept going with the tradition."

"Including taking Flintwinch for your own surname?"

"Correct. I did that as soon as I moved to Canada, though – several years before getting the post here."

"And your reasons for the name change?" Phil looked the doctor squarely in the eyes. If lies were going to start being told, such as an impropriety that might have been on his American record, they would start now.

But the psychiatrist just gazed back at him and said calmly, "My parents, of course, didn't want me to change it. However, after the war many German last names were being changed, or at least Anglicized. Also, there were already three other Jeremy Schneiders in the Canadian Psychiatric Association's Members Directory. I just thought of one of Dickens' funniest last names and presumed— rightly, I might add—that no one else would have 'Flintwinch' as a surname." He shrugged with a smile, adding, "I had it legally changed so that all my future qualifications from this country would have my adopted name on them, and when I was offered the job here, it certainly fit in well! Old Nev would have loved it."

"So all the names here are something from Dickens? I certainly recognized some, or some near ones, like 'Cad's Hill'."

The doctor, despite the worries that must be weighing down his shoulders with the present situation under his management, laughed outright. "That was one of Neville's original choices. So was the Furr-neville's Inn, of course. Furnival's Inn was another of Dickens' own residences. Bubble and Squeak was what Neville always called his little bath house and fountain out by the old outdoor pool. We just changed that to the indoor spa area. His ancestor Kate had written recipe books as Maria Clutterbuck, did you know?"

"I was aware she'd been a writer as well. The Clutterbuck name certainly sounds Dickensian! But isn't bubble and squeak something to do with cabbage?"

"Indeed. However, Monty Tigg—have you met her yet?—is the only other person to call us out on that one. Everyone else just thinks it's a fitting name for the pool and Jacuzzi rooms. Then of course all the other buildings, common rooms, and outdoor structures now have names related to Dickens as well. Tater Tots came out in the early 1950s and Neville used to adore eating them with great slabs of ham and mustard. My father would have nothing to do with the ham, of course, but he's the one who suggested that Neville name the tennis clubhouse 'Tots'n'ham Courtside', for Tottenham Court in David Copperfield."

"And the dining hall—is that a play on Scrooge's 'Melancholy Tavern'?"

"Great guess! And I'm guilty of that one, I'm afraid. Not such a skilled effort as Neville's and my dad's."

"Most amusing, though. My colleague thought he was going to be served a strange combination of garden melons and vegetables last evening. Now, I do realize the need for privacy among your guests, especially those you are treating for addictions and since many are from prominent families, or are celebrities. But how did their pseudonyms all become Dickensian as well?"

"It's really not something I'd planned, Detective Inspector. In fact, it was one of the owners' ideas. The first year we were open as a treatment and rehab center we'd already had several traditional spa guests booked from the year before, and we were all a bit worried about keeping the patients' identities confidential. So one of the owners suggested that, like Mr. Bumble in Oliver Twist, we ask everyone to take a surname in alphabetical order, as they booked, or registered. But that began to get complicated and I think it was Sela's mother, another old friend of the Hogarths, who said 'why not just have everyone choose from Dickens' characters' last names'? I mean, spoiled for choice, yes?"

"The man certainly had a talent for picking out names. I gather you're the only one here that knows the guests' actual identities? For instance, I understand from D.C. Cobalt that you are aware he is Crispin's father?"

"It is usually, exclusively, only me, you're correct. Occasionally there have been reasons to share with Sela, as she is my direct assistant. Sometimes, too, a patient will slip up in a group counseling session and the truth comes out then. We often make a pact for secrecy that very hour, though, and they repeat a mantra."

"Ah, yes I wanted to ask you more about those, but before I come to some of your techniques, let's just clearly understand about the names, Doctor. D.C. Cobalt assured me that I'd have your full cooperation in sharing any identities of guests who were top of our suspect list. Is that right?"

"I did promise him that, through one of the owners that he spoke to, yes. Still, that was before Charlie's body was found; it seems obvious now that we have two murders on our hands."

"Does that mean you're now *more* inclined to share, or less?"

"Do you know, I've thought about that all the way back from Toronto. I honestly can't say. I'm fearful for what might be going on here, what strangeness is being kept from me, from us. I can't grasp any of it. We've been doing so well and now…" The doctor put his head in his hands for a minute and closed his eyes. Then he looked up at Phil. "I'll try to do whatever I can to help, without completely violating doctor-patient confidentiality or jeopardizing the reputation of Bayham Brook House. Of course I realize that those two paths will converge, cross and probably 'double-cross' many times over. But if I have to go to a patient, or a patient's family first, or even Reverend Klassen, before agreeing to pass information on to you or the OPP, I do hope I'll be given the time to do so."

Phil remembered how he had walked across the trestle bridge earlier, and felt he was figuratively going to be attempting the same walk for many days to come—picking up one foot at a time, horizontally and deliberately, and placing it back the same careful way, desperate not to fall through the cracks, treading so cautiously, like the mime stepping through a quagmire. And the crossing taking forever, as he reminded himself to breathe.

"I will try to honor and respect your wishes to do so," he said in his most formal voice. "You mentioned Reverend Klassen. I met him briefly yesterday afternoon. You go to him often with concerns, do you?"

"I consider him a good friend, and certainly he is my personal confidante. If ever I feel like I might be about to make a wrong move with a decision about a certain method, or a stretch of some moral issue, I will ask his opinion."

"I'm hoping to stop in and interview him after we leave here today."

"I'm sure you'll find him happy to take a break from renovating their church basement."

"So Doctor Flintwinch, once D.I. Ames and I have narrowed down a few suspects, at least in the killing of Crispin Cobalt, whom everyone else here still knows as Crispin Clennam, you will allow us access to those suspects' actual last names so that we can run a check on any previous records and history?"

"Yes, as I said, I may have to verify with them, or their families, for permission—but I will endeavor to do so in a short space of time so as not to hold up this investigation any longer than necessary. I gather from Sela that you've asked everyone to remain here for the next several days? I won't be able to charge them if they are being forced to stay past their check-out times. We can only hope that the owners will be able to bear the costs of this. I don't mean to sound crass or unfeeling, of course."

"I understand. Perhaps Sela has explained that for right now D.I. Ames and I are concentrating on Crispin's death? The D.C. is a family friend of mine, I'm not sure if you were told."

"I was. Poor Charlie's murder is so unexpected also; we really had figured he'd just done a runner. He's done that from two other programs in which he was enrolled in downtown Toronto, and his family thought that must have been the case here too. But the OPP will be investigating his death, as well as looking at Crispin's again?"

"That's right, so I'm sorry if it seems like there's a lot of us creeping about here. D.C. Cobalt did speak with the Superintendent to ask if the intrusion of the OPP could be kept to a minimum, at least until the result of both autopsies are released in a few days. Both agencies have agreed to allow my colleague and me to be the primary investigators here on the scene. In this main building, at least. I'm sharing all notes with Officer Biro so that he is kept abreast of what we've learned each day."

The doctor sighed deeply. "Well, for that I'm exceedingly grateful. It will mean less disruption for everyone if you and D.I. Ames are the main faces they all see."

Phil smiled. "Well, I'm not sure Lucy Tox will be happy with that. She seems to have made up her mind that Trevor Ames and she share a recent history of some tumultuous sexual acts, and even when he's trying to rescue her from falling down several stories out her window, she'd as soon spit at him, as look at him."

"Ah, Lucy. Yes, Sela mentioned that she had to explain to you about Lucy already. Miss Tox—a Dickens name she chose herself, incidentally, but we find it *most* fitting—is definitely delusional, despite being clean for some time. Even when not suffering from misconceptions, she's still a pathological liar. She simply can't help herself. Last week she told me our brother Clark Gable was coming to stay in Room Five, since Charlie didn't appear to be coming back. She said it was a shame I hadn't ended up looking more like Clark, that he'd got all the good looks in the family. You can just never tell what Lucy will come up with next."

"Of course you've heard by now about the secret wedding between Charlie and Karen?"

"I have, but I've rung up Reverend Klassen and asked him to look into the Port Dune minister's records, make sure it was all on the up-and-up. I'm suspicious about that, though Karen did break down and show me her huge diamond ring the second I got home. She'd been wearing it on a ribbon tied to her toe, apparently, and keeping it hidden in her shoes. There will be lots of legalities to sort out if their marriage is deemed legitimate. I can divulge that Charlie's family is quite wealthy, although they'd disinherited him until he'd proven he could stay clean and sober for a minimum of two years."

"Ah, now that's an interesting point. So Karen could possibly come in to a lot of money?"

"Possibly, depending on how Charlie's family reacts to her. Karen's mother is a well-known Shakespearean actress on the Stratford stage, so Karen is hardly going to be living on the poverty line at any point. However, I guess you'd see her marrying him as an obvious motive."

"The stuff of nearly every murder mystery my godmother watches on television, Doctor. Indeed." Phil took a moment to scratch a note on the recipe card marked 'K & C Marriage'. "Now please try to be as honest and forthcoming as you can on this next question—are there any other romantic couplings or interests or jealousies among this current group? Not just involving Crispin, but anyone?"

The psychiatrist seemed baffled, then furrowed his brow in thought. "I really don't think so. There was a girl here the week before Crispin died—the same week that Charlie disappeared, in fact—who may have had a crush on Gerald, but he really didn't notice her. Her name was Daisy. Other than that, I can't think of anything. We have an artist couple here, Mitch and Jackie. I haven't had cause to speak with them much, but they seem truly wrapped up in their art and each other."

At that moment there was a rap on the office door. Dr. Flintwinch called, "Yes?" and Della's voice replied. "Tea, Doctor!" Phil got up to usher her in, then graciously helped the young woman place delicate cups and saucers, a forget-me-not tea-pot, and a petite sugar bowl and creamer on the doctor's desk.

"Thank you, Della," said Philip. "At a most welcome time as usual!"

"That's Miss Cowan, sir. She's always on top of who might need what when!" Gaily, Della disappeared again with the empty tray and Phil shut the door while the doctor poured for them both.

"Dr. Flintwinch, speaking of the artists and not having much to do with those guests who aren't here for treatment—are you aware that a number of them gather down near the brook from time to time to smoke pot?"

Sighing, the doctor replied, "I haven't caught any of them in the act, though I've actually walked Tiny, my German Shepherd, down there a few evenings to try to do so. I've posted subtle signs where I think the rehabbers won't notice, asking the guests to refrain from this, and of course it's in small print on all our brochures: 'no unlawful drugs or alcohol allowed on the property'."

"Do you think it's possible the others might be sneaking out to partake?"

"Well, we are short-staffed at the moment; we're looking to hire another orderly. However, I stay here in the building, as do Della and Clara, who would report to me should anyone be leaving their rooms or The Rookery after hours. Plus, Tiny does tend to bark if she hears the main doors open and close in the evenings."

Phil refrained from pointing out the obvious—that Charlie had evidently disappeared in the middle of the night.

"No offence, sir—but I believe I met Tiny out at the stable yesterday, and she didn't seem too interested in anything, let alone a stranger coming up from the woods."

The doctor snorted a laugh. "Bless her, she is getting on, but believe me—her ears are still good. She very much feels that it's her job to be on guard in the evenings when I bring her to the house."

"So, even someone acting as oddly as Lucy Tox, you don't think she's smoking anything besides cigarettes?"

"I don't think she even does that. I've never seen her do so."

"The reason I'm asking, is that several of us who knew Crispin have questioned why he'd be up on that monster of a bridge at what I presume was dusk? Unless he was on something that was altering his decision-making."

"Yes, I've thought about this long and hard for the last week as well. I simply can't understand it. Someone must have coerced him, but was it someone from here? Or someone he agreed to meet from outside of our little commune?"

"Everyone's allowed to use the phone in the common room, at any time?"

"Certainly, we don't like the clients to feel they are prisoners here. Although we do make it difficult for them to leave the property, even to go purchase snacks."

"Except for Charming Charlie. He seems to have been able to wind Ruth around his little finger."

"Mmm. Yes, Sela and I will be discussing what disciplinary action I may have to take with Ruth."

"So you think Crispin might have had a phone conversation with someone who enticed him to meet on the bridge?"

"It seems unlikely, but yes—I'd rather hoped that was the case. Better than if it was someone from here, I mean. But again, finding Charlie's body changes all that supposition."

"Ruth has told us that she heard Crispin, she *thought*, talking to his father right before dinner—sorry, I know the rural term is 'supper'—the night he died. D.C. Cobalt says that was not the case. Oh, and during supper there was some kind of row as it was following a group session with you?"

"I can't comment on the phone call, of course, but the squabble was pretty ordinary. Sometimes, after Group, everyone is subdued and feeling thoughtful and introspective. Other times, if some issues were raised, they will come out all fired up and full of adrenalin. Often, Lucy does her best to rile things further."

"Can you tell me about what the argument was about that evening?"

For the first time, Dr. Flintwinch looked uncomfortable. "I really can't, D.I. Steele. Not at this time, anyway. When Group gathers again tomorrow for a counseling session, I'll ask them all if they'd agree to let me share that with you."

"That will be fine, sir. Now I'm almost finished keeping you for today. As I said, I did just want to ask you about some of your more–er–interesting techniques. We witnessed firsthand how Karen was brought from near hysteria yesterday, to a measured and calm young woman. All with just a few words from Miss Cowan."

From his right desk drawer, the psychiatrist took a burgundy leather notebook and skipped several pages at the front, then ran his finger down a list of hand-written lines. "Mudfog marbles two-eight-nine? Or perhaps three-five-seven?"

"That's right. The latter, I believe."

"Well, let me explain a little background on this technique first; without going into details of each patient, I can give you a general overview of how we use the yoga-style mantras and mild hypnosis. You see, back in the 1930s, a doctor from Kentucky, Dr. Irving Vledilore, was working with Dr. Kellogg of Battle Creek. Of course, we all know of the Kellogg tradition of healthy eating—that's why he invented so many cereals, for the guests at his enormous health resort and sanitarium in Michigan. But he also concocted all kinds of experimental ideas with hydrotherapy, electrocution—not simultaneously, of course!—light therapy, and enemas. Along with Dr. Vledilore, they were also incorporating aspects of Jung's dream analysis, plus working on various forms of meditation and hypnotherapy. Kellogg didn't publish much about the latter work, but Vledilore did put out some pamphlets about the amazing results of their experiments before his death in 1947."

"I have read about Dr. Kellogg," said Phil. "And of course I studied some Jung at school. But I've never heard of this Dr. Vledilore."

"No, as I said, his work was unfinished and only published in some pamphlets he used for his local patients in Kentucky. Many were unfortunately from what they called 'The Narco Farm', a prison where they freely experimented on the inmates who were addicts. Those poor folk were often fed all kinds of cocktails of other drugs and they called that The Lexington Cure. However, my parents, Aaron and Lena Schneider, founded the Half-way House movement in Michigan and they incorporated a lot of what Vledilore and Kellogg were testing, which was mind-over-matter based. As well as introducing the Twelve Steps of Alcoholics Anonymous, naturally. They had found some of Vledilore's printed material in an old thrift store near Battle Creek and were fascinated with the results he'd reported. I was raised hearing about all these methods and naturally started incorporating it into my own counseling. When the Toronto owners bought Bayham Brook House, they'd originally thought to run it just as a recreational spa and retreat, but then one of the couples came and heard a seminar I was giving. And—voila."

"So how does it work? These mantras, and the hypnosis?"

"Well, I'm reticent to use the actual term 'hypnosis'. No one here is ever fully 'under', as is the common term, I'm afraid. What Vledilore found, however, was that because meditation can produce such a deep state of relaxation, patients are more open to suggestive behaviors, which works very well with rehabilitating those with serious addictions. During meditation, of course, one focuses all the attention inwardly, and this can eliminate the stress, the stream of jumbled thoughts and low self-esteem; it offers calm and a new confidence that many patients have never before managed to find."

Phil thought of Crispin, how his lack of confidence had plagued him since his youth, when the Cobalts had first adopted him and welcomed him into their loving home. He thought of his own sister, also loved and cherished—but he knew that so many factors could interfere with the functioning of one's psychological mind set. Then, when chemicals were also introduced into the equation...

He asked, "So there's no swinging pocket watch in your private sessions?"

The doctor grimaced, raising his eyebrows sardonically. "I'm afraid this whole hippie movement, and the yoga gurus and flower children, etcetera, haven't helped the general acceptance of actual medically proven methods of meditation and hypnosis."

"Nor, I shouldn't wonder, has the age of television."

"Correct. We have, however, found that certain mantras will assist each individual in getting to that inner place of calm and concentration, within themselves. So that they may overcome their old go-to habits of feeling they need a drink, or a shot, or a tablet. Or feeling they need to become overly emotional, or dramatic—to gain attention. That sort of thing."

"May I suggest that these techniques have not worked on Lucy Tox?"

"You may do more than suggest!" said the psychiatrist grimly. "Nothing I've tried with that woman seems to have worked, I'm sad to say. When I look at the other successes we've had in the last several years, though, those more than make up for one very disturbed patient."

"And so, 'Mudfog Marbles'? And the series of numbers?"

"Ah, well, as with any type of hypnosis—and believe me, there are many—using simple trigger words to activate involuntary hypnotic 'reflexes' in the patient's brain is a quick reminder. Sela told me that is what she needed to do yesterday with Karen when she was hysterical after finding Charlie's body. Oh, and the silly words we use? That takes us back to Dickens again. We use a combination of fun words from his literature, specific to each patient and with the addition of some noise—usually alliterative with the trigger word—to first condition the individual during their detoxification period when they are feeling ill and vulnerable. Then after that, the noise is no longer needed. So, as in Karen's case, 'mudfog' comes from Dickens' short works, named for his own town of Chatham. Because Karen comes from near Chatham, Ontario, 'mudfog' seemed a perfect choice for her. Then we use the sound of two marbles clacking together on a string when we say 'mudfog'. The numbers are relevant to the situation. It was lucky that Sela remembered the right set of numbers for that particular occasion, otherwise Karen might have become ravenous and headed to the dining hall. She used to have an eating disorder, which we've also successfully treated!"

"I see. Can you give me some other examples of these trigger phrases? You don't have to tell me to whom you've assigned them."

Dr. Flintwinch pulled the burgundy notebook toward him again. "Well, one I've used a lot for various groups through the years is 'Chuzzlewit Change'. I love the double entendre of the word 'change', of course, and it's a simple one to use at first because I always have a pocketful of loose change to rattle as the trigger noise." He reached into the top narrow pencil drawer in front of him and pulled out two halves of a walnut which were tied to either end of a string. He clacked them together to demonstrate the woody noise they made and offered, "For this we say 'Wopsle's Walnuts.'"

"I'm beginning to understand. Very ingenious, I must say. Could you share with me what Crispin's–er–words were?" asked Phil. He'd almost said *'magic'* words, but had bitten his tongue, knowing the doctor would have taken offense.

"I don't see any harm in that; the poor lad's gone now, and we aren't apt to use the phrases again until the next full group comes in for treatment." Dr. Flintwinch looked in his book, again running a finger through a long list before he arrived at Crispin's section of notes. He then reached in the drawer once more and pulled out two gaudy earrings with a large plastic lime green ball at the end of each, glittering with some sort of randomly glued sequins. He clacked the two of these together and said, " 'Boz's Baubles'. Then his own set of numbers, of course."

Phil took a last sip of his tea and stood. "One last question for today, Dr. Flintwinch, speaking of jewelry." He reached in his pocket and pulled out the tissue into which was tucked the strange pin he'd found up on the Black Bridge. He held it forward in his palm for the doctor to examine. Without being told, the other man did not attempt to pick it up. "You have any idea what this is?" asked Phil. "Where it came from? I thought maybe someone's brooch or tie-pin..."

"No, I'm afraid I've no idea. Where did you find it? Looks like a big sewing needle except the eye is broken and then twisted there."

"It's not from some specialized syringe you might keep here?" Phil purposely ignored the question about the pin's prior location.

"Oh, heavens, no. The only type of drugs we keep on the property at all are very mild sedatives, mostly Quaaludes, like the one Sela said she used yesterday for Karen, once she'd returned to her room. And those are just taken orally. There are clinics and centers starting up now who will rely on the new drug, methadone, or the old-school use of disulfiram to help with what we call the withdrawal stages. However, I refuse to mix drugs into the equation here, and that's one of the reasons the owners hired me. They wanted everything to stay as natural as possible. They believe in helping the body, as well as the environment in which we live, to be organic. It's why they insisted on the villas all being made from materials found here on the property and which would all just decompose someday."

"Doctor, you've been most helpful and have certainly cleared up a good many questions D.I. Ames, D.C. Cobalt, and I have had these last days. I appreciate your honesty for now, and while I know we're going to have to ask more personal questions about some of your guests in the coming hours, I understand you've been as forthcoming as you can be this afternoon."

The two shook hands and Phil left, feeling that he had much to share—and much to mull over within himself.

CHAPTER NINE

In the Satellite, and heading this time north to Edom's Creek, rather than straight back to a supper at Nellie's again, Philip shared with Trevor a summary of his illuminating conversation with the Bayham Brook House manager. It took the just-over two miles to the village to relay this information. They then pulled into the parking lot of the United Church, slotting the Satellite between a rusty green Ford pickup and a shining copper Camaro, where they sat for another five minutes as Trevor brought Phil up to date about his conversations with Karen and Lucy.

"Karen was still weepy today, but able to admit she'd been wrong to keep the marriage from us. Says she was just so used to being told by Charlie that it had to be a secret. She showed me the diary under the mattress—it had the wedding certificate folded up in it. She'd already taken the diamond ring from her shoe and was wearing it on her left hand when I went in. Knowing it wasn't a secret anymore made her happier, I guess. She kept twisting it 'round and 'round and I noticed that she'd been biting and peeling her fingernails again. I pointed out that Charlie wouldn't be happy about that, and that the ring would show off a lot better if she could keep her nails nicely polished and long."

"You really do have a sensitive side, don't you, Trevor?" Phil asked, smiling at his partner. *Again, the blush whenever he got too close.* "Are you going to take a stab at therapy with her now?"

"You jest. But seriously, she cheered up and said she'd get some fingernail polish as soon as she was out of her treatment. Said that sort of thing was contraband on the property, as some addicts would sniff it for a high. Can you imagine?"

"I can, yeah." *Vicki, again.* He blew her face away like the cloud of smoke Trevor was exhaling out the window of his car. "So did she tell you more about Charlie at all? Flintwinch admitted he's from a wealthy family; she might be in for a hefty inheritance."

"Geez, she never mentioned that! No, she just went on and on about how charming he could be, and thoughtful of others, and that she'd miss their talks in The Rookery when he used to hold her hand under a cushion when no one was looking... that sort of goop." Having been called out about his sensitive side, Trevor now seemed determined to swing back into 'macho' mode.

"And what, if anything, did the uncharming Miss Tox have to say?"

"She was surprisingly fairly docile. Until the very end, anyway. She told me she didn't figure she had to stay here much longer because she was 'getting better'. I had trouble not laughing at that one! She revealed that she did remember the argument she and the three male rehab. guests had had the night Crispin must have been killed. That in their group session right before supper, Gerald had called her a callous old Cruella. I had to ask what that meant and she said it was the antagonist in that kids' book about Dalmatians. I guess Disney made a cartoon about it but I was a teen when it came out, so I'd not have seen it! Of course, we only presently have Lucy's word for it that that's what started the argument, and since she's a liar, I'd say 'pinch of salt' and all that. She claims she'd made some comments in the group session, though, about all the men being rude to Karen and someone named Daisy. Don't know who that is."

"The doctor mentioned her, said she'd been here the week before Crispin died. We'll have to look into that, because really the OPP should have questioned her, and still should, especially as Charlie would have been murdered when she was still here."

"This is a crazy case, isn't it? All the suspects pretty much in one place, but no one really needing to give alibis. Because they were all either alone in their rooms and villas in the evening or, as in the case of Charlie, too many weeks have passed to get it narrowed down to a time. People won't remember. I mean, they have the same routine every evening, so who's gonna recollect details?"

"You're right, but at some point Officer Biro and his crew will be doing that regarding Squeers and we'll have to try harder to nail times down for who was where and what they might have seen when Crispin disappeared. Right now we only have Annette telling you she thinks she saw someone go past her bunk room in the early morning hours. That would have been long after when I'm pretty sure Crispin was already lying dead. What else did Lucy say?"

"Well, she says the men— Gerald, Adam and Crispin—kept arguing with her through the course of the meal, telling her to stop being such a bully. *She* says she was accusing them of objectifying the younger girls and that really they were the bullies. Anyway, the fight soon cooled down, according to her. And they went back to eating supper in comparative peace."

"We'll check with some of the others to see if that's the gist of it. Flintwinch said he'd ask them as a group if he could reveal the source to us. But for now, it sure doesn't seem to be a motive for murder, or even seething anger after the fact. Just a tempest in a tea-pot, as my godmother would say."

"Shall we go up to the manse?"

"We could, or... I hear hammering. Let's try the church basement and see if the reverend is below, shall we?"

The detectives headed for a side door and descended three stairs into the lower level of the church. Inside, a construction zone with the smell of sweat and sawdust wafting to their nostrils, greeted them.

"Hello?" called Trevor as Phil took in the wainscoting—a painted checkerboard of blacks, whites and ivories. This was untouched by the renovations, so it seemed, as were the two stained glass windows above the sink in the kitchen. However, the cupboards had been torn off the walls and were lying on the floor there, and two smaller rooms were obviously being opened to join with the bigger gathering one.

"My goodness! If it isn't the detectives, come to pay a call after all, and just in time for a Popsicle break! Come on in, and mind where you step. There's nails everywhere!"

The Reverend Klassen, still wearing his clerical collar but in shirt sleeves, shorts, and heavy work boots, went to the fridge. From the freezer section he took out four iced treats, handed two to the detectives and called "Daniel! Come on out and have a Popsicle!"

From one of the smaller rooms where a handsaw had been chugging away, a stocky shirtless figure emerged, also in shorts—snug-fitting denim cut-offs. But this muscled man was wearing no shirt and the sweat was glistening on his bare chest and dripping from his forehead. As he reached out to take a treat from the minister, thanking him politely, Phil risked a glance at Trevor and saw the flicker of attraction glinting in his eye. He stepped forward, hand extended toward the topless man.

"Hi, I'm D.I. Steele. This is D.I. Ames. We met Reverend Klassen yesterday but you are...?"

"Sorry, this is Dan Blevan. He used to work full time at the retreat but now he's doing odd jobs for the churches and a few farms in the area, and just goes back every few days as a masseuse to Bayham Brook House."

"Oh yes, I meant to get your telephone number from Miss Cowan. We had some questions for you as well as the reverend."

"Well, why don't one of you take Dan outside under that big oak by the manse? I'd offer above in the nave, but it's overwhelmingly humid up there right now and I don't want to turn on all the ceiling fans just for two people."

Philip considered as he took large, cool bites of the sweetened ice sticks. He knew what he was about to suggest could potentially be a mistake, but he'd wanted to interview the minister himself, for a variety of reasons. He said, "Perhaps Daniel will be good enough to go outside with D.I. Ames, then?" He gave Trevor a look and patted his own notes in his breast pocket, hoping that not only would Trevor remember there were some key questions they'd wanted to ask the young man, but also that it would remind Trevor to keep his mind on the job. As the two left the basement, Phil was glad to see Blevan pick up a T-shirt and toss it over his head, pulling it down to his belt.

"Let's sit here in the doorway," said the minister, pulling up two chairs and a rustic crate with a chess board on top of it. "It'll be cooler with a bit of a breeze from outside, and I'll just plug this little fan in here beside us."

Phil sat and placed some of his recipe cards on the chess board, along with his pen. When the Reverend Klassen sat, he gestured at the checkered board. "Do you play at all?"

"I like to fancy I'm not too bad at it."

"I'd love a game sometime. Dan and I play in our breaks from work, but sad to say he isn't much of a challenge for me. He usually lets me capture every one of his pawns and both his knights and rooks within the first six or seven minutes."

"We could play now, while we're talking, if you like. It actually helps me structure my thoughts sometimes."

"Ah-ha! Like Mrs. Christie's Poirot stacks his cards into towers?"

"Precisement," returned Phil with what he hoped was a Belgian accent.

As the men moved the first of their pawns and knights away from their kings and queens, Phil began. "I've spent much of this afternoon with your friend Doctor Flintwinch."

"Another strong chess player, but sadly he never has much time to play."

"He certainly seems to have his hands full with that place, and especially in recent weeks. What can you tell me about Crispin? Did you have any dealings with him?"

"I did. Enough to know that should he have wished to enter the clergy, I'd have sponsored him. The man was the essence of kindness and thoughtfulness for others. We had some lovely conversations after a chapel service once, and another after a walk we took through the woods one Sunday. I felt that his faith could have become very strong and unshakeable."

"Really? I knew him when he was a boy, and our parents are friends, as well. I hadn't realized he was particularly religious."

"I gather it was one of the things which caused him the most torment. He did pray about it, but often felt alone in that. His parents, from what I understand, did not attend church regularly?"

Phil was bewildered. "Not ever, if I remember correctly. I do think my father, who had been raised by a rather stern Anglican, took Crispin to our church once or twice when he was visiting us. But even my own family didn't go as often as we probably should have to claim church membership."

"I see. Well, I think that Crispin was just starting to feel that the United Church might be the most accepting. For him. He was worried that other denominations might judge him too much for his past—although why any self-proclaiming Christian should be judgmental at all, is beyond me."

"So, did Crispin discuss going into the ministry? Was that something he was interested in pursuing?"

The Reverend Klassen moved his rook out in a boldly straight line. "Crispin was still very confused about a lot of issues in his life. He felt that his blood parents, at least his mother, must have been quite religious; that is why he chose to believe she'd given him up in the first place. He'd told himself that her church must have stepped in. It's also why he felt he did have a relationship with God, as though it could be genetically inherited. Who knows that it can't?"

While Phil was skeptical about that point, he continued without addressing the rhetorical question. "So Crispin prayed about his addictions, and discussed his worries with you? Was he equally close to Dr. Flintwinch, do you know?"

"Jere tries hard not to get overly close, emotionally, to any of his patients. He figures that would jeopardize his professional and therapeutic relationship with them. But if he feels someone is open to it, he will recommend that they speak with me. And I'm happy to oblige, especially with someone as introspective yet outwardly giving as Crispin Clennam."

"Whom you may have heard by now is actually called Crispin Cobalt, son of the Deputy Commissioner of Police? This is one of the reasons D.I. Ames and I were sent here to continue an investigation that otherwise may have been dropped, labeled as suicide."

"I can tell you right now, and could have told the OPP if they'd bothered to ask me, that Crispin was against suicide. Because he did feel God within him, and did have that faith, he believed God would not look favorably upon someone who took his or her own life. I don't believe he thought he'd literally go to hell, mind you. That's another reason he liked the United Church—he didn't really go in for all the fire and brimstone stuff. Oops, Detective, you might want to examine that move again before you take your finger off the bishop."

Phil saw immediately to what the minister was referring, pulled his bishop back toward him, looking for a safer move. "So if Crispin didn't think he'd go to hell for committing a sin like suicide, then what did he think would be God's punishment?"

"I think he believed that there'd be an everlasting, intense feeling of disappointment, as from a parent. Which, by the way, I do think he felt from his father. Whether his father ever meant him to feel like that, I of course can't know. However, I believe he felt that he'd already disappointed two fathers on earth, and didn't want to disappoint the Heavenly one as well. In addition, he told me he was intrigued with some Buddhist practices and felt that perhaps being reincarnated and having to repeat another difficult life on this plane of existence, on this planet, could *be* the worst of punishments. No, I remember very clearly from our talks: Crispin would not have committed suicide. He believed he was getting better, was on a slow road to a final recovery, and that he could then go out and help others in some way. He was looking forward to doing that." Reverend Klassen sat back and wiped his eye, then rubbed the wet from his finger onto his shorts.

"Well, Reverend, I'd love for you to write some of what you've just told me in a letter to the Cobalts. I'll of course pass your details on to them, tonight, in fact. But it would mean so much more in the permanence of writing, something they could keep and both read whenever they wished. It would bring them comfort and assurance."

"We think alike, sir. I have actually drafted such a letter to them, and after I make some changes and wait to see what exactly the new autopsy finds, I will either send it along with you or ask for their address."

"Wonderful!" Phil said. "Thank you. And I'll just take your rook, thank you."

"Dash it! Didn't see that!"

"Is the checkerboard painting along the wainscot meant to represent your love of chess?"

"Ah, it does. But also so much more. I use chess and checkers as symbolic metaphors quite often in my sermons. Makes for some wonderful discussions afterward, as well."

"I see, like the King or Queen being God? "

"In some instances, sure. Usually it's the Queen, as she has more power and flexibility. Often, however, I'll use a lowly pawn as an example of the true meaning of overall Greatness. There are all kinds of terrific ways of comparing our relationships with each other, with Nature, and with God—to a few simple board games with different color squares! Even the black or white of rules and commandments can be meshed with gray or cream. That's why I asked for a third color in the painting on the walls there."

"And I suppose the rigidity of the squares…?" Phil thought he'd like to attend a few of this minister's sermons himself. "You can't color outside the lines, as it were? And the lines never waver?"

"Ahh, a man who appreciates symbolism. Excellent!"

"I almost got a degree in literature before I changed to law."

"Well, the law certainly has its rigidity of squares too, doesn't it? Although my congregation is probably sick of hearing me say that our love for God does not have to be a straight line, or a square square. Ho-ho! I'm betting ole Gerald has called both you and me 'squares' to our retreating backs more than once!"

They laughed and Phil went back to his queries on the case, despite yearning to carry on with the philosophical discussion. "Can you offer any suggestions as to what happened with either Crispin, or to Charlie Squeers, then, Reverend?"

"If I had drawn any conclusions at all, and of course I haven't been able to, I really wouldn't dare share them for fear of prejudicing you."

"Well, o.k., but what if you just asked some questions and I listened? Would that be safe, do you think?"

The minister thought, and made a diagonal move that Phil noticed proved he was distracted. But he purposely wouldn't act upon it. It wasn't fair to the younger man and besides, he wanted the game to last longer.

"I supp–ooose," Reverend Klassen said, considering. "For instance, I could ask you if you'd looked at the idea that someone might be so jealous of either Crispin or Charlie that they felt hatred in their hearts. Enough to kill?"

"Is there someone like that?"

"These are just questions I've asked *myself*. I've no answers, and am only repeating them aloud. I did hear this morning that Charlie and Karen had had a secret marriage, so who else might have been in love with, or relishing a relationship with, one of the dead men?"

"All right. What other questions have you asked yourself?" Phil skidded his queen over to pick up a pawn, instead of the minister's open knight.

"I've asked myself if either Charlie or Crispin, or both, could have seen or heard something that would be very bad news for someone else, if what they were doing or saying was made public."

"And dare we go a little closer to what sort of things that might involve? Purely hypothetically, of course," smiled Philip.

"How about that maybe one of the owners, or one of the couples, rather, wanted to sell out their share?"

"Is this..."

"Purely hypothetical. But if they did, and the other couple didn't have the money to buy them out, Jere and Sela's and Ruth's full-time jobs could be in serious jeopardy and the retreat business might go under. Then a lot of hopeful people might lose the opportunity to get well, get out from under the heavy weight of their addictions."

"O.K., point noted. What else?"

"Or perhaps one of the victims had overheard a phone conversation that led them to believe a crime had been previously committed by one of their group of rehabbers."

"And they'd have been killed for that?"

"It's possible isn't it?"

"Certainly. Anything is, at this point. Were you aware that Charlie was from a wealthy family and that by marrying him, Karen might become a very wealthy woman?"

"I was not. But that's certainly another type of motive, even if not *that* circumstance exactly. There may have been money involved with any sort of will, or any sort of dealing. Or for any type of 'I'll scratch-your-back/you-scratch-mine' situation, where perhaps a promise wasn't kept?"

"And again, you aren't giving me any examples?"

"I will say one thing I know. Some of the others who are there *outside* of the treatment program, the regular guests, as it were— they may not be as innocent and uninvolved as they'd like you to believe. I think the artists, Jackie and Mitch are good folk. I've known Mitch's father since I was young; he's an established tobacco farmer in these parts. However, the fellow calling himself 'Latch Lupin', I do know that he was once imprisoned for a felony that to this day he swears wasn't his fault. A bank robbery some thirty years ago down in Port Dune. From my reading of the news articles on microfiche, there was a portion of the money that was never recovered."

"That's certainly an interesting tip that calls for a follow-up."

"And Monty Tigg. She and her husband run a legitimate auction and antique business in Brownsville, but a neighbor told me several years ago that that place brought in a lot of stolen goods from Toronto. Goods that had been hauled across Lake Ontario from the States, then divided up. Of course those may be rumors. These small towns and villages are rife with harmful rumors. Plus, even if true, Monty and her husband may not know they are dealing with some items that are stolen goods. So as you can see, even these bits of questionable information are not something I feel comfortable sharing with you. Just a suggestion that perhaps it's wise to look outside the obvious—those with the addictions and emotional turmoils."

"Well, you've certainly given me something I can mull over with D.I. Ames, and perhaps investigate further. I thank you for that. Look, can we finish this game perhaps tomorrow afternoon? I might have more questions for you after I've made some phone calls, and I'd enjoy continuing down this vein, as well as looking forward to claiming your king."

"You're welcome to come anytime. Dan and I are always looking for a reason to take a break from the renovating, and a chance to cool off. Oh, and Detective? My King is always with me." Reverend Klassen offered up a wink and a grin.

• • •

Outside, Phil noticed that Trevor and Daniel Blevan were sitting on the same side of the picnic table under the huge leafy tree beside the manse. Daniel was leaning over Trevor as he wrote and Phil was partly amused and partly disturbed to see his colleague lick his stub of a pencil *twice*, just in the time it took him to walk from the basement door of the church to their shady space.

Trevor joked a few times with the masseuse before standing to leave with Phil, but once in the car and despite his years of seniority, Philip didn't feel comfortable teasing him. He'd already 'suggested' to Trevor the day before, that fraternizing with potential suspects wasn't perhaps the best idea, and he'd seen the obvious physical attraction in Trevor's eyes when Blevan had first entered the room. He'd just let it ride for now, he decided. Besides, couldn't he be called a hypocrite? Hadn't he just been playing a friendly game of chess with another potential suspect?

Instead, he told Trevor some of what the minister had revealed, especially about being positive that suicide could not have been the cause of Crispin's demise. Trevor then shared that Daniel had been 'let go' from the retreat six months ago because Sela had found some of the younger teen girls were just too attracted to him. She had written him an excellent letter of recommendation and in the meantime had agreed to let him stay on as a masseuse, but only for the non-rehab guests. Trevor said, "I mean, it's not his fault he's good-looking, is it? Seems a shame to lose a job because of how one looks."

"I expect, in an environment such as that, it's crucial that there be no distractions in the treatment of the individuals. They have enough physical and emotional turmoil to go through. And don't forget, Daniel probably isn't entirely blameless; it's possible any amount of flirting, however inadvertent, might have been going on."

"Hmm," was all Trevor said. Although it might have been '*mmm*'. Phil wasn't too sure.

They stopped at the Townsend's General Store in Sandytown—literally at the one end of the village—to pick up a new ice block for the cooler containing their camera and film rolls, and snacks and drinks for later in their rooms. Then, as they headed toward Port Dune, they pulled once again into Nellie's to grab a burger each. Upon arriving at their lodgings, they were met in the garden by Cathy Nelson, who seemed in a flutter of concern.

"Oh, did youse talk to Ruth about the wedding? She's not answering her phone and she must be home by now. I hope you ain't made her mad at me for letting out that secret."

"Miss Nelson, if she's upset now I'm sure it'll just take her a bit of time to realize that you did the right thing. D.I. Ames was the one who spoke to Ruth."

Trevor added brusquely, "She was fine. She seemed to understand that info. had to come out now."

They thanked their hostess for putting some of their soda cans in her kitchen fridge where they could retrieve them later, then headed to their rooms. Trevor said he wanted a long shower and a short nap before they gathered again to go over notes and theories that had arisen throughout the day. Phil just changed into a light-weight cotton shirt and shorts and headed back downstairs to make phone calls.

His first one was to Blue. Being careful as always about the party line, he managed to elicit enough information, carefully worded by his father's old friend, to understand that the new coroner's report on Crispin was in and that they should talk the next day about it—on a secure line. The Toronto police force would be getting a number of bills for calls from this area in a month or so, but Phil said he'd either telephone from Bayham Brook House, or possibly the Edom's Creek United Church office, where he'd be later in the afternoon. He didn't add that playing chess for a bit of relaxation as well as thought-structure, would be one of the key reasons for going there again.

His next phone call was to Daisy Culpeper, her real surname and number given him by Sela before he'd left the big house that afternoon. Daisy lived another two hours west in Windsor, right near the Detroit border, so Phil knew their interview would have to be short and only by phone. The youthful-sounding girl came hesitantly to the receiver, but gathered confidence throughout their conversation, as Phil put her at ease. She of course hadn't known Crispin, though she and her parents had read about his shocking death in the papers. She confirmed that she was there the week Charlie disappeared, but told him she'd known nothing about him, really—that "Charlie'd not have been interested in me and Karen, we were too young for him. He liked women more in their mid-twenties or thirties." Philip did not tell her about the secret marriage, but did mention Gerald's name to her, just to see if she'd respond. Jeremiah Flintwinch had suggested there might have been a crush there but if there had been, the girl certainly seemed over it now. She said "Oh, *that* guy–what a hippie! I mean, the leather jewelry and those big flowers on his shirts? Give me a break!"

Daisy swore she had heard nothing unusual the night Charlie had disappeared and simply believed what she'd been told about him; that he'd run away from other treatment programs as well. She admitted to liking Karen and spending quite a bit of time in the other girl's room, but had never noticed Charlie in the women's wing talking to her. Phil took some note of this;

obviously one of the women was lying or terribly forgetful. Daisy also said that while she hadn't met Crispin or Adam, it was true that she did occasionally feel objectified in the group sessions by comments sometimes made by Gerald and 'a few other dudes' who'd been there at the same time as she was. So 'Crazy Lucy' wouldn't have been so far off the mark if she'd accused them of this, she claimed.

Phil's next and last phone call was of course to the JUST(e)STATE. His mother answered and they spoke briefly about the heat, his godfather's honeybees and the children's lessons with Lila Sponwin beside her, offering advice. But then she wished him good luck and said she mustn't leave Lila too long, that she still hadn't even shown her to her guest bedroom yet.

"I'm sure you'd like to speak with P.J., anyway, wouldn't you, Phil?" Lary Steele teased. "Because I know she's *bursting* to talk to you!"

Phil chuckled. "Oh, put her on then!" As if he'd had any intention of hanging up.

"Phil, dear?" came the familiar voice.

"Hot enough for you, P.J.?"

"I'm acclimatizing. Did your mother tell you we had a pleasant visit with Crispin's mother today?"

"She did. I'm glad you were both able to give her some pleasant distraction."

"Well, your mother and the stables perhaps did; I'm afraid I was rather more, um–"

"Digging, by chance?"

"Tssk. I just wanted to know when she or her husband had last spoken to him."

"It wasn't the night he died, as I was given to believe by some witnesses here," said Phil.

"No. It was a few nights prior for her, and several nights before that for Blue. And–Phil?"

"You've got something, haven't you? Let's have it."

"I don't know, maybe Blue already told you this…"

"Come on! You're a tease, you."

"Well, she told me that Crispin had told *her* to let his father know that he'd have some information for him next time they spoke. But she'd thought it was something about another spa, or equipment."

"Hmm. I see. And?"

"And then she said Crispin had told his father the last time they spoke about this Bayham Brook House offering some kind of supplements, along with the counseling."

"Well, their counseling does include a type of yoga-chanting mantra and near-hypnosis. Your experimental Buddhist days in India would coincide nicely."

"Well, that all sounds relaxing and positive. But the supplements were…"

"P.J.?"

"Sharon said he'd told his father that some of them were being given some kind of drugs, if they agreed to try that part of the program. Have you not run into anything like that? No one there has mentioned this?"

There was enough of a long pause that P.J., despite often throwing her pink slipper at the television screen and snorting '*no one would ever really say that in the real world!*', said it anyway. She said, "Hello? Hello? Phil, are you there?"

When her godson spoke again, he said, "This could actually change a lot about what's going on in my head, P.J. And no, Blue hasn't mentioned it—perhaps he's even forgotten? Everyone in charge around here has been telling me just the opposite. That no drugs are even kept on the premises except some mild sedatives." He didn't mention the marijuana smokers at their circle down by the brook, nor the odd behaviors of Lucy, and even Karen and Gerald, but he was processing this new information and thinking immediately of them. He then threw into the conversation, almost as an afterthought, "P.J., will you go into Dad's library tomorrow and hunt something up for me?"

"Of course!"

She was trying to sound level and calm, but he could hear the excited upward pitch to her voice.

"Go to the west wall, where Dad kept a whole set of Dickens' works. There's a cast of characters' index in that set. Please would you go to it and look up two names for me?"

She grabbed a piece of paper from the grocery list roll on the wall and wrote the names as he spelled them out for her.

·　　·　　·

Trevor and Phil discussed the details from the day, and the case overall, for another two hours. There was nothing, however, in the nature of conclusive knowledge which could take them any further. P.J.'s potentially explosive news and the Reverend Klassen's so-called hypothetical questions were all they could rehash, and Trevor seemed as dismissive about the drugs 'supplementing' the treatments as Blue must have been to his son.

"Methadone has become common in the last few years for getting these addicts through withdrawal, you know," Trevor said. "Even if your good doctor won't admit it, they might well be dosing them up for that reason. And hey—remember the vials they were using for the memory-capsules in the dafty-crafty classes? Maybe those vials were the old empties?"

"Then why wouldn't Crispin have actually *said* 'meth' to his father? He'd been on it before, in some of the other treatment programs he'd tried."

Trevor shrugged. "Too embarrassed? Maybe was attention-seeking?"

But Phil had some other theories he needed to sleep on, before throwing them on the potter's wheel for molding. They discussed a few of the suggestions made by the minister, like Monty Tigg and Latch Lupin's possible criminal activities, past or present. Trevor licked the stub of his pencil and dutifully noted those down for further checks to be run. Then Phil asked Trevor if he thought either of the dead men might have overheard a fellow-rehabber talking about any illegal pursuits.

"Nah," Trevor said. "I think that only happens in books and silly films. If a criminal is keeping something well-hidden, he's not going to be blabbing about it where there might be a potential eavesdropper who could either blackmail him, or report him. I mean, you're being careful about the telephone and the party line here, right? And you aren't even up to anything shady!"

"Well, that's a good point. I'm not ruling it out, though. Another thing the reverend brought up this afternoon, which I know we've both considered: what about a love triangle? What if another man, say Gerald or Adam, had been in love with Karen too, and wanted Charlie out of the way? Or we really need to look at Karen herself, if she's going to be an heiress now. Do we believe she really didn't know about Charlie's family's wealth?"

"I've another option on the love triangle idea. What about if another man—say again Adam or Gerald, as they are the two in the right age bracket—what about if one of them is gay and was attracted to either Crispin or Charlie? And what if they were feeling spurned, or saw that Charlie was attached to Karen and got jealous?"

Phil waited a beat then looked at Trevor, who for once didn't blush and met his eyes steadily. "I guess we shouldn't rule that out either. What put you on to that?"

"Daniel made some comment about thinking maybe Crispin was 'that way'."

"Really? Crispin? I don't *think* so..." said Phil.

"And you'd know by what? Some sort of sixth sense?"

"I knew about you before we'd worked too many months together."

That stopped Trevor cold. His face still didn't redden, but he couldn't meet Phil's eyes now. He got up and made to leave the room. "I've—I can't talk about this now, Phil. I'm just beat. I'll see you in the morning."

Phil felt like he'd only been asleep a half hour when he heard a telephone ringing downstairs and clattering feet going to answer it. He looked at the luminous dials on his alarm clock: 1:20. He'd actually been asleep for nearly three hours, he thought, surprised. And now what? In another two minutes Cathy Nelson was knocking wildly on his door.

"D.I. Steele! Oh, D.I. Steele! That was Dr. Flintwinch calling. You got to be gettin' out there right away! Sela's mother Petra's been killed! Strangled in her bath, poor woman, poor lady! Strangled, I say!"

PART TWO

"All we have gained then by our unbelief
Is a life of doubt diversified by faith,
For one of faith diversified by doubt:
We called the chess-board white, —we call it black."
-Robert Browning, *Bishop Blougram's Apology*

CHAPTER TEN

Three days later...

Ruth McCorkle put down a saucepan, grabbed a salt shaker and, with one hand poured the salt onto the scrambled eggs while she deftly flipped bacon with the other. Where was that *dashed* Clara? She'd only asked her to run a crate of extra toilet paper rolls to the bathrooms upstairs. She should be back by now!

Dr. Flintwinch poked his head in the kitchen door. "All right in here, Ruth?"

" 'sa bit crazy, Doctor, but don't you worry none. If Clara'd get back down here, I'd manage fine."

"I just passed Della in the Bubble & Squeak. She's just finishing cleaning in there and said to tell you she'll be back here in ten minutes."

"That'd be somethin' of a relief. Don't know what any of us'd done if that girl hadn't stepped up to the plate, like, these last few days. With poor Sealie out of action, I mean. If we could'a had Daniel back temporary, that'd been good, but I guess he's too busy with all his other jobs now."

"It's just as well, Ruth. You know what I mean, don't you?"

"You stay steady, now, Doctor. You're our rock."

"Well, Sela's said she wants no more sedatives as of today, and if I know her she'll want to be back to work tomorrow. No, no more coffee thanks, I've had enough this morning. Let's not forget the OPP are finished here today. Officer Biro was just telling me.

Apparently, they've been instructed to turn it all over to Toronto, and Detectives Ames and Steele."

"Well, better the enemy you know, than all them you don't," Ruth said shortly as she dished the eggs into two huge serving bowls, warmed in the oven.

"The new guest arrives at eleven, so I'll meet her myself. I'll just work in Sela's little office here until then. Are we putting her in Lucy's old room, or one of the smaller ones?"

"I let Della make that decision, and she thought the smaller one, Room Three. She knew that even though this new lady hasn't heard about our troubles at the moment, the guests will certainly fill her in, and if she was in Lucy's old room she might feel uncomfortable."

"True enough. Well, you and the girls get on with breakfast and thank you again for all your extra hours, Ruth."

"I'd do anythin' for Sealie, or you. You know that, Doctor. Get on with you, now. I've got to get these here trollies down the hall. Monty Tigg's been helpin' me out with dishes, bless her. Though 'twould be nice if she didn't bring so many bits of straw and horse hair into my kitchen."

" Well, I'm glad to see that since the guests have had to extend their stays here indefinitely, some are at least pitching in."

Jeremiah Flintwinch pushed back through the kitchen swinger and buried himself in Sela's nook near the front door, picking up the phone to organize refunding money on yet more cancelations. Although the police had insisted that Petra's murder must not be leaked to the media, news reports about the men's deaths had been enough to scare off many booked guests, and he suspected word about Petra had been circulating, at least locally, enough to do further damage to their already much-depleted reputation. Bayham Brook was certainly lucky to be welcoming one new client today, at least.

Walter McDowell was just pushing the barn cat off a straw bale in order to lower his hefty weight on to it, when Trevor Ames strolled through the stable gate ornamented with the Furr-neville's Inn sign. He looked from Walter and the cat straight up to the little door and pulley above them. He'd have to take measurements today, from the loft to the ground, as Phil had suggested. Phil was still across the road at the Cowans, poking about in there, although they'd heard that this would be the first day since her mother's murder that Sela would not be in bed, under sedation as per Flintwinch. Trevor hadn't taken to Sela at the beginning of their week here, but now his innate sensitivity empathized with her utter despair and grief. He couldn't imagine losing someone that close...

"e-e-e-e-, y-y-y-a doin' more r-r-r-r-ounds, sir?" Walter asked, wiping his brow.

The artist, Mitch Vandenwolk—the guests' real surnames were creeping in now, at least among those not here for addiction treatments—came out of a stall with a pitchfork and an overflowing wheelbarrow. "Hi, D.I. Ames. Walt and I are just getting on with things here, hope that's o.k.?"

Trevor nodded. "Of course. Animals need looking after, whether they're in the middle of a crime scene or not."

"Well, Lucy didn't actually make this a crime scene since she didn't die, but we realize you've still got to get all the details down. I gather the provincial police are vacating today, letting you and D.I. Steele get on with things?"

"Yes. Well, Officer Biro will be actually staying on duty in one of the villas, just to keep an eye out."

Walter grunted as he tried to stand. "N-n-n-n-no more villas empty, e-e-e-h?"

Trevor pulled out his notebook. "I've marked down that he's going into a new stone cabin that isn't finished yet. Halfway down the woods side of the hill?"

"Ow-ow-owta-sight!"

Trevor was confused. Walter seemed too old to be spouting hippie jargon. He looked at Mitch to see if the artist had better understood.

"I think Walter means that villa, they're calling it 'Drury Jane', isn't going to be a great lookout for an OPP officer. It's too far out of sight of the main house and the other villas."

"Well, perhaps he'll have to talk with some of you about swapping."

"Sure. I suppose Jackie and I wouldn't mind. How close is it to being done, Walt?"

The massive, older man had now managed to rise to his feet, though was still grasping the side of the barn to steady himself. "S-s-s-stone work's done. D-d-d-did it m-meself. Just n-n-not hooked up to e-e-e-lectric." Walter moved away to take a chestnut horse from its stall to a shady paddock. Trevor's eyes followed his slow progress.

"Should he be exerting himself so much? Still doing masonry, too? I've heard he had a heart attack not that long ago."

"I don't think you could retire him. I get the impression he'd rather die on the job. Best be getting back to it myself." Mitch placed his pitchfork next to the straw bale Walter had just vacated, leaning it against the side of the stable as he pushed his wheelbarrow toward the manure pile. Trevor was about to move away when the pitchfork started to fall. He moved to grab it just as the tabby cat sprang back onto the bale, then yowled and leaped off it again, sprinting toward the tack room door. At first, Trevor thought his quick movement to snatch the pitchfork had startled the animal, but then he noticed that the loosely baled straw, greatly mashed down by the weight of McDowell, had caused a handful of Plastipack syringes, clustered tightly together, to poke very slightly through to the surface. As he bent to examine them further, he saw that one of the tiny plastic protective caps had worked its way off a needle, probably stabbing the cat when he'd landed on it. He went to the tack room, pulled out a chair and placed it firmly in front of the bale.

As Mitch pushed the empty wheelbarrow back toward a new stall to clean, Trevor called, "Mitch, do me a favor, please? Leave that work, and go across the road to Cowans'. Bring D.I. Steele back, right away." The artist looked curiously at the young detective, who had now plunked himself in front of the bale and was pulling a small pouch from his pocket. Not cigarettes, either, as apparently the city boy had enough sense not to smoke in a stable yard. But the animal-loving artist didn't ask what was going on, just nodded and left quickly on his mission.

By the time Walter came wheezing back from turning out the horse, Trevor had his tweezers and tongs spread on his lap and was leaning over the bale.

"Walter? Here're the keys to our big car. The Satellite, you know? Please go get me the camera that's in the back seat in the ice cooler. And Walter? If you can, could you please hurry?"

•   •   •

Phil and Officer Blake Biro stood outside the front of Crabapple Cottage, the Cowan's home. Biro was smoking a pipe full of tobacco that smelled of cedar and apples. Earlier that morning, Phil had helped Dr. Flintwinch walk the much-thinner, haunted-looking Sela to her back patio. He was desperate to question her, but of course Flintwinch had kept the nurse sedated for days; she slumbered in her bed continually, only being awakened for cups of beef or chicken broth soup sent over by Ruth 'to keep up her strength'. *What strength?* Phil had wanted to ask. Seeing her on the night of the discovery of her mother's body had already instilled in him the despairing fact that every single member of the human race had both a mental and a physical health that was but a few strands away from being plucked naked and bald. Sela Cowan had been understandably horrified, inconsolable and shaking violently, when they'd arrived that night three days ago; yet by then the doctor had already given her several of their 'mild' sedatives, the only drugs he claimed to keep on the premises across the highway.

But today she did seem tenuously stronger and had asked to be allowed to wake up fully and begin accepting the reality of a life without her disabled mother. Phil wished he'd met Petra before the terrible night she was killed. Everyone at Bayham Brook House swore there wasn't a sweeter, more evenly tempered woman on the planet, that no one could have wished to harm her in any way. Blake Biro was in agreement; he had met her twice in the days before Phil and Trevor had arrived on the scene and said that she was indeed a kind and generous saint, never referring to her accident or disability, although she'd been in obvious pain at times.

From Flintwinch, the detectives and the three OPP officers— including Biro, who had been phoned by Trevor after he and Phil had arrived that night of the third murder—learned that Sela had helped her mother into her bathtub, just off their tiny kitchen, then had had to rush across the road. The doctor had phoned her in a panic at about ten o'clock that night to say that Lucy Tox had tried to hang herself from the stables' loft. There was a small door up there, with a pulley just outside it, threaded with a thick rope for laboriously yanking up bales of hay one at a time. Lucy, in one of her apparent manic or delusional episodes, had left the women's wing after their group session that night and had not returned. Karen had reported to the doctor that Lucy wasn't in her room for 'lights out', and the doctor and his aged dog had gone out about the grounds, finding her on the ground, the rope still around her neck. She hadn't managed to tie-off the rope well enough and the pulley system had done its job, the noose's long length unraveling and the pulley giving way and tossing her to the stable yard's sandy soil.

Although she was off duty, Sela generally kept her walkie-talkie on or near her when at home. Flintwinch had reported to the police that she'd blurted out, through her hysteria, that when he'd radioed her to come to the stables immediately, her mother had assured her she'd be all right in the bath with her music and book for at least an hour or so. But, as she waited with Flintwinch for the ambulance to come for Lucy, whisking her away to the St. Thomas Psychiatric Hospital, it was over two hours before Sela had returned to find her mother, dead in the still-warm water in their claw-foot tub, strangled by a length of red curtain tie-back rope which was left wound about her thin neck.

Now, Blake Biro took three tiny puffs from his pipe and exhaled slowly. "I know we've been through this before, Philip, but seriously–whoever killed her, and for whatever insane reason, couldn't have *planned* it. Because if it was planned, then why not come with a prepared weapon?"

"Yes, but maybe he—or she?—did. I've had a look at the curtains hanging here, and nothing matches the cord and there appear to be no curtains missing. Flintwinch asked the two maids across the road if any drapery tie-backs were missing from there and they didn't think so. So, maybe the killer *did* come prepared."

"Well, some weapon! I guess if you're going to kill a tiny, disabled, mid-aged and defenseless woman, you don't need much." Biro angrily took another suck on the stem of his pipe.

"Hmm," was Phil's only response. He was already working on a different theory, but was no where near feeling it was time to air it.

"Well, my team have left the premises and I'd better get back to my cottage and try to get some sleep so I can begin my nocturnal guard-dog duties. Me and that old German Shepherd of the doc.'s. You'll keep me apprised?"

"Of every little thing. Promise. See you later."

The officer crossed the highway with care, looking and listening both ways first, and Phil watched him arrive safely on the other side and climb the hill toward the rear of Bayham Brook House. He then slipped back into the Cowan's bungalow, passing a small side table near the door on which were plastic flowers in a vase and a camera case with 'C' embossed into its leather. Sela, he saw, was still sitting on the back patio, just staring. He was tempted to start questioning her already, but he'd promised Flintwinch he'd check with him first before doing so. Instead, he went back to scrutinizing much of the kitchen and bathroom area. He took the menorah from the top of the refrigerator, and noted with interest that there were two mezuzah hanging in the door frames from the kitchen to the living room, and from the kitchen to the small bedroom where Petra had always slept. He strolled to the terrace, carrying the menorah.

"How are you doing?" he asked the woman, huddled in an afghan despite the August heat.

"Fine. You *will* find this guy, won't you?"

"We're working so hard on this, Miss Cowan. Believe me."

"Why've you got that?" Sela nodded to the shiny silver menorah with the candles. "I hope they've not put fingerprint powder all over it?"

"I don't want to pester you with a lot of questions just now. But I was wondering—were you and your mother Jewish? I dated a girl in high school who was a practicing Jew, but I didn't see a prayer book around here. 'Sela and Petra'. Those are both Jordan-connected names, no? But Hebrew?"

"Yes. Edom's Creek used to have a little group of us. Our name 'Cowan' is from the Hebrew name 'Cohen', you know. Edom's was settled by a rabbi, nearly a century ago. No synagogue, but we tried to keep our faith alive —at least my mother did. Until her accident eleven years ago. We didn't actually lose faith, but we–we stopped being what I guess you'd call 'good Jews'." Tears started to trickle down the nurse's face.

"I see. May I get you something? A drink? Hot or cold?"

"Well, I am warming up a *bit*," she said as she took the afghan off her shoulders and placed it on the patio table, deftly folding it first. "There's a pitcher of tea in the fridge, if you wouldn't mind." Then she said almost hurriedly, "But no ice, please. I–I don't want it *too* cold."

Phil poured her the tea into a blue plastic glass with yellow polka dots on it. He also took out an orange he spied on a shelf in the door. Finding a bread plate and a small knife he took these items to Sela and placed them on the table beside the afghan.

"I thought you should get a bit of Vitamin C into you, and some natural sugars. This might be good with your tea."

She thanked him and he told her he needed to get back to work at her kitchen table where he was organizing his notes onto more recipe cards. But he assured her he wouldn't leave the bungalow unless he'd called for someone from the big house to come over to be here with her.

He made sure he slid shut the patio door over the screen as he went back into the kitchen, however. He didn't want her hearing what he was about to do. *Why had she reacted that way to not having ice cubes in her iced tea?* It had just been a subtle shift in her stressing of words, but he'd thought she was worried that he might open her freezer.

And so of course, he went right to her freezer. The little compartment wasn't very full, and after rummaging for just seconds he spotted the clear plastic bag at the very back. It did not appear to contain foodstuffs; in fact, in it was just one item–the butt of a cigarette. It was a Belmont filter, his father's own brand that he'd seen in the ashtrays scattered around the JUST(*e*)STATE during his entire childhood. He was just about to take it out of the bag and examine it more carefully when a banging on the front door stopped him. Quickly, he stashed the bag away again, slammed shut the fridge door and hurried to see 'what was rotten in the state of Denmark' *now*.

The artist named Mitch stood there, sweaty and with ripped and stained clothing from either his paints, the grass-stains from horses' drool, or something else Phil wouldn't conjecture. He explained Trevor's urgent plea for his colleague to join him, but as Phil didn't feel comfortable leaving Sela with a potential suspect he was unsure of his next move. He asked the man to go back to the barn and tell Trevor he'd be there in ten minutes. He then picked up the phone and called Bayham Brook House, expecting Ruth or one of the maids to answer. But it was the doctor himself who picked up. He asked the man to please go to the unfinished cabin, Drury Jane, and send Officer Biro right back to Crabapple Cottage. He didn't even feel that he could leave Sela and Flintwinch alone together at this point. Any wrong decision on his part might cost someone else a life, he decided grimly.

And muttered to himself, *"Nota Bene"*. Heed well.

•   •   •

At the barn, just twelve minutes after sending Mitch back, Phil squatted and stared at the straw bale where Trevor had set up camp.

"Well, I guess there's no question. This place is using drugs in a big way, and it obviously isn't at an official or even the rumored experimental level."

"So not just a diabetic who's mislaid their supplies?"

Phil snorted and stood, knees creaking. "I don't know whether to call Flintwinch on it, or leave it between us right now. What do you think?"

Trevor always appreciated it when this middle-aged policeman, with all his seniority and experience across the country, in such a wide variety of cases, nevertheless treated his colleagues as equals.

"Well, I didn't let on to either Walter or Mitch what I'd found, so we *could* keep it to ourselves. Assuming neither of them knows about it because *they* were responsible for hiding this here. Which, you've got to wonder... We need to find out if this same bale stays here, just as a seat, or decoration or whatever. Or is there always a new one dragged here for use in the stalls every day? I can ask Walter."

"I remember there was one the first day we got here, right in that same spot. The cat was lying beside it then."

"Yeah, well we owe Miss Tabby a debt for tipping me off to it. No pun intended."

"What pun?" Phil finally had to ask.

"The tips. Of the needles."

Philip frowned. That one might have actually worked as a pun. Then he said, "*Hell*, I may have had a tip long before this, and never even gave it pause. Monty Tigg said, the day Petra was killed I think, that she'd been stung in her backside by a bee or a hornet. I'm guessing it was no such thing, that she'd had a seat here in the sun after her ride that day!"

Although Mitch and Walter were still going about the business of mucking out stalls, glancing curiously in their direction occasionally, Trevor had surreptitiously removed the cluster of syringes when they weren't looking, first taking several shots of them in situ with the camera Walter had brought from their car. The cluster, tied together with a long white string, contained twenty hypodermics, with attached needles.

"I'm guessing those vials they use for their miniature memory capsules aren't coming in empty from a hobby supply store, either," Phil said as he put the needles in the camera bag while Trevor hung the instrument around his neck.

"And do we think that Lucy Tox's outrageous behavior was actually being caused by injections of some hallucinatory drug? Or something else otherwise altering her chemical balance and creating havoc in her upper stories?" Trevor tapped his temple.

"But why wouldn't Sela and Flintwinch have caught on to that?"

"Maybe her medical files already labeled her as psychotic, and a pathological liar, or whatever, so they just assumed that was her constant natural state?" Trevor looked up again at the pulley. "I haven't got the measurements on that fall yet."

"Never mind, now. Poor woman, someone's been dallying with her mental health which was obviously close to breaking point *before* she came here."

"Yeah, and now she could be years in that Psych. Hospital."

"I know. Really only one step up from a prison, from what I've read. Thank God we think Crispin turned down whatever drugs someone's been offering here. I'm not sure his parents could have dealt with that blow on top of his murder. And while I think it's obvious now that this is not part of their treatment program, I don't know if we can totally trust everything the good doctor says on the matter."

Trevor was standing on the spot Flintwinch had shown them, where Lucy had been found. "You don't think Lucy was paid—or blackmailed—into pulling this suicide stunt as a distraction? So that the killer could strangle Petra?"

Phil nodded his head encouragingly at the younger detective. "Well considered. I wondered about it that night after we finally got to bed. *Or,* if it might have been a way for a murderer–Lucy– to get herself taken off the property? But who would want to be admitted to the St. Thomas Psych. Hospital rather than continue living in comparative freedom? Of course it would mean she had an accomplice. Plus, that would mean all her carryings-on were just blarney, as my ancestors would have called them. But I don't think she was acting, do you?"

"Nope. The Elephant Woman was one hundred percent nuts-o, in my opinion."

"Well, let's just call her—a lady who needs some help with mental and emotional issues, as well as chemical dependencies, shall we?" said Philip, tactfully. "You know how Flintwinch told us that when he'd got to her lying here that night, she'd been muttering something that sounded like 'Anita's mascara'? That she'd repeated it a few times? I've also been thinking about that. If Lucy wasn't completely just in the throes of some hallucination, of course—is it possible that Annette Micawber, and I've found out that her real surname is what she writes as: Anita *MacElburns*, is harboring more of a clue to this whole puzzle? Whether she is conscious of it or not?" The two men headed toward the car and the main building, deliberately shutting the gate in the hedge behind them as they left the now neatly raked stable yard. "I mean, what if there're drugs hidden in her make-up kit or something radical like that? She was here before, as a patient, let's not forget."

"Hmm," Trevor said, digesting this for a minute. "So you think when she told us she saw a figure go by her cabin that night that she's trying to distract us from *herself*?"

"Possibly, or perhaps she was already on to something about the influx of drugs here, and is secretly writing about *that*, but just pretending to be about to release a lovely travelogue-type article for Chatelaine. Maybe she's found a sample of the drugs and put them *into* her mascara bottle, or make-up kit to take along as proof. Remember, she was supposed to be leaving the day after we got here. But how would Lucy have found out about that? Surely a journalist wouldn't entrust her secret to *any*one, never mind the most disturbed individual on the property."

"Anita's Mascara. Sounds like the name of a racehorse. No pun intended."

Philip Steele rolled his eyes.

·　　　·　　　·

Although it was only mid-morning, the detectives decided on an early lunch and sat in the shade near the car, their backs leaning up against one of the stone pillars that supported the wrought-iron fence at the front of the property. They ate sandwiches they roughly slapped together from the bread and cold meats they'd purchased at Townsend's, which they were keeping in their big cooler in the back seat along with the camera equipment.

"When I played chess with Reverend Klassen last night, and you were out flirting with the well-sculpted Daniel—"

"Knock it off, or I'll go eat somewhere by myself."

"Sorry. Uncalled for. He won, by the way. Stalemate."

"I'll be sure to alert the media."

"Now, *you* knock it off!" Phil had to smile. "I just brought it up because we were talking last night about how this case seems to be in a 'stalemate'. Then today you find these syringes and I've got a few other new theories I'm working on in my head, having spent so much time in the Cowan house by now. "

"Such as?"

"Not sure I'm ready to shove them forth just yet. But Reverend Klassen did explain a few things to me that might be pertinent, now that we know there's an underground drugs angle. Maybe literally." Phil took a bite of baloney. "Damn, forgot the cheese, push the cooler over here please. And talk about 'stale', this bread is dreadful!"

"Klassen's enlightenments?"

"Right. Well, number one: he told me that his parents made their way here as members of the Mexican Mennonite community when he and his many siblings were just children. They came from Chihuahua, where a lot of them were being abused and wrongly accused of drug trafficking down there. It's ridiculous, of course, since they are a pacifist Christian group. Many of them have immigrated to this area in particular because there is so much work in the tobacco industry. However, Reverend Klassen has, in recent years, been looking into one or two of this large group who may have strayed from their religion and who actually *are* helping traffic drugs through the borders. Because we're so close to the American border just here, it's conceivable that there are even people from Chihuahua masquerading as Mexican Mennonites and coming through with cocaine stashed in their belongings, marijuana hidden in their foodstuffs, etc. So that's something we should think about. And can you tell me why Daniel, after being laid off from here, isn't working in tobacco himself this harvest? I gather the farmers pay huge wages through these next weeks of labor."

"He did mention it to me. We've talked about a lot of different things, he and I. But honestly, I'm just trying to feel him out about what he knows about this place."

Phil looked at his colleague and couldn't resist a sly wink. "Understood. So, what's his reason, then?"

"Just that he really loves being a masseuse and that he'd hate to lose all ties with Bayham Brook, which he would have done if he'd given up a month or more to go work in a tobacco field or kiln. He says he enjoys working with the minister on refurbishing the church basement right now, and that, together, his jobs are paying 'all right.'"

Phil asked, "Was that his newish Rally Sport Camaro in the church parking lot? I'm pretty sure it isn't Klassen's!"

Trevor looked suspiciously at his colleague. "So? It's not that expensive a car for a bachelor."

"No, but I noticed the hide-away headlights when I was walking past it, so I had a peek inside. Houndstooth seats, got a gauge-pack on the console. I'd say that's more than most laborers around these parts can afford, wouldn't you?"

Trevor shrugged. "Maybe he bought it when he was still on full salary here."

"Sure, that's likely what he did. But he's still got to make the payments. Anyway, next time I go play chess for a bit of R&R, see what more you can find out about Dan's private—*wait.*"

"What?"

"Dan. Dan. *That's not right*—oh!"

"What's not right? What's happening in there?" Trevor asked, poking his mustardy finger at Phil's forehead.

"Hmm. Yeah. Just talking to myself."

"As per usual, then."

CHAPTER ELEVEN

At eleven o'clock sharp, a long black Cadillac pulled up outside Bayham Brook House's two side-by-side red and green doors. A chauffeur, dressed in a smart double-breasted suit and cap, unfolded his tall frame from the driver's seat and went around to the back right side to help an elegant lady in her sixties from the vehicle. He escorted her to the door with the Marley knocker, left her, and returned to the car for two suitcases. Upon his return the door was swung wide and Jeremiah Flintwinch stood there to welcome his new guest.

Trevor was down by the cabins interviewing guests in their 'villas' once again, feeling them out with his new knowledge of obvious drug use, though he would keep that to himself. The detectives would share the syringe-find news later in the day with Officer Biro, but no other guests or staff would be apprised of this latest development yet. Except perhaps one, for whom it would be imperative.

Phil was pretending to be interviewing Gerald and Adam and was thus standing in the men's wing corridor, looking out the windows from above as the new arrival was ushered from the Cadillac. As the chauffeur went back to the car for her bags, Phil smiled when he saw the woman pat her suit-jacket pockets, open her purse and peer inside, then tap the glasses that sat upon her head and nod in satisfaction. He watched Flintwinch take her suitcases and gesture her inside; the chauffeur gave a small bow and returned to the car, driving away in a cloud of dry dust.

Phil left his look-out and knocked on Gerald's door.

"Morning, Gerald. I wonder if I might come in for a moment?"

"Hey, man. Peace. What's the low-down? Caught our killer yet?"

"As you know, we are still acquiring knowledge, Mr. Grewgious." The formality was settling in Phil's voice as a counter-balance to the sarcasm bubbling up through his throat. "Did you know, incidentally, that Dickens describes his Grewgious character as 'an angular man with no conversational powers'?"

"Ah, man – that's a bummer. You sayin' I can't be solid, like?"

"I would very much doubt it. But that's beside the fact. Would you mind taking off the bandage I see is still on your forearm?"

"Huh? What—no, man! That's a drag. Why'd I do that?"

"Just unravel it and I'll have a look, Gerald."

"Look, it's enough this place's been crawling with you fuzz for the last coupl'a weeks, dude. But can't a guy even be in peace in his own bedroom without you bustin' in? I'm just here lettin' my freak flag fly, ya know?"

"No doubt. But take it off, please."

Gerald looked at him, his pupils dilated. Whether because of the fight-or-flight instinct, some drug, or withdrawal from the same, Philip couldn't be sure. After a pause, with the two of them staring each other down (and Phil being disgusted by some scrambled egg from Gerald's breakfast stuck in his long, unruly beard), the hippie turned and slumped heavily on his bed.

"This isn't cool, man. What's your hang-up?"

"My hang-up is that three innocent people have been murdered in as many weeks and I'd like to solve the case before any of the rest of you are eradicated."

"God, you're such a square! You're the one with no conversational powers." Gerald had begun to strip off his bandage which appeared cleaner than when Phil had last noticed it two days ago. He moved in for a closer look as the last layers fell away and Gerald held out his untanned arm.

"Been a while since you've been wearing a bandage, I'd say," Phil stated. "You've got a pretty good tan from doing all your chores outside, playing tennis, croquet, whatever—but not there. That's more than five days' worth of white!"

"So what?"

"So, turn your arm over, please."

"No! You wanna cuff me? Take me in? Here!" Instead of turning his left arm over to expose the underside, he held both arms out in front of him, hands in tight fists, knuckles up.

Phil decided to try a slightly different tack. He sat on the man's left side and gently turned his arm over, his voice less threatening now as he said, "I've no intention of arresting you, Gerald. I just want to know what you've been shooting up and where you're getting it. I know you didn't hurt yourself on any scythe."

The man's arms were littered with track marks, some appearing to be quite recent.

"I-I, I had these needle marks when I arrived. Sela and the doc just like me to keep my arm covered so it doesn't remind me, or the others. We're not supposed to think about our past trippin', ya dig?"

"I do dig. Except *that*," Phil pointed, "and *that* one, look pretty recent to me, Gerald. And you've been here how long?"

Gerald's head hung. "Near two months."

"Not going to be getting better if you keep using, are you? I'm assuming your parents are well-heeled?"

"Gramps is, man. He's the dude keeps sendin' me to these places."

"What are you using? Is it LSD? Meth? Crack?"

Gerald shook his head and tried again. "I was doin' LSD on the streets, but nothin' since I came here. Honest! You fuzz, always gotta believe the worst of a beatnik that just wants *peace.*"

Phil made several more attempts to discover from the hippie the wheres, the whats, and the whos, but he would not get anything further today, he could tell. Plus, he heard voices down the corridor in the women's wing. Telling Gerald to re-wrap his arm as best he could, he hurried out and down to just near Karen's room.

"And this is your room, Mrs. Jellyby," Dr. Flintwinch was saying. "I'm afraid it's a bit small, but we are currently cleaning and airing a larger room for you, if you'd prefer to change over in a few days."

"Oh, I'll be fine in this one, I'm sure, Doctor."

"Well, let's put your cases in and you can freshen up, then perhaps have a swim and a whirlpool if you'd like. You can find your way back to the Bubble and Squeak?"

"Well, I don't get lost in my thirty-two room mansion, so I'm unlikely to lose my way here," the stylishly blue-haired woman said, smiling.

Oh, nice one! thought Phil, eavesdropping with smugness.

The doctor was about to usher her into Room Three when he spotted Phil, who was trying to look as though he were just heading down the stairs, oblivious to them. "Oh, Mrs. Jellyby, I'd like you to meet Detective Inspector Steele. He's here to—uh—keep us all feeling safe. I'm sure you'll be told all about it at lunch, or at supper. D.I. Steele, this is Mrs. Jane Jellyby, here for a few days to enjoy a little spa holiday."

She looked directly into Phil's eyes with a twinkle of merriment and no nervous energy that he could detect. He extended his right hand to her as he repeated her requisite Dickens' pseudonym, "Mrs. Jellyby." As she accepted his palm with her own right, she added her left hand to the top of their clasped fingers, as well. On its ring finger was a shiny, rather sizeable diamond, startling Phil for a moment. Below it, next to the knuckle, was a glistening silver band. Blue wouldn't have left out such an important detail, of course. Perhaps Sharon had even offered to lend her own rings?

Dr. Flintwinch put in, "I hope you'll be comfortable in your stay with us, ma'm. Please don't listen too much to gossip when you're with the other guests. I can assure you, you'll be safe and relaxed here for your entire stay."

Phil added, with that touch of acerbity so frequently brewing just below his surface, "Yes, 'safe and healthy' is the motto here, isn't it Doctor?"

"Tssk," tutted P.J. Whistler. "I've already heard about the murders. I do read newspapers, you know. I wouldn't have come if I'd thought they had anything to do with me. See you at lunch, doctor! Twelve-thirty, I think you said?"

•　　　•　　　•

Trevor Ames found Latch Lupin outside his mud-hut, "The Vines Villa". Grape vines roped their way across most of its wood-latticed exterior, and across a tiny little arch over the door, affording shade. He sat on the log bench there, beside the elderly man.

"Now, Latch–I understand that after being in prison you don't exactly trust a copper like me. But I'm just trying to get to the bottom of what's going on here, and who's mad enough to have killed three people, especially a disabled woman in her bathtub."

"That weren't right. Not at all." As his thick lock of nearly pure-white bangs flipped back and forth with a shake of his head, Latch stuck his tongue between his teeth and made a sucking noise.

"Well, care to tell me what you know?"

"And get killed for me efforts?"

"Surely that's unlikely, Latch. For one, how's anyone to know you're telling me? No one can hear us. Two, that killer is a lunatic, we know. But even a lunatic must know that if you've already told us, there's no point in killing you *after* the fact...which would then lead to his or her certain arrest. Because, Three: no one could get away with *four* killings in a few short weeks on the same small estate."

"I reckon he'd be willing to give it a go."

"*Do* you even know anything worth telling me?"

"Look, Mr. Ames," Trevor noted that while the older man was trying to be respectful, he was unable to go so far as to use his title. That was fine by him, so long as he started talking. "When I was shut up all them years—eight, it were, of a twelve year sentence for somethin' I never done—I read the Bible a lot and did what some say is 'findin' God'. Well, I think He found *me*, you know? He helped me get through them bad times in there. Gave me hope. I met with the chaplain all the time, and tried to help some of them other men find some solace in Our Lord, too. So I'm a good man, and a good Christian. Ask that Reverend Klassen. I go to his church, and I'm there most every Sunday. Sometimes go to Bible Study, too. I promised when I was in the slammer always to tell the truth, I've done so for over thirty year. And I ain't gonna start lyin' to you now."

"I'm glad to hear it, sir."

"I honest didn't have nothin' to do with that bank robbery down in Port Dune. But the two guys that done it, *were* friends of mine. And I did find out right after the fact, what they'd done. My only fault then was not callin' the police on 'em, and I couldn't rat 'em out like that. One of them 'ventually got banged up too, served fourteen years. He weren't walkin' with God, like, and anyway, he deserved it. But the other guy, Jed—he got clean away. And I know Jed were Walter's cousin. Walter McDowell, here, you know? So, since my wife died, I thought maybe I'd dredge up the past a bit and come here, get to know Walter better, see if he knew anything about where the rest of that money'd gone. I wasn't lookin' for the cash for myself, mind. I thought if I could find out, it might ease my own mind a bit afore my time comes to join me wife. Then, I could tell the authritties, clear my name proper."

"I see," said Trevor, dabbing his pencil stub on his tongue and making two small notations in his book.

Latch looked uneasy and pointed at the notebook. "That there's the kind o' thing might get me killed."

Trevor realized Latch was right, and put the pencil and notebook in his pocket. "I beg your pardon. Would you rather we went in your cabin?"

"Nah. I guess if it's my time to go, it's my time to go."

"So, have you found out anything from Walter?"

"Honest I'm bein' again, now, Mr. Ames. He did tell me finally just last week, mind–that he were sure Jed had said he'd taken his share and bought jewelry with it. Expensive stuff, he said. So that it could be hid better than paper. But Walter, he's hard to understand, you know? You have to wait around forever just to get a short answer out of him, even if he do be trustin' you. Jed's dead now, he said, too. That surely took a long time to get out of his lips. J-j-j-ed D-d-d-dead. Poor rotter, ole Walter. Not much of a life for him."

"No, I imagine not. But he's had a good job here for many decades, is that right? He worked here for the Hogarth family long before this was sold as a retreat?"

"That's right. He do feel at home here, I reckon."

"And he's told you nothing else about where these jewels ended up?"

"That's all I got so far. Just that Jed grad'lly turned his cash into rubies 'n' such so he could hide 'em away better, take bits back as he needed it, to sell, like."

"And when did Jed die, do you know?"

"Nope, too hard to get that outta ole Stammer Hammer. That's what we used ta call him, like. 'Cause he were always carryin' 'round his mason's hammer hooked on his pants loop. Maybe you should have him write you out a statement. You'd get that faster than tryin' to have him tell you 'bout it."

"That's not a bad idea. Maybe we will. Do you think, Latch, that the whereabouts of these jewels is why three people have died here?"

The senior man snorted. "Not hardly. But who's ta know?"

"So what else is making you nervous about talking to me? What else do you know about this place?"

Latch paused for a moment. "Well, I seen some of 'em down near the brook. Smokin' that stuff they like, you know? Them two artists, and Charlie, when he were still here, with that Karen girl. Geez, once that Monty Tigg, the horsey woman, she were down there too."

"Did you ever see Crispin down with them?"

"No sir. Not him, he were tryin' real hard to stay clean, is that what they call it? Real hard. A nice kid, that un."

"Do you think they were just smoking marijuana down there? Or was there something else, some other drugs they might have been using?"

"I don't know nothin' 'bout drugs, honest. I keep myself to myself mostly. Just swimmin', goin' in the whirlpool, having a massage now an' then. I like to read—got real good at that in prison, like. An' my Bible. An' talkin' to ole Walt out in the sunshine. I keep my nose clean, and stay away from whatever they're doin' down at that brook."

"And I'll ask again, though I know you told me when I first arrived—you can't offer anything else to help us about the night when either Charlie disappeared, or when Crispin died?"

"Sorry, Mr. Ames. I really got nothin' else. I'm a bit deaf and I sleep real good here. So hearin' somethin' I weren't supposed to hear, that's not likely. Gossip in the Melon 'n' Cauli, I just don't bother with neither. I keep my nose clean."

Trevor stood, shook Latch Lupin's hand and made his way to Mitch and Jackie's cabin, The Saffron Hill Hut. Its thick walls, with full straw bales inside the plaster, would offer a cooler alternative to sitting outside, and he hoped at least one of the artists was in, possibly with a cold drink on offer.

•   •   •

Phil hadn't found Adam upstairs in his room, but when he passed The Rookery, he peeked in and saw him sprawled on the sofa in front of a fan, book in one hand, cigarette in the other. As he entered, he also saw Monty reading. He asked if she'd mind if he spoke to Adam alone, and she was more than happy to leave them to it. "Grand day, love, innit?" she said as she exited the common room. Just as if three murders hadn't taken place right on her doorstep, Phil thought. Perhaps she was actually glad of the mandatory extension to her holiday here, being away from her husband, her clients and her business.

"Adam. I know D.I. Ames has been the one to question you before now, so I thought I'd have a chat today. You must be hot in here, even with that fan. Whew! Why don't you wear a short-sleeved shirt, or a cotton one at least?" The young man was wearing a long-sleeved polyester blouse, decorated with large paisley blotches in blue. *Surely that had been designed for a woman*, Phil thought.

"Yeah, I suppose it's a bit silly, this one. But my short sleeves are in the hamper, and since they are so short-staffed, the laundry's fallen behind."

The young man then did exactly what Phil had hoped: he uncuffed his shirt and rolled up the sleeves to his biceps. Phil leaned over him, pretending his purpose was to move away the ashtray which contained a still-billowing butt. But in doing so he had a good look at Adam's under-forearms. *Good. No track marks.*

"Adam, I see you smoke Players. Do you know if anyone here smokes Belmont filters?"

Adam put down his book and sat up, thinking. "Hmm. Gerald smokes Export A's, like your D.I. Ames does. Karen stopped smoking almost as soon as she came. I think Monty likes a cigar once in a while... no, I'm not joking, I've seen her light one up with Gerald's lighter when we're all outside on the smoking terrace, then stroll away into the night with the stinky thing. Wait, now. I think Charlie liked Belmonts. But I can't think of anyone else."

"Crispin never smoked, did he?"

"I thought you'd know that, man. The word around here is that you were friends with his family or something."

"That's right. We were asked to come and investigate his case specifically. Who told you that, do you know?"

"This little insular place, man? Gossip abounds."

"So you never saw Crispin smoking? And you two had got pretty close?"

The young wanna-be hippie hung his head, a tear starting to trickle down his freckled cheek. Angrily, he swiped it away. "He was like my best friend. He was so—just cool, eh? God, I miss him. He'd worked so hard to get himself straightened up, too. And clean."

"About that. There was no sign of him doing any drugs since he came here?"

If it were possible to sit up any straighter, the paisley shoulders did so. "There's no way any of us could get drugs or drink, if we wanted to!"

Phil looked at him carefully. "But you told D.I. Ames that Crispin's death might make you stray back to alcohol. How could you have managed that?"

Adam shrugged. "I did once hitch-hike into Sandytown, to Townsend's store. I told Ruth I was going to get myself some snacks. Now, of course they don't sell alcohol in the village, but out back of Townsend's, there were some little crates of beer I heard you could buy from the owner's brother."

"And did you?"

He shook his head. "I went around to the back, but I saw Reverend Klassen there with a few other guys and thought the better of it. I figured he must have been trying to talk them out of selling the stuff. So I just hitched back here with some sodas and chips, a few chocolate bars. They don't really like us having any junk food here, either–this whole place is supposed to be about living healthier, and more naturally with the environment and all."

"So, the smoking?"

"Ah, yeah, the doc figures first off he's helping the area by letting us keep smoking. All these tobacco farms, eh? Plus he knows there's no way we could withdraw from all our chemical dependencies in just a few months. So he lets us smoke. I mean, it *is* natural, right?"

"Up to a point. So is marijuana."

"Sh-sure." Adam seemed hesitant.

"How many smoke marijuana here, Adam?"

Again, a pause. "I really don't know for sure if they do. And if they do, I don't think it's any of us. Addicts, I mean. They keep a pretty careful watch on us after supper, and during the day we're usually busy with exercises, playing sports, or in either a private or group counseling session. It's only been since you guys came, since they found Charlie's body I guess, that we stopped having regular routines every day. Then, since Sela's mom... I don't think the doc can really manage on his own."

"Did you like Petra Cowan?"

"Didn't really know her that well. She seemed lovely, though. Sela or Ruth often brought her over to the dining hall for a meal, so we'd all chat to her a bit then. She seemed pretty groovy."

"And tell me, Adam—when you all do arts and crafts nights, have you made those little vials into memory capsule ornaments?"

"Sure. I've made three now. They're up in my room. I love doin' them. I'm going to keep them as Christmas ornaments, to remind me of my time here. I'm doing one with a Crispin-theme next. It'll have a tiny little origami in it, and a snipped off bit of film roll."

"Ever asked where the vials come from?"

"Um. No. But Crispin did."

"Did he indeed. Who did he ask?"

"I'm not sure. Della, I think. It was after one of the craft nights when Crispin came to my room. In fact that was the night we finished up our memory ornaments and also learned some basic origami from Crispin, so I remember he was late coming up. He'd stayed with Annette to help clear the mess."

"You'd been expecting him to come in with information?" asked Philip.

"Not information, no. But we often had chats in each other's rooms. We could get some pretty good philosophizing done, man. We neither of us liked the trite gossip stuff. But that one night, I remember specifically–because he *was* kind of gossipy."

"Why, what did he say?"

"He said he'd got to putting together some things in his head, and that they bothered him. He thought having those vials around was kinda weird, when we weren't supposed to have anything visually or otherwise sensory reminding us of our drug or alcohol days."

"Except for the ciggies."

"Well yeah. The 'fags', as Monty calls 'em. I guess they all call them that in England."

Phil nodded. "What else bothered him?"

"Well, he told me that Karen and Lucy and their weird ups-and-downs seemed crazy, even for people still in withdrawal. Especially Lucy. But I reminded him they were women, and just likely having their time of the months, you know? When they acted all emotional and stuff?"

"And...?"

"He said he didn't like how Gerald would disappear in the day sometimes, how he'd say he was going to do chores, or play tennis, but then we never saw him really doing those things. He'd always be a little freaky in the evenings, after those afternoons."

"The little clubhouse by the courts, what's it called?"

Adam laughed. " 'Tots'n'ham Courtside'. You been in there? Got a juice fridge, a ping-pong table and all the tennis racquets and cross-country skis for the winter guests. That's about all. Oh, and Sela has a little First Aid station out there. For when one of us gets a nick or a sliver."

Hell's Bell's, did the OPP ever search in there? He knew he and Trevor had certainly overlooked it. He took out a recipe card and made a note. *And he must get a note to P.J. as well,* ask her to fake perhaps a sprain while playing tennis one day soon.

"What else did Crispin tell you?"

Adam got serious again. "Look, man. I *wanted* him to tell me more. But about that point in our conversation, he more or less clammed up. Said he didn't want to put me in danger, knowing stuff I shouldn't. I laughed at him at the time. Now, I wish I'd pressed him harder."

"Well, did he give *any* more idea what he could have meant?" Phil knew some people with addictive personalities, and especially Crispin, could be overly dramatic and attention-seeking. It was one reason Blue Cobalt hadn't paid the attention he should have done when Crispin was trying to tell him important information about the Bayham Brook House retreat. But he was quite sure now that Crispin really had known something that probably got him killed.

"He said—he said, 'I'm going to be taking a look at those guests that like to go down to the brook. I'm going to go in a few nights. I'll let you know when, so you can cover for me if someone finds out I'm not in my room.'"

"But he never did let you know?"

Adam shook his head mournfully. "He never did. God, I wish he had!"

·　　　·　　　·

Phil and Trevor met, as planned, at one o'clock. Phil had managed to write a recipe card note to his undercover godmother, saying *'drugs here. Need 1ˢᵗ-Aid? Try court clubhse tmrrw'* and had passed it to her as he and Trevor stood outside the Melon 'n' Cauli Tavern watching the guests all pour in for lunch. She'd not even looked at him as the folded card was pressed into her hand.

The two detectives wandered out to their car, sitting again in the shade with their backs against the stone pillar that held the wrought-iron fence in place. Phil stared across the acres of lawn to the little building that was the clubhouse.

"We should just go search in there now. Sela's not back to work yet, and it'd be a perfect time."

"Yes, but Blevan's on the property. So not ideal."

"I know."

"We've got to go find Blake Biro shortly, let him know about the syringes. If we did a search in there now, someone would see us and know that we know."

"Does that really matter? Shouldn't we just get all in their faces about it now?"

"We probably should. And will. Soon. I just feel like we have a slight upper hand at the moment, and I'd like to ponder my theories overnight. P.J.'s perfectly capable of twisting her ankle playing ping-pong or something, and if Sela's back at work tomorrow as she led me to believe she will be, then P.J. will be better able to read her reactions to whatever sort of things are being kept in that First Aid station. Remember when Gerald came out that first day, and she had iodine, she *said*, all over her apron? And she'd just wrappped his arm in there?"

"Yeah, you're saying that really was blood?"

"No, it probably was iodine, but not from any cut on Gerald. She was wrapping his arm because it was full of track marks."

"Crap! So, you think she found out where he's been getting the drugs from? Been helping him cover it up?"

"Looks that way. I guess it wouldn't be good for the retreat's reputation if word of that ever got out."

"Yet neither Charlie nor Crispin's autopsies showed any traces of drugs, even though they said Charlie's body was too decomposed to know for certain."

"Right, and Crispin's fall is definitely what killed him. Not that he'd been beaten first, then tossed."

"Which I know you said was another of your famous theories."

"So there can't be wide usage of drugs on this place, then. But somehow those that want it are finding out about how to get it."

"And Crispin had been here a few months and was probably starting to get his brain sorted out. So maybe he was becoming more perceptive."

"Or maybe it was at that point he was being offered something?"

"And the weaker types, like Gerald, and Karen, they couldn't say 'no'."

"Right. About them…"

The two men then shared what each had discovered from Latch, Adam, Gerald and the artists, Jackie and Mitch. Trevor told him that the latter two had once again stated that while they did occasionally enjoy going to the brook for a few tokes, they didn't do it often, nor had they ever seen any of the 'big house' rehabbers down there. Trevor had asked specifically about Charlie or Karen but they swore they'd never seen either of them down there when they'd been sitting with others like Monty, and before her, a guest named Giselle who was another artist, a sculptor. Once, they'd admitted, Daniel Blevan had been there smoking up with them.

"Hmm," said Phil. "Wonder if that's another reason he was fired?"

"Smoking dope is just so common, I can't see why, really. I mean they are barely on this property at that point of the old road and brook. And if it's not being done with the addicts—"

"I thought you'd stopped calling them that, Trevor."

"Well, I'm trying, but sometimes it seems like the only right word."

"Well, speaking of words, remember how when we were discussing P.J. coming here, the day after Petra's murder? And Blue was getting everything organized with your Supervisor Flaherty, and making all those calls to my mom's, sorting out the details of what we needed from my dear-but-sometimes-nosy godmother?"

"I do. I'm still against the whole plan. For the record."

"Point taken. Well, I'd almost forgotten that the evening prior to Petra's death, and Lucy's little suicidal adventure, I'd asked P.J. to look up two names in my father's Dickens set. There's an index with all the characters."

"Haven't you had enough of them all, around this place?"

"Well, that's just the point. I knew Annette's pseudonym here was Micawber. I knew that was from David Copperfield. So, I wondered if she'd chosen it possibly because of the famous anagram of 'David Copperfield'."

"Famous? I must have missed that one…"

"Well, o.k., not famous maybe. But we did have a joke at my boarding school about how if you 'flipped Ovid's Cedar', you got David's Copper Field."

Trevor stared at Phil as though he'd sprung two horns from each side of his forehead. "You're kidding! At *my* school we thought we were making literary jokes if someone said, 'What did one toilet say to the other? You look a bit flushed.'"

Philip smiled. "And Ovid's Cedar made me think of the big one going up the side of the house past Karen's room. The one Lucy seemed determined to get into and crawl down."

"What's an Ovid Cedar?"

"Ovid was a poet. He wrote about taking the bark off cedar, as a symbolism for deception, confusion. Of making something appear one way, when it's in fact something else."

"O-kayyy," said Trevor.

"Well, it was just something I thought might bear closer attention. However, that night I talked to P.J. about names, I *also* asked her to look up 'MacElburns'. Annette's pen name—but as we've come to discover, her real surname."

"Is that Dickens too?"

"No, but I was sure I'd seen it somewhere. Somewhere in the last year."

"And...?"

"Well, my dear godmother remembered where. She does the same crosswords and word puzzles in the newspapers that I like to do when I get time. The Globe and Mail's, for instance. And she said that 'MacElburns' is an anagram for 'unscramble'. It was part of a puzzle a few months ago."

"Hmm. That's interesting. But I suppose a journalist might like to use that as a pen name. 'Flipping' and 'Unscrambling' words. Some people..." Trevor shook his head.

"But it's *not* just her pen name. P.J. works as a postmistress out in Victoria, in New Brunswick. She remembers a magazine coming through on someone's subscription out there. So I had one of your colleagues—Jackson, with Flaherty's permission, of course—look it up. There is indeed a new national investigative journalism magazine called "Unscramble". He called me back the other night at the church, when I was there playing chess. We'd planned a few back-and- forth calls that night, as you know."

"This whole word thing is one of your theories that you've been working on without sharing?"

"No need to pout. I'm not doing it to hurt you, Mr. Sensitive." Phil was at the point now where he felt he could ever-so-slightly tease Trevor.

"So what'd Jackson say about it, exactly?"

"'Unscramble Magazine' was only started a year ago and is primarily for articles uncovering scams, or cover-ups, or illegal doings under the guise of legitimate businesses across Canada. The editor is one Barclay MacElburns."

"Uh-huh! Father of Annette, we think?"

"Or uncle, or some such. What concerns me is that Lucy's last words to Flintwinch, at least according to him, were those strange and cryptic: 'Anita's Mascara'. So one of us needs to be off to her cabin next, find out what the hell's really going on with her. I'll bet my arse she isn't working for Chatelaine and writing up the lovely spa treatments and country walks here. And it *could* mean she's in danger, or that maybe she's dealing drugs herself, or I don't know what …"

"Well, you wanna deal with her next, and I'll go to that unfinished cabin they're calling Dreary Jane—what kind of Dickens name is *that,* anyway?"

"*Drury* Lane is an important street, and theater, in London. As far back as Dickens' time and further. I believe he lived somewhere around there, used it in his books. Plus, I'm quite sure Jane was Neville Hogarth's wife's name. So Flintwinch and Sela probably wanted to make this newest cabin in her honor, since they both would have known her."

"Right. Well, I'll go down there and let Biro know what we've found out this morning, and to be extra vigilant tonight."

"There's one more thing, to do with unscrambling words and names, Trevor."

"Yet another theory?"

"Well, you said you wanted to know."

"Touché."

"P.J. was messing about with anagrams after she figured out that 'MacElburns' one. She was amusing my mother with the fact that the JUST *(e)*STATE, unscrambled, is 'Astute Jest'. They apparently had a long discussion about whether or not my father knew that when he so-named it. I mean there've been five generations of Steeles living there, but it was my father, the lover of all things just, the lover of all things philosophical and to do with wordplay and literature, who began calling it that—back before my sister and I were born."

"So you take after your father a lot, I guess, huh?" Trevor lit up an Export.

"Probably too much. But at least I haven't had children to terrorize with over-disciplinary tactics... Sorry. Completely beside the point. The *point* is: *'Dad'*. Ruth thought she heard Crispin talking to his father Blue the night he disappeared and then was found dead next morning. I don't believe he said 'Dad' at all."

"What, then?"

"Well, brace yourself. Because it *is* just a theory, Trevor."

"Why should I brace myself?"

"Because, I know you like being with a certain someone, a certain person whose name is Daniel. Whom others call 'Dan'."

"Oh, come on!"

"No, just think about it as a cop, please. Ruth thought she heard him say into the phone, 'That's not right, Dad (or Dan). I don't think so.'"

"And then he disappears and is pushed off a bridge?" Trevor didn't normally like feeling disrespectful toward his elders, but now he looked skeptical. "You're really reaching, Philip Steele."

"I know. That's why I like to mull things over before I speak them aloud."

"Best continue that practice, then." Trevor got up, brushed off his pants, crushed out his cigarette with his heel and stomped off into the woods toward Officer Biro, who was very likely napping again ahead of a night of active patrol.

Phil put his head back on the stone pillar, wondering if he should eat something else before heading to Annette's cabin, Sorrel Close. Their sandwiches seemed many hours ago now, but more than eating, he also felt the need for a nap.

"*Shutting my eyes, surprise, surprise,*" he muttered to himself. God, when had middle-age hit him? He was suddenly amazed that the stone where his head was resting was slowly being pushed inward.

Wide awake now, as though he'd had a jolt of caffeine, he turned and squatted, fingers in the cracks, prying the rock back toward him. Not able to get his too-plump digits in between, he pulled out his pouch of small tools from his pocket and, using the blade of his jackknife, eventually coaxed the stone from its hole. There behind it was a dark cavity in the pillar about six inches by eight or nine inches. He put his hand in, felt around. It was empty. But he now knew to whom he would speak immediately after his conversation with Annette/Anita.

•   •   •

After P.J.'s lunch in the Melon'n' Cauli Tavern, (she was wholly enchanted with all these Dickens' names), a broad-shouldered woman came up behind her, pushing one of the trolleys which was loaded with their dirty dishes. P.J. stopped and turned to face her, reading her white plastic name tag.

"Hello, Ruth," she said, introducing herself as Jane Jellyby. Then she had to remind herself that in her undercover role as 'wealthy widow', she shouldn't be speaking too much with the staff. She had had this argument for several of the previous evenings, speaking with Blue and Phil over the telephone. After all, she'd said—how was she meant to get to the heart of any really juicy gossip if she put on airs and didn't speak to the help? Blue had wanted her to appear more aloof, watching from a distance, while Phil had suggested she just be more like her own character and not pose as a wealthy widow at all. In the end, she'd told Blue she would do the best she could, knowing in her heart she'd probably be offering to help wash all those dishes before this afternoon was over.

While most guests that weren't in the treatment program stayed in their own villas, the huts and cabins were all full for the moment, and this fit in nicely with their plans; they all knew she'd learn more if she had a room in the big house. But she did have one problem with that little room she'd been given.

"Ruth, I understand you're quite understaffed at the moment, and I do hate to ask. But I wonder if someone might have a moment to come and open my window for me? It seems to be stuck and it's very close in there!"

"You's won't try and hurl yourself outta it, will ya, ma'm?" Ruth asked, then covered her mouth, shocked at herself. "Oh, so sorry. It's just all getting' to me a bit around here, 'n' all."

"Do you mean that someone recently jumped from their window?"

"Oh, no, ma'm. Just, one of the doctor's patients tried to get out a top floor by climbing down a tree, is all."

"Oh, but they aren't kept like prisoners here, surely?"

"No, of course not. Just—this particular lady had some mental issues, poor pet."

"I see. It almost sounds as if she were taking drugs or something. Hallucinating or some such?" P.J. was conscious of the folded recipe card Phil had slipped her, now tucked between her left breast and her cotton bra.

"Oh, dear me, no. There'd be no way for any of them to have drugs around here! Don't you be worrying about that, ma'm." They were walking together down the long corridor, looking out the floor-to-ceiling windows at the hillsides dotted by the naturally-built villas. "Oh, there goes that nice Inspector Steele, off to question another guest, I suppose. Such a gentleman, he is."

Because she was still staring outside, Ruth McCorkle missed the older woman's head turning away, in order to hide a smile. She continued, "You're lucky you'll be the only one around here not gettin' constantly interviewed. I 'spect you've heard by now about the murders? Seems that's all anyone talks about at meal-times anymore."

P.J. cleared her throat. "I had heard about two of them. I'd read about them in the papers."

"An' that didn't cause ya to wanna go somewheres else?"

"Oh, no. I'd seen the brochure for this place some time ago and the murders only reminded me that I'd wanted to come. I expect those men were killed because they were involved in money fraud or something. And I only heard at lunch about the poor lady in her bathtub. I believe a waitress named Clara mentioned it?"

"Oh, that girl. Always got the flapping lips, her. I'll have to have a sharp word."

P.J. was hardly going to point out that Ruth herself had been the one to bring up the murders just now. She moved along toward the staircase. "Well, thank you for a most enjoyable lunch. I especially liked the orange jello and carrot salad. What do you call that?" She knew full well what it was called, of course; she often made it herself for church socials or pot-luck picnics back in New Brunswick. But she was sure her character of the rich Jane Jellyby would never have eaten such a thing.

"It's a Sunshine Salad, ma'm. Glad you enjoyed. I'll get someone to come up soon and try hefting up your window. It may even be one of the boys, as I call 'em. Gerald or Adam. You wouldn't mind that, as we're a bit short-staffed?"

"Do send in whoever's strong enough and has the time. Thank you."

And as she ascended the stairs, P.J. felt that her job had been well and truly activated.

•   •   •

Annette opened the door of her little cabin and let Phil into its cool interior. A little cross breeze blew from the window at one side facing the woods and gully, to the multi-panes on this side beside the door. Cheery red geraniums blossomed from a tiny planter in this front window and a little lace curtain flicked itself into a roll, then unfurled.

"Just wanted to get a few things straight, here, Miss MacElburns. Now, D.I. Ames tells me you said you saw someone pass by here the night Crispin died. Was that here, by this door?"

"No. I was up there in my bunk, so it was by this window at the back."

"And you wear glasses?"

"Yes, so of course I didn't have them on when I thought I saw something at 3 a.m. It was really just a shadow, but it seemed quite a bulky, big one. That's why I thought it might have been one of the horses, or a deer. I think what might have woken me up was a twig breaking. But I really couldn't see at all well."

Phil looked at her orbs, glinting a honey-gold warmth behind the lenses of her fashionable cat's-eyes. "I see you do wear some eye-shadow and mascara, Annette. Would you mind if I looked in your make-up kit?"

She stared at him, but didn't look overly shocked. Certainly not nervous. "Sure. I guess. Would you tell me why?"

"Perhaps. If I could have a look first?"

She went to the tiny toilet area that was essentially an outhouse with a separate door. Each of the cabins had these, Phil had noticed when questioning guests the day after Petra's death. The villas had electricity, but no plumbing, so an old-fashioned pitcher of water with basin, soap and towel graced each adjoining outhouse. Above this table with the basin was a small mirror. All the guests bathed, showered or otherwise cleaned themselves up in the Bubble 'n' Squeak.

Annette handed him a yellow make-up bag with a zipper, the pull being a circular hoop. Phil was seeing these more and more on the necklines of brightly striped sweaters, for both men and women. Such weird trends these days, he thought. Again, the sense of being surprised by mid-age swept over him.

He stuck his finger through the hoop, pulling the zip entirely open. Rather than pouring the contents rudely onto her little counter space, however, he took out one article at a time to examine. Ruby-red lipstick. He removed the cap, looked at it circumspectly, bent his nose to sniff at it. Did the same with another lipstick, a bright orange. He opened a little flat plastic kit that contained several colors of eye shadow, including white. Into this one he dipped a little finger, held it to his nose and sniffed it. Lastly, he took out a long tube that was obviously Annette's eye-lash paint and brush. '*Anita's mascara,*' Flintwinch had said Lucy mumbled to him. He unscrewed the lid, looked into the little tube, shook it, smelled it. He screwed it back and shrugged.

Replacing all the items back in the kit and then drawing closed the zipper again, he said inadequately, "We'd just heard something about some make-up kits."

"Were you looking for drugs? Because I've been clean for over two years, Detective Inspector. I wouldn't be able to hold down my job as a writer-reporter if I was sniffing, or shooting up, still."

"Ah. Something else I wanted to talk to you about, Annette. Your job. It's not for Chateleine, is it? Or even freelancing?"

The young woman did something very unexpected then. She removed a sheaf of papers and two rolls of film from under the mattress in the lower bunk, the one in which she didn't sleep, but on top of which was sprawled her suitcase and some books. She said, very calmly, "Is your car parked in the shade? Because I'd feel better talking to you out there. That way we can sit comfortably and still see if there's anyone nearby that could overhear."

With that, Annette MacElburns turned, papers and film clutched to her chest, and led the way out of Sorrel Close Cabin, up the steep lawn toward Bayham Brook House itself, continued marching on determinedly until she was standing beside the big Satellite vehicle.

The rolls of film. Those reminded Phil of something he'd seen earlier that day.

After gallantly opening the car door for the journalist, he took out his recipe cards and quickly scribbled: 'Blue, Camera'. And underlined the 'C'.

•   •   •

Jeremiah had been with her since one o'clock, when Officer Biro had said he really had to go and nap if he was expected to stay awake all night long. The last two nights there'd been three OPP left patrolling both sides of the road and its many acres, but now there was just to be him. So Sela had told him to telephone and ask Dr. Flintwinch to come. Not that she really needed anyone, but if it made them all feel better... Truth be told, she was pretty nervous now, although she didn't really care if she *was* the next murder victim. So Jeremiah had come, told her briefly about the new guest, a Jane Jellyby, hoping to distract her, to witness a small flicker of interest in her eyes for someone other than herself and her obvious pain. But he saw nothing in her except the dull ache of shock.

He'd made them each cucumber sandwiches with some of the brown bread her mother had favored. *"Mummy! Mummy! It's all my fault!"* Sela Cowan's mind screamed the words for perhaps the thousandth time in three days, despite all the sedatives she'd been fed.

"You don't have to stay with me, Doc. I'll be fine," said Sela dully, knowing she'd never be truly 'fine' again. "Go on back across the road and look after your guests. Tell everyone I'll be back tomorrow."

"I can't leave you, Sela. The officer asked me specifically to stay."

Her shoulders hunched as she sat in her mother's wheelchair now, playing with the brakes, restlessly pushing the foot rests up and down.

"Don't torture yourself. Sit back under the umbrella if you want to keep in the shade. What's the menorah doing out here?"

"There was a time I didn't think you'd know what the hell that was called."

"I know," he said quietly. "You probably don't remember what you told me the other day, when you were only half awake."

She stiffened. "What do you mean?"

"You said you used to call me 'Nazi', in your head; that whenever you spoke politely to me, you were all the while calling me 'Nazi'."

"I–I said that? I don't remember."

"But is that true?"

"Yeah. For years, I thought 'Schneider' was a pure German name and that the reason you'd changed it was to hide the fact that your father was a Nazi."

He picked up the menorah and carried it back into the house, saying over his shoulder, "We were just as Jewish as your family, and every bit as persecuted."

"I know that now. Mom finally told me," Sela started to sob softly again. "I'm sorry!"

"And we had nothing to do with killing your father."

CHAPTER TWELVE

After the most illuminating disclosures proffered by Annette while they sat in the car in the shade, Phil stashed the rolls of film she'd given him in their cooler with their own camera equipment and food, and hurried down the path in the direction of Drury Jane to look for Trevor. He found him, head bent to the ground, wandering back and forth in trudging little steps, as if looking for something.

"What's up? Did you tell Blake about the syringes?" Phil asked.

"Yeah, he wasn't happy I'd woken him from his nap, though."

"He wasn't really supposed to have left Sela's bungalow, but I guess he deserves to sleep sometime in a twenty-four-hour period. What are you doing?"

"Well, you're not the only one that can have theories, you know. Biro said something about hearing a horse go by down here on this path that leads to the old road. That made me wonder—that Monty woman, she's always riding out here about this time of day, so why do I never see hoof prints?"

"Ground's too dry. Need a bit of damp and mud, I guess."

"Yeah, well, I did see this." Trevor pointed to a wheelbarrow's narrow tire mark, only eight inches long, with a bit of manure and soiled straw that had fallen to either side. "What the hell's someone doing pushing manure in a barrow all the way out here?

It's not near the stables' muck heap, and it's too far from the garden to be used for fertilizer…"

"Hmm. Interesting. Let's keep it in mind. But I've just heard something *more* interesting and I don't have time to tell you all about it now, because I'm going to follow up another lead with Walter right away. But Trev—Annette's given us two rolls of Ilford film she thinks might have some important shots on them, all taken since she's been here and working on her story. Yes, for 'Unscramble'. Will you take the car and head into Tillsonburg to put a rush job on getting them developed, please? Flash your badge wherever you need to."

"Right-o. You want me to check in across the road first?"

"Yeah, not a bad idea. I'm a little nervous leaving Sela alone over there, but I'm just as nervous if a killer is baby-sitting her."

"Blake said he asked Flintwinch to go back."

"Lord in Heaven, I hope that's wise."

"Me too. I'll go check, then head into town and be back in a few hours. Oh, I saw your—saw the 'new guest' heading out to play tennis. With ole Latch."

"Ah. Perfect. Although I really wanted her to do that when Sela's back."

"Maybe she'll do that also. Gotta seem like she enjoys playing tennis every day, I suppose."

"She used to be a dancer, among other things. Luckily, she looks fit enough to pull off being an avid player."

"Back in a while. Head to the stables up that other track." Trevor inclined his head toward a path leading through a birch grove. "If you go past Dreary Jane, you'll just hear some really disgusting snores. Biro sounds like a mechanical fart machine."

●   ●   ●

Walter was sitting in the tack room polishing some metal snaffle bits that were attached to bridles strewn across the worktable. He rose as Phil entered, saying, "W-w-why'd you be takin' those ph-ph-photos of my b-b-b-ale this mornin'?"

One thing about a stutterer, it sure made it hard to tell if he was nervous about something. "We just found something of interest there. Is Mrs. Tigg out riding right now?"

"Y-y-yes. She said she were g-g-g-gonna ride down t-t-to the Otter, today, f-f-follow it a b-b-b-bit." Blushing, the man seemed defeated with that vast imparting of information.

"Good, then perhaps we'll be undisturbed for a while. To chat. Or maybe you'd prefer to write out a statement, in the form of answers to my questions. Would that be easier for you than trying to talk?"

The large man raised and dropped his broad shoulders in a shrug, hefted himself back into the chair. Philip sat across from him.

"Well, here's some paper." Removing three folded sheets of foolscap from his pants pocket and laying them in front of Walter, Phil prayed the man had basic literacy skills and that he wasn't about to embarrass him further.

"Walter, when you were a mason here and the Hogarth family was just building this place, what people that you've seen in the last few months were *also* here back then, back twenty-five years ago? Could you list them for me, please? All of them?"

He watched as the man thought, then wrote down, in beautiful penmanship, several names. Phil didn't try to read them upside down. He was pretty sure he already knew two of the names he'd see later when he read the foolscap.

"And when you were laying the foundation here, making the stone walls across the road, and the pillars out front by the wrought-iron fence, was your cousin Jed around, maybe helping you?"

Walter's chin again hung over his pen and paper, his jowls shaking slightly as he shook his head in jagged little rhythms, following the movement of the pen, deep in concentration.

"And what did Jed tell you—that you should make some little hidey-holes? For him to use? Maybe that he'd give you some money from time to time, when you needed it?"

After looking deflated, if that were possible for such a balloon-shaped figure, Walter sighed in visible relief. Once again, his ballpoint slid across the pages for quite a few moments.

"You're doing very well, Walter," Phil said, thinking, *assuming you aren't writing 'screw off, you prying bastard' over and over.* "When we're finished here, will you walk me around the property and show me all these hiding places you helped build? You only have to nod 'yes'."

The former mason-now-maintenance-man/groom stared hard at Phil. He put the top of his pen in his mouth and sucked on it thoughtfully. He clicked the pen in and out in an annoying cadence. Then very slowly, he nodded.

"Do you know if other people have been using those little holes in the years since the new owners took over? And when exactly did your cousin Jed die, anyway? *How* did he die?"

Again, the pen rattled its way from left to right across the light blue lines.

"Now, try to be honest, here, Walter. Because you're not going to be in trouble. You're really helping us find a murderer. A killer of people you cared about, right? So—did Jed leave anything in the holes when he died? Anything that you took, perhaps?"

Walter shook his head vehemently and said, "N-n-no! They was all empty for y-y-years, b-b-be-f-f-ore he died."

"O.K., write that down, because this is part of your official statement about this."

While he was doing so, Phil added, "And did you show the new owners, or Doctor Flintwinch, where they were? When the property changed hands?"

Another pause while Walter reflected. Was he thinking how much to say, or simply trying to remember? Phil decided it was impossible to tell.

When the big man had finished the answers to the last sequence, still in his rounded, slanted cursive, Phil said, "And now, just one last question. It may seem unrelated to all these others but trust me, Walter, it's not. Can you please write down where you get your hay and straw for the horses? An address, please, or phone number as well. Then we'll go out for a stroll around the place, shall we?"

·　·　·

In Tillsonburg, Trevor came out of the second camera and film-developing shop he'd tried and slumped in the Satellite with satisfaction. Phil would be pleased that Annette's pictures would be back the next day. He leaned over to put the receipt stubs in the glove compartment, then sat up again. This main street, Broadway, was in fact so broad that there was no parallel parking, just angled pull-in/pull-out spaces. Very easy to park a large car such as this one, and it allowed Trevor to sit for a few moments in the shade of an awning with 'Dor-ian's Dollhouse Tearoom' painted in flowery cursive along its front edge. As he sat smoking, having unrolled the window, he saw Reverend Klassen emerge from this small café with the lacy curtains and dollhouse in the window. He noted the minister was not wearing his clerical collar and didn't seem to recognize the Satellite. Trevor was about to call out a greeting, when something stopped him. Instead, he watched the man stride three stores down the sidewalk, turn toward a pickup and climb up into the driver's seat. It was difficult to see, as several other cars were parked between them now, but the detective inspector thought that this was not the pickup he remembered seeing on their few visits to the Edom's Creek United Church. That had been a rather rusty green Ford, and this one was a newer model, although still green. The minister backed the truck smoothly out of the parking space, and as he was about to drive past on the other side of the road, Trevor turned to look out the rear window. He noticed then that the truck was full of hay or straw bales, he couldn't tell which, and that along the side were the words: 'Klassen Farm, Edom's Creek, Ontario'.

• • •

Monty rolled over in the mud and cow pats at the top of the south bank of the Little Otter. Damn and blast that horse! She'd crossed the water here before, passed the herd of cows at a distance, and Odie hadn't spooked at them then. However, as she rose to her feet and began feeling gingerly for possible broken bones, she realized she hadn't been riding Odie when she'd been down this way. It had been the dappled mare, Sunspot. Regardless, one of the cows had let out a huge 'moo', and Odie had shied violently sideways, tossing her right out of the English saddle. He'd then fled in apparent terror back up the old road they'd just traversed. No doubt he'd already be up at the stables by now. Meanwhile, it was going to take Monty a lot longer to limp her way there. She'd landed in a heap on top of her foot, which she could feel already swelling inside the boot. She prayed they wouldn't have to cut her good leather knee-highs; they were much too expensive and her husband would not be well pleased.

She brushed off the worst of the dirt from her thighs, pulled a grasping burr from her T-shirt. About to slide down into the creek, so low at this time of the summer that she shouldn't have any trouble crossing it, she saw a bit of a leather strap with a thin buckle attached. She reached down, wincing, and picked it up. *What on earth?* This wasn't part of Odie's bridle; it was far too thin and insubstantial. None of the cows wore any sort of halters, either. Perhaps it was a strap that Bob Haggerty had once used on the gate, about forty yards down. She brushed some of the mud off it, tucked it through the belt loops on her jodhs, and began to wade across the golden-brown Little Otter.

・　　　・　　　・

Polly Jane Whistler and Latch Lupin hobbled into the 'Tots 'n' ham Courtside' building, both feeling their age after the exertion in the sun. They returned their racquets to the hooks on the wall and turning, P.J. spotted the first aid kit hanging above a small desk. A woman's flowered cardigan hung around the back of the desk chair.

"It was a lovely game, Latch. Sorry I couldn't play longer, but I'm so stiff. I wonder, if you'd like to play again tomorrow, if I shouldn't wrap my calf and ankle now, for some support."

"Could do. But o' course our resident nurse is gone."

"Oh, I could do it myself, if you think there're some elastic bandages here."

"I seen a few rolls lying about on that shelf, once, but looks like there's none there now."

"I'll have a peek in these drawers, shall I?" Without waiting for an answer, P.J. tried three side drawers on the desk; two had only stationery in them and the third was locked.

"Hmm, let's see if there are some in that box under the ping-pong table, maybe?"

But upon further examination they found only sporting supplies: ski resin, new table tennis paddles, two pairs of cross-country ski boots and several cans of both tennis balls and ping-pong balls.

"Well, let's just grab that juice from the fridge and go sit in the shade, shall we, Missus?" Latch asked. P.J. had already said she'd needed a drink when they were toweling down on the court. She hoped that this would be a good way also to see inside the refrigerator, but Latch was gallant and went to get them each a juice bottle before she could get there.

She sighed and gratefully drank her apple beverage. She'd have to try to 'sprain' her ankle tomorrow when hopefully this nurse, poor daughter of the unfortunate bathtub victim, would be back on duty.

•   •   •

Back at the Nelsons' in Port Dune that evening, Phil and Trevor made themselves comfortable in the Quay Room, as had become their habit. Cathy Nelson had said, as they'd passed her to go up the stairs, "You all don't need the phone in my parlor no more? You ain't used it…"

"… in the last coupla nights." finished her brother, sitting hunched with a coffee.

"An' if you don't, we'll like as not…"

"…go back to watching the television set in there again."

Philip assured them it was fine, thanks, to please use their set as they would do without guests about the place. He suspected that, despite the siblings' complaints about their snoopy neighbor, they perhaps *relied* on the Van Duren woman on their party line to feed interesting information back to them. Thus, he was grateful he'd remembered to use Sela Cowan's little office phone in the front hall of Bayham Brook, to call through to Blue before they'd left that afternoon. He'd been excited to add to his commentary, the finding of Monty's strap. This was the first thing he brought up with Trevor, sprawled as usual on the bean-bag chair with his feet up on the footstool and his notebook beside him.

"Right, so we've actually made some huge head-way today, I think. I know I said in the car that I'd tell you all about the strap, my theory, and what Blue said, as soon as we got settled, so here goes." Taking his sheaf of foolscap papers and recipe cards from the inner pocket of the tweed jacket he was now wearing, he emitted a slight burp and tapped his chest, excusing himself. "Those hero sandwiches and fried scallops at Nellie's are starting to get to me."

"I hear one's digestion gets worse as you get older," grinned Trevor. "Go on, what's it all about?"

"Two things I've been contemplating all afternoon and yes, one is related to Monty Tigg's strap. Poor woman, she looked a fright, didn't she, coming up out of that gully? But we should be so grateful. I don't know why the OPP didn't do a search on the other side of the creek, as well."

"They were still thinking suicide then, and by the time we knew for sure it wasn't, we were on the case and they expected us to do it, I guess."

"Well, anyway, when I was at Sela's, just before Mitch came to bring me to you and your straw bale, I noticed a camera case with a little 'C' engraved on it. I assumed the 'C' stood for Cowan, but then when Annette brought out her Ilford film, I remembered that Crispin used to use Ilford a lot. It's where I first heard of it. And Crispin, according to his father, had been feeling well enough in himself to be getting back into photography again. He had two hobbies that always relaxed him. Photography and origami. Loved them both since he was a kid."

"What the hell are you saying, that the camera you saw today at Crabtree Cottage is *his*?"

"Well, I'm pretty sure what Monty brought us is a camera strap, and while it's filthy and has been pummeled into the ground by cattle and horse hooves, I'd say it was originally the same color as the case with the 'C' on it. When I called Blue before we left, he wasn't sure himself, but checked with Sharon—and yes, Crispin indeed had a 'C' on his camera case. I also verified that his was a Minolta Repo, and it was not sent back with his other belongings, to his parents. Now, obviously we need to confirm that what's in the case I saw today *has* a camera in it, and that it's a Repo. Plus, with the quick glance I took, I didn't notice whether there'd been a strap broken, or missing, or not."

"O.K., I know I wasn't crazy about Sela at the beginning; she seemed just all too cocky and confident. But I never took her to be a killer! Is that what you're saying? That she's killed three people including *her own mother*? We've all seen the visible effects her mother's death has had on her, for God's sake!"

"Let's not jump to conclusions. But there's a few other things that came to light when I was in that bungalow today. There's a cigarette butt in her freezer, in a little plastic bag. The butt was a Belmont filter. Anyone we know?"

"Hell! Charlie Squeers! And I suppose the 'C' on the camera case *could* mean it was his, too?"

"Right. That seems pretty suspicious, doesn't it?" Phil suddenly held up one finger and quietly eased himself off his bed. Flinging open the door, he saw a pile of towels and face cloths, with two apples on top, lying neatly on the floor in the hallway. The disappearing back of Cathy Nelson was limping away, twenty feet down the corridor.

"Thanks, Miss Nelson!" Phil called brightly and she raised a hand in acknowledgement. Coming back into the room, Phil tossed one apple to Trevor and took a juicy bite of the other. "This should counterbalance my fried-food heartburn. Brother, she's good. If it wasn't for that slightly irregular step of hers, I might not have heard."

"Hold on a sec," Trevor pulled the bean-bag and footstool right up to the door and leaned back against it, his left ear pressed to the old keyhole. "Neither of 'em will be able to sneak up now! Nobody's *that* quiet!"

"Good idea. So anyway, the butt was one find. The other was that the Cowans used to be practicing Jews, but apparently have lapsed. Now, I don't know exactly how this might tie in, but I intend to have a word with Flintwinch tomorrow about it, as well as further questioning of Sela herself. And while we're on about tomorrow's agenda, Blue says to just gather everyone together and have it all out about the undercover drugs. Says to get threatening, make some promises of jail time if people don't come forward with what they know or suspect. He's fed up, and so am I, frankly. Too many secrets in that place."

"How did you know about the hidey-holes Walter was showing you when I got back from town?"

"I found one in the stone pillars, accidentally. That made me think that there were likely more. A good place to hide drugs, wouldn't you say? In this quasi-statement I got from Walter, he says his cousin Jed—whom you told me Latch told *you* about— was 'a mean man'. He writes that Jed used to tease him mercilessly, pick on him, tell him he was useless. But then he'd say his 'ole Jed' promised to look after him, would keep paying him a little salary if he'd make these holes in which to hide valuables and not tell the Hogarths. And obviously, the valuables were the jewels he turned his stolen cash into, gradually, over the years before the Hogarths even *built* Bayham Brook House. Walter says only about once a year, Jed would ask to come on the property for a 'visit' and would stroll around with Walter, who was here then grooming for the Hogarth's two horses. Jed would take out little black bags that Walter noticed once had 'some necklaces' inside, is how he put it. On top of this, in Annette's first draft of the article for their 'Unscramble' magazine—it's her older brother who's the editor, by the way—she says that indeed 'David Copperfield' was a sort of code word between herself and her brother, when she needed to phone him from The Rookery line. It stood for 'Drug Cover-up', she said. But more crucially: when she was here as a patient several years ago, she caught on to some of the rehabbers getting drugs illicitly, and watched at night when one of the others went behind the cedar tree at the side. When she snuck in behind there during daylight back then, she noticed some bark scraped away, figured it was a purposeful mark of some kind. So, Ovid's Cedar, she started calling it. When she got back here this time, she took her flashlight one night and dug around in the foundation behind the tree, right across from where the tree was bald. She found what is a hollow rectangle—almost a safe. I got Walter to show it to me, but Annette says she's taken photos which should be on the film you took in for developing. What time did you say they'd be ready tomorrow? Three o'clock?"

"That was the best they could do. Even then, it was a pretty big rush-job, evidently. Oh, and guess who I saw in town? Reverend Klassen, looking just like a regular farm hand, except that he came out of a little, frilly curtained tearoom. He was driving a different pickup, one with his family's farm name on it, full of bales."

"Interesting. Annette says we'll find a few of him in her photos as well, out on the property near the fence line, which she thought was suspicious. I suppose he was in town doing some errands for his parents? Maybe picking up more supplies for the church basement work?"

"There wouldn't have been room on that truck bed for anything major; it was crammed with bales."

"Well, I'll sort that out tomorrow hopefully, because what I suggest is this: if the pictures aren't ready until three, we have this massive meeting—which is really going to get some people squirming, and hopefully talking—about eleven. That'll give me a few hours to run out to Edom's Creek and see the reverend, get him to take me out to his father's farm. But I'll drop you at the retreat so you can spell off Blake Biro. I hope there's no major incident tonight for him; there shouldn't be—all the hidey-holes Walter showed me today were empty, so my guess is that while we're here, this scam has all gone quiet."

"Wouldn't that mean we'd be seeing more signs of withdrawal in some of them, if they haven't had their fix in a few days or more?"

"Oh, Gerald's last few injections weren't that old. I suspect he and Karen, possibly Adam and a few others who are maybe taking things orally, they'll have enough in their systems that we won't see withdrawal signs until tomorrow at least. Or, if you can hide a diamond ring away from prying eyes, you can do the same with a small stash of pills. What I don't get is that both Sela and Flintwinch *must* be in on this, surely?"

"You'd think. I mean, the signs are all there, especially if you know what you're seeing, as they do. And it's a fact that Sela Cowan was hiding Gerald's arm from the others."

"We'll get to the bottom of this tomorrow, definitely."

"You told me earlier about the retreat's bales of straw and hay coming from the Klassen family farm, but you didn't say what you actually suspect?"

"No. I didn't."

"Oh, for Pete's sake, not another theory you're keeping to yourself?"

"Well, I probably should. It's too embryonic at the moment."

"Come on, let's throw it around."

"Well, I've had two good chess games with the minister, as you know. While you've been happily shooting the breeze with Dan Blevan. In those games, we've covered a lot of topics including the persecution of some of the Mexican Mennonite families in Chihuahua. His own family, with all nine of his siblings, fled here when he was just a boy because the drugs were moving in and influencing some that 'weren't as strong in their faith', as he put it. Many were being accused, still are, who were perfectly innocent. Violence was erupting also, which they couldn't bear. But you see, I think someone who has been working at the Klassen farm has a tie-in with drugs crossing the border from Mexico. At least the syringes, if not the vials and the drugs themselves, are coming on to that farm stowed in the bales. Which must be marked somehow. Then those marked ones are getting transferred here. I'm guessing they choose mostly straw, as it's packed more loosely and won't hurt a horse as much if a stray needle becomes detached. Not that our murderer would care about the horse, just that he or she might get found-out quicker."

"Of course, there have been cases of the killers of humans who are almost sickeningly lovers of animals."

"True enough. But not, I suspect, in this case."

"Because your theory is… that the reverend and the doctor are in cahoots?"

"Unlikely, but believe me, I've given this a lot of unbiased consideration over the last few days. However, remember when Daniel was introduced to us, Reverend Klassen said he now worked for a few other churches and farms when he wasn't going in to do massages?"

Trevor raised his eyes to the older man's. "All right. Attractive as he is, I'll try to think impartially as well. Since you told me about Dan potentially being the person on the other end of the phone on Crispin's fatal night, and since finding the syringes this morning and knowing drugs must be at the heart of all this, I've given some thought to hiding places for the drugs as they're coming in. Let's say, if just the syringes and vials were coming here in the bales, that's one thing. But the drugs? They can't be out in the hot sun or in an even hotter loft. So, until you found all the hidey-holes this afternoon, which admittedly would be very cool spots in the stone and brickwork, I was thinking on my way into Tillsonburg that perhaps–hidden behind the wall of the basement in the church… The very walls they are rebuilding, maybe?"

"Well, good for you, Trevor. That's one I hadn't considered at all. But we know it's still pretty hot in that basement, and anyway, how would Dan be hiding that from the minister? Unless, again, *those two* are both in on it. Adam's seen him behind Townsend's store where they sell beer illegally. Maybe drugs too? Annette's got proof of him at dusk, skirting the wrought-iron fence where the pillars are. Now you've seen him, without his clerical collar, in town. Perhaps for immoral doings, he takes off his collar. Maybe the reverend is just one smooth talker, leading me into his complete belief in God, and being a good Christian and human."

"In fact, leading you to the very 'stale mate' you've been trying to see your way out of,—"

"Pun intended!" they both chimed together, and smiled.

"We'd better not be in the Nelsons' company too many more days. Habits are contagious, methinks. But at least you're starting to recognize an *actual* pun, Ames."

"Why on earth was Petra Cowan killed? Could she have possibly been in on the drug-running? Maybe it all started with her selling her painkillers for more money, or something? I mean, let's just assume that Charlie *had* been taking drugs, despite what his less-than-detailed autopsy could give us. Because if Karen is, might he not have been also? Maybe he overdosed, by accident? They'd have had to hide that fact—hide *him*—if so. And Crispin either had too much information, or was even trying to stop them? So, I can sort of see why they both had to be killed. But Sela's mother? I just don't get it."

"I've my own theory on that, too, but no way am I going to start— Hold on! Great Scott!"

Trevor said in a hushed voice, "What, did you hear someone out there, again?" He inclined his head toward the door as he started to rise, fingers moving to the knob.

Phil held out his hand to stop him, saying "No, no. It's just... now where're those papers Walter filled out? Here!" Snatching at the folded foolscap which he'd briefly skimmed before phoning Blue, he looked again at his very first question. "*Hell*! When I asked Walter what people he'd seen here in the last few months that had also been here when the Hogarths built the place, I expected to see Petra and Sela's names, of course. Then, this other name he wrote–I thought it said 'Charlotte'. I vaguely remember Flintwinch telling me the names of the Hogarth children and I thought they'd both started with 'ch'. Like an idiot, I didn't write those down, but I think he said 'Cheryl', pronounced as the Brits do, with a 'tch' sound, and maybe 'Char', for Charlotte? It might have also been 'Chester', the surname of one of the couples who bought this place. But they wouldn't have been here twenty-five years ago when the place was built." Agitated, Phil climbed off the bed and thrust the foolscap under Trevor's nose, pointing.

"Walter's handwriting is lovely and neat, but it's so loopy it can still be misread. What's that name right there? After 'Petra, Sela and...'?"

Trevor's mouth opened. "Looks like 'Charlie' to me, Phil. *'Charlie.'*

CHAPTER THIRTEEN

The next morning, as soon as the detectives could pry themselves away from the heavily laden table of sausages, pancakes and Bayham Township maple syrup (as well as several nosy questions from Brian and Cathy Nelson, around which they handily managed to detour), they climbed in the Satellite and headed north. Phil was driving, and dropped Trevor at the front stone pillars of the retreat, urging him to both 'guard and spy' simultaneously. They hadn't heard a report from Officer Biro, so assumed all must have been quiet in the night, and Phil asked Trevor to arrange a meeting in the 'Melon 'n' Cauli' with every person on the property, both guest and staff, full-time and part-time, for eleven o'clock. Biro would have to attend then as well, but Trevor advised that he 'might let him snore away the first few hours of the morning', at least.

Phil then headed toward the United Church in Edom's Creek. He went first to the church's basement door, but finding no one below, he walked up the incline to the manse. Reverend Klassen opened the oak portal wide, welcoming him in.

"D.I. Steele! Have you had your morning coffee, yet? I just made a fresh brew."

"I have, thanks. I was actually wondering if we might take a quick drive over to your father's farm?"

"My fa—? Sure, I suppose. What's wrong?"

Phil sat in the chair the minister had pulled out for him, in the hallway between the kitchen and the tiny, wall-papered parlor. Klassen propped himself on the telephone table's bench there, looking worried.

"Nothing's exactly wrong. Only, I've learned that all the hay and straw for the stables at the retreat are grown and baled by your father and his crew."

"Oh my. Don't scare me! With all these murders, I thought you came to say something was wrong out on the homestead."

"Sorry, I didn't mean to imply anything had happened. But there may be something connected...Look, I'll just come out and tell you, but first—have you finished all the paneling in the church yet?"

"No, there's still a half-wall of studs to cover."

"Let's walk over there and take a look, shall we? Grab your own coffee."

As the two walked to the church's social rooms, Phil told the minister about their finds the day before, and their current urgent concerns. Not willing to trust implicitly just because he liked someone, Philip closely observed the man in the clerical collar, slanting glances from under his brows and freckled forehead, walking with a slouch in order to do so.

"Daniel? You think Dan might be involved in *drugs*?"

"It's a theory we're working at the moment."

"But if he'd been stashing anything behind the walls while we were tacking up paneling, I'd have noticed. Most times I was there holding the sheets while he hammered in the finishing nails."

"Ah, that's what I wanted to check out. Have you noticed if those had more of a head on them than the usual type of finishing nails? Because if he did want to get behind there in secret, he'd need to be able to pull at least two out with ease."

"Let's look. You go along that side of the room, and I'll rub my hand down all the joined seams on this side. I expect you mean lower down?"

"Not just lower, no. He could have drugs stacked here and there, on some braces acting as shelves. And it *is* possible that he did it without you noticing, you know. All the better if he managed it, because you could swear you were always with him when boards were being nailed in. As you just did." *You could also,* Phil thought, though he didn't like to, *purposely have taken the side of the room in which you know something is hidden.* "How about you take this side, and I'll go over there?"

The minister paused and stared. "Oh, I see. You think I suggested I take that wall because I know something? Very well, good thinking." He crossed the room almost too eagerly.

Now Phil was again uncertain, but he couldn't let this show. Reverend Klassen read his mind. "Ah, you think I'm playing out some kind of chess strategy, here? That I'm double-bluffing? Feel free to run your hand down all the seams in the whole of this room and the little storage room over there, then." The minister sat down to sip his coffee, but was grinning to show he wasn't angry. *Or, more importantly, nervous.*

Philip took over ten minutes to feel each pairing of nails carefully all the way up and down the seams between the thin panels, most of which were above the checkerboard-like wainscot. He also tapped on some of the squares of the black, ivory and white checkerboard itself, then called to the minister who was now tidying in the kitchen, "How long since any of these tiles have been removed? If someone had, say, every tenth ivory one as a cubby hole behind it…"

"No such luck, my good man. If they were actual tiles, it would be brilliant of course. But those are just faux-painted to *look* like tiles. One of my sisters did it, years ago. She's an interior designer and was just starting out, wanted to practice on a big space. Then she coated them all with a porcelain finish of some kind. Pleasingly deceptive, isn't it?"

"*Far too much deception in this entire case,*" said Phil to himself and continued his search in the only smaller room remaining now that the others had been incorporated. Though not much more than a storage room, this area felt cooler and there was a fan running somewhere above his head.

He called, "What's this little fan doing in here?" It seemed odd to have a built-in fan in a storage room; it was more like an exhaust over a stove than anything.

"Oh, it blows up to my pulpit in the sanctuary. Keeps me a trifle cooler standing there with the robes on, in summer! And the other unit vents some of the hot air from the nave back down here."

Phil stood looking up at the two different units, thinking, as well as feeling cooler from the fan pointing down on him. But no matter how he figured it, he couldn't see that anything could be hidden in those two vents; they were wide open and he could practically see up to the pulpit.

When he was finished checking the nails in the new paneling in that room, all of which seemed to be miniscule and hammered completely flush with the wood, some even indented, he stuck his head through an incomplete section and looked at the unfinished side where the studs were still exposed. Then he reached in as far as he could and felt around, but to no avail. This idea of Trevor's wasn't going to wash.

However, he did notice some heavy red curtains, of a velveteen fabric, sitting on a chair, covered with a clear plastic sheet to keep the carpentry dust from them.

"Reverend? Could you come in here?"

"Sure!" The minister came and leaned on the door frame. "Find something?"

"Well, not what I was looking for, exactly. But—those red curtains, where are they from?"

"Oh, in the winters we have them hanging on either side of the sanctuary. Sometimes the kids put on little Sunday School shows up there. Also, the red is always nice dressed with greenery for Christmas and such. But in the summer we take them down. Too hot and stuffy up there as it is. We need as much air flow as we can get, believe me."

Philip slid off the plastic sheet and picked up the first set of heavy draperies. Underneath, between those and the next set, lay a red tie-back. Just the one.

He pointed. "Do you usually have two of those?"

The minister looked. "Sure. Everything has to be uniform and matched in a church, you know. As if God cares about aesthetic symmetry." He smiled a bit sardonically. "It'll be there somewhere, I imagine."

I doubt that very much, thought Phil, his heart heavy. "I've finished here, Reverend. Let's go."

Trevor's theory of drugs in the church basement's new walls hadn't panned out, but the source of a possible murder weapon had come to light as a result. As the two men set off in the minister's old truck on their way to the Klassen farm, Phil hoped his own theory about how the drug-smuggling was done would prove at least that successful.

And that he wasn't currently sitting beside a killer.

•   •   •

Polly Jane Whistler came out of the Melon 'n' Cauli, having just finished a most pleasing breakfast of fruit salad and carrot muffins. She had seen the young Trevor Ames enter the dining hall, go to the buffet table, and take a muffin for himself. She was going to ignore him completely, as she was sitting at a table with Monty Tigg and Latch. But Trevor caught her eye and gave her a quick wink which, because she was peering over her reading glasses at the time instead of looking through them, she clearly saw. When she smiled slightly, Monty said, "Thou're well-chuffed abou' summat, Jane?"

P.J. recovered quickly and simply said, "I haven't had such a tasty carrot muffin since my cook from ten years ago used to bake them. That Ruth is a marvel!"

In the corridor, trying to decide if she wanted to swim this morning and perhaps poke around in the change room's open shelves, or if she would take a stroll out to the vegetable garden and see to whom she might chat, she noticed a woman she'd not yet met, wearing a long lab coat and tight blue jeans hurrying down the hall with head bent, looking at a clipboard in her hand. P.J. suddenly became engrossed, looking at one of the tall potted plants beside the benches. She said, "My goodness, these are Fiddle Leaf Figs, aren't they? How rare, excuse me—" and she reached her arm out as if to arrest the movement of the other woman.

"Hello, I'm Jane Jellyby, I don't believe we've met?" P.J. then stared rather pointedly at the top breast pocket of the lab coat. "I don't see a name tag, dear. You are—?"

" I'm Sela Cowan. The full-time nurse here," said Sela flatly.

"Oh, my, I'm so sorry. I mean, about your poor mother. I just heard yesterday afternoon. Such a tragedy, dear."

"Thank you, Mrs. Jellyby," Sela was about to continue down the hall, but P.J. spouted hurriedly, "I wouldn't have stopped you to ask about these plants, if I'd seen your name tag. I'm sure you have more important things to worry about than telling me where to purchase some of these beauties."

"Yes, I'm afraid one of my name tags went through the wash last week and my name is now illegible. And I've lost the other. Anyway, I don't know about these plants, but you could ask a fellow named Bob Haggerty. He'd be down in the garden this morning, I imagine."

Sela put her nose back to the clipboard and scurried away, leaving P.J. to tap her lip with her index finger and stare after her.

· · ·

At ten minutes to eleven o'clock, Trevor and a yawning Officer Biro stood on either side of the doors just inside the 'Melon 'n' Cauli' Tavern, watching the crowd as they found seats or decided to have one last smoke on the small terrace adjoining the glass doors at the back of the room. Latch Lupin was reading a magazine and Trevor noticed that the ends of Phil's godmother's blue-tinted, squashed-down hair were still damp from a swim at which she'd obviously mismanaged her bathing cap.

Phil strode in just then, more rushed and distracted than Trevor had ever seen him. Leaning toward him, Trevor whispered, "Anything?"

Phil shook his head. "Dead end on both counts. Well, almost. Are you two standing guard here?" He smiled over at Biro, who raised a finger in greeting, all the energy he could apparently muster after only a few hours of sleep.

"Not really. But we just thought we'd present a bit of authority before you got here. Dr. Flintwinch, Ruth, Jackie and Mitch aren't here yet."

"Glad everyone else is. Even the Haggertys, good stuff." Phil scanned the room then walked over to Sela and bent over her, speaking softly.

"How has your morning been, Sela? Are you managing?"

Her red-rimmed eyes looked up at him and she shrugged, saying nothing.

He went on to the back of the room to speak to Bob and Martha Haggerty. Martha was not wearing her nurse's uniform; she must have joined her husband on her day off.

Jeremiah Flintwinch popped his head in between Ames and Biro and called, "D.I. Steele!" Phil jogged toward him and the doctor beckoned for him to come outside into the sunlit corridor. He lowered his voice. "Reverend Klassen is on the phone in my office. He says he needs to speak with you immediately."

Phil hurried to the door marked Chesney Fold and entered, snatching at the heavy black receiver. "Philip Steele here."

"Were you expecting Daniel to show up for your meeting? I know you gave me permission to give it a miss since I don't really work there, but…"

"I haven't checked with D.I. Ames, but he was certainly on his list of people to call in."

"It's just, I don't think he's coming. Because I just saw him drive down past the church in his Camaro, on the side road, then turn and head north, not south, as he should have done."

Phil thought for a moment, then said, "Right. Thanks, Reverend. I'll get someone on it."

Glancing at his watch, he quickly dialed Blue's number at his office. His secretary told him that D.C. Cobalt hadn't come in yet, that he was trying to spend mornings at home with his wife. When Phil got through to their home number, Sharon answered.

"Oh, Phil. How is P.J. making out? Is she quite safe, do you think?"

"Sharon, I really can't speak now, but I promise you'll both hear all about it later today. Is Blue there? It's really important!"

"Sorry, Phil, no. He popped out for some bread to do our lunch sandwiches. I can have him phone you back. Where are—"

"Rats! Gotta go, Sharon. Tell him to phone Flaherty at headquarters. I'll have to get him onto this. He can explain to Blue. Bye!"

He didn't know by heart the number of Flaherty's office in Trevor's downtown headquarters, so it took him several moments of searching through his notes to find it. When he got through to the supervisor, he spoke quickly, sharing that a suspect was possibly fleeing, either toward Toronto airport or one of the train stations along the main highway. He gave him the details on the

Camaro, although he could only remember that the license plate had started with a 'Y'. But they could easily have someone phone the Ministry of Transportation to get it, radio it out to the cars. The most important thing was that the cogs were in motion.

Feeling both relieved and on high alert, Phil made his way back to the dining hall, glancing again at his watch. It was now seven minutes past the hour. When he entered he saw that both the doctor and Ruth were sitting near Sela's table, and also noted that the artist couple, smocks stained and hands multi-colored, were in attendance as well.

"All present, then?" he said from the door, then pulled Trevor outside and told him that an all-points bulletin was out on Daniel Blevan. He tried not to notice the blink of disappointment which was his colleague's only reaction. Hastily, he moved back into the meeting.

"Now then, we've called everyone here to get to the bottom of several points that have become very apparent in the last twenty-four hours or so." He looked directly at P.J. and said, "I'm sorry, ma'm. We met yesterday, upstairs. What did you say your name was?"

"Mrs. Jane Jellyby, Officer," said his godmother primly, intentionally using an incorrect title for him.

"Well, Mrs. Jellyby. There's really no need for you to be here as you've only just come. I'm sure you've got the *scoop* on everything that's happened here the last few weeks, but really — please feel free to go about your *business*."

As P.J. got up to leave the dining hall she realized she daren't pass too closely to Phil, who stood in the middle of the room, all eyes upon him. But she took a chance that no one was watching Trevor Ames as she slipped him a tiny piece of paper, reading '*r.r. pin—nametag? Sela!*'

She headed out the double doors and then leaned back against the wall, panting in excitement. She had hoped Phil would do this, but she'd wanted to be there to make sure that if she *was* excused, everyone would hear. It had to look normal, natural. He really hadn't needed to emphasize two of their cue words, which they'd set up on the many phone calls between herself, Blue and Phil in the days following Petra's murder. She'd been almost expecting them, if he released her from the meeting as she'd hoped. 'Scoop' meant 'Snoop' and 'Go about your business', meant 'go poke around in someone else's.' Problem was, she didn't know what was top priority. Perhaps Lucy's vacant room. She'd been suspicious that it was taking so long to clean and 'air' it, before offering it to her. Then, if she could get in, she might try Gerald's room...

In the meantime, Phil was allowing himself to get angry, deliberately raising his voice to create tension. "Everyone here is keeping some secret. Everyone. Even if it's just that your last names aren't your own. Obviously you've been told to do that, here. Of course we understand about the need for privacy. But that's rather back-fired on you all now, hasn't it?" He allowed a brief pause as his eyes scanned the room, letting the point sink in.

"How many of you knew what Charlie's real surname was, I wonder? Obviously the good doctor was aware, as he is of all of yours. And Sela must have. But how about you, Ruth? And Bob and Martha? This is a small rural area, so I'm sure you all knew that the young Hogarth boy, Charlie, was back here where he'd grown up, to try to get clean on his family's former estate. The boy named 'Charles', of course, for his father's favorite author."

Phil wanted time for the gasps and exchanges of glances; Trevor and Blake Biro had been instructed to circle the room, watching for reactions that seemed out of the ordinary. Trevor, he knew, had not had many minutes to fill Biro in once the sleepy officer had been shaken awake. But it would have been enough time to ensure that this small back-up team would not be looking surprised themselves, and could keep poker faces as they watched their roomful of suspects.

"Sela grew up here with the Hogarth children. You can't make us believe that she didn't know Charlie, no matter how many years may have passed, no matter how many hard drugs had ravaged his face, since she'd last seen him." Philip took a moment to look at Sela, who had her back turned to him, face leaning on her hand. "And Charlie's secret wife Karen—do you really want us to believe that you didn't know Charlie had grown up here and that his family still had lots of money in the pot?"

Karen rose to her feet unsteadily. *Drugs, anger, or nerves?* Again, it was hard for Phil to tell, as she hollered at him. "I didn't know! Of course I knew his name was Hogarth, 'cause that's mine now, too; it was on the marriage certificate. But I didn't know the Hogarths lived *here*. I'd never heard that name until a few days before our wedding." Karen started to flap her hands and sniffle. Trevor walked to her, took her arm, and encouraged her to sit back down, gallantly handing her a clean, folded handkerchief from his pocket.

"And Dr. Flintwinch, you must have known that Charlie would be recognized by at least some of the staff who've lived in these parts most of their lives?" Phil didn't want to give away the fact that it was Walter's written statement which had led him to this theory about Charles Hogarth, son of Neville and Jane, brother to Cheryl. "Didn't you think that would be a breach of the confidentiality, to have him be recognized here?"

"I was very worried about it, indeed," said Flintwinch. "I had tried to persuade Mrs. Hogarth and her daughter and daughter's husband that this was not the place for Charlie, that he needed to be somewhere where he could feel safely anonymous, and as if he were starting fresh. But they were determined that it would be better for him to be in some place 'comfortable' and familiar. And they thought it would help if his childhood friend Sela was here to help make him better." Sela gave a whimper at that point; Flintwinch leaned across and patted her hand.

"Then there's another big secret that many of you have been keeping, isn't there? I don't expect you all to raise your hands and tell us how many of you knew of, or were actually taking, drugs since you've been here. Drugs being sold to you by some unscrupulous staff, or members of this community. But I know for a fact that there have to be five of you in this room, minimum, who know this."

The room erupted.

"Drugs? What drugs?"

"What'd he say?"

"No one's allowed any drugs here, we can't even have aspirin in our rooms!"

Phil noticed that Trevor and Blake were doing an excellent job looking for the people who were either sitting still and not reacting, or who were leaping out of their seats and over-reacting. He himself noticed that Dr. Flintwinch was rubbing his temples and shaking his head slowly back and forth, head down.

"I'll be speaking to Doctor Flintwinch and the two nurses in private, immediately following this meeting, but—"

"I don't know what you're talking about, Detective! I know nothing about any drugs, I can tell you that!" Martha Haggerty said staunchly.

"Well, then, Martha, you're free to make that abundantly clear in your written statement. But I feel that the rest of you, whether rehabilitation patients, regular guests, or other staff,"—here Phil looked hard at Della and Clara—"will need to think long and hard before you decide to keep anything more from us about the drugs that have been coming onto this property. We've found syringes out at the stables—"

"I reckon them's for t' horses, innit?" Monty Tigg seemed genuinely confused.

"Not in bundles of twenty hidden in straw bales, ma'm, no."

More gasps. Phil continued, "and we've found many of the hiding places in stone and brick work around the property, places that would have made ideal spots for temporarily stashing the drugs until they were sold on, or taken either orally or by injection by the very people who were meant to be getting rid of the foul stuff forever." Phil felt Annette's eyes on him and knew she was praying that her own cover wouldn't be blown. She'd have a better story than ever for the family-run 'Unscramble' magazine, once this case was solved and put to bed.

"D.I. Ames and I will be available to any of you all afternoon if you'd like to come and tell us what you know, or what you've suspected. Officer Biro will be asleep this afternoon, but you can speak with him tonight if you'd rather. Alternatively, you can write up your statement and simply hand it to one of us. But," and here Phil raised his voice again and looked his most belligerent, "we do expect some of you to come forth and admit what you've so obviously been keeping from us. And what was more than likely the reason poor Charlie and Crispin were killed, and Sela's mother as well, however indirectly. Now I just want you all to sit here and ponder that for a moment while I have a word with D.I. Ames. Outside, here." Phil stepped out through the back doors onto the small patio where many of the guests smoked. Trevor followed and Phil closed the door firmly, leaning against them.

"I'm about to wrap it up. You have anything to add in there?"

"Nope, good job rattling the bars of the cages, though." Trevor stood directly in front of Phil so that no one watching from inside would see him hand over the tiny piece of paper. "Your godmother handed this to me before she left the room. Mean anything to you?"

Phil read it, then swore under his breath. "Damn, if that little woman hasn't sorted that clue for us, I'll just bet. She means the weird pin with the curly-cue that I found up on the railroad bridge might be from Sela's name tag, which I gather is missing."

Trevor stared at him, his eyes growing bigger. "You mean...?"

"I mean, we *have* to get a look in her house today while she's over here working. I've got to look at that camera case and get back in her freezer for that butt we think was Charlie's. Listen, Trevor, trot upstairs and find P.J., will you? Tell her to get back to her own room, wherever she is, 'cause I'm about to dismiss this meeting. Tell her it's more crucial than ever that she 'sprain an ankle' on the tennis court right after lunch. Not so much so that she can get a look in Sela's first aid supplies out there, but to stall her while I'm over the road in her cottage."

"Right-o."

"We'll see if we can grab a bite here, then I'll have the big talk with Flintwinch, and you just follow Sela from a distance. We won't try to question her just yet, or even get a statement. We need evidence, not just all this conjecture. I'll take our camera over there and get some shots in situ. As soon as I'm done with the doc, and once I've seen P.J. head to the court, I'll scoot across the road."

"Right. I'll go pull Mrs. Jellyby from out of someone's closet."

Phil was not about to use that inappropriate point in time to mention that Trevor was actually *missing* a pun there, and regarding his own personal lifestyle too. "I won't let anyone out of this dining hall until you come back and give me the nod so I know P.J.'s tucked up in a corner of her own room with a book. Innocent as Shirley Temple."

●   ●   ●

"I honestly had no idea. Truly," said Jeremiah Flintwinch in 'The Fold' a half hour later. "I can only say how horrified I am to realize this has, in *any* way, been going on under my stupid nose, and for how long? Lord, what a complete idiot you must think me. Obviously, there were things I couldn't quite make sense of here and there—behavioral patterns that didn't really fit. For instance, if we used hypnotherapy on someone like Karen, it would seem to send her into a highly agitated state of emotions, so we would discontinue it, just go back to mantras and concentration exercises with her."

"What about before this group of patients? You didn't notice obvious signs then? And how about the radical behaviors of Lucy Tox?" Phil planned to remain very skeptical of the psychiatrist's seemingly earnest statements of innocence.

"I can go back through all my notes for years, and show you the red asterisks I've inserted wherever there's something I've questioned. But I would often attribute these things to either the typical schizophrenic or psychotic behaviors that would exhibit with patients already diagnosed by preceding doctors, as in the case of Lucy, *or* to strong withdrawal symptoms from a number of different street drugs, or even to some of our more unusual techniques which we're trying to incorporate here, experimental as some of them may be."

"You didn't find it strange to see, especially in your private sessions, that eye-pupils might have been dilated when they shouldn't have been, that a hand might be shaking, or that in the middle of a humid Ontario summer, forearms were covered by long-sleeved shirts?"

"Of course, to all the above! But they could also be explained away by withdrawal symptoms. And the coverings, if I ever asked, simply a way to prevent sunburn and heat rash as they went about their outdoor chores. Now you tell me that there were drugs and vials and paraphernalia being stashed all over the property in little hiding spots in foundation walls, in the pillars of the fence line?"

"Correct, and thanks to Walter finally deciding it was time to tell all, we've found most of them, I believe. Empty, of course. Except I think there's likely one or two in those stone walls over at Crabtree Cottage as well. I may have to ask Walter to escort me over there in a few hours. I'll get to Sela in a moment, but for now can you tell me more about Charlie Hogarth? Because of course we're right, aren't we? That *was* the Charlie about whom Walter was referring on his statement?"

"Yes. Of course I couldn't divulge that to you before, nor did I see how it was relevant. The Commissioner of the OPP was told of his identity by me personally, in Toronto, the day Sela called me there to inform me his body'd been found. But she always acted as though she didn't know him as anything more than Charlie Squeers. It would have been years since she'd laid eyes on him. And while the Hogarths and my own parents had been friends after the war, we weren't so close in recent years that I'd have recognized Charlie myself after nearly two decades. In fact, most of the organizing of him coming here was achieved through the Hogarth daughter, his sister Cheryl, and one of the new owners, Donna Lawton. The tennis player, you know? Those two knew each other through the circuit apparently, so I had very little to do with him being brought here, and he and I never discussed our parents or our past. As you know, it's part of our policy *not* to produce reminders of patients' pasts in any way. Because therein lies the root of all their evils, all their triggers. We concentrate very much on focusing on the present, and just a little, on the future."

"You mention your parents, the Schneiders, Doctor. I have to ask—were they connected to the Nazi party in some way? Is that the real reason for your name change, and for you coming to a different country, to separate yourself from them?"

"Good God, no! But I've only just found out this week that Sela had been under the impression that we were. For years! When she was under sedation from the Quaaludes and Mandrax I was giving her during those three days after she found her poor mother, she told me she was sorry she'd ever suspected our family of having been responsible for killing her father. He was in Auschwitz, you know. Just as my great-uncle and aunt were. Arbeiter Cohen. Of course Sela never knew him, but her mother told me once that even as a little girl, she'd always felt his loss deeply, that she had a lot of anger about the war, that she probably should be given some 'help' in that aspect of her life. But again, my stupidity! I wouldn't have had time to treat her professionally myself, nor would it have been appropriate. But I should have helped make sure she had a colleague..."

"So your family was also Jewish?"

"Of course. Certainly."

Phil now remembered, feeling a little foolish, that the doctor had stated that his father wouldn't have eaten ham, but had had fun naming the clubhouse the 'Tots'n'ham' for his friend, who loved the meat fried up with the then-new 'Tater Tots'. "It seems that Sela has actually held a grudge against you for years, though, until recently?"

Flintwinch stared. "That–that's what it sounds like. According to what's been admitted to me this week. I never dreamed, of course...she's a good actress. I always thought we were well-matched co-workers, even friends."

"You do see where I'm going with this? It seems obvious to me that she's been involved in bringing drugs on to the property, then secretly selling them, or at least doling them out to the patients. Perhaps to see you fail? To see the retreat fail?"

The psychiatrist took several moments to register this. He blinked, raked his hand through his dark curls, shook his head.

"*Sela*? Sela is a nurse."

"There are as many nurses dealing drugs today as probably anyone. There are just as likely to be evil agendas among the nursing profession, as any."

"But Sela really does love trying to help others. I've seen it. She's full of compassion..."

"If she was being paid a good sum to sell drugs to addicted people who just had to have a fix, and if she felt she could somehow get back at you for what she perceived was your family's crime against her own..."

"*Hell!* Her mother's surgery! She's been trying so hard to save up enough to send her mother to New York. She hated seeing her mother in pain. I can actually see her doing almost *any*thing if it meant that she could alleviate her mother's pain."

"Which is why it seems unlikely that she could be our murderer."

"You–you think Sela Cowan is the killer of three people? Including her own beloved mother? Impossible!"

"Doctor, at the risk of pointing out the glaringly bloody obvious here, you've been pretty naïve in regard to other aspects of this case. Could you not also be mistaken about this?"

Flintwinch squeezed his eyes closed and simply shook his head again.

"I have a lot more questions for you, but perhaps you'd save us time in that respect if you simply started writing out a statement, covering everything you now understand to be truth, in hindsight. We have a full afternoon ahead of us. I'd like you to try to keep your patients indoors here today, if you can. No chores, no activities. It's probably safest if everyone just sticks to his or her room, or The Rookery if they must. I realize you can't ask this of your other guests, those not here for treatment. But I wouldn't even advise swimming in here."

"Do you think we're all still in danger somehow? You're not serious?"

"I'm deadly serious. Deadly. So is someone else. Sela Cowan hasn't been acting on her own, no matter what her motives. Please start on your statement."

•   •   •

No sooner did Philip Steele step away from the doctor's office than he was met by Bob Haggerty, looking extremely out of place indoors, wearing a straw hat and earth-soiled overalls. "I've been waiting to speak with you, Detective."

"Yes, Bob?"

"Actually, I think I'd best show you. After what you were saying in the meeting, I don't guess I oughta be keepin' this to myself any more. Even if I'm wrong…"

"I have a few minutes, Bob. Lead on."

Phil followed the farmer to the top of the hill above Drury Jane, from which he could indeed hear the sound of damp snoring. Haggerty didn't seem to notice, but stomped on until he was part way down the hill, well off the trail.

"Look. I've been worried about this for a few weeks now. I should have said something, earlier, maybe, but I just thought it was another of the many experiments in health foods and natural eating, and stuff, that they like to do here." The farmer pointed to a slapped-together pyramid of old panes of glass erected in a spruce glade, under which were growing orange-red mushrooms, polka-dotted with little white spots. All around were drying mounds of manure, and Phil instantly remembered the small spills of straw and horse fertilizer Trevor had found near the trail, with just the tiniest indication that a wheelbarrow had been pushed there.

"Pretty mushrooms, Bob. Like the little toadstools you see in children's books with fairies perched on them. Or under them. What's the concern?"

"Well, for one thing – why didn't someone tell me about this? I'm supposed to be in charge of everything edible that's being grown here. This seems kinda secret, doesn't it? Hidden away, like? And while there *are* mushrooms that are perfectly edible that look like that, these little jobs *aren't*, I'm pretty sure! See those additional yellow dots in some of the white? Look here—" Bob pulled out a small handbook from the apron pocket of his overalls. "I looked this up when I first found this set-up, and I brought the book today, in case I got a chance to show you at the meeting. Now, after what you've told us… Well, look!"

Phil took the book and, following Bob's dirty finger, read the paragraph:

Amanita muscaria (red fly agaric). "*This mushroom has a red or orange cap with small white plaques. . .In recent years, the consumption of it has increased among young people due to its hallucinogenic properties. Although the prevalence of its consumption is lower than that for marijuana and hashish, it is presumed that in the future there will be more patients poisoned by these toxic hallucinogenic mushrooms... Amanita muscaria is considered one of the most remarkable and beautiful mushrooms. Its consumption is sometimes used for its psychedelic effects*" *causing a state of euphoria or exhilaration.* *

Amanita Muscaria. Anita's Mascara. *I'll be damned,* thought Phil. *Lucy Tox, her Dickens surname an actual clue to the very toxins she was ingesting, had been trying to lead them to this, in her last words to Flintwinch.* And there he'd been, like an idiot, rummaging through Annette/Anita's make-up bag! Would Trevor ever let him live that one down? Never mind Polly Jane! Ruefully, he suspected that if he'd even mentioned 'Anita's Mascara' to her, she'd have suggested it sounded like a poisonous fungus.

"Well, good for you, Bob. This could be part of the case, indeed. Who's to say that all manner of drugs in varying stages of development aren't being sold right here to some of the patients, or *from* here to members of the public as well? How did you stumble across this in the first place?"

"I got here really early one day a few weeks back. I had an agricultural society meeting that afternoon, so wanted to get all my work done before I went. But my wheelbarrow wasn't in the garden *or* out at the stables, where it sometimes is, if we've been bringing loads of old manure down for the veggies and herbs. I happened to ask that Crispin fellow if he knew where it might be, as he'd been assigned to garden duty with me that week. He said he'd seen it lying over here by where they were working on Drury Jane. So I figured maybe Walter was using it to help the builders on the stonework. That's the work he still loves best, you know, masonry. Even though it's all too heavy for him now. But later in the day I asked him, and he said no, but that he'd seen it just down the trail from here. I went snooping, and I found—this."

"Great work, Bob. I hope more come forward this afternoon with some tales of drug-use or other suspicious activity. You've never run across a syringe or even a little needle when dealing with the straw?"

"Needle in a haystack sort of thing?"

"A little more literal."

The farmer took some time to digest this. "They smuggling stuff in, in the bales, is that it? No sir, I never have. But then I only use straw at the very end of the season, to cover the garlic and onions and such. They'd know that would be when I'd need it, and probably not do it then."

Phil thanked the farmer again and they parted company. Up near the parking lot, he drew their camera from the ice chest in the back seat of the Satellite. He saw Trevor in the distance, wandering about with a hoe, poking along at the flower beds that surrounded the Tots 'n' ham. Camera around his neck, Philip approached his colleague.

Lowering his voice, he said, "Are you looking for something in particular?"

"No. Just looking busy." Trevor nodded at the clubhouse wall, keeping his own voice sotto voce. "Sela's in there on her own, and Latch and 'Mrs. Jellyby' are with Jackie and Mitch. They're going to play doubles, I guess."

"Any word about Blevan?"

"Nothing yet. I told Ruth and the doctor that we might be expecting a call. Doc gave me one of their walkie-talkies."

"I'm worried the reverend might have put us on a false trail."

Trevor looked at him calmly for a beat. "Are you saying that after all your inferences about my getting too buddy-buddy with a suspect, it might be that you've done the very same?"

Philip shrugged. "I just know I'm more suspicious of everyone right now."

"Well, add another to your list. Walter just came up to me and stuttered out that the reason he thinks he had his heart attack back in January is that he saw his dead cousin Jed. Jed appeared to him out at the stables and threatened him by making a cut-throat gesture. Walter now admits he *did* take one black pouch full of jewels after his cousin died. I guess you scared that out of him, even though it's not relevant to the drug-trafficking."

"O.K., but I'm not adding a ghost to an already enormous list of suspects. The OPP, or the Port Dune police, or whoever's dealing with that old robbery can have at him when we've got these murders solved." Philip looked over his shoulder, then lowered his voice even further. "Listen, I've got a lot to tell you, but crucially, I have to grab a few shots down there," he nodded in the trail's direction to Drury Jane, "and then head across the road. P.J. knows to give me about five minutes after she sees me head toward the highway?"

"Yup. I told her upstairs that you wouldn't be going the regular route, down the hill and out through the gate. Did you know that's what the funny little elevator was for, by the way? So that Sela could push her mother's wheelchair straight across the road, into the laundry and games rooms below, then they'd raise her up to the main level to access the dining hall."

"I figured. O.K., I'll make it look like I'm snapping photos along the main drive and just make my way across the road and hike back down the highway where Miss Cowan won't see me if she looks out. But hopefully P.J. will keep her too busy. Stay sharp!"

Trevor went back to poking in the shrubs with his hoe. Phil snapped seven shots, all from different angles, of the mushrooms and their tented greenhouse. On the way back up the trail, hearing Officer Biro's snores still emanating from the unfinished wall of the stone cabin, he suddenly had another thought and hurried back to Trevor again.

"You mentioned the elevator just now," he said, in lowered voice again. "While P.J.'s having her ankle treated, will you get in the house and check the floorboards in it, poke with your hoe up into the top above the cage part? That's one of the last places no one's searched around here, and I wonder…"

"Brilliant. Yeah, those OPP wouldn't have done it, and we sure as hell haven't thought of it."

"Just, if you do find something, presume fingerprints, right?"

"Of course."

"O.K., I'm off now. I'll make a big fuss of my camera and some shots around that forsythia, when I first make my way down the lane. So dear old blue-bonnet, sharp-eyed Susie out there sees me leaving."

CHAPTER FOURTEEN

"Oh, my, oh, ouch! That's it, right there! Ooo, I think it may be swelling!" P.J. harkened back to last winter when she'd tripped on her fuzzy pink slippers and broken her ankle. As the pain was still somewhat fresh in her mind, especially remembering the way Doctor Graham had twisted it this way and that when examining it, she was better able to pretend she was genuinely in distress.

"Thanks, Latch. You may all go on back to the house. Just let the doctor and Ruth know I'll be a little while tending Mrs. Jellyby before I come back in," said Nurse Cowan tiredly.

"Should 'a wrapped it yesterday, I guess, Missus," said Latch as he made to leave the Tots 'n'ham, after hanging up all four racquets on the wall. "She near-as sprained it out there *then*, Sela."

"Well then, you probably shouldn't have played today."

"Oh, I do love my tennis, and it's one of the reasons I chose to come here, you know. Playing on a clay court is always a treat! Ooo, ow!" P.J. threw in for good measure as Sela squeezed her ankle.

"Just leave your foot here on this stool. I'll go get the wraps— I keep all my bigger bandages in the washroom."

Which would explain why I couldn't find them yesterday, thought P.J. In a speedy move reminiscent of her days being dipped in the Lindy Hop, Phil's godmother threw herself onto the floor and searched underneath the small kneehole in the nurse's desk. Bingo! She spied a little package taped to the far back corner. But she knew she didn't dare explore further as she heard Sela returning.

"Mrs. Jellyby! Are you all right?"

She hadn't even had time to get back into her chair and prop her foot up again, so Polly Jane Whistler stayed silent and still for a moment, prone on the thin carpet.

"Mrs. Jellyby!" Sela tapped her cheeks lightly and P.J. slowly opened her eyes.

"Ooo, oh the pain! I must have fainted! Have you some ice I could put on it before we bandage it?"

The nurse helped her to her chair again, biting her lip, and tenderly helped her to put her foot back on its rest. "Just a moment, I think there're some ice cubes in the little freezer of the bar fridge here." Sela crossed the room and P.J. eyed the locked drawer she'd found yesterday, wondering how she could get the nurse to open it as well. But she was out of ideas. Except...

"What about a painkiller? An Aspirin or two?" she whimpered.

"Oh, let's just see how the ice works first, shall we? And then I'll strap it up firmly for you so we can get you back to the house. There's an elevator in there you can use to get up to your room. There now, I've put these cubes into a bag. Let's just hold this on the ankle bone until it starts to numb up a bit."

•   •   •

With the maids and Ruth in the kitchen, and most of the addicts—or whatever he was meant to call them—up in their rooms, Trevor figured it was a perfect time to search the elevator. He presumed the doctor was in his Chesney Fold, or possibly The Growlery as he'd noticed both doors were shut when he'd passed them, feeling a little conspicuous as he was still toting around a hoe.

He pulled the antiquated cage doors open and stepped in, using the hoe first to see if any floorboards on the elevator's bottom surface might be loose. Finding it completely solid, with nary a creak, he next pushed upward with the hoe, forcing wooden square panels of the ceiling up. But he could see the open air and daylight from the upper story through them, so it would appear there was no cubby hole between the elevator's cage and the upper cables and mechanism. However, that made him wonder. Leaving the interior of the elevator, he went down the corridor to the Bubble and Squeak, also empty as per Phil's and Doctor Flintwinch's instructions. He walked to the side of the pool and yanked on the ladder that went into the deep end. It pulled up off its metal holders and he retraced his steps, caring not about the chlorinated drops of water he was leaving behind him, to the elevator's cage where he hung the hooked top of the ladder on the cage doors. He then grabbed his hoe again and climbed the four steps of the ladder so that he could peer on top.

At that point Ruth McCorkle bustled down the hallway pushing a trolley toward the dining hall. Pausing, she looked up at him and remarked, "Detective Inspector Ames, you ain't got a workin' noggin', if you think that's safe! Wan' me ta hold that ladder for ya?"

"That's all right, Ruth. Thank you. I'm perfectly secure."

"Well, on your head be it! An' you just might end up on it, too!"

She clattered away again and Trevor was glad they'd had the meeting that morning; at least she didn't want to know what he was searching for. That, it now appeared, was patently obvious to all.

He craned his neck. There was something dark in the far back, he was sure of it. Now, if his hoe could just... could just reach... *There*! He had it! He hooked the blade of the hoe around the package and drew it toward him. *Gloves,* dammit. Where were they? Holding on to the cage doors with his right hand, he thrust his left into his cargo pants pocket, at the side of his knee and pulled out a pair of plastic gloves. He then picked up the small cardboard box, perhaps eight inches long, tucked it under his armpit and descended the ladder. Kneeling on the floor, he yanked the top open and was just pulling out a plastic-wrapped square of white powder when, through the glass side doors of the corridor, hobbled Mrs. Jellyby, her arm across the top of Sela Cowan's shoulders. Sela took one look at what Trevor had in his hand, blanched, struggled out from under her patient's arm, and fled the scene.

·　　·　　·

Phil let himself in the back patio doors of Crabtree Cottage. He knew they'd likely be unlocked and, even if the front door had also been so, he preferred to do this without someone from Bayham Brook House looking across and seeing him enter. He'd decided that for the sake of a future court case he wouldn't remove any evidence, but would instead take many photographs. He wasn't worried about not being given permission to search; danger was too imminent for all involved and Blue had reiterated that such decisions would be to his own discretion.

The camera case was still on the little side table by the front door. Taking one thin leather glove, as he preferred to use, from his interior jacket pocket, he opened the case, already feeling unhappy at its weight. It was empty. Where *was* Crispin's actual camera, then? He placed the case back down and began snapping photos of it, noting with some satisfaction that it certainly looked as though the strap for the case had been roughly detached. A little ripped edge of the dry leather on the back side of the case was also photographed from several angles. *And*, it appeared to fit the width and similar color of the strap Monty Tigg had brought up from the creek, now locked securely in an evidence box in the trunk of the Satellite, along with the pin with the odd curly-cue. Which reminded Phil of something else he wanted to check…

Touching nothing, he moved to the bedroom he knew to be Sela's and looked on her dresser. A few pieces of costume jewelry and a small bottle of inexpensive perfume were all he saw there. Still wearing his glove, he pulled open the drawer of the one end table beside her single bed. A paperback novel, two mints, a candle, a used handkerchief and a spare light bulb were all that rested there. Swiftly, knowing his time could be limited, he moved to the laundry room, a little cupboard just off the bathroom. The washing machine was low enough to allow a disabled person to put clothes in and out. Beside it was a shelf with laundry soap and a small dish of coins. Also inside the dish was a white thinly laminated plastic nametag. The name itself had been completely rubbed off in the hot water of the washing machine. Flipping it over, however, he shook his head when he saw that the pin was indeed the same shape and length as the one he'd found on the Black Bridge. His godmother had nailed it. The little curly-cue spiral was what attached it to the back of the plastic, allowing it to hinge open and shut. Sela's other tag, assuming each staff member was issued two, must have come off on the top of that towering monstrosity stretched across the valley. In some kind of struggle? The same struggle that had also broken the strap on Crispin's camera case?

Phil made his way next to the refrigerator. Pulling open the door, he took the police-issued camera in one hand, and with his other gloved one, reached into the freezer and pulled the bag with the cigarette butt toward him. He began snapping pictures, being sure to get the 'Belmont' printed on the stubby golden brown end. He sniffed it. Ah, how that aroma brought back instant memories of his father! Freezing it this way must keep the scent fresh. Is that why Sela kept it here? And her mother would never have been able to reach this high, so she must have felt it a private safe spot.

He studied the bag more closely. It seemed to have been molded once around other objects. Whether these were food items that they'd used it for previously, or possibly the vials, full of some drug like the methadone which was often used for the treatment of drug addicts, but *not, supposedly* at Bayham Brook House. The vials which, once empty, were being put back into circulation as craft projects for the guests to fill with memory items, or natural sands and feathers, etc. for their hanging glass ornaments. Phil almost shook his head in disbelief at this blatant abuse of the authority given a member of the medical profession.

He was just shutting the fridge again, the menorah jiggling on top, when Trevor Ames burst through the front door, breathless.

"Phil! Cowan's on to us! She's on the run! Let's go, and you'll need that camera! Between Polly Jane and me, we've found quite a hefty stash of coke. We'll want photos right away. I've woken Biro. He's called in his colleagues and he's got everyone under guard in The Rookery!"

·　　·　　·

Later that evening, having made the requisite telephone call to Cathy Nelson to explain that they wouldn't be back at their lodgings that night, and with OPP and the local towns' police forces on the lookout for both Dan and Sela, (though the Cowan car was still sitting in the driveway at Crabtree), Trevor and Phil flipped a coin for who would get The Rookery sofa and who would be in Lucy Tox's old bedroom. Phil won the toss and would thus be upstairs in the room next to his godmother, who still insisted on remaining undercover. Someone from Biro's contingent had come by for the two stashes of cocaine that had been revealed to them, but Phil fretted that there were yet more drugs hidden on the property. He hadn't asked Walter to show him if there were any holes in the stone wall at the Cowan's place, for instance, and he suspected there might be, given that the two properties were developed at the same time.

Dr. Flintwinch entered, his brow in a permanent pucker now, and half-moon shadows of navy blue puffed under his eyes. He held out his hands to them.

"Here, you'd better each take a walkie-talkie. Channel Two, I'm on tonight. I gave one to Officer Biro last night, so we're all on the same. Problem is, Sela must still have hers, so she could be listening in. The staff channel is usually Three, but it wouldn't take much for her to figure out we'd change that."

"Good thinking, Doctor. Thanks." Phil didn't like seeing the man many had described as practically a hero, merely a week ago, looking this beaten and dejected. Jeremiah Flintwinch no longer appeared self-assured, confident or even handsome.

"I've brought you each some of my pajamas. I've given Tiny to Officer Biro, more for company than because I believe she's much use as a guard dog anymore. Poor thing, if her hearing had been what it once was, I may have clued in to whatever nighttime illegal activities have been going on here, for God knows how long." His shoulders hunched.

"Thanks, Doc," said Trevor. "I was just going to sleep in my clothes, ready for action if need be. But I'll be a lot more comfortable in these."

Flintwinch nodded. "You can find some blankets in the storage cupboard just outside the Bubble and Squeak main doors. And D.I. Steele, I believe the bed in Room Four was made up some time ago."

"Yes, well I'll head up now. Trev, you called Flaherty, and he was going to update Blue and Sharon, right?"

Trevor nodded. Then he said, "Doctor, could I just have a last word with Phil, here? Then we'll be off to sleep, if any of us can do so tonight. On top of everything else, it sure is humid out."

"I'll say goodnight then. I hope tomorrow brings an end to all this nightmare." The doctor walked out, closing The Rookery door behind him. Phil crept to it, opened it quietly and stared at the psychiatrist's retreating back as he disappeared around a corner, heading toward his own suite.

"My word, you really are getting more and more suspicious of everyone, Phil."

"I feel like I can't trust my own instincts anymore. It was you who first took a dislike to our Nurse Cowan. I figured her for a fine, upstanding member of the medical profession."

"Yeah, but I'm the one that was more or less swept away by Daniel Blevan and his good looks and easy-talking. And Phil—it was that which I wanted to tell you about. I-I think maybe I'm the reason poor Petra Cowan is dead."

"What are you saying, exactly?"

Trevor lit one of his Export 'A's, happy at least that he was allowed to smoke in the room in which he'd be sleeping. "Well, that first day we met Dan, and I sat with him out at the picnic table, I–I may have let slip that we'd been wondering about Sela, and whether she'd been feeding them meth on the side, just to help ease them in their withdrawal instead of relying only on the mumbo-jumbo stuff the doc seems to like."

"Oh, Trevor…"

"I know, I know. But honestly, I *was* just trying to find out if he knew more himself, feel him out. But I've been thinking about this a lot today and I guess, well—it's looking more and more that if both Sela and Dan are involved in this drug-dealing scam up to their ears, then maybe Dan got worried she was going to rat him out. Maybe he went there that night…"

"To kill Sela. Yes, I always had a feeling it might have been a case of the wrong Cowan being killed."

"You're joking! You mean you've thought—mistaken identity all along?"

"It's one of the theories I was mulling over that I didn't want to share yet. Especially as I thought you might have reason to blame yourself. They looked much the same from the back, Sela and her mother, and it's the back of the clawfoot that faces the door. Both long-haired brunettes, and with the mother's hair up in a bath cap, as it was…"

"When you told me earlier about finding the other red tie-back, I figured then that this was my own fault. Maybe I should resign from the…"

"Stop it, Trevor. You're still young, and you're obviously incredibly good at this job or you'd have not already been made a D.I. We're none of us infallible, you know. We all make mistakes in judgment, no matter our age or experience. But that's not to say—"

Phil was cut off by an excited tapping at the door and the doctor poked in his head again.

"D.I. Steele. Reverend Klassen's on the phone for you!"

"Sleep tight, Trevor. Don't think any more about it. Coming, Doctor! May I take it in 'The Fold'?"

"Yes, Reverend?" he said into the receiver on the doctor's desk moments later.

"Philip!" Apparently the minister had left off the use of titles in his excitement. "I got thinking about why you were asking me about those fans that vented up and down from the pulpit. So tonight I went in there—"

"Bit risky, Peter, to go in there at all, at night, with a couple of killers on the loose." Phil thought he might as well ignore titles as well.

"The doc told me about Sela. I'm pretty devastated, to say the least. But listen, I got thinking that those drugs need to be kept in cool spots, mostly, don't they? I mean, don't they go off, lose their color, their potency, whatever, if they're somewhere hot?"

"That's the theory we've been following in trying to find them, certainly. Although a few warmer hiding spots have come to light today that must have been temporary, since there've been police on the grounds."

"Well, add to that one more. I guess Daniel thought the fan would keep them cool enough in the sanctuary! Would you believe I did my sermon last Sunday from a pulpit full to the brim with little bags of methadone? It's stamped right on them. *Hundreds* of bags, Philip. Hundreds!"

·　　·　　·

Philip tossed and turned a lot in the first few hours he was in bed. He was worried about the Reverend Klassen staying at the manse alone. Having now decided that since no police blocks had found Daniel Blevan and his sporty Camaro, the car must have been hidden somewhere, and the drug-dealing masseuse trying to flee the area incognito. But worse than this thought was the one that he wouldn't leave thousands of dollars of drugs hidden in several spots around the church and the retreat. He wouldn't leave them all for Sela's monetary gain, Phil was quite sure. He couldn't know that they were on to her involvement as well, and he wouldn't leave them when he'd probably now need access to funds, since his bank account was frozen as of that morning. Phil had tried to persuade the minister to come and join them at the retreat, where at least there was safety in numbers, but the reverend had only promised to lock his doors and windows, and to sleep with a baseball bat under his pillow. He was going to be stifling in there like that, thought Phil as he flipped over in the big bed and turned over his pillow to find a cool spot for his cheek.

He must have fallen asleep, perhaps was even dreaming...because he woke with a start, disoriented, shaking his head to clear what felt like an addled brain. Someone was prodding his shoulder.

"Phil, Phil!" his godmother was hissing, standing over him in a sleeveless cotton nightgown. "There's something rattling that big tree, the one outside my window!"

Alert now, Phil realized she was talking about the tree Annette had dubbed "Ovid's Cedar". The tree that stretched, skinny yet graceful, right up to just between Karen and P.J.'s windows. He followed her quickly as her bare feet padded back to her square little bedroom. Without turning on a light, they both peered over the sill of the open window. The tree seemed as still as could be, the outside air hot and also motionless.

He drew P.J. back inside. "Are you sure there wasn't just a breeze blowing it? Maybe a big bird had just flown in and out of it?" He kept his voice low.

Shaking her blue waves vigorously, his godmother said, "No, Phil, I saw the shadows of the tree dance across my wall first, and that must have meant there was some kind of flashlight out there, too. I wasn't asleep yet, so I'd not been dreaming."

"All right, of course I believe you. I'll just grab my shoes and the walkie-talkie and go investigate."

"I'm coming with you!" she hissed.

"You most certainly are *not*!"

But as he headed down the stairs with both a penlight and the two-way radio in his hands, he could hear her pitter-pattering behind him in what she called her 'house shoes'. He wondered about waking Trevor, as he passed the door to The Rookery, but thought the better of it. He'd only be a few minutes; besides, Blake Biro and the dog Tiny were somewhere about out there. He'd be safe enough. He turned at the door and shook his finger sternly in P.J.'s face. "You are to stay right here. If I'm not back in five minutes, and I mean a full five, you may go and wake up Trevor. But you aren't to walk across this threshold, hear me?"

The wavy blue hair bounced up and down again, this time in agreement. Her faded eyes were wide with both excitement and fear. For him, he knew, not for herself.

He trod softly out the corridor's glass doors and padded through damp grass around to the side of the house where the tall cedar rooted right beside the foundation of the upper-hill stories of the house. He paused, listening, not daring yet to turn on the penlight. If Blevan had returned, why would he be checking the safe-like hollow in the wall behind the cedar, the one which Annette had apparently photographed, in photos that no one had had time to drive to Tillsonburg today to retrieve? Surely Dan Blevan knew that all the hidey-holes had been empty these last several days, that Sela—or perhaps even he himself—had hidden the drugs under her desk in the clubhouse and on top of the elevator, instead?

Well, he decided, if someone had been behind that tree causing it to shake a few moments ago, they were certainly gone now. A rumble of thunder sounded in the distance. He snapped on the little flashlight and moved behind the tree, shining the light to see where the bark had been peeled. *"Ovid's Cedar Flipped is David's Copper Field,"* he muttered in their old school-boy chant. Wait—*flipped!* What if it wasn't the hollow that Walter had shown him, that Annette had discovered, and which they'd all found empty? What if 'flipped' didn't just mean twisting around letters, but also… after all, it wasn't just boarding school boys and journalists who knew the old anagram joke. He followed his pen light from straight across from the bald spot on the skinny trunk, to the stone foundation. Yes, there was the stone, which, when removed, exposed the safe-like metal box inside. But, with a little struggle, a little effort on his part considering the penlight now in his mouth and the walkie-talkie weighing down the doctor's pajama bottoms so that the detective was afraid he'd soon be exposed in his underpants, he managed to flip the interior box over on its side, as if it was skewered on a rotational device. Another hole, below the first, became visible. He took the penlight from his mouth and shone it in, leaning over the stones to peer into the maw. He was aided by a sudden flash of sheet lightning, another roll of thunder ominously accompanying it.

A bulky package tied with twine lay inside, stacked full of white squares in plastic bags. And on top of the strung-together package was an envelope. Addressed to him.

CHAPTER FIFTEEN

Phil only scanned the letter from Sela Cowan, as he sat in The
Rookery with Trevor and P.J., an olive-colored afghan from the
D.I.'s make-shift bed now wrapped around her 'for decency'. He
read a few bits of the long epistle aloud to them, but then scanned
down to just a few lines before her signature and said shortly,
"Trev, get dressed. Pull your pants on over the pajamas. We've
got to *go!*"

With that, and not caring that he was only in skimpy pajamas
himself, he led them on the run—outside where the rain had
started to pelt down, then past the unfinished Drury Jane, radioing
as he ran, "Biro, this is Steele. Return to your cottage and find us
below. Over."

"I'm three minutes away. Be right there. Over." From the
man's breathless words, the D.I.s could tell he had already started
to run.

Phil slipped on the muddy trail as the rain poured harder. He
nearly went down, but Trevor caught his arm as it flailed behind
him, saving him from splatting to the ground. Philip half slid/half
ran, pulling both of them down the slope, calling "Over here, over
here, *the mushrooms!*"

But when they got to the little spruce glade just off the trail,
where the tee-peed old windows made a greenhouse over the
poisonous fungi, lightning flashed onto the drenched body of Sela
Cowan, crumpled on the ground beside them, vomit seeping into

the soggy earth beside her head. She was utterly comatose, eyes bulging, yet with a faint pulse, which Trevor discovered while Phil radioed again.

"Doctor, if you're awake, and can hear this, call for an ambulance and get yourself down to below Drury Jane. You'll see our flashlights shining, we're just off the trail."

At that moment Blake Biro and the enormous shepherd, Tiny, arrived, the dog on a long leash and barking in excitement. *If only she'd done that fifteen minutes ago,* thought Philip fleetingly— when Sela Cowan, likely already drugged for more than an hour or two on the beautiful but deadly amanita muscaria, had decided to put her joint suicide note and entire confession into the topsy-turvy vault behind the cedar tree.

·　　·　　·

The ambulance attendants, having slipped down the now-treacherous slope with a stretcher, were doing their best to revive the comatose nurse. However, they offered little hope as their vehicle sailed away into the dark night of streaming rain and occasional hail, toward Tillsonburg Hospital. The two Ontario Provincial Police officers who had been across the road guarding Crabtree Cottage in case Sela returned there, had been told by Blake Biro to go home.

Back inside now, bundled into yet more of the doctor's dry clothing, the three policemen sat sipping strong, hot tea made by Polly Jane, who'd helped herself to Ruth's big kitchen. The psychiatrist and his sopping dog (the latter overjoyed at being allowed into The Rookery where she was never normally permitted), both had blankets from Trevor's sofa thrown over them. The inquisitive young journalist, Annette 'Unscramble' MacElburns, had joined them, coming up the hill from Sorrel Close, which was the closest cabin to the edge of the gully and from which she'd heard the shouting and squawking walkie-talkies. Only Adam Tetterby, from those on the floors above, seemed to have heard the siren or been awake to notice the flashing lights. The thunder and lightning must have camouflaged them and Philip considered this was for the best. Monty Tigg, her ankle still hurting from her riding fall, had taken a sleeping pill she'd had Ruth sneak her from her own home, P.J. had reported. Thus, it was just Adam who sat with them in striped jogging pants and a T-shirt, looking dazed.

"She won't make it," Trevor said dully. "We lost our little window of opportunity to arrest her, make sure she pays for what she's done."

"I can't believe," said Flintwinch. "I simply can't..."

P.J. spoke up now, all thoughts of the wealthy widow Jellyby surrendered. "I think maybe, dear—the letter. From the beginning, straight through?"

Phil put his mug of tea down on the coffee table, where two other steaming mugs and several cigarettes resting in ashtrays gave the illusion of a central warmth, as in prehistoric days around the fire.

He looked at Adam, Annette, Officer Biro, and the psychiatrist. "First, to avoid any further confusion, let me introduce Polly Jane Whistler. She's here as a freelance agent of the Toronto Police force, under the authority of Deputy Commissioner Cobalt who, Adam, was actually your friend Crispin's father. And yes, earlier I discovered this case," Phil held it up then placed it back under the coffee table, "of what appears to be either heroin or cocaine packages, in a secondary secret compartment of what is already one of many secret hideaways built into the foundations and walls of this property by the original mason, your very own Walter McDowell. At some point I'll find out why he didn't care to share with me that the little safe inside this particular one spun around to reveal a larger cavity below, but suffice to say— many of these secret holes have been used for the spate of recent drug-trading that's been transpiring. With this premises as its base."

Phil looked away from Dr. Flintwinch, whose head was turned from them all, staring out the French doors at the pounding precipitation, common after weeks of unrelenting humid Augusts.

"On top of this package was an envelope addressed to me, and it was due to its last few lines that we realized Sela Cowan had overdosed." He directed his gaze at Annette, saying, "When I asked to see your make-up bag earlier it was because Lucy's last words to the doctor had been what sounded like, 'Anita's Mascara', but was in fact 'Amanita Muscaria', a potentially poisonous mushroom that has been growing here, probably as part of the drug-dealing scheme. I glanced at the last few lines of Sela's letter, realized she'd eaten these hours before starting to write her statement out, and that she was going back for more. I'll read the entire statement now, as Polly Jane has suggested. It's time the entire truth was heard, I think."

Philip unfolded the three thick pages of hand-written, blue-inked scrawlings and began.

" 'D.I. Steele, and to whomever else in the Ontario legal system this may concern; I, Sela Rachel Cowan, formerly Cohen, write this tonight on a stolen watercolor pad I sneaked from Saffron Hill Hut when Mitch and Jackie Vandenwolk were up at the main house. I am giving my full statement and confession while hiding in the loft of the stable, as I see my own dear Crabtree Cottage is now being guarded by OPP and I realize I will never be able to set foot there again. After my dearest mother's death, I'm not sure I care.

Having grown up on this wonderful property, with the patronage of the Hogarths whom I worshipped, I realize that I actually led quite an entitled childhood. Cheryl, Charlie and I were happy as youngsters, playing together in the woods and fields, despite several years difference in our ages; this was the countryside, after all, and you played with the only people near you. When I was about eleven, and Charlie thirteen, we started spending more and more time together, without Cheryl. I adored him, and he told me he loved me too. We had our lives all planned together, here. He said he would inherit the estate someday, and of course we would both live here, in the big house, and raise lots of children and perhaps adopt some as well—there'd be plenty of space for kids to have their own rooms, and grow up with the horses and other animals. As we grew into our teens, we dated, kept each other company constantly at Tillsonburg High, sat on the bus together to and from school, and when he could drive and his father gave him his first car, we went back and forth to town in that, sometimes taking Cheryl along, but usually just us. We were always together and our parents seemed happy and comfortable with this.

After his graduation, Charlie started at Western University and I finished high school myself, then began my nursing course. But we still saw each other all the time on weekends, one evening at least a week. We loved each other so much, wrote letters to each other nearly every day when we were apart, telephoned whenever we could manage it.

But then something went wrong with Charlie. He said things had been going stale between us, that he needed something fresher. While I started training work at London hospital, he dropped out of university just before he would have graduated. He began taking drugs, which of course I didn't know at the time or I would have tried to help him. If he'd have let me. But he likely wouldn't have, I realize that now. I don't blame myself, although I perhaps should have gone to his parents and told them about his drug use as soon as I did cotton on to it.

Charlie just kept saying that our relationship had become uninspired and stale, that he wanted to experiment more with life, with other people, with the world. But even though he said that, *he was seeing less, growing less. His world got smaller and smaller as he was basically living on the streets of London.*

Then, I guess to find help for him, or at least get him away from his druggie friends, his mother and father moved him to Toronto and he started the first of many programs which were meant to treat his addictions. But that was over ten years ago, and it's obvious that none of those programs helped. Right before Neville Hogarth died of his cancer, just over five years ago, he let it be known that if Charlie couldn't pull himself up, get over the addictions, he was disinherited. So Bayham Brook was left to Jane and to Cheryl, our little Crabtree Cottage already having been gifted to us. Suddenly, about two years ago, Charlie wrote to me. He asked if I could travel into Toronto to see him, and so one weekend I took the train in. He lived in a little run-down hovel off Yonge Street; you'd never have known his family were so well-off. His face was emaciated and pock-marked. I barely recognized him. But since then I've gone faithfully into the city at least once a month to try to help. And by helping, I thought I was doing the right thing by putting him on meth, which was what all these new treatment centers have been trying. Even though Jeremiah Flintwinch and his parents believed in a more natural, more Buddhist-based way, I just wanted to see him get well, and fast. I wanted to see him better. I still loved him so much, and he seemed to love me back again, too. What an idiot I was to think that!

His mother and sister wrote and told me that if Charlie could get clean and sober with my help, that they'd negotiate a deal with the new owners who were trying to make a go of Bayham Brook House—just as a spa-retreat then, in those first early days. They didn't really think it would make it as a retreat; a little too far from both London and Toronto, they thought.

My own mother was starting to suffer badly from pain then, from her accident. She needed a surgery that no one here could do. And let me just say, although I know differently now, that for much of my life, knowing the Schneiders vaguely through the

*Hogarths, I was under the mistaken impression that they'd been
Nazis. My father was tortured and murdered at Auschwitz. My
dear mom had loved him so much, just worshipped him—and they
took him before he could escape with us. And killed him. I wanted
to hurt any Nazi I ever met. I hated them! HATED them! I never
went to the synagogue after my mother's accident, and I just kept
finding more and more hate in my heart. I hated the boys who'd
drunkenly hit her on the highway, I hated Charlie for saying we'd
gone 'stale', and those other addicts for getting him onto drugs. I
despised these new owners who, although they'd given me a job,
were never here to help properly manage the place. Jeremiah and
I had to try to keep it going alone, which left me little time or
energy to spend with my mother, and the salary they gave wasn't
enough to let me save the thousands I'd need to get her to New
York City, to pay for her surgery and the six months of
physiotherapy she'd need down there afterward.*

*It was at about this time that Daniel Blevan was hired on here
as a full-time orderly and masseuse. I was receptive to all he had
to say, to offer. I needed more money, I needed to see this place
fail so that Charlie and I could own it again, see our childhood
dreams come to fruition, and if I could hurt the Nazi, Doctor
Flintwinch, into the bargain— that would be icing on the cake. (I
do want to say that I'm sorry about ever believing what I'd come
to discover about the Schneider family. My research had been
weak and biased. Jeremiah is a good, well-intentioned man as are,
I know now, his parents. I'm sorry for the damage I've done in
ruining his reputation.)*

The lights flickered as the storm surged on. Phil paused here
because the psychiatrist looked as though he wished to speak.
Beating at the windows like tiny white fists of anger, the rain had
again changed to hail. Flintwinch had turned his back on the
French doors, and the flashes of lightning put him in an obvious
spotlight as the bulbs in The Rookery all faded to a dull glow

before springing to life once more. Ever the alert hostess, Polly Jane saw that many tea cups were now empty and said she'd just go make another huge pot of the stuff. She grabbed the teapot and its cozy then hurried out, the olive home-knitted blanket still draped around her shoulders, clashing with her blue-tinted hair and the glasses perched as ever atop the candy-floss-like puff.

Flintwinch cleared his throat. "I'm still in shock, I guess. Can't quite realize that someone could have hated me so much for years, could have worked side by side with me for so long, and known me a little even in the decades before, yet still thought I was evil. When, as it turns out, I guess she had such hatred in her own soul that she turned to evil herself."

"It's certainly one for the reckoning of our Reverend Klassen, methinks," said Phil.

Adam spoke up. "I'm in shock, too. Sela has been a blessing around here, helping so many of us, always supportive, seemingly so generous of her time. I honestly didn't know about the drugs, have never been offered anything myself... thank God."

Phil thought of the irony of Della once saying, having brought them beverages that Sela had suggested: "*That's Miss Cowan, sir. She's always on top of who might need what, when...*"

Officer Biro still seemed to be stuck several pages back. "Do you mean to tell me that little old lady is here working undercover? Why the hell didn't anyone tell *me?*"

"Sorry, Blake. We did discuss letting you in on it, but it just seemed like the fewer people who knew, the fewer chances for her cover to be blown, and thus for her to be in danger. We were fairly certain she'd only be here for a few days, and we did need someone on the inside."

Annette took a pen and small notebook from her raincoat pocket. "Does anyone mind if I take some notes? I'm going to forget details if I—"

Just then the lights went off completely and a shriek was heard from the corridor. Also, a clanging grind. Della burst through the door holding a lit candle in a candlestick, panting. Her light summer robe, Phil noticed even in the candlelight, was on inside out. The lapels were missing, tucked underneath her, and the tie was nowhere to be seen. Flintwinch and Trevor lit two other candles on the mantle as Della babbled, "Quick! Oh, do come! He's got Clara! They're in the elevator and it's stuck!"

Rushing to the corridor with candles and flashlights in hand, they arrived just twenty feet from the main staircase and looked up to between the floor that they were on, (the second story if counted from the bottom of the hill, but really ground floor from this level) and the next story, that of the main guest bedrooms. Della and Clara stayed, of course, in what had once been the servants' quarters, on the very top floor.

Della pointed to the elevator, stuck about thirty feet from their heads. Whimpering came from the cage but they could see nothing. The young girl lowered her voice now, saying to Phil, "That Dan Blevan! He's in there with her. He has a knife! He made Clara go with him, and then the power went out!" Her teeth started chattering with nerves and a tear rolled down her face.

"Daniel Blevan. It's over!" Phil called up into the dark. "Toss down your knife, *now.*"

"Nothing's over, Steele. I've got boxes here that belong to me, and I aim to get 'em back. And this little girlie's my ticket out!"

Phil looked at Trevor, their eyes met, and when Phil jerked his head toward the elevator, the younger D.I. knew that his hours spent talking to the good-looking jack-of-all-trades would not have been in vain if he could make a crucial connection now.

"Hey, Dan. It's Trev. Let's just take a breath, here, o.k.? Let's just think about this."

Phil opened his arms and tried to herd the others back toward The Rookery. Della and Annette went obediently inside the common room again, but the door remained open as Flintwinch, Tiny, and Blake Biro stood under its frame, still watching and listening, each man holding a flashlight on the scene as Phil went back to Trevor's side. Trevor shone his own penlight up into the elevator doors, the elaborate wrought-iron, folding cage doors from which now poked two faces: Clara's, terrified, a knife at her throat and Dan's, his muscled arm wrapped around her neck with hand tightly clasping the knife's handle.

"I want my stashes back. That bitch Sela took some, I know. The one I had in her stone wall across the road. Plus, I had a package above this rig here, and one in the clubhouse. Where the hell are they?"

Trevor was doing remarkably well, his voice calm, his demeanor not vibrating with the intensity Phil felt within himself.

"I'm afraid we found all your stashes, Dan. Two of the boxes we got this afternoon have been sent away with the cops already, but we do have one down here in The Rookery now. Just found that under one of the hidey-holes at the cedar. Probably you didn't even know about that double-decker affair, did you? Sela must have stowed that one in there herself."

"I want it. Go get it, now, or this little maid gets an ear lopped off. And that'll be just the beginning!" Clara screamed and then was cut off mid-exhale as Blevan choked her more tightly with his arm.

"I'll go bring it out for you, Dan," said Phil. "You just keep calm up there. When the power comes back on, that elevator's going to jerk hard. You'd better not hold so tightly to her or you'll cut her without meaning to. Just loosen up a bit, huh? I'm going for your box now."

As Phil turned to go back down the hall toward The Rookery, the lights and power switched back on with a dramatic roll of thunder in the distance, followed by yet another flash of lightning outside the floor-to-ceiling-length corridor windows. He heard the elevator grind, then shift its cables into gear and start to descend. He gestured at Biro to grab the box from inside the room, and turning, was just in time to see the elevator land squarely on their floor. Trevor remained motionless as Dan Blevan pushed aside the doors and stepped forward, Clara in front of him, wild-eyed and whimpering in her nightgown.

The telephone started ringing in Chesney Fold, just as Dan and Clara passed that closed door and he gave a slight start, proving he wasn't as cool and in command as he was pretending to be. It kept ringing, and Tiny, finally feeling the anxiety of everyone else in her home, started to bark. Phil backed up to show he wasn't going to interfere with the forward progression of the man with the knife and the teen-aged girl. He heard Jeremiah Flintwinch behind him say softly to his dog, "Tiny, Gashford Grip! Four-nine-two, Four-nine-two, Gr-ri-ip!!" And at that moment, a flurry of blue and olive flew around the corner from the kitchen pushing a trolley full of cookies and teapot. *Bam!* The trolley crashed into the back of Blevan, the teapot full of boiling brew as well as the baked goods, sliding forward and hurling its contents over him, just as Tiny rushed forward and grabbed Dan's pant leg, growling ferociously.

Obviously burned, and being tripped up by the German Shepherd, Blevan dropped the knife and started howling as Phil and Trevor moved in to restrain him. P.J. Whistler raised her right arm with winged blanket like a protective mother bird and brought it around the now-sobbing Clara.

·　　·　　·

It was three a.m. The same group (minus Della, Clara and several others from upstairs who had come down upon hearing all the extra commotion), was now crowded into the kitchen, perched upon various pieces of hard wooden furniture in Ruth McCorkle's abode. "Closer to the kettle," stated Polly Jane practically, "since there's no tea-pot anymore. And no smoking in *here*!" She waggled a finger at Trevor and Adam.

The OPP had come for Blevan and the last remaining box of drugs. They had also been dispatched to pick up the meth found in Klassen's pulpit. Trevor had tried to convince everyone to go back to bed so that they themselves could get some sleep, but Blake Biro had pointed out that his unfinished cottage, Drury Jane, was likely flooded after the downpour of the night, and everyone else felt too wired on adrenalin.

"We'd like to hear the rest of Sela's letter, D.I. Steele," said Annette. "If we may."

The ringing phone that had startled Dan Blevan had carried on trilling away every ten minutes, until Dr. Flintwinch had finally answered it. A hospital administrator had been on the other end, announcing the death of Nurse Sela Cowan. It had not come as a surprise. She had meant it to be that way; she'd been granted her final wish.

"Well, the letter is of course evidence, and her official statement. But since I've already started it and you all deserve to know, seeing as how you've vested interests, I will. However, first I must know, Doctor. What did you say to Tiny to make her charge like that?"

"Oh, I didn't really expect it to work. Early on when my parents were experimenting with hypnotherapy and the use of repeated positive affirmations and mantras, they tried some phrases out on their dogs. So, when I first came here to work, before we'd really started to offer treatment programs, I taught Tiny using a Dickens alliterative like what we'd later use on our patients, Sela and I. Grip, you know, was Charles Dickens' raven and Neville Hogarth used to have a crow he called Grip as well. I thought the double meaning was humorous, so I paired it with one of his characters from Barnaby Rudge. I couldn't remember the numbers I'd used for 'bite', though. 'Four-nine-two' must have just meant, 'grab a pant leg'. But, timed with Mrs. Jelly—I mean, Mrs. Whistler's brilliant actions, Tiny's redeemed herself as a guard dog, in my eyes at least."

"She didn't even glance at the cookies raining all around her!" Adam said, impressed.

"By the way, I'm not actually married, Doctor. Nor do I live in a thirty-two room mansion," smiled P.J. "But I do accept your compliment."

"And of course, compliments from us all," Phil said. "It was very brave of you, P.J...And perfectly timed."

"Oh, I'd actually been waiting behind that corner for some moments, waiting and listening. Luckily Ruth has this gas range, so the kettle was still able to boil without electricity, and thank goodness she had candles hanging from the beams so I could see in here when it all went dark. Now this time, I've made cocoa. Who wants some, while Phil reads?"

As she poured hot chocolate into their mugs brought from The Rookery, Phil removed the letter from inside his borrowed sweatpants' pocket.

" 'It was at about this time that Daniel Blevan was hired on here as a full-time orderly and masseuse. I was receptive to all he had to say, to offer. I needed more money, I needed to see this place fail so that Charlie and I could own it again...' yes, yes, ah–here we are: 'Dan was very persuasive about the drugs he was bringing in to the country, from both the Windsor and Niagara borders. He has some Mexican contacts on the American side, posing as coming through with forged immigrant-status Mexican Mennonite papers. I'm not sure how he connected with them. And no, I don't know all the details of his business, but I do know that while he used his hands as a masseuse and a handy-man, he was best at using his malicious brain at being a discreet drug dealer. He was forceful when he needed to be, making sure both Walter and I had showed him any hiding places in the walls and pillars that we remembered. But he was also conniving and even charming. He persuaded me that the meth was the best way to make me extra money, that it wouldn't hurt the ones who seemed to really need it for their withdrawal symptoms. Oh, I wasn't stupid enough—and neither was he, when he still worked here full *time—to just up and offer them to anyone. He expected me to worm out the ones who might be most willing to pay for this 'extra treatment', as I'd call it.*

But after a year of working just with methadone, I realized how much more money was to be had by also selling coke, heroin, or even the Qualuudes, the one legal drug the doc did allow on the property—but only in monitored doses at the most crucial times. I learned how to use the hypnotherapy to my advantage too. I could use certain trigger words to lull some of our patients, trusting dopes that they were, into believing that what I offered them was an easier way to becoming clean and sober, without all the nightmares that go with withdrawal. People like Gerald just wanted to pretend they were getting better, without any intention of doing so. So, because I was getting closer and closer to seeing my poor mother have her surgery, I just kept shooting them up, if they needed a fix, then hiding their arms. Or sometimes, like with some real stoners like Lucy or Gerald, I'd inject their feet. They always had to pay me on-the-spot, and I'd just stash the cash in my little locked desk drawers in both the Tots'n'ham and the main house, until I could get it to the bank. I couldn't leave it at the cottage in case Mother would find it. I'd always planned to tell her that I'd won money from that new New York state lottery they've started, you see.

After a while, Dan wanted to start sending more and more drugs here to keep cool until he could sell them on the street. He shipped in syringes and glass vials and hid them out at the Klassen farm in bales, making sure they'd get transferred here by marking the twine with bread clips, and making sure he was always the one that volunteered to stock up Walter's supply for Furr-neville's. I don't know how he always managed to be there at the right time, but he managed it. He always took his sandwiches in bread bags, when he was at the farm, so if anyone ever asked he could just say the clips were from when he'd sit on the bales eating his lunch. We had a slick little system, you know. And I'm not really sorry. I helped a lot of people deal with a lot of pain, and all to help my mother deal with less. In the end, of course, I caused her—much worse.

Charlie coming here was his sister Cheryl's idea. I was happy to keep trying to get him clean by visiting him in Toronto once a month, but Jane and Cheryl insisted he be in a residential program, and that they'd heard good things about what their old friends' son, Doctor Flintwinch, was incorporating here. They thought it might tempt Charlie to get clean and stay that way, if he could have the dangling carrot of his very own property, be in a place he felt perfectly comfortable, and even have a bit of the cock-of-the-walk as he strutted around. Even though he couldn't tell anyone his family used to own it. I really thought he'd fallen back in love with me by this point. We were so close again, so much like we'd once been all those years ago... we took walks, went riding on my days off, and it was all wonderful again.

Until Della told me she'd seen a big diamond ring on Karen's dressing table one day. I knew she'd had a crush on him, but I hadn't realized he was also wooing her, the bastard! She was years younger, and so immature! Whenever I'd be home with Mother, he'd be over here getting all close and cuddly with Karen, and making arrangements to get his mother to mail him a family heirloom—I bet Jane and Cheryl even suspected it was for me! I was furious! After all we'd shared, and all I'd done for him! I snooped around a bit, found the marriage certificate and that was it.

On the very night I found out for sure that they'd had a secret marriage, I was removing some of the old used syringes and packing materials to bury down in the woods, where Dan said we had to keep them well covered, in a big hole on the slope, when Charlie startled me by jumping out from behind a tree and asking what the hell I thought I was doing. I guess he'd been spying on me for a while, don't know what he thought he'd do with the information, but it just made me so angry. Every ounce of love I'd *ever felt for him had turned into rotten hatred. I broke off a half-dead branch and just let him have it. I hit him right across the temple, twice, he dropped the cigarette he was smoking and fell. I grabbed the filter, stubbed it out and put it in my pocket as a memento of the old Charlie, the Charlie I'd loved for so long. Then when I realized he was unconscious, I was still so full of hatred that I ran up to the clubhouse and got out some of my kit which I kept for Gerald and Lucy. And I shot Charlie Hogarth full of heroin. Then, I trekked home, thankful my mother took sleeping pills every night, and called Dan. He parked on the highway and we hiked in and buried Charlie right there on the slope.*

I was also grateful that the doc's dog, Tiny, was old and never heard anything from the main house. In the old days, she probably would have, but she's aged fast. Little did I know that someone else had *been sniffing around, was ready to bark.*

I never even felt that bad about Charlie. I didn't allow myself to. He'd done it to himself, ruined us both, all our plans and hopes for the future. I was on such a destructive path now that I just didn't care.

But I didn't expect to have to kill again, or be in at the kill. However, Crispin must have seen or heard enough about the drug-dealing that he called Dan a couple of times and told him he was going to have to report him. Dan thinks Crispin saw him stashing packages in the pillar one night, and we found out later that he had photographed our greenhouse and the mushrooms we were experimenting with. We were going to sell those for a pretty penny, because the feeling of euphoria they can give if they're doled out in small dosages, is supposed to be fantastic. I don't know if Crispin knew I was involved, and I don't know why he didn't just report Dan instead of only threatening to. I don't think he intended to blackmail him, or us. Maybe it just gave him some kind of feeling of control. I know that addictive personalities always need to be controlling when they are sober. But whatever his reasons, Dan told me we had to shut Crispin up. He had me do some of his trigger words that night, the last time Crispin phoned him. I often had to tell Mother I was working late, but that particular night I really hated to; I'd only been home long enough to see she was o.k. for supper and came straight back. Doc Flintwinch was in a small group session with Lucy, Gerald and Karen. Adam was in his room, and so I asked Crispin to get his camera and come down to The Rookery, said I had an important job for him to help me with. As soon as he came in I said, 'Boz's Baubles, Eight-Six-Four', a couple of times, which almost immediately put him into a semi-hypnotic state. Dan had told me not to give him any drugs, we didn't want them found in an autopsy, if there was to be one. But the trigger words worked a treat. I told Crispin to follow me and, as Dan and I had planned, I led him up the back way, across Blackfriar's Bridge and up to Bloomsbury Ridge. We didn't speak, but once we started to go across the railroad tracks and onto the Black Bridge itself, Crispin seemed to come to a bit, asked me where we were going, pointed out it was almost dark. So I said that I wanted him to use his excellent photographic skills and his good telephoto lens and try to get some shots of the group that were at the bonfire pit smoking joints. Then we could catch them in the act and the Doc and I could put an end to that aspect of what was wrong on this place. I knew Crispin would fall for it, because obviously he didn't like the illegal stuff going on with the drugs, anyway, all high and moral and mighty as he'd seemed to suddenly become!

And he did. Followed me like a puppy right across the bridge to just over half way. Then I had him kneel down to shoot some pictures. Only two people —Jackie and Mitch, Crispin said—were at the pit at that point. I leaned over him and pretended to be pointing, knowing that the two people at the pit wouldn't be able to make us out with the naked eye, and if they did, we could just laugh, say they were high. So when he could hear there were no cars coming and just as it was so dark no one could really see a thing, anyway, Dan came from the other side—he'd parked over on the Haggerty's side, and been waiting for us, crouched in the little safety balcony—and grabbed Crispin's camera from him and just shoved him over. Only thing is, Crispin clutched at us, must have ripped the strap from the camera when he went, and he must have pulled my nametag off as well, because there was a little tear in my uniform top and I never did see that tag again. He did holler a bit as he fell, but it just sounded like an owl. Mitch and Jackie never looked up.

I picked up the camera case from the tracks, and Dan took Crispin's camera. A few days later he developed the pics himself, which is how he knew that the mushrooms had been found. He was always sneaking down there in the middle of the night tending those dratted mushrooms, going right past Annette's cabin. I warned him she was a reporter, but he wouldn't take the longer pathway. Anyway, he dropped me off at home that night and we never talked about it again, just kept trying to carry on as best we could with things once all the cops started crawling around. And I'll admit that I did wait several hours after the Haggertys found Crispin before I finally told the doctor. I was scared, needed time to think, because we didn't think his body would have been found that fast. But the rest of that procrastinating, that was just chance working in our favor.

Of course most of Dan's shipments had to be stored elsewhere for a while. I kept some in the hole in our stone wall, and even in my freezer at home for a few days. That's where I've been keeping Charlie's last cigarette, too. When I smelled it, it smelled just like my Charlie, the Charlie I'd loved since we were kids, the one who'd been my kindred spirit...until he'd announced that we'd gone stale. Well, the joke was on him, then, wasn't it? Because by the time he was found, he was far from fresh and pleasant, and I guess enough time had passed that the heroin in his system didn't even show up for the coroner.

I thought we were going to get away with it, I really did. And when you'd all left, I was going to tell Dan we had to stop. I didn't care if he kept selling to kids on the street, but I wanted out. I had nearly enough money to get Mom to New York and to pay for her operation and that's all that mattered. But something must have happened. Dan must have freaked out, decided he couldn't trust me, that I was ready to blab or something. Because the night Lucy tried to hang herself, Dan must have presumed it was me in the bath and that my mom was already tucked up in bed with her sleeping pill.

If I planned to live longer I might try killing Dan myself, to get back at him. I'm pretty sure I could just stab him with some of his own heroin and give him a lovely overdose, the evil son-of-a-bitch. He took the only person in my life who meant anything to me, after Charlie was gone.

What I did, I did only for love. The love of my mother, trying to get rid of her pain, and the love for a man I had thought loved and worshipped me back.

I've spent most of the afternoon and early evening writing this, D.I. Steele. I'm now going to inject myself with the last dose of methaqualone on the property, which I know the doctor has kept in my desk in the Tots'n'ham. If I can get in there again with no one seeing me. Doc was mostly giving me the oral Quads, this week, to keep me sedated. I did appreciate that, you can tell him. But I'm sure there's one injectable vial of the beauty left. Then I'll put this with the package I removed last night from our stone wall, to put in the secondary secret hole that only Walter and Charlie and I knew about because Walter's cousin had asked for it especially to be made that way—and many years later, Walter showed us. He was proud of that. I expect you'll figure it out, or Walter will show you eventually. Then you've got my statement in full.

So as soon as I've hidden it, I'll go down and finish off with some lovely mushrooms; those will leave me feeling like I'm floating in the clouds, talking to my mother and the Charlie of old, again.

Signed, Sela Rachel Cowan.

EPILOGUE

"Sure you want to do that?" Reverend Peter Klassen said, as Phil slid his bishop confidently across the diagonal.

"*Darn.* No, you're right. Thanks for that." He slid it back, resumed studying the board for his next best play.

"How's Clara after a few days of adjusting now?"

"I think she'll survive. Turns out she had a bit of a crush on Daniel. So Ruth has told us now."

"Ah, that Ruth McCorkle. Always full of information, but often after the fact," said the minister, smiling.

"We'd noticed, yes." Phil moved his knight up one, over two.

"I presume that after he'd traded cars with his friend over in Brownsville, that's how Dan persuaded Clara to let him in? Played on her heartstrings? Since the doors are always locked at nine..."

"Della says he just showed up on their floor with the knife, wanting them both to go look on top of the elevator for him, fuming because he'd lost some 'parcels.'" Phil snorted. "Makes them sound as innocent as a day in my godmother's post office in the hills of New Brunswick."

"I'm sorry I didn't get to meet her, she sounds like quite a woman."

"Indeed she is. Brave, too!"

"All that *and* she can beat you at chess? I'll have to invite myself to your Toronto farm to have a game with her before she leaves."

"You might be sorry. She really is a stronger player than I."

After the reverend moved his king out, it was Phil's turn again.

"So the car picked D.I. Ames and your godmother up this afternoon?"

"Yes, Trevor had a lot of paperwork from the case to go over with his direct boss, so he had to head back." Phil grinned, adding, "Crispin's father didn't spring for the limo this time, as it was no longer necessary for their cover story; P.J. was most disappointed."

"And what time will you head back tomorrow?

"I've a little more paperwork to go over with Jeremiah and Officer Biro. Then, I guess—in the mid-afternoon. That's *if* I can get an early enough start after being battered with yet another barrage of questions from the Nelsons. They are pretty devastated that a lot of their tobacco was ruined by hail the other night, so Brian's mostly moping around the house now. It was bad enough with two of us there to deflect their curiosity. With Trevor gone now, it'll be only me tonight—I'm defenseless!"

"I don't know them at all, but Ruth mentioned once that her cousins like to speak at the same time."

"More like constantly finishing each other's sentences. Practically *interrupting* the other to finish a phrase first," Phil said.

"Funny. My siblings and I used to argue a lot, say we were never on the same wavelength at the same time. None of us, not even with my own twin. Seems like the Nelsons are just the opposite."

"They are something of—Peter, did you just say you have a twin?"

"Sure. Mom has nine kids, with two sets of identical twins. My twin is Paul, but we've never been close, like you always hear twins are supposed to be."

"So that wasn't you in town the other day, sans your dog-collar?"

"Nope. I haven't been off the property in days, not even to visit sick parishioners."

Phil chose his words carefully. Up until this very moment, he'd still had some niggling doubts about the man he wholly wanted to trust. "Have you ever been behind Townsend's store in Sandytown? Where they supposedly sell beer?"

"Do they? I haven't heard that—no, if I just need a loaf of bread or something, I use the Edom's Creek General right here."

Philip pulled a stack of photographs from his inner jacket pocket. He shuffled through them, and pointed to two very dark pictures. "That's not you either, then, is it?"

The minister squinted at them, holding them up to the light, twisting them slightly. "Goodness me, no. That isn't me, but I can see why someone would think it is. These are awfully dark, but that looks like Paul. Have you thought this was me all along?"

"We only picked these up from the developer yesterday, but they were taken by Annette with her telephoto. Does your brother work on your parents' farm?"

"Of course, as do the two boys still in their teens. My youngest sister lives at home, too and helps my mother with all the meals."

"Peter, you'll have to excuse me a minute or two. I've got to make a phone call."

The minister swallowed hard. He was a highly intelligent man, Phil knew; he could see that knowledge was slowly dawning on him, and pain hitting him like a back-handed slap.

Reverend Klassen stood abruptly. "I see. Yes, well—I've got another hammer I wanted to get from the manse. I'll be back in five minutes, is that long enough?"

"Sure. And Peter, you can't—"

"Don't worry. I won't be making any calls myself."

As soon as he'd disappeared through the back door of the manse, Phil picked up the telephone in the nearly remodeled church basement kitchen and dialed the Bayham Brook House number. Della answered, and Phil asked her to go find Officer Biro, quickly.

Moments later, he heard the OPP officer's voice. "Yes, Philip?"

"Blake, I've just found our missing link. Reverend Klassen has a twin brother that works on the family farm up here in Edom's Creek. I'm pretty sure he's the primary agent Blevan's been using to bring the drugs in from the Mexican contacts at the border. We knew there must be someone else involved on this side, and having him right there on the Klassen farm, not just as a temporary hired hand, but a permanently established member of the family, just makes more sense. I'll let your department go grab him, get the questioning started. I expect it won't take much to break him now that his two main cohorts are gone. I've got to stay here at the church for a while."

"So that wasn't the minister in those photographs out by the highway?" asked Blake Biro.

"No. Annette's done well to get so much proof for our court case; it was just a question of which Klassen was actually involved in the trafficking. Go get him."

Phil hung up the phone and went out into the sunshine, blinking. He saw the minister returning slowly with a hammer. If this had been one of his godmother's much-loved television mysteries or novels, he'd now be alone, confronting yet another criminal with a deadly weapon. But he no longer had the gut-punched suspicions about the man he'd so wanted to call 'friend'. Instead he met him half-way and slung an arm around the other man's shoulders as they walked back together to their chess game.

"I suppose I should have known when you and I went out there. I was praying it was just Dan involved, and when we didn't find anything in the bales that day…"

"I know. You thought it was bad enough just to think your handyman was involved," said Phil sympathetically as they sat again on either side of the squared board.

"But when you've got nine siblings, all very different from one another, I suppose the odds are there will be one bad apple. Poor Mom and Dad. I'll give it a few hours, then I'd better get out there and do some consoling."

"You don't seem entirely surprised, Peter."

"No. I guess I'm not. Paul was always a brat, had lost the Faith—if he'd ever had it. I'd just never have thought *this* of him. The irony is that I've been actively trying to find out who in our Mennonite community has turned to this life of crime. Some sleuth I'd have made!"

"Do you want to talk about it?"

"Not really, thanks. Dad already had his nose out of joint realizing he'd been duped by someone he trusted. But I think that was mostly because he didn't like what he considers his 'nice tight baling' going to Bayham Brook House as anything less than packed solid. What's he going to think now, when he finds out his own son has been an instigator, a dealer?" The minister shook his head slowly as he moved out his queen.

"I don't think Walter ever noticed. About the bales, I mean. Bit of an enigma, that fellow." Phil was trying to change the subject, and the reverend happily accepted the diversion.

"Isn't he? I suspect he harbors a lot more secrets that will go to the grave with him. He isn't the type to communicate anything if he isn't asked a direct question."

"If I didn't love anagrams, I'd never have found that last bundle of drugs, or Sela's confession. Even Annette was amazed that the name she thought *she'd* devised for that hiding place had been taken so literally by someone else. Flip it. Of *course* Neville Hogarth, the Dickens obsessive, must have had Walter build it that way."

"Ovid's Cedar, Flipped. David's Copper Field. So clever. But yeah, Phil. You would have found it."

"Glad you have so much faith in me. Your turn, by the way."

"It's not the faith I have in you," stated the minister as he put his hand on his knight, then changed his mind and moved his bishop only two squares. "It's the faith I have in the big guy upstairs." Peter Klassen pointed upward.

"You've got *another* body-builder hiding drugs in your sanctuary up there?" Phil grinned.

"Hmm." Evidently, laughter would not come to the minister's lips today; Phil couldn't blame him. "No, it's just that I asked the Lord to help us get through that night with no more innocents being hurt, and with all the drugs being recovered so that they couldn't hurt any more poor souls by being sold on, distributed to the masses. I know drug trafficking's never going to stop, but I just had to ask that what was in our own midst might be found and confiscated. I asked that of God right before He sent me back to the church to unscrew the panel of my pulpit. Not to put too fine a point on it, I might add—at the very first roll of thunder."

"I see why you have so much faith, if coincidences like that keep happening to you."

"You may call it that if you like, Phil! I know differently in my heart. And I have to accept now that a wound within my own family is part of God's plan to finish cleaning up this mess."

"Good for you, and very stalwart. The world needs more true Christians like you, no matter what our religious beliefs are. I'm sorry I was a bit suspicious of you. It's just, a lot of little signs, and if you'd been double-bluffing…"

"Oh, the way you were going on about not letting me help you search these walls! I understand now. I guess it just never came up that I had an identical twin."

"One who even shares your initials. Annette handed over to me some film and her notes the other day. In her notes was a scrap of paper which she said Crispin had folded up one evening in an origami craft class, then threaded as a swan ornament and presented to her. It was only after Petra was killed that she thought to unfold it, on a 'hunch', she said. He'd written, *'should anything happen to me, tell police—D.B., P.K.? S.C.? J.F.?'* "

"And of course you assumed the 'P.K.' was me?"

"As possibly Crispin thought as well. But don't take it too personally. I've suspected Flintwinch even more. Now, I just feel like he's a deflated man. I'm not sure how he'll pick up and keep going."

" 'Oh, how the mighty are fallen'," murmured the minister. "Never mind, I'll be here to support him. He *is* trying to do good things there. I think sometimes he can just be a bit tunnel-visioned. A bit like an absent-minded professor, you know?"

"Well, his crazy mantras and trigger-words and hypnotherapy tactics... I think that's got to stop. It's done more damage than any good, as far as I can see."

"I'll have a word. Maybe there's some kind of middle ground. But what will happen when Annette's article in 'Unscramble' comes out, I wonder? Your go, again."

Phil studied the board; it looked like the reverend was going to put him in checkmate again, in three moves. "I've given her the exclusive scoop so that in turn she can make sure it's public knowledge and emphasize that all the traffickers are gone and drugs are banished forever from Bayham Brook House. She even said that she would still do a write-up for Chatelaine, lauding all the virtues of the place as a spa/retreat, if not as a treatment center, just yet. Donna Lawton's going to come next month to do a demonstration tennis match as well."

"Ah, well that should help, then. And I had a phone call from Karen this morning. She's hoping with some of her inheritance from Charlie, to buy Crabtree Cottage, rename it 'Hogarth House', and offer it as a special family home for those who want to be close to their teens while they are going through treatment."

"Lovely idea," said Phil. "Not sure how much the doctor will like that as he and his family seem pretty firm about wanting to keep the past, including families, *out* of the addicted person's life while they are rehabbing. Look, I'm just going to put my queen back here, and if you take her, so be it."

"Hold on, that's the phone. It's probably for you. Seems like you've used this line more in the last week than I have in a month."

"Shall I get it then?"

"Go ahead. I'm taking your king in two moves."

"I saw."

In the kitchen again, Phil picked up the receiver and said "Edom's Creek United."

"Phil, it's your mother."

"Hello, Mom. Anything wrong?"

"Well, not with me. Actually things are really looking up today, thanks to you. I've had a call from a Montaglia Parker, she says you'd know her as 'Tigg', who wants to come and start volunteering with the disabled kids for L.A.R.Y. *And* she says she'll be sometimes bringing along her friends Jackie and Mitch. She explained that you've been telling them all about the great therapeutic benefits for the children, and since they like working with horses, anyway, they've decided to give it a go. This Jackie is an artist, I guess? She told Mrs. Parker to tell me to pass on to Sharon and Blue that she's done a portrait of Crispin from a photo her husband took of him, won't they be pleased? Oh, and someone named 'Latch' is interested in coming to help out too. But more to meet Oliver and discuss getting his own honeybees. What kind of name is Latch, for goodness sakes?"

"I'll tell you all about these characters when I'm home tomorrow, Mom. At least what P.J. hasn't already told you."

"Sad to say, her news isn't quite so good. Here, I'll let her tell you. See you tomorrow, son!"

P.J. came on the line. "Oh, Phil dear. I'm afraid I have to fly home tomorrow morning and won't see you again this trip. Very disappointing, dear, but needs must!"

"Why, P.J.? What's happened now?

"Oh, that Mary Henry! My friend Betsy Lawford telephoned this afternoon and goodness, that phone bill will certainly be costly! But she wanted to tell me that Calpurrnia was run over today. She thinks that evil Mary did it, too, but of course there's no proof. Mary may be an excellent postal worker, but she's no friend of mine, and she's certainly no lover of animals. My poor Cal! Anyway, the vets have him, and have set his broken leg, but he's hissing at everyone and causing a colossal ruckus, apparently. Even your playmate of old, Chet Anderson, has been called in on the case. The vets also think this was no accident and that Chet should investigate. Tssk, I could just strangle that woman!" P.J. then seemed to have remembered Petra Cowan's fate, and the inappropriateness of such an exclamation. "Well, I'm sorry, Phil, but that cat was probably just minding his own business looking for mice in the ditch. And Mary never did like him!

Now, I hear that some of the Bayham Brook folk will be coming to help your mother with her program here. Isn't it lovely how murder can bring people closer together?"

THE END

ACKNOWLEDGEMENTS

I would like to acknowledge the contributions of budding author Carriann LeBlanc and Susan Biro (formerly of the Ontario Provincial Police, whose surname is used as a nod to the family including her sister Judy) for researching certain procedural details, and to Matthieu LeBlanc for relating the amusing tale of a real-life character and his 'puns'.

As always, many thanks again to Marlene Joy Cehovin, an exemplary line editor. She catches every little mistake; sometimes I just choose not to 'correct', as the incorrect version may be more in keeping with a character's dialogue, or is simply less awkward-sounding to our modern ears. Star Beta-reader Richard Reich again 'clued in' for 'clue-outs' and I thank both for their dedicated nose-to-the-grindstone team efforts throughout all of 2022's creative projects, especially.

I would like to acknowledge the generous authors who have read this book and offered wonderful cover blurbs. They are Leigh Turner, Remy C. Garner, Sherry Hobbs and Karen K. Brees.

Real-life Names' Wordplay:
For some anagrams, acronyms, and 'unscrambling': to Lesa Jordan Speller for volunteering to be an anaGramma'd character and thus starting the whole Jordan=Jewish/Edomite connection, and to Annette Maeckelbergh for also lending her name (as well as her unfailing support as the unofficial J.Ivanel Johnson Fan Club President). Remembering with gratitude and warmth the important offerings to decades of dedication to therapeutic riding of both Lida McGowan at Cheff Center, Battle Creek, MI (Kellogg's scholarship through the NARHA of old) and Lelia Sponsel of CANTRA in Ottawa, ON. These two formidable women are an amalgam of the character 'Lila'. Remembering the

inspirational horsey-bookish-artsy Reid family, and the days of their **R**iding **E**xperiences for **I**ndividual **D**evelopment, to ARCH (Avon Riding Center for the Handicapped) and to SARI (Special Ability Riding Institute, in memory of their daughter Sari Greenberg). Thanks to Peg Andrews for offering her Uncle Walter as the mason, since he really did work on "The Parcel" outside of 'Sandytown', whereas, despite relatives of relatives being from a Hogarth family from the area NONE of them was intentionally featured. The Hogarth name was only used because of its connection to Dickens, and the first names of the Hogarths were chosen for other obvious reasons.

Every author tends to thank at least one English teacher from his or her past, and every actor/playwright acknowledges at least one Drama teacher. Ian Moir is that one teacher for both, for me. He and his wife Doreen, collectors of many beautiful, historical items including antiques and dolls, were the inspiration for the name and decor of 'Dor-ian's Dollhouse Tearoom'.

Straffordville

Once again, I want to acknowledge my grandmother, Victoria Ivanel Johnson, (1906-1992) for first introducing some of this series' characters, and for plotting/drafting the first in the series, (now published by Black Rose Writing as Just A STILL LIFE) as far back as 1947, setting it in the original Sandytown (Straffordville, ON) in Bayham Township, where she was born and raised. To see photos of her, and read more about her, visit this page and scroll to bottom:

https://mckencroftproducti.wixsite.com/jivanelauthor/still-life

Also very much a part of the Straffordville, real Eden, Tillsonburg and Bayham connections is the Howey family. The use of the name 'Della' is a tribute to them and my family's own close attachment to our much-loved Della Lorraine. Bob Haggerty is a tribute to Bob Howey. We shared a birthday and that good gentleman-farmer just passed away this year. I wish he could have lived just a little longer, to know how important his character would be to helping solve this mystery! His love of gardening is a particular salute here.

Thanks also to Cheryl Ward for permission to play with the pronunciation of her first name, and to use "Townsend" and "Townsend's Store", which did exist during my youth in that village.

"Something Written in the State of (New) Denmark"

While Shakespeare's Hamlet quote (see below in 'Quotes Referenced' section) is something more 'rotten', I'd like to thank Cindy Jensen, local unofficial JUST *(e)*STATE mystery series agent/promoter and her sister-in-law Heather Jensen, for their continual support of their non-Danish neighbor— the writing hermit on the hill... *"she only talks on the phone if her husband's lost in the woods again!"*

Readers and Fellow Authors – Finally, to all the readers of my work, especially those interested in this cozy mystery series. Thank you for your purchases, your words of encouragement asking for more, your photographs sent to me of you reading my novels or anthologies, your review–writing (it is your short reviews, especially on Amazon.ca/.com/co.uk that can make all the difference in sales for any writer! If you haven't already, please do so!) and your blurb writing, invitations to podcasts, blog interviews or just some sharing on social media. These make all the difference! Thank you so much! - *j.i.j*

QUOTES USED OR REFERENCED IN THIS NOVEL

"Care is heavy; therefore, sleep you. You are care, and care must keep you."
–Thomas Dekker

"Stand guard at the portal of your mind."
–Ralph Waldo Emerson

"You can have your droll name again... setting you apart,"
–Charles Dickens, *Little Dorritt*

"Far from the madding crowd"
–Thomas Hardy title, but taken from Thomas Gray's poem *Elegy in a Country Churchyard*

"The most difficult thing is the decision to act, the rest is merely tenacity. The fears are paper tigers."
–Amelia Earhart

"Something is rotten in the state of Denmark"
–William Shakespeare, *Hamlet*

"An angular man with no conversational powers", re: Grewgious
–Charles Dickens, *The Mystery of Edwin Drood*

Information on the mushrooms: from an article published online 2021 Feb 2. doi: 10.12890/2021_002212 The Deceptive Mushroom: Accidental Amanita muscaria Poisoning by Francesca Irene Rampolli,[1] *Premila Kamler,*[1] *Claudio Carnevale Carlino,*[1] *and Francesca Bedussi*[2] from the National Library of Medicine, https://www.ncbi.nlm.nih.gov/pmc/articles/PMC7977045/

'Oh, how the mighty are fallen'… from Samuel 1:19
"A gazelle lies slain on your heights, Israel.
How the mighty have fallen!"

NOTE: - part of the historical information on the Doctors Vledilore/Kellogg partnership and experimental work is real, part of it has been fictionalized. Also, although Aaron and Lena Schneider are fictitious characters, there were several well-meaning couples around the Great Lakes States in the 1960s who were leading the way with residential rehabilitation/addiction/treatment centers and half-way houses, many begun on rural farms and properties.

ABOUT THE AUTHOR

J. Ivanel Johnson is the pen name for an author/playwright living with disability who now resides on a remote farm in the Appalachians of New Brunswick. She strives always to write about marginalized and culturally-diverse characters, many based on people from the First Nations, inner city or mountain communities where she has previously lived and taught across the UK, USA and Canada (including in SW Ontario on a rural property such as the one described in this novel.)

Her historical Canadian musical Rough Notes, also set in both New Brunswick and Ontario, was just workshopped professionally thanks to a national grant, and the first book of the *JUST (e)STATE* mysteries (actually taking place after *Just A STALE MATE*, in 1971) came out in September of 2022 by Black Rose Writing.

NOTE FROM THE AUTHOR

Word-of-mouth is crucial for any author to succeed. If you enjoyed *Just A STALE MATE*, please leave a review online—anywhere you are able. Even if it's just a sentence or two. It would make all the difference and would be very much appreciated.

Thanks!
J. Ivanel Johnson

We hope you enjoyed reading this title from:

www.blackrosewriting.com

Subscribe to our mailing list – *The Rosevine* – and receive **FREE** books, daily deals, and stay current with news about upcoming releases and our hottest authors.
Scan the QR code below to sign up.

Already a subscriber? Please accept a sincere thank you for being a fan of Black Rose Writing authors.

View other Black Rose Writing titles at
www.blackrosewriting.com/books and use promo code
PRINT to receive a **20% discount** when purchasing.

www.ingramcontent.com/pod-product-compliance
Lightning Source LLC
Chambersburg PA
CBHW050146120726
47903CB00002B/512